"DISMISS THE CASE!"

Judge Bagby shook his head. "The prosecution has proven a murder. It has proven that the defendant was in the cabin where the murder was committed at the time it was committed, that the defendant's fingerprints were on the murder weapon and that there was blood on her clothing.

"It certainly seems that there is sufficient evidence, unless of course the defense wishes to call witnesses."

"The defense does," Perry Mason said.

"Then go ahead and call your first witness."

"I call Lieutenant Tragg."

Two Complete Novels by
ERLE STANLEY GARDNER

PERRY MASON

2 in 1

The Case of the Mythical Monkeys

The Case of the Fabulous Fake

🅿 A KANGAROO BOOK
PUBLISHED BY POCKET BOOKS NEW YORK

Distributed in Canada by PaperJacks Ltd., a Licensee
of the trademarks of Simon & Schuster, a division of
Gulf+Western Corporation.

PERRY MASON 2 IN 1

POCKET BOOK edition published August, 1977

The Case of the Mythical Monkeys
William Morrow edition published 1959

POCKET BOOK edition published August, 1961
7th printing........................June, 1977

The Case of the Fabulous Fake
William Morrow edition published 1969
2nd printing........................June, 1977

ISBN: 0-671-81453-2.

FOREWORD

THE AVERAGE citizen little realizes the extent to which forensic medicine, also known as legal medicine, plays a part in his life.

While the forensic pathologist deals with those who have died violent or unexplainable deaths, the things that he discovers have saved many, many lives and will save many more lives.

Then there is, of course, the interesting and controversial question of how many murders go undetected simply because those communities where there are no adequate postmortems fail to realize that murder has been committed.

During the past few years, I have seen legal medicine grow considerably in stature, and there has been an increasing understanding of its importance on the part of the public. This has been due in large part to the caliber of the men who are leaders in the field and the zealous devotion of these men to their profession.

Take, for instance, my friend, Dr. Joseph A. Jachimczyk, who is Forensic Pathologist in the Office of the Medical Examiner of Harris County at Houston, Texas, and who is not only a Doctor of Medicine but holds a Bachelor of Law degree as well.

Dr. Jachimczyk is carrying on activities that would keep four or five men fully occupied if they worked on any kind of conventional schedules with weekends free and ordinary vacation time.

Dr. Jachimczyk works day and night. He is generally on duty seven days a week, and a vacation is unknown to his schedule.

Not only is he making great sacrifices to carry out his work, but also his family is joining in those sacrifices.

So many times I have found it to be true that the wife and family of a forensic pathologist forego social life, become accustomed to telephones ringing at all hours of the night, and can only "look forward" to Saturdays and Sundays as no different from any other day except that the death toll is heavier on those days.

Yet these people cheerfully make such sacrifices.

The forensic pathologist needs to have the skill of a hospital pathologist and in addition an encyclopedic knowledge of crime. For the most part, his pay is far less than that of a hospital pathologist and he never knows at what minute he will be dragged from bed and find himself racing through midnight streets to the scene of a crime.

If more of us could only realize how great a debt of gratitude we owe to these men, it is quite possible there would be better pay and better hours. However, as long as there is such a shortage of competent men who are adequately trained, it isn't going to be easy to get any relief from the tension under which they work.

But, getting back to Dr. Jachimczyk, perhaps some of the cases he has handled would serve as a better illustration of what I mean than any amount of general discussion.

There was, for instance, the time he was called upon to examine a thirty-seven-year-old man found dead in bed, apparently of a heart attack. The man was reputed to have effeminate mannerisms, but aside from that there was nothing to arouse suspicion. There was no evidence of any disorder; no external signs of any traumatic injury.

Yet, a special dissection of the neck showed that the man had met his death as the result of a traumatic injury, which left no external signs.

Once it was established that death was in fact due to violence, the perpetrator of the violence was discovered, and then it was found that he had probably had something to do with two other deaths within the preceding six months, and the man *admitted* being responsible for ten other deaths in another state.

Here, then, is an authentic history of a dozen murders which went undiscovered until it happened that Dr. Jachimczyk was called in.

The man is now in prison, and it is quite possible that more than another dozen murders were prevented by Dr. Jachimczyk's skill.

Another case is that of a young girl playing in a yard. Suddenly and without notice she had a convulsive seizure and died shortly afterward. Ordinarily, the diagnosis would have been meningitis, but here again careful autopsy disclosed a dislocated neck of a type that was possible only with trauma. Shrewd investigation disclosed that a short time before, an angry relative had "bounced" the little girl up and down, trying to vent her rage upon the helpless youngster. This had caused the injury which had caused her death.

Or take the case of the man who was found dead in bed with no evidence of violence, no blood on any of his underclothing. An attending physician made a diagnosis of heart attack, but Dr. Jachimczyk was not satisfied with the situation. Through careful dissection, he found that an ice pick had inflicted a stab wound in the chest. Investigation led to a young woman who finally admitted the crime and, incidentally, admitted that she had murdered two other people in another state in this same manner without the authorities even suspecting they were dealing with murder.

It would be possible to go on almost endlessly showing the manner in which a competent forensic pathologist can protect the living through an examination of the dead.

The average citizen has more at stake than he realizes. He

should know more about legal medicine and the part that it plays in his life.

And so I dedicate this book to my friend,

Joseph A. Jachimczyk, M.D., LL.B.

—Erle Stanley Gardner

CAST OF CHARACTERS

x

1

GLADYS DOYLE had started her secretarial duties with Mauvis Niles Meade in January. Now, on the sixth day of February, she realized that after a full month of what she had described to a friend as a "cheek by jowl" existence, she knew virtually nothing about the person for whom she was working.

There had been letters, of course, and visitors. But a secretary-companion, hostess and general assistant to a person who had written a book which had been a run-away best seller certainly should have known more of the private life of the author by that time.

Miss Meade kept herself barricaded behind a wall of steady reserve which Gladys found completely baffling.

On taking up residence in the Los Angeles penthouse apartment, Mauvis Niles Meade had advertised for an experienced, good-looking secretary, hostess and companion, not over twenty-four, not under twenty-two, poised, close-mouthed and diplomatic.

Gladys Doyle had secured the position. Miss Meade had explained it was a twenty-four-hour-a-day job, had given Gladys a beautiful corner bedroom in the penthouse apartment, and work had started the next day.

The work had consisted largely of writing short letters, terse telegrams, answering the telephone, making appointments for publicity interviews and serving as a gen-

eral watchdog to keep Miss Meade from being disturbed
when she didn't want to be disturbed.

The literary gossip in the newspapers was that Miss
Meade was busily engaged writing another book.

If she was writing such a book, Gladys Doyle certainly
saw no evidence of it.

Not a great deal was known about Mauvis Meade's
background. Because of the nature of her best-selling
novel, *Chop the Man Down,* it would hardly have been
tactful to make too searching inquiries.

The book dealt with a small-town girl who went to the
big city, who was buffeted around by fate, who took a
"fix" at the behest of a sophisticated weekend companion,
who faced the usual economic and moral problems con-
fronting a young woman who finds it necessary to finance
an expensive dope habit.

Then suddenly her beauty got her involved with an unscrupulous individual who became infatuated with her.
This infatuation turned to love—a love so strong that he
saw to it that not only was she cured of the dope habit
but that word was passed around the underworld that a
death sentence awaited anyone who ever again supplied
her with dope.

The heroine's radiant beauty also attracted a shrewd,
powerful lawyer who had considerable influence. That influence began to make itself manifest in an unexpected
manner.

While some of the background pertaining to the central
characters seemed at times highly colored by a juvenile
imagination, there were flashes of grim reality indicating a
firsthand knowledge on the part of the author. No one
questioned the authenticity of the romantic portions of
the book. As one reviewer put it, they "reeked of reality."

Now, on this Friday afternoon, Gladys Doyle, answering Miss Meade's summons, carrying her shorthand note-

book and pencil, found Miss Meade stretched out on a chaise lounge, a cigarette in the long, carved ivory holder.

"How much expense money have you, Gladys?"

"About fifty dollars."

Mauvis Meade opened her purse, took out a roll of bills the size of her wrist, peeled off three one-hundred-dollar bills, folded them the long way, scissored them between two fingers of her right hand and extended them to Gladys.

"You'll need more. Take this."

Gladys took the three hundred dollars, made a notation in the notebook, waited expectantly.

"I want you to keep a date for me."

"A date?"

"A date," Miss Meade repeated. "Sometimes I wish I'd never sold those damned motion-picture rights."

In view of the fact that it was rumored she had received a cool two hundred and seventy-five thousand dollars for those motion-picture rights, Gladys could think of nothing to say. Apparently no reply was expected.

"The man's name is Edgar Carlisle," Miss Meade said. "You'll have to get in touch with him at the Summit Inn. I told him I was going to be there skiing this weekend, but I don't feel like it.

"Take the station wagon and your skis—I have a suite reserved at the Summit Inn. It's held for me every weekend, whether I use it or not, and paid for by monthly check, so don't bother with hotel bills. Just sign chits for anything you want.

"Carlisle will call the suite tonight, after you get up there. Explain to him that it's impossible for me to be there, that you're my assistant. Find out what it is he wants—it's something to do with publicity in connection with the picture release."

"How much will I tell him?" Gladys asked.

"Use your judgment," Miss Meade said. "Anything in connection with publicity that will help the sale of the book is all right. As far as the picture is concerned, I tried to hold out for a percentage. They wouldn't stand for it. They made a cash price and let it go at that. I think my agent fell down on the job on that one.

"I'm not going to break my neck doing a lot of fool things to publicize the picture. I'm willing to be reasonable, but that's all.

"The outfit Carlisle is with isn't philanthropic. They've worked out something that will publicize the picture, and that's all they're interested in. You're going to have to be tactful and diplomatic and smart. Change his proposition around so it will call for a minimum of work on my part, will publicize the picture, but will also help the sale of the book . . . and there's one more thing, Gladys."

"What?"

"This man is young and, from the way he talks over the phone, I think he's a wolf."

"And I'm to be distant and cool in a personal way, but attentive in a business way?" Gladys asked.

"Good heavens!" Mauvis Meade said. "I don't give a damn what you do. I was just trying to point out the attractive side of the chore.

"Now, here's another thing, Gladys. Coming back down the main road Sunday evening—and you'll stay until Sunday—the traffic is almost bumper to bumper. It's a mountain road, and driving it will wear you out. There's a short cut you can take coming down. It's a road that's surfaced until you are seven miles from the Inn. Then you've got ten miles of dirt road, but it's not bad. It brings you in on the other highway—there's a little map in that desk drawer. Hand it to me, will you?"

Gladys went to the desk, opened the desk drawer, found a folded piece of paper and brought it over to Miss Meade.

"Don't try to go *up* on this road," Mauvis warned. "It's dirt part of the way, and muddy after this last storm. Coming down it is easy, going up is different. The road is steep in places.

"You have your notebook. Take these directions . . . Leave Summit Inn on the main highway, go into the main part of town. Two blocks past the post office turn to the right, then after five blocks, turn left. This is a narrow, surfaced road which goes for about a mile on a fairly easy grade, then turns to the right and starts winding down the mountain. Set your speedometer at zero at the post office. At nine and seven-tenths miles, you'll come to a fork in the road. Take the right-hand turn. At fifteen-point-three miles, you'll come to a fork in the road. Again take the right-hand turn. After that, keep on the road until you come into the main highway. Don't turn on the main highway, but cross it, keeping on the same road, which you will find is surfaced after it crosses the highway. This is a rather narrow road winding among orange groves for three miles until it hits the main freeway to Los Angeles."

Mauvis Meade handed the map back to Gladys. "Put it back in the desk."

Gladys returned it to the desk drawer.

"You have the clothes you need?" Mauvis Meade asked.

Gladys nodded.

"Skis?"

"I'm an enthusiast," Gladys said.

"Leave at three o'clock this afternoon, Gladys. Return so that you're here late Sunday night. Be sure you have your key. Don't leave Summit Inn until *after six o'clock Sunday night* . . . Stay at Summit Inn until *after* six o'clock Sunday night."

"And I'm to start up at three this afternoon?"

"That's right. You're to take the station wagon. I'll have the garage fill it with gas and check the tires. You won't need chains. Have a good time. That's all. I'm going to be out the rest of the day. Answer the phone, tell anyone who calls I'm not available until Monday, that you don't know where I am.

"Now you'd better go pack some things. It isn't going to hurt to use a little glamour on the weekend. Cheese-cake will go nicely with the job you have to do. I've made an appointment for you at the beauty shop at twelve-thirty, so you'd better have an early lunch. The tab is all arranged for. Have a good time, dear."

Gladys accepted her dismissal, packed her suitcase, had lunch and went to the beauty shop. She returned to the apartment only long enough to have a bellboy take her suitcase down to the station wagon, which was fully gassed and waiting in the garage.

It was then Gladys found that someone had torn the page out of her notebook which contained the directions for the short cut down the mountain.

Miss Meade was gone. Gladys felt with annoyance that there was no reason why anyone should have torn that page from her notebook. Gladys had already entered the three hundred dollars in her expense book, she wasn't apt to forget the name Edgar Carlisle, and, of course, she knew all about the Summit Inn, the swank hotel on the snow-clad summit of the mountain ridge.

There was, however, the question of the short cut back down the mountain. She didn't fancy fighting her way through a stream of Sunday traffic.

So Gladys went to the desk, opened the drawer, found the map and made notes from it. The map she found was complete only as far as the second fork in the road. An arrow indicated the turns to be taken.

Gladys wondered why Mauvis Meade had given her three hundred dollars in cash if she was to charge every-thing at the hotel, and wondered why she had been twice cautioned not to leave the Summit Inn until after six o'clock Sunday evening. These, however, were minor matters.

A job which included an all-expense skiing weekend at the exclusive Summit Inn, negotiations with an attractive young man who was "something of a wolf" certainly was better than a nine-to-five job in a humdrum office.

Gladys' trimly shod foot was eager as it pressed on the car's gas pedal.

2

THE SKIING WEATHER was perfect. Edgar Carlisle was young, handsome, considerate and evidently not at all put out that Mauvis Meade had failed to keep her appointment. It was quite apparent that he felt the matter could be safely entrusted to the discretion of Miss Meade's secretary, and his manner so indicated. Moreover, Carlisle had obviously had an expense account which he wished to use, and Gladys had a very enjoyable time.

Despite Miss Meade's warnings, Carlisle was not especially wolfish. He was essentially masculine and kept pushing his way, trying to find out just where the no-trespassing signs were. But, having found the boundaries, he respected the signs, and all in all Gladys had such a good time that she didn't leave the Summit Inn until after dinner Sunday night.

It had clouded up and had started to snow at four o'clock in the afternoon. Gladys knew that she should have secured chains and gone on down the main highway.

But there were no chains in the car. It was almost a certainty they really wouldn't be required as a matter of safety if she was careful, but the road patrol was very strict on weekends, and, with snow on the highway, chains were required.

Gladys was pleased that she had a short cut which would take her down the mountain on a road that was not patrolled, and so she started blithely out on the journey, setting her speedometer at zero as she left the Summit Inn post office, making the proper turns and finally starting to wind down the mountain.

It was snowing hard at this elevation and she drove very cautiously, keeping her car in the lower transmission and driving with the throttle instead of keeping it in the higher gears and using the brakes. She was an experienced mountain driver and she had no particular fear of accidents.

It was as Mauvis Meade had said. There was virtually no traffic on the road. She met two cars coming up the surfaced road; then, after the hard top ceased and she came to a graveled road, she met no one.

The snow turned to a hard, pelting rain at the lower elevations. At the second fork in the road, Gladys hesitated. It looked very much as though the main graveled road was the one to the right. But the map had plainly shown an arrow indicating the left-hand fork. After some hesitancy, Gladys took the left-hand fork, and for the first time began to feel a little uneasy.

It was now a wild, stormy night. After the first mile the road rapidly deteriorated. It became simply a plain dirt road—muddy, slippery, winding and twisting down the side of the mountain above a small stream which had cut a deep canyon.

Here and there were rather high centers in the road, and Gladys had to crowd the wheels up to the bank on the curves in order to avoid those high centers and keep out of the well-worn ruts.

She felt certain now that the map had been wrong, that she should have kept on the right-hand fork. And, thinking back, she began to question in her mind whether Mauvis Meade hadn't *said* the right-hand fork when she had been dictating directions. But the map itself quite plainly had shown an arrow indicating the left-hand fork.

In any event, Gladys was trapped now. There was no place to turn around, and in the darkness it would have been all but impossible to have backed up the narrow, winding road.

At first Gladys had been afraid she might meet someone on the narrow road. Now she was beginning to wish that she would meet someone. She felt terribly alone in the pelting rain as she eased the car down the narrow mountain road.

The headlights showed a sharp, right-hand curve ahead.

As Gladys entered the curve she came to a point where she literally could not see the road. The curve was sharp enough so that the hood of the car obscured the road on the right. On the left the beam of her headlights was swallowed up in the darkness of the canyon. It was at this point that the car swerved and settled. Gladys knew she had hit a soft spot, and, in panic, gave the car a sudden burst of gas.

She felt the machine lurch, skid, then Gladys was suddenly conscious that the spinning wheels were digging into the ground. She eased off on the gasoline.

By that time it was too late. She was stuck and knew almost instinctively that her situation was hopeless.

With a weary sigh, she left the motor idling while she got out to survey her predicament.

It was difficult to determine all the details in the darkness, but apparently a culvert had washed out; a stream of storm water splashing down the hill above had started flowing down the road and had made a mudhole some twenty feet long. Gladys had apparently applied the power at just the wrong time. As her left front wheel had pushed against a rock, the rear wheels in the soft earth had dug a hole in which the car rested.

Gladys knew it was dangerous to try to back up in the dark on account of the curve, but she decided to try it. She got back in the car, put the transmission in reverse, eased on the throttle.

The car slowly began to move.

Gladys gave it a little more throttle, moved back until she began to get a headway. For a moment of swift elation she thought she was out of it, and then the front wheel struck the hole which had been dug by the spinning back wheels, and the car settled.

She could go neither forward nor backward.

She had no flashlight, the night was dark as velvet, the rain was pouring down, and as Gladys got out of the car for the second time she realized it was a cold rain, a rain which a thousand feet higher up the mountain was falling as snow.

She got back in the car, shut off the motor and the headlights. Without a flashlight, she knew it would be hopeless trying to extricate herself. She would have to wait until daylight or until help came.

She settled comfortably on the seat, but within fifteen minutes the car began to get cold. At the end of half an hour, she was cramped and chilled.

She started the motor, knowing how dangerous that was, yet determined to run it in a short burst so that she could get enough heat in the car to warm it up. It was a choice between the danger of carbon monoxide poisoning on the one hand and pneumonia on the other.

At the end of five minutes, the warm air flowing along

her ankles from the car's heater made her more comfortable and she shut off the motor.

Almost at once the car started to cool.

Twenty minutes later, Gladys determined that anything was better than sitting there and becoming chilled to the bone. She got out, slogged through the mud halfway up to her knees to open the back of the car and grope around for the jack, yet when she found the jack, she was, she realized, no better off than she had been before. She was going to have to scour the mountainside to find brush and rocks she could put under the wheels so as to get a solid foundation for traction. She decided to try walking.

Once she had decided to walk, she knew there was no help up the road until after she had climbed some seven miles, the last three or four of which would be through snow. So she decided to go around the curve and walk downhill. The road certainly must go somewhere and there was always the possibility that there would be some habitation.

She realized now that she must have taken the wrong road back at the last fork. The sound of the stream tumbling over rocks in the canyon far below, the pelting of the rain and the sighing of wind in the trees were the only noises she could hear. There was no sound of a motor anywhere.

Walking in the darkness, Gladys realized the danger. It was so dark that she literally had to feel her way a foot at a time. There was not even enough light to show the tree-clad ridges silhouetted against storm clouds. There simply was no light at all.

For the first time, Gladys felt a surge of panic. It was possible that she might have real difficulty extracting herself from this situation. If she had to turn and climb back up the grade, it would be daylight before she could reach Summit Inn . . . Of course, when she got to the point where the rain had turned to snow, she felt that the white

ground would reflect at least some clue to the location of
the road. Here there was a distinct possibility that her
next step would plunge her into the canyon.

Suddenly, Gladys caught her breath. From the darkness ahead came the gleam of a light.

For a moment she thought it might be an automobile
approaching, then she saw that it was a steady, stationary
light shining through the trees and apparently not too far
away.

She didn't realize the extent of her panic until she had
experienced the feeling of relief which swept over her.
She wanted to shout, wanted to run, but instead she con-
trolled herself and continued to feel her cautious way
along the road.

By the time she reached the cabin, she was wet and
cold. Her numbed feet stumbled up the rough board steps
from the road to the little level place where the log cabin
nestled under pine trees.

The light she had seen came from a single electric bulb
shining through a window on which there was no shade.
There was someone inside moving around. She could see
a shadow moving on the wall.

Then she was pounding on the door, crying out,
"Hello, hello, inside. Help me please!"

She heard some article of furniture being moved. In the
back of the house a door was slammed shut. Then steps,
and the door leading to the rustic porch was opened.

The light behind the man in the doorway showed him
only in silhouette. She saw that he was tall, with broad
shoulders and wavy hair. He was evidently young, but his
voice was uncordial and sharp with suspicion.

"Well, hello," he said. "What are *you* doing *here?*"

"Please," Gladys said. "I got on the wrong road. I was
coming down from Summit Inn. There's a place two or
three hundred yards up here where a culvert has washed
out and a whole stream of floodwater has softened up the

road. I blundered into it without seeing it on account of the curve, and . . . well, I'm stuck."

The man hesitated so long that for a moment Gladys was angry, then he said, "Well, come in. At least you can get warm here."

He stood to one side and she entered a rough, rustic cabin, furnished simply but tastefully.

Warmth and the aroma of fragrant tobacco smoke enveloped her as she entered the room.

"Stand over there by the stove," the man said. "You're rather wet."

She smiled at him. "Perhaps if your wife—"

He shook his head. "I have no wife. I'm here alone."

"Oh," she said.

She took a good look at him then—a man perhaps twenty-eight or thirty, with a straight nose, a prominent chin and an uncompromising stiffness in his manner which showed resentment.

"Do you, by any chance, have a phone?" she asked.

"Heavens, no!"

"You have electricity."

"Electricity which comes from a battery which is charged by a windmill so I try to conserve the light as much as possible."

The stove was a big fifty-gallon gasoline drum which had been converted into an oil-burning stove. It gave out a steady welcome heat.

Gladys could see steam rising from her clothes.

"Look," she said, "I *have* to get back to Los Angeles tonight. I'm due there right now. Do you suppose you could . . . ?"

She was interrupted by the determined shake of his head.

"But why not?" she asked. "I'm willing to pay, I'm willing to—"

"It isn't a question of money," he said. "In the first

place, you need daylight for a job of that sort. If that culvert is washed out, that road up there must be a mess."

"It is," she said, looking down at her mud-stained legs and soaked shoes. "Where does this road go? On down the mountain?"

"That's right. There's a public camp ground and picnic facilities a mile and a half down the canyon."

She had a sudden wild surge of hope. "I'll bet you have a jeep," she said. "You could go up and hook onto my car, and . . . and there must be a way down here to turn around and—"

Again she was interrupted by the shaking of his head.

"But you must have *some* car. You're not marooned out here. Any car could pull me downhill out of the mudhole. Then I could get down to the camp grounds. There must be a good road from there."

"As it happens, I have no car tonight," he interrupted.

"No car at all?" she asked.

"No car at all."

"But how in the world could you be here without having a car? You must have driven here. You didn't—"

"I don't think there's any call to discuss my personal affairs," he said curtly.

"But obviously," she said, throwing out her hand in a gesture, "I can't stay *here* all night."

He gave a faint shrug with his shoulders, a spreading motion with his hands. "What would *you* suggest?" he asked.

"Well," she said hotly, "you're a great big strapping man. If you don't have a car that can tow me out, you certainly have a raincoat and boots, and you can go there and . . . I'll help. I'm already soaked anyway, and we can jack the wheels up, and—"

"It's a job for daylight."

"Surely you have a flashlight."

"But no spare batteries—by daylight I can perhaps

help you extricate your car. I'm sorry, but I can't do it tonight."

"Won't you please understand that it's highly important—"

"I'm sorry," he interrupted, in a tone of finality. "I have recently recovered from pneumonia and I have no intention of going out and slogging around in the cold mud and getting wet to the skin trying to get some social butterfly out of a mudhole. Furthermore, I don't know what you're doing down here, and, frankly, I'm not satisfied with your explanation."

"I haven't made any," she flared.

"That's right," he said quietly.

"I tell you, I got on the wrong road."

"All the way down the mountain?"

"I was trying to take a short cut."

"Why didn't you keep on the graveled road?"

"Because my directions said I was to turn here."

His eyes held a light of mocking triumph. "Oh, so you *were* to turn here. Then you didn't take the wrong fork. May I ask who gave you those directions?"

She said, "I don't know as I can quote your exact words, but I'll try . . . I don't think there's any call for us to discuss my personal affairs."

He smiled at that.

"If you have any whiskey in the place, you might at least buy a girl a hot toddy—and if I'm going to stay here all night, I warn you that any person who tries to make unwelcome advances is in for the surprise of his life."

He said, "I'm not going to make any unwelcome advances. I'm not going to make any advances, period. As a matter of fact, your showing up here is damn inconvenient and I'm still not satisfied with your explanations. What's your name?"

"What's yours?"

"Call me John."

"What's the last name?"

"There isn't any."

"Call me Gladys," she said. "And the last name is none of your business."

"Well," he said, "we seem to be getting on. I'll get some hot water going and we'll try a toddy."

"And don't load it," she warned.

She watched him as he moved about the place. He had a big frame, but there was a spring to his step and his motions seemed perfectly co-ordinated.

This man, she decided, had trained himself in co-ordination. He was either a juggler, a football player, a boxer or perhaps all three.

"Am I going to sit up by the stove all night?" she asked.

"There are two bedrooms here," he said. "They're unheated. There are plenty of blankets. There's a bathroom which does not have hot water. There's a coil of pipe inside the stove here, and—"

"Wonderful," she said. "If you have no objection, I'm going to have a hot bath."

"A hot shower," he corrected.

"All right, a hot shower."

"When?"

"As soon as you get that hot toddy, and as soon as I can get these wet clothes off."

The toddy was good. After she had finished it, she bolted herself behind the bathroom door, got out of her wet clothes, enjoyed a hot shower, dried herself with a rough towel, looked into the adjoining bedroom he told her she was to occupy, and shivered with the cold air which greeted her.

She started to put on her wet clothes, then hesitated. After all . . . She crossed over to the bed, pulled off one of the heavy blankets, put it around her shoulders, wrapped it around her arms, picked up her damp garments, unlocked the bathroom door and entered the living room.

"I'm going to dry out these clothes over the stove," she said. "I've taken the liberty of using one of your blankets as a combination dressing gown, cocoon, and—"

She broke off as she saw that she was addressing an empty room.

She pulled up a chair close to the stove, spread the wet clothing over the back of the chair so close to the stove that the garments started to steam. Then she settled herself in another chair, pulled the warm blanket tightly about her skin and relaxed in the warmth.

The aftereffects of the hot toddy made her feel warm and relaxed. After a while she began to feel drowsy.

She turned her clothing on the chair, toasting first one side and then the other, until finally it was dry.

She was just about to put it on when she heard the pound of steps on the porch, then the door opened. A draft of cold air entered the room.

Her host was peeling off a raincoat that was glistening with rain, stamping wet feet encased in high leather boots on the floor.

"Well," she said, "look who's taking chances with his pneumonia!"

He looked her over with an impersonal appraisal which somehow bothered her more than if he had tried to grab at the blanket. "I see you've made yourself right at home."

"I'm decent," she said defiantly.

"I didn't say you weren't."

"I'm not going to sit around in wet clothes."

"No one asked you to. It's a free country."

"And I've told you I know how to take care of myself and don't appreciate unwelcome attentions."

"Look," he said irritably, "you're a good-looking girl. You've probably never had the opportunity to associate with men who thought about anything except making passes. Now, I didn't invite you here. Your presence happens to be distracting and annoying. I've offered what hospitality I can. There's a lock on the bedroom door. Now then, sister, curfew is ringing as far as you're concerned. Take your clothes and go on into that bedroom, lock the door, get into bed and go to sleep."

"What were you doing out in the rain?" she asked in sudden suspicion, and then felt herself flush as she remembered the uncurtained window in the bedroom. "Were you . . . were you spying on me?"

He merely indicated the door to the bedroom. "Curfew is ringing," he said. "All little girls are off the street. Go in and go to bed."

"I'm not going to have you treat me like a child."

"Then quit treating me like one of these Hollywood wolves," he said. "For your information, I don't go around making passes at every girl I meet."

"How very interesting," she said sarcastically.

He strode over to the chair, scooped up her clothes, ran his hands down the garments, said, "They're dry now," walked over to the bedroom door, flung it open and tossed the clothing on the bed.

"All right, Gladys," he said.

She looked at him defiantly.

He took a step toward her, and suddenly she realized that he intended literally to put her in the bedroom if she didn't go by herself.

"Good night, John," she said with exaggerated politeness.

"Good night, Gladys," he said, and his voice was that of a man who was getting rid of a distracting influence, whose mind was already starting to cope with some more interesting problem.

3

■

GLADYS TURNED on the small light globe as he closed the door. She looked at the window which was devoid of shades or drapes, and as she slipped out of the blanket, felt as though she were standing naked on a public stage with a spotlight on her.

She made a lunge for the light and switched it off. Standing nude in the cold darkness, she adjusted the blanket over the bed, then crawled under the covers and slept.

It wasn't until she wakened sometime in the small hours that she realized she had, after all, forgotten to lock the bedroom door. It was, she decided, an unnecessary precaution.

Lying there, she thought she heard the sound of an automobile engine. She stretched, yawned, propped herself up on one elbow, held herself in that position for a while, then dropped back to the pillow and almost instantly sank into the warm oblivion of slumber.

When she awakened again it was daylight. The storm was over, and her wrist watch showed it was seven-thirty.

There was a fur rug by the bed and it felt good to her bare feet. She dressed hurriedly, tentatively opened the door to the living room. She knew that the automatic oil feed would keep the big stove going and she was looking forward to the warmth.

The room was cold and empty. The stove had been

shut off, and there was about the whole room an air of vacancy.

"John," she called.

There was no answer.

She opened the door, looked out on the porch.

"Oh, John!"

Her voice was swallowed up in the still mountain air.

She went back and regarded the closed door of the other bedroom with exasperation.

"John, what do we do for eats?" she asked. "I'm famished."

When there was no answer, she turned the knob of the bedroom door. She half expected to find it locked—it would be just like him.

The bedroom door swung open, and Gladys looked inside. "Well," she said, "come on, sleepy head. I'm a working girl. What do we do about——"

Suddenly the breath went out of her at what she saw lying on the floor.

It seemed that she stood there for ages, holding the cold iron latch of the door in her hand.

Then she screamed.

After that she had a vague recollection of kneeling, of blood, of a lifeless arm, of a small-caliber rifle lying near the open window which she picked up and dropped. Then she found herself fleeing from the cabin, running blindly up the muddy road.

4

■

DELLA STREET, Perry Mason's confidential secretary, said, "There's a very excited, very bedraggled young woman in the office who says she has to see you at once on a matter of greatest importance."

Mason raised his eyebrows.

"Her name is Gladys Doyle," Della Street went on. "She is employed as a secretary-companion and hostess by Mauvis Niles Meade—you remember, she wrote the sensational novel, *Chop the Man Down.*"

"Ah, yes," Mason said, "a veritable smorgasbord of smooch, seduction and smut. And as such, of course, a runaway best-seller. You say Miss Doyle looks somewhat bedraggled?"

"That's a mild name for it. She looks as though she had had to walk home from a ride in the rain and had just got here."

"How old?"

"Twenty-two or three, attractive, good figure—"

"I'll see her," Mason announced.

Della Street smiled.

"Not because of the beauty," Mason said, "but because she's disheveled. If a girl of that description intended to vamp a lawyer into working on her case without adequate compensation, she'd have gone to the beauty parlor first. From the way you describe her, it's either a genuine emergency or she intends to pay for the services in cash."

21

"That's an angle," Della Street admitted. "I was only thinking of curves. I'll bring her in."

She went to the outer office and returned with Gladys Doyle.

"Good Morning, Miss Doyle," Mason said. "Miss Street said you have a matter which you consider extremely urgent."

She nodded.

"Care to tell me about it very quickly?" Mason asked. "Then I'll know whether I can be of any assistance. Just hit the high spots and you can elaborate later if it turns out I can handle your case."

"I went skiing over the weekend," she said. "I was with a man about whom I know very little. It was a business appointment for Miss Meade."

"And you walked home?" Mason asked, glancing at the mud-stained wreck of her shoes.

She shook her head. "I tried to take a short cut. My car got stuck in a mudhole. I came on a cabin. There was a man in the cabin. He was about twenty-eight or so, rather good-looking and exceedingly independent—I had to spend the night there in that cabin."

Mason raised his eyebrows, said, "You were alone with him?"

"Yes. There was nothing else to do. I—"

Mason said, "I think, Miss Doyle, you'd better go to the police."

"Please let me finish," she said. "He insisted that I go to bed in one of the bedrooms and lock the door. When I got up this morning, there was no one in the house. I called, then opened the door to the other bedroom and looked in. There . . . there was a dead man lying on the floor."

"The man who was in the cabin with you?" Mason asked.

She shook her head. "No, this was someone else. I . . .

I'll try to just hit the high spots if you'll let me finish, Mr. Mason."

"Go ahead," Mason told her, his suddenly alert eyes showing his keen interest.

"I ran back up the road, hardly knowing what I was doing—I'd left my car bogged down in a mudhole. When I got back to my car, it had been hauled out of the mudhole, turned around, pointed back up the grade. Whoever had done it had been considerate enough to leave it on the upgrade side of the mudhole. The ignition keys were in the lock. It was all ready to go."

"So what did you do?" Mason asked.

"I went."

"You know this man was dead?"

She nodded.

"How do you know he was dead?"

"His color, his . . . the general grotesque stiffness and . . . and the blood on the floor. I knelt beside him to feel his pulse, and—"

"Blood?" Mason interrupted.

She nodded.

"Go on," Mason said. "What did you do? Did you come directly to me?"

"No. I went to the penthouse apartment where I work —Mauvis Niles Meade."

Mason nodded.

"The place was a wreck, Mr. Mason. Drawers had been pulled out, clothes had been jerked out of the closet, papers were lying around the floor—you never saw such a mess."

"And Mauvis Niles Meade?"

She shook her head. "Not a sign of her. She said once that if she ever got into any trouble she knew you could get her out. So, now that I'm in trouble . . . well, here I am."

"Well," Mason said, "you do seem to be in quite a

predicament. Before we call in the police we'd better get
certain things established. Why didn't you call the police
as soon as you found the dead man—I mean as soon as
you got in your car and got away from there?"

"Because," she said, "I suddenly realized what a position I was in. I don't want anyone to know I spent the
night in that cabin if I can help it."

"Why?"

"The notoriety, for one thing. But mainly, I guess, the
utter implausibility of it all. I never did find out the man's
name. He called himself John. That's all I know. Apparently this other man must have been dead by the time
I got there, lying dead in the bedroom, and . . . well, of
course, you can put two and two together, John must
have known about him.

"I sensed almost from the moment I entered the place
that my presence was embarrassing and he wanted to get
rid of me.

"You can put yourself in my position, Mr. Mason. My
clothes were wet, I was soaked. I went into the bedroom
and stripped down to the skin. There were no shades on
the window, and I suppose he was standing right outside,
watching every move I made. I don't suppose he was interested in the spectacle of nudity so much as in seeing
whether I was curious about that other bedroom."

"You say there was a lock on the door of your bedroom?"

"A bolt—on the inside of the door."

"After you went to bed . . . you had locked your door,
of course."

She flushed, then suddenly laughed. "I guess one is
supposed to tell the truth to a lawyer."

He nodded.

"Actually, Mr. Mason, I didn't lock it. When I woke
up and remembered I had neglected to lock the door, I

thought I had just forgotten it. Now that I think it over I'm certain I didn't forget it on purpose."

"You mean that you—"

"Heavens no," she interrupted. "It was just that he was so smugly superior that subconsciously I wanted to have him make a pass so *I* could have the pleasure of being the one who turned *him* down. That would have been better than to have *him* ignore *me*.

"After all, I'm not dumb enough to think that I'm completely repulsive. I have a good figure. I was virtually certain this man had been watching me through the uncurtained window. If he had seen me moving around in the nude, then had entered the house to find me clothed only in a blanket, and had curtly sent me to bed and told me to bolt my door . . . well, I guess a subconscious resentment kept me from doing it. I really wanted him to make a pass."

He studied her thoughtfully.

"Now that," she said, "is being devastatingly truthful. I wouldn't admit all that except to a lawyer."

"John didn't become amorous?" Mason asked.

"Not in the least. His reactions were thoroughly abnormal, if you know what I mean. Perhaps I should say completely preoccupied."

"No passes?"

"Absolutely not. And that's a treatment—well, it's rather unusual as far as I'm concerned."

"I can imagine," Mason said dryly.

"Here I was," she said, "clad only in a blanket which I was trying to keep around me as best I could . . . I wasn't certain I could handle the situation, but I certainly expected there'd be a situation to handle . . . and I wasn't going to stay out all night in the cold rain.

"Instead of what I expected, he simply sent me to bed. I suppose after I went to bed he went out and managed to extricate my car . . . And the way he did it . . . I mean,

the way he left it would certainly indicate that he was trying to tell me that, for my own good, I'd better not say
anything about having been there.

"He told me he didn't have an automobile, but he certainly didn't walk to the place. I'm almost certain I heard
an automobile sometime in the small hours of the morning when I woke up. I suppose he took his car up, pulled
my car out of the mudhole, then drove the car down to
the wide place in the road in front of the cabin, turned the
car around and took it back up . . . " Her voice trailed
away.

"It was on the upper side of the mudhole?" Mason
asked.

"Yes."

"How did he get it through there?" Mason asked. "If
you got stuck going down, it must have been quite a job
to get through going up."

"Perhaps he had a jeep. Perhaps he was a good dirt
road driver. He certainly looked capable."

"Did you look for jeep tracks? This morning, I mean."

"I didn't look for anything, Mr. Mason. I just wanted
to get away from there, and . . . and something's happened up at Miss Meade's apartment. It's a wreck. Someone has been in there looking for something. Clothes have
been pulled out of the closet, drawers have been dumped
on the floor, papers have been scattered all over the place.
It looks as if a hurricane had spent the weekend there."

"Can you describe the exact location of this cabin?"
Mason asked.

"Yes. I've drawn you a little sketch map from memory.
Here it is. I spent the weekend at the Summit Inn. This is
the short cut I took coming back. Mauvis Meade told me
about the short cut."

Mason took the map. "You'd better tell me a little
more about Mauvis Meade, about your job and the weekend at Summit Inn," he said.

Gladys told him briefly what had happened. When she had finished, Mason said, "Here's what you do. You have some other clothes there in the penthouse apartment?"

"Yes, of course. I just didn't stop to get into them when I saw what had happened. I took one look and then came running here. I was told to be back last night, that is, to be back Sunday night."

"Go back to the penthouse apartment, get out of those clothes—no, wait a minute. You give Miss Street the data on the size of clothes you wear. Get a new outfit. It probably won't be the best-looking outfit in the world, but— Do you have money or a charge account in any of the stores?"

"I have money."

"All right," Mason said. "Get an outfit. I'd prefer not to have you going into the store for the try-ons. Now, wait a minute . . . let Della get something that will fit you. Perhaps Della has some clothes in her apartment you can borrow. You're just about the same size. Get some clothes on, go back to the penthouse apartment, call in the manager, tell him that you're very much concerned, that you think perhaps Mauvis Niles Meade had some kind of tantrum and threw things around. But you can't be certain, and the fact that she isn't there causes you some uneasiness. She *was* intending to be there?"

"I'm quite certain she was. She told me she had something very important for me to do this morning."

"All right," Mason said. "Now sit down for just a minute before you go."

Mason picked up the telephone, called Homicide headquarters at the Police Department and asked for Lieutenant Tragg. When he had Tragg on the line, he said, "Lieutenant, this is Perry Mason talking. You co-operate with the county authorities pretty much?"

"We work together," Tragg said. "What's the matter? You got another body?"

"I have another body," Mason said.

"You certainly collect 'em," Tragg said dryly. "Some day I'm going to get one of the tabulating machines at the department to find out whether you've been there first on more than fifty per cent of our cases, or whether—"

"I *haven't* been there first," Mason said. "I haven't been there."

"So?"

"I'm going to co-operate with you, and I want you to co-operate with me. I'm telling you there's a body out in a cabin on a dirt road down from Summit Inn. I'm protecting a client."

"You're supposed to turn over all the facts to the police," Lieutenant Tragg said.

"You're the police," Mason told him, "and I'm turning them over."

"Not this stuff about your client."

"I'm not supposed to turn that over to anyone."

"Your co-operation!" Tragg groaned. "It's too bad there isn't a television set on this telephone, Mason. You could see me drawing my right forefinger across my throat when you mention co-operation."

"Nevertheless," Mason told him, "that's what you're getting."

There was silence for a moment, then Tragg said, "Just where is this cabin?"

"Take a pencil," Mason said. "I'll give you directions on how to get there."

After a moment Tragg said, "Okay."

Mason gave him a complete description of how to get to the cabin.

"How did your client happen to know all this?" Tragg asked.

"Not telling," Mason said.

"You'll have an appointment with the grand jury," Tragg promised him.

"All right, I have an appointment with the grand jury."

"You'll be testifying under oath," Tragg warned.

"That's where you're wrong," Mason told him. "I'll be under oath, but I won't be testifying. I'll claim professional privilege."

Tragg thought that over, said, "Okay, we'll look into it," and hung up.

Mason turned to Gladys Doyle. "All right," he told her, "get started. Now, when you're questioned about the cyclone that hit the apartment up there, tell them that's the way it was when you came in."

"If they ask you a lot of details about *where you'd been* and *when* you got back, tell them the truth about the time you first found the apartment had been robbed. Then tell them you went out to try to find Miss Meade. Don't tell them where you went, just say you went to see someone you thought could tell you where Miss Meade was.

"Then tell the police you don't want to make any statement at all until you have contacted Miss Meade. You can say you were working on a confidential matter for her over the weekend.

"If they continue to press you, get mad and clam up. Tell them they're being impertinent."

"And I'm not to mention Summit Inn or the murder?"

"Hell, no," Mason said, "and don't keep thinking about it as a murder. It was probably suicide."

5

■

IT WAS LATE in the afternoon when Gertie, Perry Mason's receptionist, announced over the interoffice communicating system, "Lieutenant Tragg is here to see Mr. Mason." And then added, almost in the same breath, "He says he's coming in."

Mason looked up from the papers on which he was working as the door opened and Lieutenant Tragg, walking with his characteristic shuffle, head thrust slightly forward, long, firm mouth twisted in a slightly whimsical smile, said, "Hi, Perry . . . just happened to be in the neighborhood, thought I'd drop in and pay my respects and talk with you a little bit about that murder case out in Pine Glen Canyon."

"Glad to see you any time," Mason said. "Of course, some day I hope you'll learn to follow the conventional custom of being announced and then waiting until you're invited in."

Tragg shook his head. "That would be bad business, Perry. If we did that, we'd spend half our time cooling our heels in somebody's reception room, waiting for him to put through a telephone call to his lawyer and find out what to say. And if that lawyer happened to be Perry Mason, the man might not say much by the time we finally were invited to come in.

"No, it's better this way, Perry. Just bust on in, keep

your hat on, try to give the impression of being a little boorish, but all the time boring toward an objective."

"Suppose I happened to have a client here?" Mason asked.

"So much the better," Tragg said, positively beaming. "It would convince the client of the efficiency of the police. And I think at the moment you have a client that I'd like to know a whole lot about."

"I probably have several you'd like to know about," Mason commented wryly.

"I stand corrected," Lieutenant Tragg acknowledged, bowing. "And how are you this afternoon, Della?"

"Very well, thanks," Della Street said.

"The police are plodders," Tragg remarked, apparently apropos of nothing.

"Oh, I wouldn't say that," Mason protested. "They're very efficient."

"Efficient is right," Tragg said, "but their efficiency relates to plodding. It comes as the result of plodding. Take this Gladys Doyle, for instance."

Mason kept his face without expression. "What about her?"

"Funny thing," Tragg said. "She's working for this novelist, Mauvis Niles Meade. Seems she'd been away for a weekend, came home and found the apartment all torn to hell, things scattered all over. The place was wrecked."

"Notify police?" Mason asked.

"She notified the manager, and the manager thought things over and then gave the police a ring."

"Well?" Mason asked.

"She was asked the usual questions about when she discovered the crime and where she'd been—said she'd been away for the weekend, doing some confidential work for Mauvis Meade.

"Well, we started checking on the time element. Now, as nearly as we can find out from the doorman and the garage man, she expected to be back last night and at work at nine o'clock this morning. She didn't get in until after nine, and then she dashed right out."

Mason listened attentively but said nothing.

"Police looked around and tested the place for finger-prints. It was just a chore for the detail in charge of burglary, but when they asked Miss Doyle about where she'd been and she became coy, the police questioned the man at the apartment garage. He said Miss Meade had left instructions that Miss Doyle was to have the station wagon and it was to be put in good shape with oil and gas and antifreeze in the radiator because Miss Doyle was going to the Summit Inn. A routine check at Summit Inn showed she'd checked out after dinner last night.

"Well, of course, burglary detail started questioning her in considerable detail after that. We try not to be arbitrary and not make nuisances of ourselves. Ordinarily when a good-looking girl is out overnight and doesn't want to discuss the matter, we just look the other way.

"But there was this murder out there in Pine Glen Canyon, and a person *could* have driven down that way from the Summit Inn, and Miss Doyle had told someone at the Inn she was going to take a short cut she knew about . . . Well, anyway, the burglary detail notified Homicide."

"Very efficient of them," Mason said.

"Well, we try to keep from kicking ourselves as much as possible. If I run into something that looks like a lead in burglary, I always give the department a ring. If they get anything that looks as though it might be tied in with a homicide, they get in touch with me."

"I'm sure they would," Mason said.

"So I told them to look over Gladys Doyle's clothes, just for the purpose of seeing if there were any blood-stains on them. We wanted to get the clothes she'd been wearing, naturally."

"And?" Mason asked.

"No bloodstains," Tragg said, "but as a matter of routine we put them in ultraviolet light and infrared light—a lot of things come out that way—you know, quite a few of the cleaners nowadays are using marks on clothes that are invisible to the naked eye, or virtually so, but come out with startling brilliance when ultraviolet light is turned on them. They're printed in fluorescent ink."

"And?" Mason asked.

Tragg grinned and hitched one hip up on a corner of Mason's desk, sitting there swinging his left foot slightly.

"The number didn't agree with the other cleaning marks and we got the idea that perhaps she might have borrowed some clothes from someone on account of bloodstains on her garments.

"So naturally we looked up the cleaning mark and darned if it isn't the cleaning mark of Miss Della Street.

"Well, of course, the way we work, you know, Perry, we put two and two together and make four. Then we get another two somewhere and that makes six. After a while we pick up another two and we get eight."

"I see," Mason observed noncommittally.

"So I thought Miss Della Street might want to tell the police why she gave this Gladys Doyle some of her clothes to wear."

Tragg looked over at Della Street. "It would be right interesting if up in Miss Street's apartment we found clothes that belonged to Gladys Doyle and found some bloodstains on them."

"Want to look?" Mason asked.

"We're looking," Tragg said.

"Rather highhanded, isn't it?" Mason asked.

"I don't think so," Tragg said. "Under the circumstances, we decided it would be a good idea to get a search warrant and take a look. I'm sorry, Miss Street, that I have to seem a little abrupt at times, but you know how it is. A man gets a job and there are certain duties and obligations that are part of that job. Now, my job is to investigate homicide. I'm working for the taxpayers. You're a taxpayer. I hope you'll understand. I'm trying to help *you*.

"Here's a murder case that Mr. Mason called to our attention. Presumably, he had a client who had seen the body, so when we find one of Mason's clients wearing the clothes of his secretary, we start putting two and two together, like I said."

"I don't think Miss Street is going to like that," Mason said.

"I'm quite sure she isn't. Women don't like to have police officers prowling through their apartment, looking for things. I'll tell you this, Della. I told the boys to be very careful and not to do any general prowling around, just look for the clothing we wanted."

The telephone rang.

Della Street picked up the receiver, said, "Hello." She extended the telephone to Tragg. "It's for you, Lieutenant." Her voice was acid.

Tragg eased himself over along the edge of the desk, picked up the receiver, said, "Tragg speaking . . . You did, eh . . . ? When . . . ? That's good. Thanks a lot."

Tragg hung up the telephone, turned to Della Street and said, "They found Gladys Doyle's clothing out there. They'll take it to the laboratory to be examined. You can get it back after they're finished with it—unless, of course, they find something significant."

Tragg elevated his left knee, caught the leg just below the kneecap in his interlaced fingers, beamed at Perry Mason and said, "So I thought perhaps you'd now like to tell me whether Gladys Doyle was the mysterious client who told you about the murder in Pine Glen Canyon."

"Because she borrowed Miss Street's clothes, that makes her a murderer, does it?" Mason asked.

Tragg grinned. "Now you're jumping at conclusions, Mason. I didn't say that, didn't say anything like it. But you'd be surprised at what the laboratory can find out from those clothes—clothes are composed of microscopic fibers, you know, and if you come in contact with other persons, you're apt to get fibers from the suit the other person is wearing."

Della Street said to Lieutenant Tragg, "Well, thanks a lot for telling me, Lieutenant. It would be embarrassing to go home and find things all twisted around and—"

Tragg shook his head slightly. "No call for you to say anything like that, Miss Street. I'm talking with your boss. We'd dislike very much to get *you* mixed up in any murder case or catch *you* suppressing evidence or anything of that sort. We know that anything you did, you did on instructions, so naturally we thought we'd like to find out what those instructions were. I think it would be a lot better for Perry Mason to tell us . . . You know, concealing evidence can be rather serious at times and—"

"And neither Miss Street nor I would think of it," Mason interrupted. "Now, as I remember it, Tragg, in order for a person to become guilty of concealing evidence so that it's a crime, he has to know that it's evidence and has to conceal it.

"I'm quite certain that if the police found any clothing belonging to Gladys Doyle out at Della Street's apartment, they found that it hadn't been concealed at all but was right out in the open. Now, you say that the clothing is evidence in a murder case, but unless there are bloodstains or significant fibers on that clothing, it isn't evidence of anything, it's just clothing."

"That's what comes of having a trained legal mind," Tragg said, getting to his feet and shuffling toward the door. "I thought Perry could answer the questions for you, Della . . . Just happened to be in the neighborhood, Mason, and thought I'd drop in."

He went out.

Mason and Della Street exchanged glances.

"Well, Chief," she said, "the fat seems to be in the fire."

"I'm afraid," Mason told her, "the fire's in the fat."

"Think we should take a run out to the Meade penthouse apartment and see if our client is available?" Della Street asked.

Mason shook his head. "We can find her just as quick sitting right here. She's undoubtedly in custody. They won't let her telephone for an attorney unless they charge her with something, and if they decide to let her telephone, we'll get a ring."

"And in the meantime?" Della Street asked.

"In the meantime," Mason said, "we get hold of the Drake Detective Agency and start Paul Drake looking around."

"Want me to give him a ring?" Della asked.

Mason nodded.

Della Street put through the call and after a moment said, "Drake is on his way down."

The Drake Detective Agency, with offices on the same floor as Mason's offices, remained open twenty-four hours a day. Paul Drake, who did all of Mason's investigative work, sometimes shuttled back and forth between his office and Mason's as many as a dozen times a day.

Within a matter of seconds after Della Street had hung up the telephone, Drake's code knock sounded on the door of Perry Mason's private office and Della Street let him in.

Paul Drake, tall, loose-jointed, easy-moving, contrived somehow to give the impression of being indifferent to his surroundings, yet managed to see everything.

"Hi, beautiful," he said to Della. Then to Perry Mason, "What is it this time?"

"This one," Mason said, "has everything—sex, sophistication, mystery and melodrama."

"Shoot," Drake told him, sitting down in the big overstuffed leather chair, then after a moment twisting around so one upholstered arm supported his back while his long legs were draped over the other arm.

Mason said, "Mauvis Niles Meade, who wrote a novel, *Chop the Man Down,* has a secretary, Gladys Doyle. Police have picked up Gladys Doyle, at least for questioning, in connection with a murder which took place in Pine Glen last night."

"Where's Pine Glen?" Drake asked.

"Out on the slope of the mountain between Summit Inn and—"

"Oh, yes, I know the place," Drake said. "A wild canyon that runs down the mountainside. There's a public camp and picnic grounds called Pine Glen, which takes its name from the canyon."

"There was a murder out there last night," Mason said. "I'd like you to find out all you can about it, Paul—just pick up what the police are doing and I'd like to get some background on Mauvis Niles Meade and find out where she is now. Her apartment seems to have been pretty thoroughly ransacked over the weekend."

"I can tell you a little stuff about Mauvis Meade right now," Drake said.

"What?"

"Her novel got pretty close to home, Perry. There are some of those things a woman just doesn't make up out of whole cloth."

"So?" Mason asked.

"So," Drake said, "the rumor is that some big shot is pretty unhappy about some of the things in the book."

"What sort of a big shot, Paul?"

"A lawyer," Drake said.

"What sort of a lawyer?"

"I wouldn't know too much about it, Perry. I've just heard rumors, that's all. I guess you'd call this guy a mouthpiece."

"What could have been in the book to make a lawyer unhappy?" Mason asked.

"Have you read the book, Perry?"

"No. I understand generally it's the story of a woman who got around."

"It's all of that, and among the men the heroine knew was a lawyer. Now, I understand this lawyer is a real character. He made a play for Mauvis Meade and everything was hunky-dory for a while . . . and then Mauvis blossomed into a novelist and that was bad."

"The lawyer talked too much?" Mason asked.

"To Mauvis, yes. At least some of his clients are reputed to think so."

"What was the specialty of this lawyer?"

"Investments."

"What sort of investments?"

"You'd better read the book, Perry."

"I will, but tell me generally what sort of investments?"

"Suppose we call them razzle-dazzle investments. Suppose a lawyer has clients who make big money out of gambling, bookmaking, numbers, and perhaps a little smuggling."

"Go on," Mason said.

"Well," Drake said, "I'll ask you a question. What does a man do with this dough after he's made it? He can only spend so much."

"The Government likes to have a big part of it," Mason said.

"That's the point, Perry. A man who makes a million out of doing something illegal doesn't intend to turn around and pay nine hundred thousand of it to Uncle Sam in the form of taxes. Having violated one law to make a million, he'll violate another to save nine-tenths of it."

"The Government usually considers its wants are paramount," Mason said dryly.

"That's right," Drake said, "provided the Government knows about the million, provided the Government can find the million in the first place. Now, that's where a lot of this razzle-dazzle comes in. If you don't use banks, if you do business on a cash basis, and if you have enough people shuffling things around, it's sometimes rather difficult to prove anything. And if some of the dummies are good-looking babes who can put on an act in front of a jury, it sometimes becomes even more difficult to tell where the razzle begins and the dazzle leaves off."

Mason thought things over for a minute, then said, "Mauvis Meade shouldn't be too difficult to find."

"She shouldn't, for a fact," Drake said. "I don't think they'd like it if she was hard to find for very long at a time. Have you tried the easy way, Perry?"

"What do you mean, the easy way?"

Drake pointed to the telephone.

Mason said, "She was missing shortly after noon, but it's an idea, Paul. I suppose when she shows up the newspapermen will keep her busy for a while."

Drake said, "This Mauvis Meade has a penthouse apartment out at the Sitwell Arms. How long's your client been working for Mauvis Meade?"

"About a month, I think."

Drake said, "You know, Perry, this client of yours could have been hand-picked."

"By whom, and for what?"

"As a patsy," Drake said, "and by some smart lawyer who wanted to get himself out of a jam with some unconventional clients."

"Then Mauvis Meade would have to be in on it," Mason said.

"Is there any definite assurance that she isn't?" Drake asked.

Mason thought the situation over for a few moments, then turned to Della Street. "Della," he said, "I think Paul Drake has a point. Ring up the Sitwell Arms Apartments, say that you're Mr. Mason's secretary, that Mr. Mason is very anxious to get in touch with Miss Meade just as soon as she returns. Emphasize that I want to talk with her in person and at the earliest possible moment."

Della Street nodded and reached for the telephone. As her fingers rapidly spinned the dial, Mason turned to Paul Drake. "In the meantime, Paul, find out all you can about the general setup and about the murder. If we could possibly locate Mauvis Meade before the newspaper reporters get hold of her, it would—"

Della Street broke in excitedly, "Chief, she just came in! The switchboard operator says she went up to her apartment about five minutes ago. The operator's ringing the apartment now."

Mason reached for his telephone and at that moment, Della Street said, "Miss Meade, this is Perry Mason's office. Mr. Mason wants to talk with you. Will you hold the phone please?"

Mason said, "Hello."

A throaty feminine voice said, "Well, well, Perry Mason. And how do *you* do, Mr. Mason?"

"Nicely, thank you," Mason replied. "I'd like very much to see you."

"And *I'd* like to see *you*."

"You're in your apartment now?"

"What's left of it, yes. It seems that while I was gone someone else moved in. Someone who was a very careless housekeeper. My possessions are scattered to the four corners. The manager of the apartment is surveying the damage."

"He's there with you now?"

"Yes."

"Will you do this?" Mason asked. "Will you ask him not to notify anyone that you have returned until after I can come and talk with you? Your secretary, Gladys Doyle, is in trouble. I'm representing her. I am assuming that you'd like to co-operate."

"How long will it take you to get here?"

"I can get there pretty fast," Mason said.

"Well . . ." She hesitated.

Mason placed his hand over the mouthpiece of the telephone, said to Della Street, "I'm not going to plead with her. We've made the suggestion. We'll let it germinate."

The silence on the telephone became embarrassing.

Suddenly Mauvis Meade's voice said, "Are you still there, Mr. Mason?"

"I'm waiting."

"All right," she said, "get out here right away. I'll tell the manager not to let anyone know I'm here. I'll talk with you first. The apartment is Forty-six A. Just come right up. Don't wait to be announced."

"And in the meantime," Mason asked, "will you ask the switchboard operator to disconnect all calls until I get there?"

"I'll think that one over," she said. "You'd better come right away."

"I'm coming," Mason promised.

The lawyer slammed up the telephone, glanced at his watch, said, "I'll have to fight traffic. You close up the office, Della. Paul, you'd better keep yourself personally available until I get back."

"I'll be in my office," Drake said.

"And I'll be right here," Della told him. "I'll close up the office, if you want, but I'll be waiting."

Mason patted her shoulder, said, "Good girl," grabbed his hat and shot out of the door.

6

■

THE ELEVATOR EASED to a crawl for the last few feet of
its climb, then came to a stop. The door slid back, Mason
entered a small vestibule. On one side was a door bearing
the sign, "Roof." On the other side a door had the
number 46A.

Mason pressed the mother-of-pearl button and heard
chimes on the inside of the apartment.

A moment later the door opened and a chestnut-haired
beauty attired in black silk lounging pajamas, holding a
cigarette in a carved ivory holder in her left hand, smiled
up at Perry Mason with impudent eyes and said, "Well,
you look just like your pictures—strong, rugged . . . and
intensely masculine. Come in, Mr. Mason. As you can
see, the place is a wreck. I've straightened out a few
things, but it's going to take a whole day to get things put
back in any semblance of order. Damn it, I wish I had
Gladys here to help. How long are the police going to
hold her?"

"That depends," Mason said, following Mauvis Meade
into the apartment.

The lounging pajamas had been tailored to sleek
smoothness over her body, and Mauvis Meade, leading
the way through the reception hallway, walked as though
she was accustomed to having men's eyes centered upon
those curves and had no objection.

She led the way into a living room and indicated a chair. "Sit down, Mr. Mason. Want a drink?"

"Not right now. I'd prefer to cover as much ground as we can before we're interrupted."

She raised her eyebrows. "You think we'll be interrupted?"

"I'm afraid we may be."

She said, "That pile of stuff over there on the floor came out of the dresser drawers. I haven't had a chance to put it back . . . Would you like to try one of my cigarettes, Mr. Mason?"

He said, "I'll stay with my own brand, if you don't mind."

He took a cigarette case from his pocket, tapped a cigarette on the edge of the case, lit it and said, "How much do you know about the situation in which Miss Doyle finds herself?"

"Very little," she said. "I was scheduled to meet Edgar Carlisle, who's from the movie studio that bought movie rights to my book. He wanted some co-operation on publicity. I didn't know whether I cared to give it to him or not.

"They bought movie rights to the book, but they didn't give me a share of the gross, which was one of the things I wanted. As far as I'm concerned, they've bought something. It's theirs. I'm not going to put myself out for them.

"I intended to be up at the Summit Inn this weekend, but then I decided not to go. I'd told Carlisle I'd meet him up there, and so I told Gladys to go up in my place. In case you hadn't noticed, Mr. Mason, Gladys is rather easy on the eyes and I think she knows her way around. I gave her a rather generous expense allowance, told her to take the station wagon and go on up."

"You also told her about a short cut coming back?"

"That's right. That Sunday traffic can be deadly coming down the mountain, particularly when there are good skiing conditions. The short cut is a dirt road, but I've made it under all sorts of conditions."

"Do you know what happened?" Mason asked.

"Only generally. The manager tells me that Gladys got off the road, got stuck, spent the night in a cottage and found a body—at least that seems to be what the police claim."

"How did you happen to discover that short cut?" Mason asked, making the question sound casual.

She regarded him for a moment, then stretched back against the cushions of the davenport, the sheer silk straining across her full breasts as she pressed her shoulders back against the cushions. Her large, dark-brown eyes surveyed him appraisingly. The long-lashed lids lowered and then raised with provocative deliberation.

Instead of answering the question, she said, "*I* thought *I* might need an attorney, so I mentioned to Gladys that if I ever got in any kind of trouble, Perry Mason was the man I wanted . . . so now Gladys is the one who gets in trouble and *she* ties you up."

"What do you mean, I'm tied up?" Mason asked.

"She's your client?"

Mason nodded.

"You're going to represent her?"

"If she's charged with anything, I am."

"And, of course, while you're representing her you couldn't represent any client who might have conflicting or adverse interests?"

"That's right, generally speaking."

"What a sap I was," she exclaimed.

"Why?"

"To mention you to Gladys."

"Are you," Mason asked, "in a position where you're going to have any conflicting interests?"

"How do I know? My crystal ball is no bigger than yours, Mr. Mason—probably not as big."

"Does it require a crystal ball?"

"It requires looking into the future, and I don't like to do that without a crystal ball."

"Just why did you think you might need an attorney?" Mason asked.

Her smile was arch as she turned her head slightly to one side. "Aren't you being rather naive, Mr. Mason?"

"Am I?"

"I think so, particularly under the circumstances."

"You don't think you should tell me?"

She shook her head.

"You feel there may be a conflict between your interests and those of Gladys Doyle's?"

"I don't think I care to amplify my statement, Mr. Mason. I'll just say that I think you're being rather naive and let it go at that."

"Very well," Mason said, "let's act on the assumption, then, that you're a witness and I'm interviewing you."

"A witness to what?"

"To whatever you know."

"All right. What do I know?"

"Let us begin at the beginning," Mason said. "You have written a highly successful novel?"

"That," she said, "is something that we can . . . let's see, I believe stipulate is the word the lawyers use."

"Would you care to tell me what figure you received for the movie rights, for instance?"

"The newspapers have insisted that I got two hundred and seventy-five thousand dollars cash."

"And we may assume that the newspaper accounts are not too far out of the way?"

"Newspapers try to be accurate."

"And your royalties?"

"Well," she said, "royalties from the hard-cover edition have been very satisfying. However, the paperback edition which is coming out is going to be the main source of income. It's no secret, Mr. Mason, that I have been given a guaranteed royalty for a period of ten years, payable in ten annual installments."

"You think your book will be selling for ten years?"

"Probably not, but I'd rather have the income spread out over a period of ten years than take the royalties in a lump and turn them all over to the Government."

"And, of course," Mason said, "you'll be writing other books."

"Well," she observed thoughtfully, "I'm not so certain."

"Surely," Mason said, "you'll follow up your success."

"After a while, perhaps, but . . . you see, Mr. Mason, I'm under no illusions as to the literary quality of my book. You know, people essentially are hypocrites. They love to lecture about morality, but they love to read about immorality.

"An attractive young woman can write a story about a heroine whose clothes keep coming off and describe the resultant consequences in detail. People are shocked. But people love to be shocked.

"If you'll notice the best sellers and analyze them carefully, you'll find that most of the sex books written by attractive women whose photographs look very seductive on the dust jackets are the stories that sell in the big figures.

"Women readers love to read about sex from the standpoint of a woman. Men like to look at the dish pictured on the cover and wonder just how it happened that she learned all those details about the things which are described in the book and which nice girls aren't supposed to know. It makes for speculation—and sales.

"A woman can do that with a first book. When she tries to follow it up with another book, the public doesn't react so well. The first venture into sex is seduction. The second is commercialized mental prostitution—if you get the distinction."

"You evidently have this all figured out," Mason said.

"I've figured it all out, Mr. Mason. I wrote the sort of book I did deliberately and carefully. I studied the market. I studied the books that have become runaway best sellers. I did a certain amount of research work, a certain amount of field work on the subject of sex."

"All the time intending to write a novel."

"All the time having this in the back of my mind. Of course, I had other things as well."

"I believe you described certain characters in your book," Mason said, "certain powerful, ruthless men."

"Powerful men are *all* ruthless," she said, "particularly where sexual conquests are concerned. They're accustomed to having what they want. They get it by one means or another. People like to read about that. People also like to read about the woman in the case, not a young woman who fumbles through the first adolescent adventures of life, but about a young woman who is demurely conscious of her charm, who attracts the attention of the strong, determined male who goes about getting what he wants in the world of romance with the same ruthless determination with which he batters down his rivals in the world of business.

"And then, of course, your girl has ultimately to acquire an ability to appraise the type of merchandise she has to offer and to capitalize on it at the end in a truly feminine way. If she can't have marriage, she intends to settle for material benefits. People like that."

Mason studied her with interest. "Why?" he asked.

"Probably," she said, "because every woman who is respectably married wonders just how much success she would have had if she had strayed from the straight and narrow path and become a courtesan— I think the temptation is more universal than perhaps we realize."

"That," Mason said, "is to my mind rather a sordid appraisal of literature and of life."

"It's a damn good appraisal of the literary *market*," she said, "regardless of literature *or* life."

"And you went into it deliberately?"

"I went into it deliberately," she said mockingly. "Or you might say that I used the literary field of exploitation in order to get my financial returns for the manner in which my own charms had been exploited by the ruthless male."

"Is that true?" Mason asked.

"I said that you might assume that it's true."

"I'm interested," Mason told her, "because I think that the experiences Gladys Doyle had last night are perhaps tied in, in some way, with her employment with you."

Mauvis Meade shook her head, her smile mocking.

"You don't think so?" Mason asked.

Mauvis said, "Gladys Doyle is a young woman who knows her way around. She's attractive, poised and . . . well, let us say provocative."

Mason's eyes narrowed, "Your advertisement asked for exactly that sort of a secretary."

"That's right. Do you want to make something sinister out of the ad?"

"I don't know," Mason said. And then added after a significant pause, "Yet."

"Well, don't try it," she said. "The answer is perfectly obvious. With the background that I had set up and the type of publicity I intended to use, I certainly didn't want to have some mousy little nincompoop tapping out correspondence on a typewriter but not having the faintest idea of what actually went on in the world, of what was beneath the surface."

"And," Mason said, "you directed Gladys Doyle down the mountain on a short cut."

"I did."

"And the directions were such that she was certain to blunder into this cabin on the Pine Glen road?"

"Now there, Mr. Mason, you're one hundred per cent wrong. You're—"

The door chimes sounded once. Then, after a brief interval, twice. They were followed by the sound of knuckles.

"I was hoping we could finish this phase of the inquiry without interruption," Mason said.

"I know you were—and I'm not certain that I want to finish what you call this phase of the inquiry, Mr. Mason. I have been looking forward to meeting you, but I'm not certain the experience is exactly as I had planned it. I was hoping that you could protect me and now, thanks to a stupid remark, I find that I have disqualified you from—"

Again the chimes sounded and again there was an insistent pounding on the door.

With a lithe motion, Mauvis Meade got to her feet, went past Mason to the entrance hallway, opened the door and said, "Well, you might at least follow the rules of the house and be announced on the telephone. There's no need to break the door down."

"I'm sorry, ma'am," Lieutenant Tragg's voice said, "but I'm Lieutenant Tragg of Homicide and it's part of our policy not to be announced. I'm coming in, if you don't mind. I want to talk to you."

"I'm not alone," Mauvis Meade said.

"So much the better," Tragg said, walking on in. And then, catching sight of Mason, "Well, well, well, Perry Mason! Well, this *is* indeed a surprise, Mr. Mason. I seem to keep running into you."

"You do, for a fact," Mason said.

"Well, I won't be bothering you any more, Mason. There's no need to detain you."

Mason shook his head. "I'm sorry, Tragg, but this is one time I'm not leaving. I am, at the moment, engaged in getting some very essential information from Miss Meade. I have no objection to sharing that information with you, but you're not going to have an exclusive on it."

Lieutenant Tragg surveyed Mauvis Meade with thoughtful, appraising eyes, took in the manner in which she was dressed, the swelling curves so daringly displayed, the indolent, almost impudent manner in which she tilted her head slightly to one side, her chin up as she looked at him with a half-smile. She raised her eyelids with exaggerated slowness.

Tragg said, "I think Miss Meade and I want to talk privately, Mason, and I don't have time to postpone my discussion until you and she are finished."

"Miss Meade," Mason said, "gave Gladys Doyle directions for taking a short cut down the mountain from Summit Inn. Those directions included taking the road which led down to Pine Glen."

"They did not," Mauvis Meade said with quiet, firm insistence.

Tragg grinned.

"And I say they did," Mason said. "Mauvis Meade had a sketch map which she showed to my client. I am stating to you, Lieutenant Tragg, officially, that this map showed that my client was to go down the Pine Glen road. In doing so, she was following directions and instructions given her by her employer, Miss Meade.

"Now then, Lieutenant, if you want to try and get rough about it and have me thrown out and then Miss Meade should take the witness stand with any different story, I'll use this interview to show bias on her part."

Tragg, easing himself into a chair, looked at Mauvis Meade meditatively. "That true?" he asked at length.

"It is not true, Lieutenant Tragg."

"You told her about a short cut down the mountain?"

"I told her about a short cut down the mountain. The

Pine Glen road turns to the left at the fork. I told her to take the right-hand fork at the Pine Glen turnoff."

"What about this sketch map?" Tragg asked.

"That is right. I gave her directions from the sketch map."

"And the sketch map shows that she was to take the right fork?"

"That is right."

Tragg grinned. "Let's just take a look at that map, Miss Meade . . . Under the circumstances, Mason, sit down. Just stay right here. I think it will be a lot better for you to see the evidence right now than to claim it's been tampered with later on."

"The map is in the other room," she said. "It may take me a little time to find it. The place has been thoroughly ransacked."

"That's all right," Mason said, "we'll help you hunt."

"You will not!" she said with sudden vehemence. "There are some things on which a woman is entitled to privacy. You do not search my apartment—either of you."

"You go get the map," Tragg said. "We'll wait right here."

Tragg settled back in his chair and smiled at Mason.

Mason watched Mauvis Meade glide from the room.

"Nice work, if you can get it," Tragg said.

"She seems to have been quite successful in getting it," Mason said.

"You misunderstood me," Tragg told him. "I was talking about your client and the map."

"My client," Mason said, "went to that cabin because she was directed to go down that road."

Tragg grinned. "Your client went to that cabin for reasons of her own—not that it makes a great deal of difference."

"You'll be surprised how much difference it can make."

They were silent for a few moments, then Mason frowned and glanced toward the door through which Mauvis Meade had vanished. Abruptly he got to his feet. "I think," he told Lieutenant Tragg, "that, even at the risk of invading a young woman's privacy, we should assure ourselves that evidence is evidence—let's take a look."

Tragg grinned. "You're out of line, Mason. We made our choice when she went through that door. You don't realize what can happen on a deal of this kind—think of newspaper headlines: AUTHORESS ACCUSES POLICE OFFICER OF BARGING INTO BEDROOM. Then there'll be a photograph and below that will be the caption: MAUVIS MEADE SHOWS HOW SHE WAS STANDING POISED IN FRONT OF MIRROR WHEN POLICE LIEUTENANT TRAGG BURST INTO BEDROOM. ' "The only difference between the picture and what Lieutenant Tragg saw is the amount of clothing I had on," Miss Meade said.'

"Then the chief reads those headlines and the people read the headlines, and it makes a nice spicy story and—"

"But it shouldn't take her that long to find a map," Mason said. "The hell with the headlines! I'm inviting you to come along, Lieutenant."

Tragg simply crossed his legs and settled himself in the chair. Mason strode across to the closed door, had raised his right hand when the door was suddenly opened.

Mauvis Meade, standing face to face with Mason, smiled seductively. "Why, Counselor," she said, "how impulsive!"

"The map," Mason said.

She started to hand him a paper but Tragg was out of his chair and across the room with surprising agility.

"Hold it," he said. "Keep that map in *your* possession, Miss Meade. We'll let Mason take a look at it and then *I'll* take the map into *my* custody."

"Good heavens!" she said. "It isn't that important. It's just a sketch map showing the road down the mountain. Here, Mr. Mason, you look over this shoulder and you, Lieutenant Tragg, can look over the other shoulder."

She sidled up close to Mason, pressing against his arm as she held out the map.

Tragg looked over the other shoulder.

The map showed an oblong labeled "Summit Inn," and then another rectangle showed the location of the post office. There were two intersecting streets past the post office, then an arrow showing a turn to the right, then five intersecting streets and an arrow showing a turn to the left. A series of winding curves went past the written figures five miles. A fork showed in the road with the figure, 9.7 miles, and an arrow indicating the right turn. Farther down the paper there was another fork in the road and the figure 15.3 miles. Again an arrow indicated the right-hand fork, then the road went on down to the extreme lower left-hand corner of the paper where diagonal parallel lines were labeled "Main Highway." The arrow went straight across the highway.

"Well," Tragg said, "that's very interesting, very interesting indeed. Now, just which is the Pine Glen Road, Miss Meade?"

"You set your speedometer at zero at the post office," she said. "The fork of the road here at fifteen and three-tenths miles is where you turn left, I believe, to go down to Pine Glen. The road I always take is the right-hand fork."

Tragg extended his arm. "Now, Miss Meade," he said, "if you'll just put your name down in the corner of this map and the date and the time, I'll take the map, and in that way there won't be any chance of confusion."

"You'll have to loan me your pen," she said, laughing. "I don't keep pockets in these lounging pajamas."

Tragg reached for his fountain pen.

"Hold it," Mason said.

Tragg looked at him speculatively.

Mason's hand reached out, took possession of Mauvis Meade's right hand. He held up the middle finger, then the forefinger.

"How does it happen you have these fresh inkstains in between these two fingers if you don't have a fountain pen available?"

"I don't know," she said shortly. "Those stains have probably been on there for some time. I didn't wear these lounging pajamas all day. Did you want to make a search for a fountain pen, Mr. Mason?"

Mason abruptly dropped her hand, walked to the door, pushed it open.

"You can't go in there," Mauvis Meade said angrily.

"I'm in," Mason told her.

The room was equipped as a study, with a writing desk in one corner of the room. The desk had been opened, papers from the various pigeonholes had been thrown helter-skelter onto the folding top which swung down on hinges to form a writing table. The contents of the drawers below this folding top had been dumped on the floor. The drawers themselves were lying bottom side up.

A fountain pen with the screw cap removed was lying on the part of desk used as a writing table, and a pad of paper was near the fountain pen.

"Don't you go near that desk! Don't you touch those papers." Mauvis Meade shouted angrily.

"I'm taking a look," Mason said.

"You get out of here!" Mauvis Meade said angrily. "You can't do this to me."

Mason said, "Miss Meade, you drew that map just now. You either couldn't find the original map or you didn't want to find it, so you made this one. The map that you used in giving directions to my client showed that she was to turn left at the fork fifteen and three-tenths miles from the post office."

"What are you trying to do?" she asked angrily. "Are you trying to drag me into this?"

Tragg, standing slightly to one side, listened to every word of the conversation, watched every move made by Mauvis Meade and the lawyer, but said nothing. His face was twisted into a smile.

"I'm trying to get at the facts," Mason said, "and I want the facts. I'm warning you, Miss Meade, that you can't get away with this. You didn't have any ink on your fingers when you entered this room. When you came out with the map you had ink on your fingers. That pad of paper there on the desk is exactly the same size as this map which Lieutenant Tragg is holding. That pen had been knocked on the floor and left lying on its side. Some of the ink had leaked into the cap. You can see that there's ink on the barrel of the pen where it screws into the cap and that the ink is still moist. You picked it up to draw this map."

"You are trying to involve me," she said to Mason. "You are smart, you are dangerous. All right, Mr. Perry Mason, I'll tell *you* something. I, too, am smart. I, too, am dangerous."

Mason said, "I am calling on you here and now, in the presence of Lieutenant Tragg, to produce the original sketch map, the sketch map which you had in your hand when you told my client where to turn."

"Your client!" she said scornfully. "Your client is a fool! Where are the notes that your client made from the dictation that I gave her? Let her produce those notes. They will show that she was to turn right at the point in the mountain where the Pine Glen road turns off the main graveled highway."

"Those notes were torn out of her shorthand notebook," Mason said.

"Phooey!" Mauvis Meade exclaimed. "You are a lawyer. You are supposed to be smart. You are supposed to be skeptical, yet you fall for a story such as that . . . you men!"

"Perhaps," Mason said, "her shorthand notebook is here. Perhaps we should look for it."

"All right," she said, "a good idea. Let's look for it."

"Where is her room?" Mason asked.

"This way," Mauvis Meade said.

The exaggerated undulations of her walk were now no longer evident. She strode straight-backed across the room, jerked open a door and entered the bedroom of Gladys Doyle.

Here everything was in order.

"Well!" she said, standing in the doorway and letting her voice show such startled surprise that for the moment it seemed almost overdone. "Here," she said, "we have apple pie order! The rest of the penthouse is torn up in a frantic search, but there was no search in this bedroom. It is almost as though the persons making the search knew that the thing they were searching for would not be in the bedroom of Gladys Doyle. Doesn't it seem so to you, Lieutenant?"

"I'm here only as an observer at the moment," Tragg grinned. "Go right ahead. If you want to look for the shorthand notebook used by Gladys Doyle, it's all right with me. As yet, I haven't a search warrant. In view of Mr. Mason's activities, I'm going to see that the place is guarded until we do get a search warrant."

"Well," she said, "you don't need a search warrant. I'm giving you authority to search. There is the shorthand notebook."

She walked over to a stenographic desk on which there was a typewriter and paper, picked up an opened shorthand notebook, whipped it closed and handed it to Lieutenant Tragg.

"All right," Mason said, "show me where she made the notes."

Mauvis Meade opened the book, riffled through the pages. "This is correspondence we did last week," she said. "This is . . ."

She paused as the neat shorthand notes terminated and the next page was blank.

"But this was the notebook she used," she said to Lieutenant Tragg. "I am certain of it. She had it in her hand."

"How does she take dictation?" Tragg asked, looking at the notebook speculatively. "With a pencil, a pen or . . . ?"

"With a ballpoint pen," Mauvis Meade said.

Tragg reached out, took the notebook, tilted it slightly, inspecting the blank page. Then he said with sudden interest, "Come over here a minute."

Tragg turned on a piano light with a flexible spiral tube in the handle. He adjusted the light at just the right angle, said, "Miss Meade, would you mind turning off the main switch?"

She walked over to the door and clicked the main switch.

"Now, if you'll step over here, please," Tragg said.

She came over to stand at Mason's side.

Using the illumination from the single bulb in the piano light, Tragg tilted the notebook so that it was on one side and the light spread smoothly across the page.

"This is an old police trick," he said. "Quite frequently a person writing on one page leaves an indentation on the page directly beneath . . . there seems to be something here which . . . I think we can bring it out in the lab."

"Yes. You can see lines there," Mauvis Meade said. "There certainly are lines."

"There certainly are," Tragg said. And, abruptly snapping the shorthand notebook closed, slipped it in his side coat pocket.

Mauvis Meade said indignantly, "I'm not going to have her drag me into this thing. You examine the indentations and you'll find I was telling the truth. I told her to take the right-hand fork."

Tragg looked around him, said, "It certainly is an interesting fact that nothing has been disturbed in Gladys Doyle's room."

"That's an insult," Mason said.

"Who's insulted?" Tragg asked.

"You are. The police are. The idea that anyone would be so dumb as to think the police would fall for anything so terribly obvious is an insult."

"I know, I know," Tragg said, "but I've been insulted by experts, and there's always the possibility someone making a hurried search knew the article he was after wasn't in Gladys Doyle's room and therefore didn't waste the precious time he had at his disposal looking for it there."

Mauvis Meade, who had been looking around, said, "I notice there are some papers in her wastebasket. If the *room* hasn't been disturbed, the probabilities are the *wastebasket* hasn't either."

She reached gingerly into the wastebasket, said, "I hope I don't come up with a lot of moist chewing gum, and . . . *here's* that page out of the shorthand book, Lieutenant! *Now* we can see who's right and who's wrong."

She smoothed out a crumpled page from a shorthand book, said, "Here it is, right at the top of the page. 'Received three hundred dollars expense money' and the date, and here are the directions—they're in shorthand. I can't read her shorthand very well, but I can manage to make it out . . . Yes, here it is, right here."

Mauvis Meade held a pointed fingernail on the page.

"There you are, right there. I know enough about her system of shorthand to know that that's the sign for right. She's to turn right at that fork in the road."

Tragg folded the paper, put it in his pocket, started methodically looking through the wastebasket.

"There may be some things here she wouldn't like to have you see," Mauvis Meade said. "A girl's entitled to have her privacy respected."

Tragg kept right on with the search.

The telephone rang. Mauvis Meade said, "Pardon me," and went to answer the phone.

She was back by the time Tragg had finished inventorying the contents of the wastebasket.

Tragg looked at her sharply. "Bad news on the telephone, Miss Meade?" he asked.

"Good heavens! Am I *that* obvious?"

"You look as though somebody had socked you in the stomach with a wet towel."

"I . . . it's a personal matter."

"How personal?"

"Very personal. I . . . I'm afraid I've been under too much of a strain for the past few hours. I guess I'll . . ."

Again the phone rang.

Mauvis Meade looked helplessly at Tragg.

"Want me to answer it?" Tragg asked.

She hesitated a moment, then shook her head, got up and went to the phone.

"Sure looks as though that last phone call gave her a lick right between the eyes," Tragg said conversationally to Mason. "We'll have to go about finding out who it was and what was said."

"This call is for you, Lieutenant," Mauvis Meade called out.

Tragg strode out into the other room, took the telephone from Mauvis Meade's outstretched hand, said, "Yes, hello, Tragg speaking . . . the devil . . ."

He was silent for a few moments, then said, "All right, I've got it," and hung up.

He turned and frowned at Mason speculatively. Abruptly he said, "Well, I have work to do. I'm leaving. I think, Mason, since Miss Meade is beginning to feel the strain under which she's been laboring, it would be just as well if you left when I did."

Mauvis Meade nodded. "I don't want anyone here—I don't want to see anyone. I . . . I guess I'm more tired than I thought."

"You certainly don't need to see anyone you don't want to," Tragg said sympathetically. "Come on, Mason."

Mauvis Meade saw them to the door, then slammed the door shut. They heard the sound of a bolt shooting into place.

While they were waiting for the elevator, Tragg said thoughtfully, "I wonder what that telephone call was. It seemed to upset her a lot."

"*I'm* wondering what *your* call was," Mason said.

Tragg grinned. "Did I seem upset?"

"No, but you're mighty thoughtful."

"I'm always thoughtful," Tragg said. "And when *you're* on a case, Mason, I get very, very thoughtful indeed."

7

PERRY MASON latchkeyed the door of his private office. Della Street, who had been seated at the telephone, jumped up with an exclamation. "Gosh, am *I* glad to see *you!*"

"What's happened?" Mason asked.

"I've been working the telephone overtime. Mauvis Meade said you'd left and she didn't know where you were going. She thought you were with Lieutenant Tragg."

"You didn't call Tragg, did you?" Mason asked.

"Heavens, no! I called your apartment, I called the garage, I called the gasoline station where you usually get filled up, I called the parking lot—"

"I got hung up in traffic," Mason said. "What's happened?"

"Paul Drake has a break. He has a line on the identity of the corpse. He wants you to call him the minute you get in—I'll give him a buzz."

Della Street sent nimble fingers flying around the dial of the telephone and a moment later said, "Paul, he's here. He just came in.

"Paul's coming right in," she said to Mason, hanging up the telephone.

"How did Paul happen to get a line on the corpse?" Mason asked. "And are we ahead or behind the police?"

"Apparently we're ahead of them—at least Paul thinks

we are. That's why he was in such a hurry to get hold of you. He didn't know whether you'd want to pass the information on to the police or not."

Mason's eyes narrowed. "I don't see how Paul could have any information the police haven't," he said, "however—"

He broke off as Drake's code knock sounded on the door.

Della Street opened the door.

Paul Drake had discarded his pose of easy nonchalance. His voice was crisp and business-like. He kicked the door shut with his heel, walked over to sit on the corner of Mason's desk and said, "I think we've got the corpse tagged, Perry."

"Go ahead," Mason said, "tell me about it."

"His name is Josh Manly—full name, Joseph Hanover Manly, but he signs it Jos, period, and then puts a capital H, period, so his friends call him Josh. He lives in a bungalow at 1220 Ringbolt Avenue. He's been staying in that cabin up there off and on for several months."

"Why does he have a place on Ringbolt Avenue and then spend so much time in a cabin at Pine Glen Canyon?" Mason asked.

"That's one of the things I haven't been able to find out yet. Probably there's a woman in the case."

"There are probably at least *two* women in the case. Okay, Paul, let's go."

"My car or yours?"

"Mine."

"Take Della?" Drake asked.

Mason hesitated.

Della Street caught his eye and nodded vehemently.

"Okay," Mason smiled, "take a brief case and a couple of shorthand notebooks, Della . . . It may be quite a while before you get anything to eat."

"That's all right, Chief. I can wait."

"All right, let's get started."

Driving out the freeway, Mason said, "Tell me how it happened, Paul."

"Just legwork," Drake said. "I put men out covering the place and trying to find out all they could.

"There wasn't any chance of finding any physical evidence the police didn't have. Our only chance to get ahead of them was in the field of interpreting the evidence, taking the physical facts and finding out what they really meant.

"One of my men prowling around the back of the cabin, just giving it a once-over, noticed a neat stack of firewood that had been sawed into lengths for a kitchen stove and then split into small sticks."

"So what did he do?" Mason asked.

"So," Drake said, "the first thing he did was to get a tape measure and measure the pile. He found from the way the supports had been placed to hold up the ends of the pile that it must originally have held a full cord of wood. About a quarter of a cord had been used.

"If the owner of the cabin had been gathering logs, sawing and splitting them, he would have got up more than a cord to last through the winter. The fact that the entire pile of winter wood was limited to one cord indicated the wood had been purchased from a dealer and the party living in the cabin intended to buy a cord at a time —which meant he was assured of good wood of uniform quality and that he could get prompt delivery.

"So when my man had carried his reasoning that far, he got out of there fast and started asking questions about who had wood for sale around that part of the country. He found a man named Atkins living down the Pine Glen road had wood for sale. My operative went down and got to talking with him.

"Atkins remembered all about the transaction—even gave a pretty detailed description of what Manly looked like. Manly had paid him by endorsing over a check and Atkins wasn't too sure whether he wanted that check. So he jotted down the license number of the car Manly was driving, a jeep station wagon with four-wheel drive. The check cleared all right, but Atkins was able to rummage around and located the license number for my operative. So we traced the car registration and it's this guy, Manly, living at 1220 Ringbolt Avenue in Terra Vista.

"The cabin is heated with an oil stove, but the cooking stove burns wood. Apparently Manly had been up there for brief intervals for several months. At first, he'd gone around and rustled up what wood he could, using dead branches and sawing up a few fallen logs, then he drove into Atkins' place and made arrangements to buy a cord of wood."

"Good work, Paul," Mason said. "Know anything about what we'll find at the address?"

"Not a thing," Drake said. "It's just a street number as far as I'm concerned."

Mason drove with swift skill through the traffic. At length he turned the car and said, "This is Ringbolt Avenue . . . It's a good-looking neighborhood."

Street lights at the corner showed the house numbers in hundreds painted on the street signs, and Mason ran quickly to the twelve hundred block.

"This looks like the place," Drake said. "The one over on the right, Perry, third from the corner."

"There's a light on," Mason said. "I guess somebody's at home."

"It'll be our luck to have the police there ahead of us," Drake groaned. "Of course, it was just a pile of stove wood, but my man recognized it right away as a clue, and it's a cinch that some of the police officers will."

"No police cars," Mason said. "So far, so good."

He eased his car to a stop at the curb.

Mason led the way up to the porch and rang the bell.

After a moment the door was opened by a woman who could well have been beautiful at one time but who evidently had been too busy or too frugal in recent years to keep up her appearance. Her brunette hair was stringy, her blue slacks were old and faded, her short-sleeved blouse was opened deep at the throat. Her sole concession to care for her personal appearance was that she was wearing rubber gloves to protect her hands.

"Good evening," Mason said. "Does Mr. Manly live here?"

"That's right."

"We'd like to see him."

"He isn't here."

"Can you tell me where I can reach him?"

"Tucson."

"Arizona?"

"That's the only Tucson I know of."

"Can you tell us where we can reach him there?"

"No."

"It may be rather important," Mason said.

"I'm sorry."

"Is he staying at one of the hotels there?"

"I don't think so."

"With friends?"

"No."

"Where?"

"Probably a motel. He'll stay at one place one time and another place another."

"I gather, then, he makes rather frequent trips?"

"You gather a lot, don't you?"

Mason smiled affably. "You're Mrs. Manly?"

"That's right."

"I'm Perry Mason, a lawyer. This is Della Street, my confidential secretary, and Mr. Drake."

"You're Perry Mason, the lawyer!" she exclaimed.

"That's right."

"Well, for heaven's sake! What in the world brings you out here? Well, don't stand there. Come on in. Now, why in the world would you want to see Josh?"

"He may be a witness," Mason said.

"Well, come on in and sit down. I was just cleaning up the kitchen. Things are a mess and I'm a mess, but do come in and sit down . . . I've read about a lot of your cases, Mr. Mason. I'm fascinated by courtroom stuff, and murder cases always interest me. I told Josh once that I felt that when I died I was going to be murdered—made him mad. What's he a witness to, Mr. Mason?"

She stripped off the rubber gloves, shook hands with each of them in turn.

"Do sit down and make yourselves at home . . . you *would* have to catch me looking like this!"

She laughed nervously, glanced at her hands self-consciously, then as she noticed the smudged finger tips, hastily put the rubber gloves back on.

Mason caught Della Street's eye and shook his head, indicating she was not to take notes. He waited until they were settled comfortably in chairs in the compact living room, then asked, "What business is your husband in, Mrs. Manly?"

"He's a sharpshooter."

Mason raised his eyebrows.

"Buys and sells and makes deals."

"What sort of deals?"

"Heavens, I don't know. I don't ask him about his business and he doesn't ask me what I put in the dishes I cook. He brings home the money, I keep the house."

"Was your husband ever in trouble?" Mason asked.

She looked at him sharply. "Now what makes you ask *that* question?"

"I was just trying to get information."

"Well . . . you'd better ask him about that."

"I want to. Now, can you tell me when he left for Tucson?"

"This is Monday. He left . . . let's see . . . Wednesday."

"That was Wednesday of this last week, the fourth?"

"Yes."

"Was he driving a car?"

"Yes."

"His own car?"

"That's right."

"A jeep station wagon, is it?"

"A jeep? Heavens no. It's an Oldsmobile. He doesn't have any jeep. What gave you that idea?"

"Somehow I gathered the impression he was making mining deals," Mason said smoothly. "In that case I reasoned he'd be driving a car he could use on the highway or in the desert, and so I quite naturally thought of a jeep station wagon.

"That's what comes of deductive reasoning. Sherlock Holmes was the only person I ever knew of who could do it. I try and fall flat on my face."

She laughed. "It was fine reasoning if you hadn't got off on the wrong foot at the start, Mr. Mason. I don't think Josh ever dabbles in mining deals. He goes in for quickies—you know, the sort of deals where he can get a quick turnover on his money.

"Frankly, I don't know too much about his business, and I don't want to know too much. I know he always has cash available and he buys for cash and sells for . . . say, maybe I'm talking too much . . . I've heard so much about Perry Mason I sort of feel you're one of the family."

"Thank you," Mason said. "Has your husband been making frequent trips to Tucson?"

"He's out all the time, working on deals. I never know when he's going or when he's coming."

"How does he get a line on these deals of his?" Mason asked.

"He has friends that keep him posted. The phone will ring and he'll go out, maybe for a day, maybe two or three days. Sometimes I know where he is, sometimes I don't."

"He doesn't call you up long distance?"

"Why should he?" she asked. "He knows where I am. He knows what I'm doing . . . I don't always know what he's doing, but . . . well, he's a man. He travels and lives out in the world. I'm a housekeeper. I stay home and take care of the place."

"Do you have a car when you're staying home, for shopping and things?"

She nodded. "I guess you'd call it a car. It runs, gets me down to the market and back. Say, you're asking lots of questions."

Mason laughed affably. "Well, a lawyer has to, you know."

"Yes, I suppose so. My gosh, Mr. Mason, I don't see how you do all the things you do. You stand up in court and somehow always seem to catch the witnesses that are lying and make them tell the truth and . . . do *you* lead an exciting life!

"Della Street is your secretary. I've seen her picture with you lots of times."

She turned to Paul Drake. "What do you do?"

"Drake's an investigator," Mason said.

"He works for you?"

"Sometimes."

"Private detective?" she asked.

Mason nodded.

"Well, you must have something in mind, coming out here. Ask me. Maybe I can tell you."

"Do you know your husband's friends and acquaintances?" Mason asked.

"The folks next door and . . . my husband is away a lot and we don't have any social life, to speak of."

"How about his business acquaintances?"

She motioned toward the telephone and said, "About all I know is that the telephone rings and somebody wants him."

Mason thought for a moment, then said, "I'm going to ask you a personal question, Mrs. Manly."

She laughed. "That's all you've been doing ever since you walked in."

"Does the telephone ring and people want your husband when he's not here?"

"Heavens, Mr. Mason, how would they know he was here if they didn't telephone?"

"I was just wondering," Mason said. "You get a good many calls, then, when he isn't here, and—"

He broke off at the look on her face.

"Well, now, that's funny," she said.

Mason waited.

"Come to think of it," she went on, "when he's here, the phone is ringing all the time. People are calling up and wanting to talk to him . . . when he isn't here, the phone hardly ever rings."

"These people that talk with him," Mason said, "are they men or women?"

"I don't know," she said. "He answers the phone when he's here . . . oh, once in a while if he's busy or something I'll answer the phone, but he doesn't like to have me do it. He usually takes the call himself."

"Men or women?"

"Men mostly. Why?"

"I was just wondering," Mason said. "Usually a wife is a little more curious about her husband's business."

"I'm not. His business is his business."

"Even when a woman calls up?" Mason asked.

"It's business," she said. "Josh is a live wire. If some

woman makes a play for him, he'll brush her off unless there's an angle. And if there's an angle, he'll turn it into money. That man has the sharpest mind I've ever seen. He hears some casual remark and the first thing you know he's out buying and selling."

"Does he hold property and—"

"Not Josh," she interrupted. "He handles everything for a quick turnover. He doesn't buy until he knows where there's a chance to sell . . . he doesn't try to get rich on any one deal, but we get by all right. He keeps turning things over and he deals for cash."

"Do you know if he's acquainted with any writers?" Mason asked.

"Writers?"

Mason nodded.

"Heavens no! At least I don't suppose so, Mr. Mason. I've never asked him. If he wants to tell me anything, he can tell me. If I wanted to know anything I'd wait until he did tell me."

"Do you know if he ever goes up in the mountains?"

"In the mountains?"

"Yes."

"You mean just to stay?"

"Camping," Mason said.

"Heavens no. Josh is the poorest camper on earth. He wants comforts. Why in the world would he go camping, Mr. Mason? He can't do any business out camping. I've told you he isn't interested in mining deals."

"I'm just trying to get a line on his personal habits," Mason said. "Now do you have any pictures of him— photographs?"

Her eyes narrowed. "I have a picture or two, but . . . look here, Mr. Mason, I don't think Josh would like to have me give you a whole lot of information."

"It might save a lot of trouble," Mason said. "Or, I'll put it this way. It might save a lot of time. You see, Mrs.

Manly, I'll be frank. I don't know whether your husband is the man I'm looking for or not."

"But you know the man you're looking for?"

"Yes."

"Can you describe him?"

Mason glanced at Paul Drake.

Drake took a notebook from his pocket.

"About five-feet-ten, chestnut hair, about a hundred and seventy-five pounds," Drake said.

She shook her head emphatically.

"No?" Drake asked.

"That doesn't fit my husband at all. He's six-feet-one, he weighs—I think it's a hundred and eighty pounds, and he has rather light hair."

"Well, of course," Drake said, glancing at Mason, "you can expect a certain number of mistakes in a description. How old is your husband, ma'am?"

"Thirty-two."

Drake sighed and shook his head. "The man we're looking for is at least fifty."

Her laugh showed a certain amount of relief. "Well, my husband is thirty-two and he's built like an athlete. He looks like a football star."

"It's strange that there'd be such a coincidence on names," Mason said. "Did your husband say anything to you about seeing an accident at Pico and Western about five or six days ago? That, I guess, would be just before he left for Arizona."

"Not a word."

"But would he necessarily have told you about it?"

"Not necessarily, but he certainly would have told me, that is, if it had been a serious accident. Was anybody hurt?"

"A car tried to make a left turn without a signal," Mason said. "It was a pretty bad smash-up."

"Where would my husband have been? In one of the cars that was hit?"

"No, two cars behind."

"Did anyone talk with him?"

"No one talked with him," Mason said, "but he chatted briefly with a bystander, told the bystander his name was Manly and that his first name was Joe. He said he'd seen the whole thing, and then traffic was cleared and he jumped back in his car, drove around the wreckage and sped away.

"We'd like to find that witness very much indeed."

"I suppose you're running down all the Joe Manly's in the city."

"We certainly thought we were on the right trail here," Mason said.

"Well, I'm sorry. You've drawn a blank."

"When do you expect your husband back?"

"I don't know. He's usually gone four or five days when he goes to Arizona, sometimes a week. I don't think he's ever stayed longer than a week."

"Then he'll be back by Wednesday or Thursday?"

"I think so, but I'm certain he's not the man you're after."

"Well, thank you," Mason said.

They left and she stood in the doorway watching them.

It wasn't until after they were in the car with the motor started that Mason said to Paul Drake. "How about the description, Paul? Does it tally?"

"He's the guy, all right," Drake said. "The body is that of a man around thirty to thirty-three, the height is six-feet-one, the weight is a hundred and eighty-nine pounds and he has light hair and blue eyes."

Mason sighed. "All right, Paul, we know the corpse. Now we've got to find out everything we can about him."

"And using the information his wife gave us as a starting point, that's going to be a real chore," Drake said.

"How much time do you suppose we have?" Mason asked.

Drake said musingly, "We haven't any time. If he's thirty-two he's done military duty somewhere. They'll have his fingerprints. Tragg'll be out here any minute now."

"And when he arrives," Della Street said, "and finds that you have been there . . . well, Tragg will be wondering how *you* made the identification."

"We'll have to tell him sooner or later," Mason said, "or he'll think my client gave me a tip."

"Business in Arizona," Mason observed. "Goes down there frequently . . . what's the best guess on that, Paul?"

Mason drove in silence.

"Well," Drake said, "you know what it means, Perry— women."

Mason said thoughtfully, "Let's keep it in the singular and say woman, Paul, but let's not jump at conclusions. Start some men looking around in Arizona . . . and we've got to talk with your man who got the information. Where can we find him?"

"Right at present he's up at the camp and picnic grounds," Drake said. "His name's Kelton. I told him to go up there and wait. He has a jeep."

"Good work, Paul. How much of a drive is it up to the camp site?"

"Not much. The road's surfaced that far. We can make it within half an hour from here."

"Eats?" Della Street asked.

"Later," Mason said. "Let's go, Paul."

8

■

MASON, DELLA STREET AND PAUL DRAKE found Kelton waiting at the Pine Glen camp site.

"Can we get up to that cabin?" Mason asked, after Drake had performed the introductions.

"Sure," Kelton said, "if you want to ride in my jeep. You can probably make it with your car, but the jeep is a sure thing."

"All right," Mason told him, "take us up there. I want to look around. How about the police?"

"They've left," Kelton said. "They've fingerprinted everything, photographed everything and were finished with the place by three o'clock this afternoon."

They crowded themselves into Kelton's jeep.

Kelton eased the machine into motion.

"Got plenty of gas?" Mason asked.

"Nearly full," Kelton said.

Drake grinned and said, "That's one thing about a good operative, Perry. They *always* go off a job with a full tank of gasoline."

"Well," Kelton said defensively, "you have to. You can't make a report stating that you started tailing someone who was important and then ran out of gasoline when you were halfway to where you were going. They'd fire you for pulling a stunt like that quicker than anything."

"How long will it take?" Mason asked.

"Not long. It's only a mile and a half from the camp-ground to the cabin."

Mason braced himself, clung tightly to the seat supports and closed his eyes. His face showed the extent of his concentration.

Kelton put the car into the lower gear ratio, left the shifting lever in high. The car twisted its way up the road. Kelton fought the steering wheel over the slick places, kept the wheels churning steadily through the soft places, never applying too much pressure on the gasoline pedal but keeping the car moving at steady speed.

"You've evidently done quite a bit of mountain driving," Mason ventured, studying Kelton.

"Lots of it," Kelton admitted. "I like it."

"Where did you drive?" Della asked.

"Idaho and Montana, ma'am."

They were silent for a few moments, then Kelton swung the car sharply to the left, said, "This is the best place to park—there's been a lot of traffic here. The cabin is about a hundred and fifty yards farther up the road . . . some of this ground is still pretty soft. Miss Street is going to get her shoes muddy."

"Perhaps you'd better wait here, Della," Mason told her.

"Not even if I have to buy new shoes," she said.

She flung open the door of the car, jumped to the ground. "Come on, let's go. And quit worrying about my feet."

Kelton had a small fountain pen flashlight and he used this to light the way up the road.

The weather had cleared and the stars were blazing steadily down through the pure mountain air. There were a few rather soft places in the road, but it had dried out somewhat and the swollen stream down in the canyon, roaring over the rocks, was the only real reminder of the storm.

They worked their way up to the cabin.

Kelton said, "We can get in this window—this is the south side. It's a window that opens on the bedroom where the crime was committed."

"Now look, Perry," Paul Drake said, "I don't know just where we stand on this. Do we have any right to go into that house?"

"Not a bit," Mason admitted cheerfully. "Who owns the cabin?"

"I don't know."

"Who's living here?"

"Apparently no one. According to the police, someone has it rented, but no one has been really living here. They keep blankets on the beds and pillow slips on the pillows. Evidently it is some sort of an overnight rendezvous."

"Love nest?" Mason asked.

"Hard to tell," Kelton said. "Police just aren't satisfied. They think they'll find out a lot more when they identify the corpse. Apparently he spent some time here.

"There were quite a few provisions on the shelves, but there's no refrigeration and everything in the line of food is canned. There's coffee, powdered cream, sugar, canned butter . . . a fair supply of hooch—everything a party would need for a weekend."

"Fingerprints?" Mason asked.

"Very few. The humidity was bad. They got some prints, I understand, but not very many and not any that were any good."

"How about the discarded bottles and cans?" Mason asked.

"There aren't any. Apparently they were all hauled down to the picnic grounds and put in the trash containers there.

"In short, the cabin is something of a mystery, but police are working on it. They hope to have something soon."

"I think that, under the circumstances, we can take a look inside," Mason said. "I'm representing a young woman who's accused of committing a murder here . . . I might be guilty of trespass, but . . . well, I want to take a look around.

"How did you say we get in?"

"This bedroom window. There's no lock on it," Kelton said. "It works with gravity. You just push the window up and prop it with something."

"Got something to prop it with?" Mason asked.

"There was a stick around here in the mud somewhere," Kelton said, "standing before the window on the south side . . . wait a minute, here it is."

He stooped, picked up the stick, raised the window, propped the stick in under the sash.

"Just the right length," he said. "Want to go in?"

"*I'm* going in," Mason said. "Give me a boost up so I can get my foot over the sill."

He crawled in through the window.

Della Street laughed nervously. "Give me your hands, Chief, and let Paul give me a boost. I'm coming in, too."

She scrambled in through the window. Drake followed suit, and then Kelton jumped up, caught the sill, and with the aid of the others, was pulled through the window.

"Lights?" Kelton asked.

"How's your flashlight? The batteries fresh?" Mason asked.

"The batteries are fresh, and I have spare batteries in my pocket."

"All right. We'll use your light," Mason said. "We won't use the lights in the place."

"Here's where the body was lying," Kelton pointed out, the beam of his flashlight showing a sinister red stain on the rough pine boards. "Now, you notice these beds have no sheets, but there are nice, clean blankets. There are pillow slips and they're clean.

"There's an oil tank out there and a stove which works with a gravity oil feed and warms the place. There's a fireplace in addition to that, and then there's a wood cooking stove. The other bedroom is back there, and the bathroom is between the living room and this other bedroom. The bedroom on the south opens into the living room—evidently when the place was built this bedroom and the main living room were all there was to the cabin. Then they added another wing on the north and west with the bathroom, and the other bedroom opening out from the bathroom."

"You've been in here before?" Drake asked.

"Sure," Kelton said. "I cased the place."

"How thoroughly did you search?" Mason asked.

"I didn't search. I just looked the place over to get the lay of the land. I was trying to find something that would give me a line on the person who owned the place."

Mason said, "They've dusted everything for fingerprints?"

"That's right."

They moved around through the rooms, their steps echoing in the grim silence of the cabin.

"What's up here?" Mason asked, standing by the kitchen stove and pointing to a cupboard which was closed off with sliding doors.

"A cupboard with lots of canned provisions," Kelton said. "I understand the officers found a beautiful new tea-kettle up there—stainless steel and copper-bottomed. The teakettle on the stove is a big aluminum kettle that they evidently kept full of water whenever there was a fire in the cooking stove. That other teakettle apparently hadn't ever been used."

Mason slid back the panel doors.

The beam of the flashlight showed the shelves, illuminating a rather nondescript array of containers of different sizes bearing labels printed on them—FLOUR,

SUGAR, COFFEE, TEA, MATCHES—and row after row of canned goods.

"Where's that teakettle you were talking about?" Mason asked. "The new stainless steel one?"

"I think they found something on it," Kelton said. "They took it to Headquarters."

"What would a *new* teakettle be doing up there?" Mason asked.

"That's a point," Kelton said. "I understand it was a new kettle that apparently had never had any use— Now, all these other pots and pans and stuff represent an assortment of battered equipment which probably has been with the cabin ever since it was built."

They looked the place over, then crawled out through the window.

"How about underneath the house?" Mason asked. "Anything under there?"

"Just an assortment of junk," Kelton said. "The place is built on a pretty good slope. On the east the distance between the floor of the cabin and the ground is enough so a person can stand up without hitting his head. It's a mess under there, an old casing or two, some junk, a few boxes and stuff like that. On the west the floor is within two and a half feet of the ground. That board is loose. You pull it back and you can get under."

"Let me have your flashlight," Mason said. "I'll take a look."

The lawyer pulled back the loose board and eased his way under the house, prowled around, sending the beam of the flashlight darting this way and that, presently emerged carrying a can marked "COFFEE."

"It's like that one in the cabin," Della said.

Mason examined the can. "It is, for a fact."

He used a handkerchief so that he would leave no fingerprints, took the top off the can.

Mason held the flashlight over the can, then gingerly lifted a cloth out of the interior.

"There's something heavy in this cloth," he said.

"That's a woman's scarf," Della Street said.

Mason lifted out the printed silk scarf. "Oh-oh," he said.

"What?" Drake asked.

"A scarf with the traditional three monkeys, see no evil, hear no evil, speak no evil," Mason said. "Now what's this?"

He lifted the cloth from the can. There was a sag in the bottom of the scarf where something heavy had been deposited.

Mason unfolded the scarf. "Well, well, well," he said, "a box of .22 long-rifle shells."

He took the cover off the box, looked at the neat array of shells arranged in rows, the copper alternating with the lead.

"Some missing?" Drake said.

Mason nodded, counting the shells, said, "Seven missing."

"That accounts for it," Kelton said. "Those are the same shells that were used in the murder, all right. The gun held seven. There were six in the magazine. One had been fired and ejected."

Mason thoughtfully replaced the cover on the cartridge box, put the cartridge box back in the scarf, folded it all together and dropped it in his pocket. Then he replaced the cover on the coffee can, still taking care to leave no fingerprints, and replaced the coffee can under the house where he had found it.

"Now what are you going to do with that stuff?" Drake asked.

"I don't know," Mason admitted at length. "I'm going to evaluate it."

"That's evidence, Perry. You've got to turn it in."

"Evidence of what?"

"Evidence of a murder."

"They don't need any evidence of a murder," Mason said. "They've proven the murder. They've got the corpse."

"You know what I mean. It's evidence linking someone with the murder."

"Who?"

"*I'm* not making any guesses," Drake said. "However, the police will."

Mason thought for a moment, then said, "The police aren't going to know anything about this, Paul, at least for a while. I want you folks to promise that you'll say nothing about this to anyone."

"We can't," Kelton blurted.

"Why not?"

"That would be suppressing evidence."

Mason said, "You simply keep your mouth shut. I'll take all the responsibility. Say you're acting on my orders."

Kelton started to say something, then checked himself.

Mason nodded. "I've got to do it, Paul. I'll take all the responsibility."

"Well, okay," Drake yielded halfheartedly. "Kelton, don't say a word about this to anyone."

"Come on," Mason said, "let's get out of here."

9

RETURNING TO THE CITY, Della Street said, "I suppose there are rather late but satisfying eats in the offing."

"Your supposition is entirely correct," Mason said. "I think we're making progress. I'd like to keep one jump ahead of the police, but we certainly *are* going to eat."

Paul Drake smacked his lips. "Now this," he said, "is something I like. Usually you and Della Street are out in one of the fine restaurants enjoying a New York cut with potatoes au gratin and a carefully selected bottle of vintage wine, while I'm sitting in the office with a hamburger in one hand and a telephone in the other. The hamburger comes from the restaurant a block away and is soggy by the time I get it. By the time I'm half through, the bun has turned into a paste. I'm still hungry but I can't go the rest of it, and I throw it away.

"Half an hour afterward I'm reaching for the bicarbonate of soda. An hour after that I'm weak from hunger.

"Tonight, knowing that I'm eating on an expense account, I'm going to give my stomach the surprise of its life. I'm going to have a jumbo shrimp cocktail, consommé, a salad with anchovies across the top, a New York cut, medium rare, lyonnaise potatoes, the best red wine they have in the house, a side dish of creamed onions and some hot apple pie alamode."

Drake settled back in the seat and let his face relax in a smile.

"Don't," Della Street begged, "you're giving my mind St. Vitus' dance trying to count calories."

"Don't count them at a time like this," Drake told her. "When you're eating on an expense account with a client who usually keeps you on a diet of soggy hamburgers and lukewarm coffee, you want to go the limit."

"How about the Golden Fleece?" Mason asked Della Street, while Drake was still engaged in his mental drooling.

"Fine," Della Street said.

"It's only a few minutes from here," Mason told her.

"Then what?" Della Street asked.

"Probably," Mason said, "we call it a night. There's not a great deal we can do at the moment. Tomorrow, if I can find any opportunity for sabotaging the case the police have worked up against Gladys Doyle, I'll file a writ of habeas corpus. I'll insist either they charge her or let her go. They won't want to charge her with the evidence they now have—at least I don't think so."

Mason drove to the Golden Fleece and surrendered his car to a parking attendant. A deferential headwaiter greeted Mason obsequiously.

"A table for three?" Mason asked.

"There is *always* a table for Perry Mason," the headwaiter said.

He seated them at a table near the dance floor, summoned a waiter and directed him to take good care of Mason and his party.

"You wish drinks before seeing the menu?" the waiter asked.

Mason glanced at Della Street, nodded, said, "Bring a Manhattan for the lady—what do you want, Paul?"

"A *double* Manhattan, sweet," Drake said.

"I'll take a Bacardi cocktail," Mason said, "and then you can bring the menu."

"Now, wait a minute," Drake said. "I have a horrible

hunch about this thing. I would prefer to give my order right now. I don't need any menu and I know what you and Della are going to eat—I have a hunch we may have to bolt this meal, if we get it at all."

Mason's eyes narrowed thoughtfully. "Hold everything for a minute, waiter. Call your office, Paul. Let them know where we are and see if there's a report on anything urgent."

"You wait right there," Drake said to the waiter. "I'll be back and confirm that order."

Drake started for the phone booth and the waiter said to Mason and Della Street, "I'll bring the menus. Shall I bring the drinks now?"

"Hold the drinks," Mason said, "until he gets back from the phone—but you can bring the menus."

Mason smiled across at Della Street. "Paul can't believe he's really going to relax and have some good food . . . Can we make yours a double Manhattan?"

"Well," she said, hesitating, "I . . . No, thanks, Chief, I guess a single will do. We'll let Paul do the celebrating."

The waiter brought menus. Mason studied his menu carefully. Della Street glanced at it, made up her mind, folded the menu, put it to one side, looked up toward the phone booth, said, "Oh-oh."

"What's the matter?" Mason asked.

"Paul," Della Street said. "Look at him."

Drake was hurrying toward their table.

"Something new?" Mason asked.

Drake said rapidly, "I hate to tell you this, Perry. It may make a difference."

"Shoot."

"You told me to put men out on all phases of the case," Drake said, "and I sent a man up to Summit Inn to check on Gladys Doyle's time of arrival and departure. I also had a man phone in to the American Film Producers

Studios to get Edgar Carlisle's address so I could talk with him."

Mason nodded.

"The point is," Drake said, "they don't have any Edgar Carlisle."

"What do you mean?"

"The studio has reported to the office in answer to a specific question that it doesn't have any such individual in its publicity department. The publicity department reported it had long since given up trying to get co-operation out of Mauvis Meade. She sold her movie rights for a flat sum and there's been quite a difference of opinion between her and the movie company as to what she should give in the line of co-operation.

"Quite naturally, the studio feels that the publicity it's going to give her will help sell the book and that she should co-operate. She's adopted the position that because she isn't sharing in the profits made from the film she's going to be hard to get.

"Apparently the studio decided that it doesn't need her as much as she needs it."

Mason said, "You'd better sit down and we'll get the order in—"

Drake interrupted, still standing, "I've got my office waiting on the line. Here's the point. My man up at Summit Inn did a little checking around after the studio advised him that Edgar Carlisle wasn't with them. He found Carlisle bought gas at a Shell Service Station up there on a credit card, so we now have his address here in Los Angeles."

"Where is it?" Mason asked.

"An apartment at 1632 Delrose," Drake said.

"Shucks," Mason said, "that's within half a mile."

The lawyer was thoughtfully silent.

"Is it *that* important?" Della Street asked, after a swift glance at Paul Drake's face.

"It's that important," Mason said, pushing back his chair.

"I was afraid of that," Drake muttered to Della Street.

"We'll be back," Mason told the waiter. "Reserve a table for forty-five minutes from now. We're on our way."

"We could at least have the cocktails," Drake pointed out.

Mason shook his head. "Then we'd be interviewing a witness with liquor on our breaths. You can't tell where this man fits into the picture. If he isn't connected with the studios, if he was up there under false pretenses . . . well . . ."

"You mean you're going to give him a rough time?"

"Rough time, hell," Mason said. "I'll make him the murderer before I get done if this thing keeps going the way it's headed. That's why it's absolutely imperative that we get to him ahead of the police and that we don't have anything to drink. Come on, let's go."

They hurried out of the restaurant, redeemed their car and drove in silence the half-mile to the sixteen hundred block on Delrose Avenue.

Paul Drake said, "That's the place we want, Perry . . . and here's a providential parking space. It's about as close as you can hope to get."

Mason eased the car into the parking place. They walked up to the apartment house. Mason consulted the directory in the front and pressed the button opposite the name of Edgar Carlisle.

"The chances that he's home are only about one in a hundred," Drake said.

Mason nodded and pressed the button again.

When there was no answer, Paul Drake took a key from his pocket and said, "Almost any key will work this outer door, in case you want to go up."

"Hold it," Mason said. "It's all right under ordinary

circumstances to take a chance on giving Lieutenant Tragg the right answers to his questions, but this time the situation may be a little different. Let's just try pressing the wrong button by mistake."

Mason pressed three or four buttons. Finally someone buzzed the door open.

The three of them walked into the lobby of the apartment house.

"What now?" Drake asked.

"Now," Mason said, "we go up to the second floor and go down to Apartment 242, just to give it a once-over."

"Now look," Drake protested. "I don't want any funny stuff, Perry."

"You're altogether too sensitive," Mason said. "However, this is once I'm inclined to agree that extreme caution is indicated. Let's take a look."

They climbed the stairs, then walked on down the hall.

A door abruptly opened. A beautiful blonde, attired in a tight-fitting suit, sized Perry Mason up, smiled and said, "Were *you* the one who buzzed my apartment?"

Mason bowed deferentially. "It was a mistake. Forgive it, please. I didn't realize until afterward that I had the wrong apartment."

"Oh." Her face showed disappointment.

After a thoughtful moment she said, "You *did* have the wrong apartment?"

"We *did* have the wrong apartment," Della Street said in a tone of finality.

The young woman slowly closed the door.

They walked on down the corridor.

"Let's hope she didn't recognize you," Paul Drake said.

"Well," Mason said, "she—" Abruptly he broke off and said, "Paul, there's a light in 242. You can see a faint thread of light coming through at the bottom of the door."

"Well," Drake said, "you don't suppose our man is

home but not answering the bell, do you? Gosh, Perry, let's not discover another corpse!"

The trio moved on cautiously.

Behind the somewhat flimsy door of 242 a typewriter was going noisily. They could hear the rattle and bang of the keys, then the sound of the carriage being slammed back. Once more the typing reached a crescendo, then faltered, slowed to a stop. There was a period of silence.

Mason glanced at Della Street.

"I don't think it's a touch system," she said. "It sounds like a high-speed, four-finger system—and it's evidently some sort of an original composition."

Mason nodded, hesitated, then raised his hand and tapped gently on the door.

The typewriter once more exploded into noise.

Mason tapped again.

The typewriter stopped abruptly. Mason knocked a third time and steps came banging toward the door.

The door was jerked open and a man's angry face confronted them. "How the hell did you get in here?" he demanded. "When I don't answer my bell it's because I don't want to be disturbed! Now beat it!"

"Edgar Carlisle?" Mason asked.

"Yes, I'm Edgar Carlisle and I'm working. Now beat it."

He started to close the door. Drake eased a shoulder and arm in the door. "Wait a minute, buddy," he said. "Take a look at this." Drake flashed his badge showing that he was a licensed private detective.

"Now, wait a minute, wait a minute. What's all this about?" Carlisle asked.

"We have a few questions to ask you."

"Get lost," Carlisle told him. "I'm working against a deadline and I haven't got any time for questions. Come back when I'm finished."

"How long is it going to take you to finish?" Mason asked.

"A little after midnight."

"Well, then, it won't get finished," Mason told him. "The police will be here before then."

"The police? What the hell are you talking about?"

"Mauvis Meade and murder," Mason said.

Carlisle blinked his eyes as though chopping the information into separate statements by using his eyelids as punctuation marks.

Abruptly the significance of what Mason had said soaked in. "Mauvis Meade and *murder*?"

"Your weekend at Summit Inn," Mason explained. "Your representation that you were with the publicity department of American Film Producers Studios, and the murder of an unidentified corpse on the mountain."

"Who . . . who the hell are you?"

"My name's Mason," the lawyer said. "This is my secretary, Miss Street, and Paul Drake. You have already seen Paul Drake's credentials as a private detective."

Carlisle's face showed that anger was giving way to consternation. At length he said grudgingly, "Well, come on in. Just what are you people trying to put across?"

Mason said, "You represented yourself as being connected with the publicity department of American Film Producers Studios."

"I did no such thing. I said I was getting publicity for the American Film Producers Studios and, damn it, I am! What's more, I didn't get anything of value as a result of any impersonation. I can make any statement I want to, just so I don't get someone to part with something of value on the strength of it. You go see a lawyer if you don't think I'm right."

"I'm a lawyer," Mason said, "and I don't think you're right, not in *this* instance."

Carlisle said, "I didn't impersonate anyone or anything.

I simply made a statement and, as it happens, the statement was true."

Carlisle looked Della Street over in a swift head-to-toe survey which evidently resulted in a change of heart on his part. His eyes showed sudden and unqualified approval.

"All right," Carlisle said, closing the door. "You've interrupted my train of thought and you've delayed the delivery of the article, so we might just as well take time out to get acquainted."

Mason walked over to the typewriter, looked down at the sheet of paper.

"It will cost you twenty-five cents to read that in *Pacific Coast Personalities*," Carlisle said. "For your information, I don't like to have people read my material before it's printed."

Mason paid no attention to him but stood looking down at the paper in the typewriter. When he had finished reading he sat down and said, "So you're doing an article on Mauvis Niles Meade."

"I'm doing an article on Mauvis Niles Meade," Edgar Carlisle repeated.

"And you rang her up and told her you were representing American Film Producers Studios?"

"I told her nothing of the sort. I rang her up and told her I was getting some publicity for American Film Producers Studios, that I understood she spent her weekends at the Summit Inn, that I was going to be up at the Summit Inn and I wanted an interview."

"And what did she say?"

"She said she'd be there."

"But she didn't show up?"

"She didn't show up. She sent her secretary, Gladys Doyle."

"And from Gladys Doyle you got enough information for an article?"

"That's right."

"What makes you think *Pacific Coast Personalities* is interested in such an article?"

Carlisle said angrily, "Because I'm a professional writer, because the article has been bought and paid for and I have a deadline delivery date of tomorrow noon, in case that means anything to you. The name of Edgar Carlisle is fairly well known as an article writer in movie, television and similar magazines. Now, I'd like to know by what right you come barging in here asking questions."

Mason said, "As I told you, my name is Mason. I'm an attorney. I'm—"

"Wait a minute!" Carlisle exclaimed. "You're not *Perry* Mason?"

Mason nodded.

"Good Lord," Carlisle said. "Of course you are! I should have recognized you— Hang it, I knew there was something familiar about you. My gosh, you're *the* Perry Mason. I've been trying to get up my nerve to approach you to get material for an article for I don't know how long. Well, can you beat that!"

Mason said, "All right, I'll assume for the moment that you're acting in good faith as a free-lance writer. Now suppose you tell us about that trip up to Summit Inn."

"Why?" Carlisle asked.

"Because," Mason said, "after leaving Summit Inn, Miss Doyle lost her way. She got stuck in a deep mudhole, spent the night in a strange cabin, woke up in the morning and found a murdered man in the bedroom. There's every reason to believe that you were instrumental in getting her up on the mountain and there's a distinct possibility that Mauvis Meade was the person who was to have been trapped, or perhaps the person who was to have been murdered."

"Good Lord!" Carlisle exclaimed.

"Now then, you say that you are working for *Pacific Coast Personalities?*"

Carlisle nodded.

"You have an order for an article?"

"From Dale Robbins himself. He's the editor and publisher. There's a Tuesday deadline. That is, it has to be put in the mail tomorrow noon."

"And addressed to *Pacific Coast Personalities?*" Mason asked.

"That's right."

"You were commissioned personally?"

"That's right."

"You talked with Mr. Robbins personally?"

"Yes."

"Personally or over the phone?"

"Well, it was personally," Carlisle said, "but the conversation took place on the telephone."

"Do you know Robbins when you see him?"

"Sure—that is, I've met him. He probably wouldn't remember me. I met him at a writers' club meeting."

"Suppose you tell me exactly what happened."

"Well, it was Thursday afternoon. The telephone rang and it was Dale Robbins on the line. He congratulated me on an article I'd had published in *Television Personalities of the Day*. He said some nice things about it, the sort of stuff that makes a writer feel good. He said it held the reader's interest right from the start, that I had managed to show a real character with a very skillfully painted word picture, that I hadn't used all the trite clichés that made things so completely unreal. He said that as soon as he read it he felt that I could do an article on Mauvis Meade."

"Go ahead," Mason said. "What happened after that?"

"Well, he told me that he'd give me a firm order for such an article and that he'd pay a thousand dollars for thirty-five hundred words. He said that I could consider myself on the staff of *Pacific Coast Personalities* for the purpose of the article, but that he didn't want Mauvis Meade to know that—that he felt that she would start posing if she thought she was giving just another interview. He said she had been rather difficult at times, on interviews, and I knew that to be a fact.

"He suggested that I meet her up at the Summit Inn. He said she had a room up there that she kept on a monthly basis, that she was up every weekend, that I could call her and make an appointment to meet her there. He suggested that I explain to her I was getting publicity for something in connection with the sale of her book or her picture, and get her to co-operate with me on that basis and so get the facts I needed. He said he didn't give a hoot *how* I got the facts just so I got something that was colorful and had what he was pleased to call the 'Carlisle touch.'

"He said Mauvis Meade was good copy because her book was filled with sex and that she was a sultry babe herself. He said he wanted a catchy title like 'A Weekend with Mauvis Meade' and that if I could legitimately contrive to give the readers an idea that she was a hot number without going too far it would be a swell approach.

"He said he definitely wanted something different, something with a warm, personal touch. He wanted his readers to feel her vibrant personality."

"What did you do after talking with him?" Mason asked.

"Well, in the first place I told him that I'd have to have some expense money and he said that would be no obstacle. He asked me how much I needed and I told him he'd better send me three hundred and fifty dollars to bind the bargain and give me some expense money, that I'd submit an account with the article, that any amount that was left over would be credited against the payment he was to make."

"That was satisfactory?"

"That was satisfactory."

"And he sent over the money?"

"He said he'd have a messenger on the way with the money inside of an hour and he was as good as his word. I didn't make a move until after the messenger arrived."

"With a check?" Mason asked.

"With an envelope containing three one-hundred-dollar bills and one fifty-dollar bill."

Mason's face showed skepticism.

Carlisle said suddenly, "When you stop to think of it, that was a funny way for them to do business. I . . . I guess they wanted me to get busy right away."

"Undoubtedly," Mason said. "So what did you do?"

"I got in touch with Mauvis Niles Meade and . . . well, I led her to believe that I was with the publicity department of the studio, all right. I was very careful what I said, but I know that she got the impression I was . . . well, that was it."

"All right, what happened?"

"I made a date with her for the weekend at the Summit Inn."

"Then what?"

"After I got up there I got a phone call from her. She said that she couldn't make it but that she was sending her confidential secretary, Gladys Doyle, up there, that Gladys could get the proposition I had in mind thoroughly thrashed out and then bring it back and submit it to her and that Miss Doyle would co-operate with me up there on any information that I needed."

"Well?" Mason asked.

"At first I was sore," Carlisle said. "I saw my chance at the article I wanted going out the window. Then all of a sudden the idea hit me right between the eyes. It was made to order.

"There'd been too many interviews with Mauvis

Meade, and she's rather difficult at times. She needs a public relations man in the worst way, but she won't get one . . . well, I'd have a new approach.

"I'd write an article entitled 'A Weekend with Mauvis Meade's Secretary.' They said the secretary was some dish and I took along my camera and got some swell art. At least I think I did. The films are being developed.

"I stole a little cheesecake, and this secretary was class. She told me a lot—a lot more than she knew she was giving out. Of course, she didn't know I was doing that sort of an article, but I got a regular blank-check authorization from her. She said she'd been instructed to cooperate in every way, and believe you me, I got some swell stuff."

Mason said, "If your story is true, it's interesting. And if it isn't true, you're up to your neck in murder."

"It's true."

"How can I verify it?"

"Call Dale Robbins."

"You call him," Mason said. "I'll talk with him."

"I don't know where I can get him at this hour, but . . . I'll try."

Mason said, "It happens that I have done some work for Dale Robbins—do we have his phone number, Della?"

She nodded.

"We have it here?"

Again she nodded, taking a notebook from her purse.

Della Street crossed over to the telephone.

Edgar Carlisle was at her side instantly. "It's all connected with the outside," he said solicitously. "Here. Here's a chair that is nice for telephoning."

He seated Della Street, stood by her shoulder looking down at the telephone.

Della Street waited, her hand held over the telephone.

"Did you get a worthwhile story out of Gladys Doyle?" Mason asked Carlisle.

"Did I!" Carlisle said, turning to Mason. "I talked to that girl about Mauvis Meade on a day-to-day basis, and really turned her inside out without her knowing it. She—"

He broke off and whirled back as he heard the whir of the dial of the telephone, but by that time Della Street had completed half of the number and was holding her left hand so that it obscured his view of the dial of the telephone.

After a moment, Della Street said, "Hello, this is Della Street, Mr. Mason's secretary, speaking. I'd like to . . . yes, that's right, Mr. Robbins . . . Mr. Mason wants to talk with you. He wants to ask a question. Just a moment, please."

She handed the telephone to Mason.

Mason said, "Hello, Mr. Robbins. I wanted to ask you a question about the magazine."

"Well, hello, Mason," Robbins said. "This is indeed a pleasure. What can I tell you about the magazine? Advertising rates? Publicity? Circulation? Net profits? What do you want?"

"I want to know about a man named Edgar Carlisle," Mason said.

There was a moment's hesitation, then Robbins said, "Well, I can't tell you very much about him. He's a writer who does some pieces on personalities. It just happens he's never done anything for us. Frankly, we'd be inclined to buy something from him if he wrote anything that was down our alley . . . he's a free lance. He's considered a fair writer in his particular field, but I don't know a great deal about him. I can find out a good deal by tomorrow if it's important."

"Have you ever talked with him?" Mason asked.

"Me? No . . . now wait a minute. I think I did meet the

guy at a writers' club meeting one night. Sort of a get-together where editors and writers were meeting socially . . . I think I did."

"You haven't commissioned him to write an article for your magazine within the last few days?"

"No. Definitely not."

"How about any of your assistants? Would they have—"

"Not without my knowing it, Mason. I keep a close watch on such things. We're a healthy magazine and I want to keep it that way. We can let an inventory pile up awfully fast, and personalities change a lot these days. We like to buy on a hand-to-mouth basis as much as possible. We have a few dependable writers we can call on in case there's an emergency shortage of material. We—"

Edgar Carlisle came pushing forward. "Here, let me talk with him," he said.

"Just a moment," Mason interrupted. "I'm here with Mr. Carlisle at the moment. He tells rather an interesting story which may have some bearing on an investigation I'm conducting. He wants to talk with you personally."

Mason turned the phone over to Carlisle.

"Hello," Carlisle said. "This is Edgar Carlisle, Mr. Robbins. I was telling Mr. Mason about the arrangement I had with you on the Mauvis Meade story."

Mason, watching Carlisle's face, saw the expression change.

"Why, Mr. Robbins," Carlisle exclaimed, "surely you remember commissioning me to do an article . . . you sent me three hundred and fifty dollars by special messenger. . . . No, it wasn't a check, it was in cash . . . Well, I thought it was strange at the time, but I talked with *you* . . . well, anyway, the man on the phone said he was you . . . well . . . I see . . . Well, good heavens, *somebody* commissioned me to write an article for *Pacific Coast Personalities* and gave me a firm commitment . . . That's right . . . thirty-five hundred words . . . yes sir. The price was a thousand dollars . . . Well, I thought so at the time, but . . . but I've received three hundred and fifty dollars and have an expense account and . . . you're certain? . . . Look, Mr. Robbins, would you check in the morning? . . . I see . . . Well, of course, if that's the answer, that's the answer . . . You want to talk with Mr. Mason again?"

Carlisle said, "Okay, just a minute," and handed the phone over to Mason.

"Hello, Robbins," Mason said. "This is Mason again."

"Look," Robbins said. "I don't know what this guy is trying to pull. It's phony, whatever it is. That is, the deal is a phony. Carlisle may have been victimized. Of course, there's nothing to prevent anyone from calling up and saying that he's Dale Robbins of the *Pacific Coast Personalities*, but I'd like to get at the bottom of this. I certainly don't like the idea of some free-lance writer feeling he's been given a firm commitment on a story. I don't like the idea of having it appear we do business that way, and I certainly don't like the idea of incurring the ill will of professional writers. After all, we depend on them to get out a magazine, you know."

"You had no understanding with Mr. Carlisle?"

"Definitely not. And I'm satisfied that no one connected with the magazine made any such arrangement. Moreover, if any advance payment had been made, you can readily realize that it would have been made by voucher and not in the form of cash sent over by messenger. Someone is doing something here I don't like. I wish you'd check into it if you can conveniently."

"We'll let you know," Mason said, and hung up.

"Well," he said to Carlisle, "that seems to dispose of that."

Carlisle seated himself in front of the typewriter as though his knees had buckled. "I'll be damned!" he said.

"You didn't see the person who talked with you? You didn't—"

Carlisle shook his head, said, "This is all news to me. I'm completely flabbergasted. My gosh, fifteen minutes ago I was going like wildfire on a story that was almost writing itself, and now I'm left high and dry . . . I guess I'll go out and get drunk."

"I wouldn't do that," Mason said. "You're going to have to answer some questions, probably from the police. You don't know anything about this money?"

"No, it came by messenger. At least, the man who brought it in wore the uniform of a messenger service."

"Would you know the man if you saw him again?"

"Sure, I would. I think you'll find it was a regular messenger service, though. The fellow looked . . . well, rather typical, and it seemed to be a routine job with him. He had a book for me to sign and I noticed that the book simply called for one envelope so I signed the receipt and he handed me the envelope."

"How old was he?"

I would say he was somewhere in his fifties. A short fellow . . . looked as though he might have been a former jockey . . . one of those leathery faces, small but strong, if you know what I mean."

"Well, I guess that's it," Mason said. "That disposes of one phase of the case."

"Can you tell me what this is all about?" Carlisle asked.

Mason shook his head. "Not right now, I can't."

"Is there any objection to my getting hold of Gladys Doyle and asking her?"

"Not in the least," Mason said, "if you can locate her."

"She's still working for Mauvis Meade, isn't she?"

"I believe she is still an employee of Miss Meade's," Mason said.

"This is a great disappointment to me," Carlisle said.

"I thought I had a whale of a story. I thought I'd made a new magazine market in an interview with the head guy himself. I'd put a new ribbon in the typewriter, opened a fresh box of carbon paper and had mentally spent the dough I was going to get by making the down payment on a sports car.

"Now you come along and spoil my dream and ruin my story."

Mason smiled. "Your story isn't ruined."

"Shows all you know about writing," Carlisle retorted. *"Pacific Coast Personalities* wouldn't touch it with a ten-foot pole—not now."

"Go ahead and finish it," Mason said. "You'll find you can sell it to a newspaper and *then* to a magazine later on."

"Are you crazy?" Carlisle asked.

Mason walked over to the door, held it open for Della Street and Paul Drake, said, "I don't think so. You'd better finish your story." He held the door open and they walked out, leaving Carlisle standing in the doorway, watching them as they walked down the hall.

10

"WELL," DRAKE SAID, as they got into Mason's car, "we seem to be making headway."

Mason said thoughtfully, "I feel like a horse on a treadmill. We get going faster and faster, and yet we're no nearer our objective. Right now we need to know *why*

Manly was killed, and then we have to know *who* killed him. The more information we get, the more complicated the thing becomes."

"But we eat?" Della Street asked anxiously.

"We eat," Mason said. "After all, we have that table waiting and there's only so much we can do on an empty stomach."

"Well, that's a relief," Drake said.

They returned to the Golden Fleece, had their cocktails and ordered dinner.

It was as Mason was cutting into his steak that he became thoughtfully silent.

"Go ahead and finish it," Della Street said.

"Huh?" Drake asked, looking up from his steak. "What's the matter?"

"The boss," Della Street said, "is getting an idea. He's thinking he should be someplace else at the moment."

"Where?" Drake asked.

"Mauvis Meade," Mason said.

"Well, it's too late to go calling now," Drake told him.

"Why Mauvis Meade?" Della Street asked.

"I have just thought of something," Mason said.

"What?" Della Street asked.

"Do you remember the copy of *Chop the Man Down* that you got for me?"

She nodded.

"And the photograph on the dust jacket, the photograph of Mauvis Meade standing at the rail of a yacht?"

"In a typical pose," Della Street said to Paul Drake by way of explanation. "Lots of wind and very little restraint."

"Yes, yes, I remember," Drake said, wolfing his steak.

"It doesn't affect your appetite any."

"Certainly not. It increases it," Drake mumbled, pushing food into his mouth. "That guy's ready to take off, Della. We'd better load up with groceries."

Abruptly Mason shoved his plate away, pushed his chair back from the table. "Will you take care of the check, Della? Take my car and go home. I'll take a taxi. You can drop Paul at his office. Paul, I want men working on Manly. Find out everything you can about him. Check in Tucson and Phoenix. See if you can pick up any sort of a trail there."

"What about the dust jacket on the book?" Drake asked, washing down food with a big swallow of wine.

"Quit gulping, Paul," Della Street said. "He's going to leave us to finish the meal. You'll get indigestion and be taking soda bicarb again."

"Heaven forbid," Drake said. "What about the dust jacket, Perry?"

"It was all legs and eyes," Della Street said. "That girl tried so hard to be a vamp . . . I guess that was supposed to be a private yacht she was on, wasn't it? Her skirts were blowing and . . ." Abruptly Della Street broke off. Her eyes widened.

"What?" Paul Drake asked.

"She was wearing a scarf that was blowing in the wind," Della Street said thoughtfully. "Is that what you were thinking of, Chief?"

Mason nodded.

"A scarf," Della Street said, "that had some printed figures on it."

"Can you remember those printed figures, Della?" Mason asked.

She shook her head. "I'm doing well to remember the scarf. The pose was enough to make any woman angry. She just used the idea of the yacht as an excuse for showing all the leg that law allowed . . . But there certainly was a scarf blowing back in the wind, and her hair was blowing—of course, they had the wind to account for the skirts whipping. But that scarf certainly did have some printed figures on it."

"What a break it would be," Mason said dryly, "if it turned out that *that* was the scarf we found out there in the murder cabin."

"*Under* the murder cabin," Drake said.

"Under the murder cabin," Mason agreed thoughtfully.

"You'd better finish your dinner," Della Street said.

Mason shook his head, arose, smiled at them, said, "See you in the morning, folks."

"You can't get in this time of night," Della Street said.

"On the contrary. This is just the break I need in order to get in," Mason said. "That clerk at the desk has been watching police go by all afternoon and evening. You know the policy of the police from our own encounters with our friend Lieutenant Tragg. They don't like to be announced. They think it gives the suspect too much opportunity to collect his or her thoughts, or perhaps call a lawyer, so they go barging past everyone and right into the private offices or right up to the door of the penthouse apartments."

"You mean you're going to impersonate an officer?" Drake asked.

"I won't impersonate an officer," Mason said, "but I'll amble along, not too fast and not too slow, acting as though I were doing a job. And nobody's going to stop me. It's a crime to impersonate an officer. It's not a crime to act like one. I'll get to the apartment and . . . well, then we'll see what happens."

"She may be in bed," Della Street said.

Mason put his hand in his pocket. "Paul," he said, "you take charge of this scarf and the box of .22 shells— remember that at some time we may have to introduce these articles in evidence, in which event we must be able to account for possession so we can furnish a chain of identification.

"Take these articles up to the office, lock them in the safe, and . . ."

Drake vehemently shook his head. "I was willing to stand by while you took that, Perry, but I'm not going to touch that evidence with a ten-foot pole. I wouldn't have it in the office. I don't want it in my custody."

"Why?"

"Why!" Drake exploded. "Good heavens, the stuff is evidence and we've taken it into our possession. We're concealing it from the police."

"Evidence of what?" Mason asked.

"Evidence of the identity of the person who committed the murder, of course."

"We don't *know* that."

"Well, it's a reasonable assumption."

"But don't you think we'd better wait until we know it before we turn it over to the police?"

"That's just an excuse," Drake said.

"Nobody knows we have it," Mason said. "Just the four of us—you, Della, Kelton and myself."

"And four is too damn many to know a thing like that," Drake said. "We're monkeying with dynamite. I'll admit that you probably have something in mind, Perry. You're going to pull a fast one and you'll come out on top of the heap or you think you will. But the point is, suppose the police get wise to the fact that we're holding this before your plans mature. *Then* where does that leave us?"

"It leaves us in a most embarrassing situation," Mason admitted.

"Exactly," Drake said, "and it's that situation I don't want to get caught in. You keep your scarf and shells."

Della Street said quietly, "I'll take them, Chief."

Mason hesitated a moment, then handed them over to her. "I hate to drag you into it, Della, but I don't want to take those things up to Mauvis Meade's apartment with me. I might get accused of trying to steal the scarf and plant the shells, and there's always a possibility that I may be stopped and searched before I get out of there."

"I understand," she said.

Mason left the Golden Fleece, hailed a taxicab and went to Mauvis Niles Meade's apartment house. "Put the meter on waiting time," he told the cab driver. "I may be in there anywhere from two minutes to an hour."

He handed the driver a ten-dollar bill, said, "This will be a guarantee that I'm not walking out on you."

"I'll be waiting right here," the cab driver said.

Mason entered the apartment house, walked at a steady, even gait toward the elevator.

The night clerk at the desk looked up expectantly.

Mason didn't even vouchsafe him a glance but walked over to the elevator.

The clerk hesitated for a moment, then, with an almost imperceptible shrug of his shoulders, turned back to the work he was doing at the desk.

Mason entered the elevator, said to the operator, "Up—all the way."

"Penthouse?" the operator asked.

"You heard me," Mason said, "*all* the way up."

The operator said, "Yes, *sir*," and the cage shot upward.

Mason tapped on the door of Mauvis Meade's apartment, waited a moment, then tapped again.

The door was flung open. "Well, it's about time you got here," Mauvis Meade said. "We . . ." Her voice trailed away into dismayed silence as she saw Perry Mason. "*You* again!" she said.

"In person," Mason said. "I want to talk with you."

"You've already talked with me."

"I want to talk some more."

"Why?"

"For one thing," Mason said, "I want to get you straight. You've found that it's good business to adopt the pose of the sophisticated woman-of-the-world, the babe who has all the curves and knows all the angles—and somehow or other, I have an idea that it's pretty much of a pose with you, that you decided you could make money by writing a daring book and then give the impression of having a sultry personality."

"Indeed," she said.

"And I think that's why you've been somewhat difficult on publicity interviews," Mason said. "You're afraid you'll betray your true character. You're not the sort of girl you'd like to have the book reviewers think you are."

"How interesting," she said.

"Isn't it?" Mason said. "Do I come in and talk it over, or do we discuss it here in the hallway?"

"You come in and we talk it over," she said, standing to one side and holding the door open. "You've challenged me, so I have the choice of weapons."

She had taken off the lounging pajamas and was dressed in a strapless gown that seemed held in place by a miracle of mechanical ingenuity. Her shoulders and the swell above her breasts gleamed seductively in the soft light.

She said nervously, "I am a little jumpy tonight. Newspaper reporters and police officers have been wearing out the carpet."

She seated herself on the davenport and indicated that Mason was to take a seat beside her.

As Mason seated himself, she looked up at him and gave that characteristic slow raising of the eyelids.

"Now, look," Mason said, "it's going to help a lot if you get over the idea that you have the only curves in captivity. You have a nice chassis, but, after all, it's standard equipment as far as I'm concerned. I'm interested in protecting a client, and I'm interested in a murder case."

She regarded him archly. "You're taking the wrong

tactic, Mr. Mason. The challenge alone is enough to make me practice all the seductive wiles I've been studying so assiduously."

She moved closer.

Mason made a gesture of impatience. "Do you," he asked, "happen to have a copy of your book handy?"

Her laugh was throaty. "That's like asking a salesman if, by any chance, he happens to have his samples in that leather bag he's carrying."

"I want to look at it," Mason said.

She regarded him thoughtfully, said, "Well, you don't need to be so damn impersonal about it."

She sulked for a moment, then got up, crossed over to a bookcase, pulled out a book and all but tossed it in Mason's lap. She stood before him, not seating herself, looking down at the lawyer.

Mason took the book, turned it over to the photograph on the dust jacket.

"Oh," she said, as she saw him studying the photograph, "then you *are* interested. That's better. The legs *are* nice —don't you think?" She seated herself beside him once more.

"This scarf," Mason said, "it's very interesting—is that a monkey shown on the scarf?"

"That's right. That's a printed silk scarf I got in Japan. It has the three monkeys, see no evil, hear no evil and speak no evil." She laughed again and said, "I thought it was particularly appropriate for a woman author who had seen all, heard all and was telling damn near everything."

"That scarf interests me a lot," Mason said. "I wonder if I could look at it."

"Why?"

"I want to see the scarf."

"I heard you the first time. But *why* do you want to look at it?"

"There's something about it that interests me. It may

be . . . well, I'd like to see if there's anything on it showing any data about its manufacture, whether there's a
stock number or anything, so I could duplicate it . . ."

She shook her head. "You're not going to duplicate
that. Not in this country. I got the scarf in Japan, and it's
the only one I saw. I saw it in just this one store. It fascinated me and I bought it."

"You don't think there are any others?"

She shook her head.

"Then I'm going to have to bother you to look at
yours."

"My, but you're insistent," she said. "Do you always
get what you want—with women?"

"Very seldom," Mason said.

"All right. I'll get it for you. You wait right here."

She left the davenport, went through the door into the
bedroom and Mason sat, waiting. After a while, he lit a
cigarette.

At one time he thought he heard the rumble of a masculine voice.

Then Mauvis Meade was back. "I'm sorry, Mr.
Mason," she said, "I can't find it. You'll have to give me
a raincheck on it. I'll dig it up for you later on. You see,
things are in a terrible mess. You understand. Somebody
really went through the apartment like a whirlwind—all
except Gladys Doyle's room."

Mason nodded.

"Why do you suppose that Gladys Doyle's room was
immune from search?" she asked meaningly.

"I'm not certain that it was."

"What do you mean?"

"My idea is that whoever searched the apartment was
looking for some one thing and was in a terrific hurry.
That person didn't have time to be tactful. He or she had
to dump things out of drawers, pull things out of closets,

paw through papers and just keep moving. There was no time to make a surreptitious search."

"And then when this person came to Gladys Doyle's room?"

"It might have been," Mason said, "that, as you pointed out to Lieutenant Tragg, the room was not searched because the person knew that whatever he or she was looking for wouldn't be in that room. Or it *might* be that as soon as the person started searching her room, that person found whatever it was that was wanted, and, therefore, left the apartment without carrying the search any further."

Her index finger started making little patterns on the arm of the davenport.

"Well?" Mason asked.

"Sometimes," she said, "I think you're awfully damn smart."

"And at other times?" he asked laughingly.

"And at other times I'm sure of it," she said.

"Can you tell me when was the last time you remember seeing that scarf?" Mason asked.

She pursed her lips. "I had it on for that photograph. Of course, Mr. Mason, that photograph was a fake. That is, it was made in a studio. Those are stock props and they had a fan. The idea was to show lots of leg, and they didn't want to have it look like posed cheesecake, so someone decided to have me on a yacht with a wind, and then catch the photograph at just the right time. My gosh, I'll bet they took fifty photographs before they got the one they wanted."

"The others not revealing enough?" Mason asked.

"Some of them were not revealing enough, and some were altogether too damn revealing. The idea was to get the skirt with just the right swirl in it so that you could look at it and know that as it continued blowing it was going to . . . well, you know. You build up suspense that way."

"You had the scarf on then," Mason said. "That photograph was taken some weeks ago, wasn't it?"

"Yes, months ago."

"And when have you had the scarf since?"

"Oh, I have had it two or three times—I loaned it to Gladys once—why is it so important?"

"It could be very important," Mason said. "I . . . are you alone, Mauvis?"

"Why, Mr. Mason, what gives you that idea?"

"I'm just wondering. The manner in which you're holding your head. You—"

"Look, Big Boy," she said, "aren't you getting a little proprietary? Do you have any right to chaperone me or censor my company?"

Abruptly the door from the bedroom opened and a paunchy man in his late forties, with cold, hard eyes, stepped out. "I'll take it from here, Mauvis," he said.

Mason said, "Well, good evening . . . Dunkirk, isn't it? . . . Gregory Alson Dunkirk."

"That's right," Dunkirk said.

"And you seem to have been following the conversation," Mason said.

Dunkirk stood with no change of expression. "That's right, Mason. I had the room bugged. I thought it might be a good precaution, under the circumstances."

"And what are the circumstances?" Mason asked.

"As though you didn't know. You know, Mason, I don't think I like the idea of you coming in here and cross-examining this girl."

"I'm sorry," Mason said.

"I think you owe her an apology."

"I'm not apologizing," Mason said. "When I said I was sorry I meant I was sorry you didn't like it."

"You're representing Gladys Doyle in this thing. Now,

you're pretty smooth and pretty resourceful. Once you start, there's no telling where you're going to stop."

"I usually try to get at the truth before I stop," Mason said. "I find the truth is rather a powerful weapon."

"It depends who's using it," Dunkirk said. "The trouble with these powerful weapons is that a great deal depends on which way they're pointed. I'm taking over here. I'm going to give Mauvis a little protection."

Before Mason could say anything, there was a quick knock at the door.

Mauvis Meade looked at Gregory Dunkirk, a glance of swift interrogation, then at some invisible signal she received, she hurried to the door and opened it.

A big, grinning, bull-necked individual with a cauliflower ear, a broken nose and smiling eyes set beneath beetling brows, said, "Hi, Mauvis."

"Well, it took *you* long enough to get here," Mauvis Meade said.

"I came as quick as I could."

The big man moved easily into the room. "Hi," he said to Dunkirk.

"How are you, Dukes?"

"Pretty good," the man said.

Dunkirk said to Mason, "Meet Dukes, Mason. I think his name is Lawton, but everybody calls him Dukes."

"How are you," Mason said, getting to his feet and extending his hand.

Duke reached out a big paw and scooped up Mason's hand, his lips twisted into a grin. "Hi, Counselor," he said, and exerted pressure.

Mason fought back against the crushing fingers until he reached a point when he seemed to have used his last ounce of strength. The grinning Dukes abruptly released his hand.

"Mighty glad to know you, Counselor."

"And who, may I ask, is Dukes? And how does he fit into this picture?" Mason asked.

Dunkirk said, "Dukes is a bodyguard. He's going to take care of Miss Meade for a while and see that she doesn't have a lot of unpleasant interruptions. You'll pardon me for being personal, Mr. Mason, but you're classified as an unpleasant interruption."

"Indeed," Mason said.

"No hard feelings personally."

Mauvis Meade smiled up at him.

Duke Lawton's face lit up. "You want him out?" he asked, jerking his thumb toward the door and leaning slightly forward so most of his weight was on the balls of his feet.

"No, no," Dunkirk said. "He's leaving. No rough stuff, Dukes."

"Okay. Anything you say." Dukes said good-naturedly, and walked over and held the door open.

Mason said to Mauvis Meade, "I'm sure you're going to be well taken care of, Miss Meade."

"Thank you," she said demurely.

"And all that reasoning about that person making the search," Dunkirk said to Mason, "you know you *could* be awfully wrong about that."

"And I could be awfully right," Mason said.

"I wouldn't bank on it," Dunkirk said.

He turned and said, "Dukes." He said it with quiet authority, as one would talk to a well-trained dog.

Dukes Lawton snapped to alert interest. "Yeah," he said.

"Mr. Mason is leaving," Dunkirk said. "He isn't coming back any more unless I'm here, or unless Miss Meade's lawyer is here. Do you understand that?"

"Sure."

"And I hope *you* understand it," Dunkirk said to Mason, his eyes hard.

Mason bowed. "I take it, then, that Miss Meade is mixed up in this a lot deeper than appears on the surface."

"She will be by the time you finish trying to get your babe out of it," Dunkirk said. "Now get this, Mason. I've always had a lot of respect for you. You don't handle my kind of stuff or you'd have been my mouthpiece. But you and I could have trouble. You stay away from Mauvis Meade and you and I'll get along all right."

"Did it ever occur to you," Mason said, "that you are taking the exact course which is going to direct suspicion to Miss Meade? Did it ever occur to you that if, for any reason, I wanted to pull her into this, you have given me the most beautiful build-up in the world? Did it ever occur to you that I was trying to give her a break and now you've spoiled it?"

Dunkirk said, "Don't pay any attention to him, Mauvis. What he's saying now is not for my ears but for yours. He's using me as a sounding board."

Once more Dunkirk said, "Dukes," in exactly the same tone of voice he would have called to a dog.

"Uh-huh," Dukes said.

Dunkirk motioned with his thumb.

The grinning Dukes placed a hamlike hand between Mason's shoulder blades and exerted gentle pressure. "Good night, Mr. Mason," he said.

The pressure increased. Mason had to move quickly to keep from stumbling.

The door slammed and a bolt shot into place.

11

PERRY MASON sat in the visitors' room at the jail and surveyed Gladys Doyle with keen eyes.

"I want you to tell me the truth," he said.

"The absolute truth, so help me."

Mason said, "An attorney is confronted with a lot of alternatives in a situation of this sort. For instance, I could sit tight, hoping that you'd answer questions and persuade the officers that you were innocent.

"On the other hand, I could have advised you not to answer any questions and trusted to luck and the fact that the officers couldn't uncover enough evidence against you to justify them in bringing a charge against you.

"You understand that?"

She nodded.

"All right," Mason said. "Now, I had a third alternative, and it's the one I elected to use. I'm trying to force their hand. I filed an application for a writ of habeas corpus. The judge issued an order of habeas corpus, which means that the police have to produce you in court and show cause why they're holding you. If they can't show cause, you're released. Therefore," Mason went on, "the police will probably see that a complaint is filed charging you with first degree murder. They won't wait for a grand jury indictment.

"The advantage of that course," Mason said, "is that when the case comes on for a preliminary hearing, I have an opportunity to see what the evidence against you really is, to cross-examine witnesses before anyone knows just how their testimony is going to fit in with other testimony. In other words, before anyone has had a chance to coach them so that the case against you is airtight. There are lots of little holes that can be uncovered in a preliminary hearing, in a situation of this sort.

"I hope you have enough confidence in me to agree that it was the proper thing to do."

"Anything you say, Mr. Mason."

"Have you seen the morning paper?"

"No."

"There's a photograph of the victim in the morning paper," Mason said. "They've photographed the features and retouched the eyes so as to give the corpse a lifelike appearance. They feel that someone is certain to recognize him."

Mason unfolded the newspaper and held it up against the heavy plate glass through which the interview was taking place.

Gladys Doyle looked at the newspaper picture with considerable interest.

"Do you recognize the man?" Mason asked.

"By that do you mean did I ever see him in his lifetime . . . before I found him lying dead in the cabin?"

"That's right. Did you know him, did you ever see him in life?"

She shook her head.

"Now, this other man who was in the cabin when you arrived. Had you ever seen him before?"

"I'm certain I had never seen him."

"Have you thought of anything, any clue which would enable us to locate him?"

"No. I've been trying. There was nothing I could put my finger on. I can't remember anything except what I've told you already."

"All right," Mason said. "Now I'm going to approach the corpse from another angle. I want you to think carefully before you say anything. Does the name Joseph H. Manly mean anything to you?"

Her face was completely impassive. She slowly shook her head.

"Not a thing?" Mason asked.

"Not a thing."

"You don't know him?"

"I never heard of him, as far as I know."

"All right," Mason told her. "I have every reason to believe that the victim is a person named Manly. I think we got that information in advance of the police. However, I think the police know who he is now and are withholding information from the newspapers because they don't want us to take advantage of it."

"You mean they may know who he is already?"

Mason nodded. "I'm inclined to think they do. However, they haven't announced it. They're acting on the assumption that the identity of the murder victim is a mystery. Now, there's another thing. They have found the murder weapon was the .22 rifle that was lying on the floor of the bedroom. You picked up that rifle?"

"Yes. Things were all pretty much of a whirl in my mind, but I'm quite certain I picked it up."

"When?"

"Just after I found the dead man. I saw the rifle and, as nearly as I can recall the situation now, thought that I could use it in case—well, you know, if the murderer was still in the cabin. Then I went into a panic and put it down where I'd found it."

"And, in so doing, quite probably left some fingerprints on it," Mason said.

"But, Mr. Mason, that was long after the man was killed. It must have been."

"I know," Mason said patiently. "*You* know when you

picked it up. You'll say, 'Why, that was a perfectly natural thing to do, and those fingerprints were left on there long after the man was murdered.' The trouble is, fingerprints aren't dated. If you left any fingerprints on that gun and the police can develop those latent fingerprints, there's nothing to show whether the fingerprints were made before the man was killed or afterward. Now, about that map and the directions which Mauvis Meade gave you. I'm going to tell you this, Gladys. Mauvis Meade is playing some sort of a very deep game.

"I want you to think back to the time when she gave you those directions. I want you to tell me whether she told you to turn to the *left* at that fork in the road or turn to the *right*. I'm not going to take any advantage of you, Gladys. I'm going to tell you that the police have in their possession what seems to be the original pages of notes which you made, giving directions, and it shows that you were to turn to the right at the forks in the road rather than the left."

Gladys Doyle's face suddenly showed consternation.

"Yes?" Mason prompted.

"She did, Mr. Mason. I remember now! She *did* tell me to turn to the right there at that last intersection, but . . . well, when I wanted to get my directions, I went to my notebook and found the page was gone. Someone had torn it out, so then I went to the writing desk where she had the map, took the map out and made notes of the route I was to follow from the route that was shown on the map. And I'm willing to stake my life that the map actually showed the road to the left—that is, the arrows on the map showed that the left-hand road was the one to be followed."

"You *are* staking your life on it," Mason said. "I want you to be sure."

"I've given it a lot of thought. I'm certain. I will tell

you this, though, Mr. Mason. I'm beginning to believe, the more I think of it, that when she looked at the map and told me the road to follow, she told me to turn right at the forks."

"Would you know the map if you saw it again?"

"Certainly I would. It was in Mauvis Meade's handwriting. It was in ink, and there were some red arrows that were made showing the direction to be taken coming down the mountain . . . Now, here's something else. I'm inclined to think there was a picture of some sort on the back of the piece of paper, a pen-and-ink sketch of a house. I didn't really look at it. I just remember it was there."

"And you'd know this map if you saw it again?"

"Absolutely. I made notes from it, just brief notes of the distances and the turns as shown by the arrows."

"You are completely positive that the arrow *on that map* showed you were to take the left-hand fork in the road, the one that goes down the Pine Glen road, down to the cabin where you spent the night?"

"I'm absolutely positive."

"Here's something else I want to ask you," Mason said. "Was there anything in your bedroom there at the apartment in the penthouse that might have been of particular interest to some person who was trying . . . well, let us say trying to get an intimate line on Mauvis Meade?"

She started to shake her head.

"Now, wait a minute," Mason said, "before you answer that question do some thinking. You had been taking quite a bit of dictation from Miss Meade. Is there anything in your shorthand notebook, anything in perhaps some of the older shorthand books that you had filled up and discarded?"

"Well, of course, there were letters, correspondence and notes."

"How much?"

"Quite a bit. I . . . I can't remember all of the different things."

"You're going to have to try and remember them," Mason said. "Try to think over the things you had taken in shorthand—Now, I have a theory that whoever searched that penthouse was looking for some specific paper. He tried to find it in Mauvis Meade's quarters. Then, when he couldn't find it, he got the idea of going to your room and looking in your shorthand notebooks. He probably found it there."

"Then he would necessarily have had to read my shorthand notes," she said, "or . . ."

Mason saw the expression change on her face. "What is it?" he asked.

"Well," she said, "this may or may not be important. Last week . . . let's see, it was Wednesday, I think . . . Wednesday of last week, Mauvis handed me a sealed envelope. It was addressed to me and was in her handwriting and it had on the envelope, 'Personal and Private Property of Gladys Doyle.' "

"A will?" Mason asked.

"She didn't say. I assumed it was instructions as to what I was to do in case . . . well, you know Mauvis Meade is rather unpredictable and . . . I don't know. I had an idea from what she said it might be she was intending to elope and get married, or something of that sort."

"What did she say when she gave you the letter?"

"She told me that if anything happened to change my status I was to open that letter."

Mason thought that over, then said, "Did you look for that envelope when you went back to the apartment after you had returned from the mountains?"

She shook her head.

"Or when you returned the next time after you had borrowed Della Street's clothes?"

"No," she said. "I just didn't look for it. I . . . I guess I should have when I found the apartment all torn up and Miss Meade missing, but to tell you the truth, I never thought of it again until you started asking me about it."

"You haven't told the police about it, or—"

"No. I tell you, I haven't thought of it."

"All right, then," Mason said, "don't think of it. Forget it. Say nothing about it, nothing to anyone. Understand?"

She nodded.

"All right," Mason told her, "that's all we can do at the present time. I'm going to demand that you be given a preliminary hearing. At that preliminary hearing, I'll probably let them bind you over to the superior court for trial. I'm using that strategy to find out what evidence they have against you.

"I want you to understand what I'm doing. I want you to give me your confidence."

"You have my confidence, Mr. Mason. I'm willing to do anything you say."

"All right," he told her. "Keep a stiff upper lip."

"What do I do about reporters and persons who want to interrogate me?" she asked.

"Simply smile at them and tell them that now that you have formally been charged with murder, your attorney will do all the talking, that you'll do your talking from the witness stand in the courtroom at the time your attorney tells you to."

"No other comments?"

"Oh, general comments," Mason said. "Talk about anything except the case. The newspaper reporters will like you if you're good copy. Give them something to write about. If they want to know about your experiences in jail, if they want to know about working for Mauvis Meade, or anything of that sort, tell them anything that will make a good story. Just be sure that you stick to the facts.

"Some of the female reporters, the kind that are known as sob sisters, will want to know about your early life, your childhood, your schooling and all of that, and there's no reason on earth why you shouldn't tell them."

"Nothing about the case?"

"Nothing about the case," Mason said, and got up, nodding to the matron that the interview was over.

Mason took a taxicab back to his office.

Della Street was waiting for him.

"You have an anonymous letter," she said.

"Another one?" Mason asked. "We're always getting them."

"This one has something that *may* be pay dirt. It came special delivery."

Mason raised his eyebrows.

"A letter," she said, "which encloses a map. The map purports to be the work of Mauvis Niles Meade, and it is claimed the lettering is in her handwriting. The map shows the road down to the murder cabin and a sketch of the cabin on the back."

Mason's eyes narrowed. "Let's take a look, Della."

She brought him the envelope which had been addressed on a typewriter. The message on the inside read:

Dear Mr. Mason:

If you are going to represent Gladys, you had better have this map. It was made over a year ago by Mauvis Meade, when she first began to take an interest in the cabin above Pine Glen. All of the lettering is in her handwriting and the sketch of the cabin that is on the back was made by her because she thought the place was rustic, quaint and artistic.

We're sending you this map because you may want to use it on cross-examination. We have no further use for it.

Don't be misled by nylon stockings, curves and tears. Go in there fighting and you'll be surprised what you uncover.

Mason regarded the envelope, the letter and the enclosed map thoughtfully.

"Get Paul Drake for me, Della. Ask him if he can come over right away."

Mason resumed studying the letter carefully and was still studying it when Paul Drake tapped on the door to the private office.

Della Street let him in.

"Hi, Perry," Drake said. "Did you do any good with Mauvis last night?"

"It depends on what you mean by doing good," Mason said. "She's becoming pretty well entrenched, what with a professional wrestler and fighter for a bodyguard and Gregory Alson Dunkirk in the background."

"Dunkirk!" Drake exclaimed.

"Evidently he's the prototype of the big shot Mauvis Meade's heroine got tangled up with in *Chop the Man Down*," Mason said.

"*He* got tangled up with *her*," Drake said. "Have you read the book?"

"Not yet. I've glanced through it, reading a page here and there . . . I identified that scarf all right. It's not only the one pictured on the dust jacket of the book, but Mauvis Meade says she purchased her scarf in Japan, that it was exceedingly difficult to find one, that she doesn't think any more of them are in this country."

"Oh-oh," Drake said.

"Just how much do you know about Gregory Alson Dunkirk?" Mason asked.

"Not a hell of a lot," Drake said. "About what everybody else knows. He's dynamite, he's poison, he's powerful politically, he's unscrupulous, he's rich, and he's clever. I understand the income tax people have never been able to get anything on him—believe it or not, people make him gifts. They pay the gift tax and they're very reticent about their reasons for making the gift later on. But it's all regular, as far as a bookkeeping transaction is concerned."

"Well, he's taken charge," Mason said, "and he's hired a bodyguard. From now on, I don't think people are just going to barge in on Mauvis Niles Meade.

"Now here's something that came in the mail today. A very nice anonymous letter containing a document in which I think you'll be interested. Be careful about fingerprints, Paul, because I want to have you examine the document for prints by iodine fumes."

Paul Drake picked up the letter, holding it gingerly by it's two corners, his fingers touching the extreme ends of the paper.

"You can develop prints on paper?" Mason asked.

"Sometimes, if you're lucky. The iodine fumes every once in a while will give you a fingerprint."

"Let's try it on this," Mason said, indicating the paper.

"What about the map?" Drake asked.

Mason shook his head. "We're sitting tight on the map, Paul."

"When you spring it at the hearing, if your client's fingerprints are on there, the police will dig them out."

"Let the police dig them out, then," Mason said. And then added, "I could play it dumb, you know."

"How do you mean?" Drake asked.

Mason grinned. "I could put the defendant on the stand and get her to tell about the map that gave her di-

rections down the mountain, and then say to her, 'Is this
the map you saw?' and hand it to her before anyone could
recover from their startled surprise. Then Hamilton
Burger would say he wanted to see it, and she'd hand it to
him, and then Burger probably would give it back to her
before it occurred to somebody that it would be a good
plan to test it for fingerprints. By that time they couldn't
tell a thing about it, not as far as the defendant was concerned. Her fingerprints would be all over it and Burger's
as well."

"Are you going to try that?" Drake asked.

Mason grinned and said, "I never know *what* I'm going
to try."

Drake's face was concerned. "Perry, I wish you'd get in
touch with the police on that scarf and that box of .22
shells."

"Why?"

"Because I'm scared," Drake said.

"Sit tight," Mason told him. "You haven't seen anything yet. Now, Paul, I want to find out what typewriter
was used in writing this letter. Call in an expert on questioned documents and get me all the dope."

"That's easy," Drake said. "A good expert can look at
that document and tell you right away what make of typewriter and what model of typewriter was used."

"Okay, get busy, Paul."

"And you'll tell Tragg about that scarf and the box of
shells?"

Mason shook his head. "I can't tell him now, Paul, or
he would haul us over the coals for withholding evidence.
The minute I let it appear that I think it's evidence, I've
crucified myself. As long as I play dumb and pretend I
didn't think it could possibly be evidence, they have to
prove that I knew it *was* evidence—"

"Don't be silly," Drake interrupted. "You can't pretend
to be that dumb."

"Well, let me ask you a question," Mason said. "Why would the murderer have used that stuff? How could it have fitted into the crime?"

"That's easy," Drake told him. "When you carry a box of .22 shells in a purse, the box slides open and the shells dribble out. But when you wrap the box in a scarf, then you can put it in the purse and carry the shells without spilling any."

"So you carry them to the scene of the crime," Mason said, "crawl underneath the house and plant the stuff in a can?"

"Well, you can't explain everything in a murder case," Drake said. "But my pet guess is that whoever killed this guy was waiting under the house for the propitious time. It was dark underneath the cabin and on that low side of the hill a person could sit in there, sheltered from the rain and with warm clothing could have been as snug as a bug in a rug."

"You keep on reasoning like that," Mason said, "and you'll reason yourself right out of your license. It shows that you not only thought the stuff was evidence but had reasonable grounds in support of that belief. Personally, I just refuse to admit even to myself, much less to you, that it's evidence."

"Just a coincidence," Drake said sarcastically.

"That's right," Mason told him.

"Well, I am looking forward to hearing Hamilton Burger examine you on the witness stand when you try to play innocent and he turns loose his heavy sarcasm . . . You're sitting there under oath, trying to explain to the judge that you thought it was just a coincidence . . . how nice!"

"You get busy on that letter," Mason told him, "and forget about hanging black crepe all over the office walls."

Mason returned to his work, as Paul Drake, carrying the typed letter, left the office.

Later that afternoon Drake called Mason. "No fingerprints on the letter, Perry. It was written on a Remington machine, a model that was first put out five years ago."

"No prints at all?" Mason asked.

"None at all, Perry, which was surprising in a way, because a new ribbon had been put on the machine just before the letter was written. Ordinarily the new ribbon would have rubbed off on the operator's fingertips.

"Here's something else about the machine. It's probably not a machine in a business office because it's rather badly out of alignment. It's evidently used by someone who bangs away at high speed and may occasionally pile up the type, but this particular letter was probably written by a professional because the touch is remarkably uniform.

"That's about all the information the expert on documents can give us. There's nothing unusual or distinctive about the paper that was used."

"And no fingerprints at all?"

"Not a one."

"Okay, Paul," Mason said, "we'll have to take it from there and carry on."

12

JUDGE ARVIS BAGBY took his place on the bench and said, "This is the time heretofore fixed for the preliminary hearing in the case of the People of the State of California versus Gladys Doyle. Are you ready, gentlemen?"

"The defense is ready," Mason said.

Harvey Ellington, one of the more promising young attorneys in the district attorney's office, said, "The People are always ready, Your Honor."

"Very well. Proceed with the case," Judge Bagby said. "Now I want to call to the attention of counsel that we are getting a terrific backlog of cases here, and there is some criticism of the courts because of delays in the administration of justice. I am going to ask you gentlemen to co-operate with the Court and with each other in trying to get the nonessential parts of the case out of the way.

"Now then, gentlemen, in view of that situation, are there any matters on which we can have a stipulation which will save time and eliminate the necessity of proof?"

"I'm quite certain we can save time with several stipulations, Your Honor," Ellington said. "I have here some maps, a small scale map showing the road going up Pine Glen Canyon from the last paved highway; I have larger scale maps showing the location of the cabin; I have general maps showing the roads leading from the vicinity of the cabin up to the crest of the mountain, and, in particular, to the Summit Inn resort, which is, of course, a very popular resort for skiing; I have photographs of the cabin, both of the interior and the exterior; and I have a map of the cabin.

"The photographs were all taken under police supervision by a police photographer, and we can vouch for their accuracy. The large scale maps were prepared in the office of the county surveyor, and the small scale maps were taken from the official records. I take it there will be no objection to introducing these various documents in evidence, and that it will not be necessary to put the individuals on the stand who can testify to the authenticity of those maps."

"That's quite all right," Mason said. "On the strength of counsel's assurance, I will stipulate those documents may go into evidence."

"Now then," Ellington said, "the cabin in which the murder was committed is owned by Morrison Findlay. Some months ago, Mr. Findlay received an offer to rent that cabin for a hundred dollars a month. He rented the cabin and, thereafter, received a hundred dollars on the first of each and every month, so that the rental was paid up in full, in advance. Findlay had acquired the cabin in a real-estate deal some months earlier and had made an inspection trip to the cabin at the time the deal was completed. Aside from that, he had only been at the cabin twice, and, after the lease was made, Mr. Findlay did not go to the cabin at all. Therefore, he can shed no light on the crime except to give us a background as to the ownership of the cabin, the fact that it was leased and that the rental money was paid regularly. I will state further that the cabin was rented by a person giving the name G. C. Challis, that the rental deal was made over the telephone, that Mr. Findlay was busy at the time, that he made no attempt to get in touch with the person renting the cabin, but stated that a rental of a hundred dollars a month would be satisfactory and that the tenancy could commence at such time as he received a hundred dollars rental in advance covering the first month's rent and another hundred dollars covering the last month's rent.

"I can assure counsel that we have investigated those facts and they are true, and I will ask counsel to so stipulate."

Mason said, "Before I make a stipulation, I will ask counsel if Mr. Findlay made any attempt to get in touch with Mr. Challis."

"I don't think Mr. Findlay made any attempt to get in touch with the person renting the cabin," Ellington said.

"Does he have the address of Mr. Challis?"

"He has an address which came on envelopes in which the rental was mailed," Ellington said. "The address was that of a secretarial agency which furnishes office space to persons who wish a mailing address or minor office services."

"You have investigated that address?" Mason asked.

"Of course. The police have made an investigation."

"And have talked with Mr. Challis?" Mason asked.

"It has been impossible, so far, to find the person who paid rental on the cabin," Ellington said. "I fail to see that it is particularly important. We would like to talk with this person, and it may be that later on it will appear that the identity of this person is of some importance, perhaps of considerable importance. But at the time, we have been unable to find this person, and, for the purposes of this preliminary hearing, it is entirely immaterial.

"As Court and counsel both realize, it is only necessary to show that a crime was committed and that there is reasonable ground to believe that the defendant perpetrated the crime. We are prepared to make that showing at this time.

"We also feel that, at this time, there is no use going into a lot of collateral matters."

"I take it counsel will be willing to stipulate as to the matters outlined by the deputy district attorney," Judge Bagby said.

"I will stipulate that Morrison Findlay is the owner of the cabin if I am assured that such is the case."

"I can assure you such is the case," Ellington said.

"I will further stipulate that it may be deemed that Morrison Findlay was on the stand and testified, on direct examination, to all the facts set forth in the deputy district attorney's statement," Mason said.

A look of quick relief flashed over Ellington's face. "Very well," he said, "that disposes of the ownership of the cabin then, and—"

"Wait a minute," Mason interrupted. "I don't think you were listening very closely, Counselor. I stated that I would stipulate that Findlay could be deemed to have been on the stand and testified to these facts in direct examination. Now then, I have the right of cross-examination. I want to ask Mr. Findlay a few questions on cross-examination."

Ellington frowned. "But we've given you all the information, and—"

"That's my stipulation," Mason said. "I'm representing a defendant in a murder case. I'm willing to save time on matters which are nonessential, but I'm going to find out whether matters which are seemingly nonessential are in fact nonessential, and I'm going to cross-examine Morrison Findlay, one way or another. Either take my stipulation or go ahead and put him on the stand and show your chain of title and then I'll cross-examine."

"The procedure is rather unusual," Ellington said, "but I have no other alternative except to agree to the terms imposed by counsel."

"Very well," Judge Bagby said. "Mr. Findlay will be

deemed to have given the testimony contained in your statement, subject to cross-examination by the defense. Now, Mr. Findlay is in court?"

"He is."

"Then let him take the stand for cross-examination," Judge Bagby said.

Morrison Findlay, a middle-aged, sharp-eyed man with bushy eyebrows, took the witness stand and looked expectantly at Ellington.

"Mr. Mason will question you on cross-examination," Ellington said. "We have stipulated as to your testimony on direct examination, Mr. Findlay."

Mason rose to face Findlay.

"In discussing this stipulation with counsel, Mr. Findlay, whenever I referred to the G. C. Challis who had rented a cabin from you, I referred to the individual as being Mr. Challis. On the other hand, I couldn't help but notice that whenever Mr. Ellington had occasion to refer to this individual, he said 'the person renting the cabin' or words to that effect which did not disclose the sex of the individual.

"Therefore, Mr. Findlay, my first question on cross-examination is whether the G. C. Challis who rented the cabin from you was a man or a woman."

Findlay glanced swiftly at Ellington, then said, "It was a woman."

"Did she give you any first name?"

"No, just the initials—G. C. Challis."

"Wasn't that rather an unusual way to rent a cabin?"

"Very unusual, Mr. Mason."

"Why did you do it?"

"Because the cabin was worth, at the outside, perhaps thirty dollars a month. I got the cabin on a trade and it is carried on my books at a nominal valuation. The cabin is on five acres of land, and the land itself may eventually have some value, but the terrain is mountainous, there is

only a small flat around the cabin, the scrub timber is of
no great value except for purposes of ornamentation and
holding the soil in place. Under the circumstances, a
hundred dollars a month was very, very satisfactory to
me."

"And you received the money each month?"

"Yes, sir."

"By check?"

"No, sir."

"Not by check?" Mason asked, raising his eyebrows.

"No, sir. I received it in the form of cash."

"How did you receive it?"

"Each month I received a letter bearing the return address of G. C. Challis. In the letter was invariably one
one-hundred-dollar bill and a brief note stating rental of
cabin for October, November, December, or whatever the
month was."

"The rent was in advance?"

"In advance."

"You received the letters by the first?"

"Yes, sir."

"Did you make any attempt to trace this mysterious
tenant?"

"Only to the extent of looking up the address that was
on the letter."

"And you found what?"

"That the address was that of a secretarial service
which rented out office space and furnished a mailing address to persons who wished to receive mail. I gathered
that Miss Challis, or Mrs. Challis, whichever she was, did
not care to have me know anything about her. In view of
the fact that the rental was coming in promptly every
month, I made no attempt to get any further information.
Frankly, I felt that any attempt to do so would be considered as prying on my part and might very well result in
the loss of my tenant."

"The first remittance contained two hundred dollars?"

"That is right. Two one-hundred-dollar bills, with a notation stating that the bills covered the first month's rent, which I believe was the month of September, and the last month's rent."

"Was the last month specified?"

"No, it was just described as the last month."

"Then you rented the cabin in September of last year?"

"No, sir. It was the year before."

Mason's eyebrows raised in surprise. "This has been going on for more than a year, then?"

"Yes, sir."

"How were the notations on these letters made? In feminine handwriting?"

"No, sir, on a typewriter."

"And you saved those letters?"

"Certainly. I endorsed upon each letter as it was received the amount of the cash remittance which was appended to the letter, and made that in the form of a notation."

"Did you ever send any receipts?"

"I did the first two months. I acknowledged receipt of the money and then received a telephone call stating that that wouldn't be at all necessary, that I was a reputable businessman and that my word was good. I was advised that it cost the recipient of the letters twenty-five cents for each letter that was received and forwarded to her and that there was no need of throwing twenty-five cents to the birds, as she expressed it."

"Over the telephone?"

"Yes."

"Did you have any idea whether it was a long-distance call or a local call? In other words was there any clue as to the location from which this person was talking?"

"None. I have every reason to believe it was a local call

because there was no announcement of a long-distance call."

"The whole situation was rather mysterious," Mason said. "Did you so consider it?"

"I so considered it, Mr. Mason."

"And did nothing to clarify the mystery?"

Findlay smiled, a tight-lipped smile which emphasized the shrewdness of his eyes. "I felt that I was getting perhaps twenty dollars a month for the cabin and eighty dollars a month for minding my own business."

"What gave you that impression?"

"Just the manner in which the deal was handled."

"So you minded your own business?"

"Yes."

"Now, have you brought those typewritten notes that accompanied the rental remittances to court with you?"

"I have."

"Produce them please, and I wish to have them introduced in evidence."

"No objection," Ellington said.

Findlay handed the clerk of the court the documents, fastened with a rubber band.

Mason took advantage of the delay to bend over Paul Drake.

"Paul, get your handwriting expert up here. See if the typewriter is the same one that typed the anonymous letter. Go phone your expert right away. Tell him to step on it."

Mason straightened, turned to the witness.

"Have you," he asked, "ever heard the defendant, Gladys Doyle, talk?"

Findlay hesitated a moment, then said, "Yes."

"The police arranged for you to hear her talk?"

"Yes."

"Was her voice the voice you heard over the telephone?"

"I don't think so."

"That's all," Mason said. "I have no further questions on cross-examination at this time. I do state to the Court, however, that before the case is concluded I may want to test Findlay's recollection of the voice he heard over the telephone by asking him to listen to other feminine voices."

"You can make him your own witness, if you want to do that," Ellington said. "We would like to have your cross-examination concluded at this time."

"Under the peculiar circumstances of this case," Mason said, "we feel that we are entitled to ask Mr. Findlay on cross-examination to listen to the voices of every female witness who may be called to the stand and determine whether the voice he heard over the telephone was the voice of such witness. I am going to ask Mr. Findlay this question."

Mason turned to the witness. "Will you be willing to remain in court during the hearing in this case and listen to the voices of the female witnesses? If you hear any voice that impresses you as being the voice of the person with whom you talked over the telephone, will you then advise me?"

"That's objected to as not proper cross-examination," Ellington said.

"It may not be proper cross-examination for the purpose of providing the identity of the voices," Mason said, "but it's proper cross-examination to show bias or interest on the part of this witness, and I'm going to insist that I have the right to do this."

"I'm going to let the witness answer the question the way you have asked it," Judge Bagby said, "because this obviously is a rather peculiar and very interesting situation. As far as the Court can tell at the present time, it may have some very significant bearing on the issues in the case, and the Court, of course, realizes that in a case of this sort the defense is proceeding blind. The prosecution knows generally what its case is and what evidence it has to produce."

"Very well, Your Honor," Ellington said reluctantly, "I will withdraw my objection to the question."

"Are you willing to do that?" Mason asked Findlay.

"I'm willing to do it, if necessary," Findlay said, "although I am a rather busy man and I dislike to spend more time than I have to in the courtroom. Because the question has been raised as to my bias or interest, Mr. Mason, I will state that I think you should know the prosecution had me listen to—"

"Now, just a minute, just a minute," Ellington interrupted, jumping to his feet. "We feel that the witness should be instructed, Your Honor, not to volunteer information but only to answer questions. We move to strike out any rambling dissertation as to conversations which took place with the prosecution, and, incidentally, we object to this part of the witness' answer on the ground that he obviously was on the point of repeating hearsay evidence."

Judge Bagby looked at Mason with a twinkle in his eye and said, "The Court will sustain the position of the deputy district attorney, at least at this time, on the grounds that the witness was about to volunteer a statement not called for in a question and that that statement quite obviously related to hearsay evidence."

"Yes, Your Honor," Mason said, smiling faintly. "Let me ask you this specific question, Mr. Findlay. You listened to the defendant's voice to determine if her voice was that of the person giving the name of Challis over the telephone?"

"Yes, sir."

"Did you listen to anyone else?"

"Yes, sir."

"To some woman?"

"Yes, sir."

"Who?"

"To a Mrs. Joseph Manly."

"Anyone else?"

"Yes."

"Who?"

"To the voice of Mauvis Meade."

"Anyone else?"

"No. Those were the only voices."

"And did you recognize the voice of any of those persons as being the voice of the person giving the name of G. C. Challis over the telephone?"

Findlay crossed his legs and shifted his position on the witness stand. "I will state this," he said, "that I was unable to make any positive identification of any of the voices."

"But short of a positive identification," Mason said, "did any of the voices sound familiar to you?"

"Well, yes."

"Whose voice?"

"That of Mauvis Meade."

"That sounded like the voice of the woman who called you and gave the name of G. C. Challis?"

"Well, I couldn't be positive. I told the police that I wouldn't identify the voice, but since the question has been asked in the way it was asked, I will state that I . . . well, I'll put it this way. I am not sure that it was Mauvis Meade who called me on the telephone and gave the name of G. C. Challis. On the other hand, I am not at all sure that she was *not* the person."

"Thank you," Mason said. "That's all."

The lawyer turned to Ellington and said, "And in view of the circumstances, the defense feels that even in the interest of expediting matters, it cannot enter into any further stipulations in regard to testimony."

Ellington flushed. "Call Mrs. Manly to the stand."

Mrs. Manly took the witness stand and was sworn.

"You are the widow of Joseph H. Manly?" Ellington asked.

"Yes."

"Your husband is dead?"

"Yes."

"When did you last see your husband alive?"

"It was, I think, on the fourth of this month."

"Did you subsequently see his body?"

"I did."

"And when was that?"

"That was on the following Tuesday."

"At what time?"

"In the morning."

"Did you identify that body?"

"I did."

"What body was it?"

"It was the body of my husband, Joseph H. Manly."

"I show you a photograph. Can you identify it?"

"It is a photograph of my husband."

"We ask this photograph be received in evidence," Ellington said.

"No objection, Your Honor."

"Very well," Judge Bagby ruled, "it may be received in evidence."

"Cross-examine," Ellington said.

Mrs. Manly turned to face Perry Mason as he arose.

"You told me that your husband was in Tucson?"

"Yes, sir."

"Did you know that he was not in Tucson?"

"At the time I made that statement to you, Mr. Mason, I was quite positive that my husband was in Tucson, Arizona."

"You had no reason to believe he was elsewhere?"

"No."

"In view of the fact that you told me he was in Tucson, I

will ask you if you have subsequently uncovered any information which accounts for the fact that he was not in Tucson but was in a cabin within a short distance of your residence."

"I don't know what in the world he was doing there," she said. "I have absolutely no idea what caused him to go to that cabin."

"No further questions," Mason said.

"Call Dr. Samuel G. Cleveland," Ellington said.

Dr. Cleveland came forward, qualified himself as an autopsy surgeon in the office of the county coroner, stated that he had performed an autopsy on a body which he identified as that of the body taken from the mountain cabin in Pine Glen and which, he stated, was the same body which had been viewed and identified by Mrs. Manly.

"How did that man meet his death?" Ellington asked.

"He met his death by a gunshot."

"What kind of a gun, if you know?"

"A .22-caliber high-velocity bullet of the type known as a .22 long-rifle."

"Where was the wound, Doctor?"

"He was hit in the left temple. The bullet ranged slightly upward. There was some considerable hemorrhage, and, in my opinion, death was virtually instantaneous. The man was unconscious from the moment the bullet hit him and died within, I would say, a matter of . . . well, probably a matter of seconds."

"Now then, did you make any test to determine the time of death?"

"I did, yes."

"What was the time of death?"

"The man died within one hour of the time he ingested a meal consisting of meat which was a beef of some sort, probably a steak, and French fried potatoes. There was a sauce, probably catchup, that he had put on the meat.

"I place death within not more than one hour and not less than forty-five minutes of the time such meal was ingested."

"You, of course, don't know of your own knowledge what time the meal was ingested?"

"No, sir, I only know that death occurred within those time limits."

"What have you to say with reference to temperature of the body and *rigor mortis*?"

"We took body temperature. *Rigor mortis* had begun to develop. However, as far as time of death is concerned, these were far less satisfactory means of proving the time of death. The period of time from the ingestion of the food in question is the most accurate means we were able to discover in this particular case as fixing the time of death. In view of the fact that it is, I believe, known when the food was taken—"

"Never mind volunteering any information, Doctor," Ellington said. "I am simply asking you what you learned as to the time of death."

"Yes, sir. It was within a period of forty-five minutes to an hour after the meal was ingested. The processes of digestion are such that, with a meal of that sort, we are able to make a very accurate determination as to the relative time of death."

"Cross-examine," Ellington said to Perry Mason.

Mason arose to cross-examine the doctor. "Doctor," he said, "do you have, perhaps, in the back of your mind an idea or an opinion as to the exact time of death?"

"Well . . . yes, I do."

"What time is that?"

"Now, just a moment," Ellington said. "I object to that, if the Court please. The question has already been asked and answered by the doctor. He has placed the time within forty-five minutes or an hour of the time the

the Mythical Monkeys   141

last meal was ingested, and he certainly can't place it any
closer than that."

Mason said, "I object, if the Court please, to the deputy district attorney rushing to the assistance of the witness
and calling his attention to the way the prosecution would
like to have the question answered."

"I'm not rushing to his assistance," Ellington shouted.

Mason grinned. "Then why didn't you let the doctor
answer the question in his own way?"

Judge Bagby said, "Gentlemen, let's abstain from personalities. Dr. Cleveland, can you answer that question?"

"Yes, sir."

"Answer it then."

"I think the decedent met his death at a period of from
forty-five minutes to an hour after he ingested the last
meal," the witness answered.

"Now then, Doctor," Mason said, smiling and urbane,
"do you also have in mind right now some opinion as to
the exact hour of the day that the decedent met his
death?"

"Well, of course, I don't have any evidence—that is,
any evidence that could be presented in a court of law
that would enable me to answer the question."

"I'm not asking you about where the evidence came
from or anything," Mason said. "I'm simply asking you if
in your own mind, at the present time, you have an idea
or an opinion as to the hour of the day at which the decedent met his death."

"That's objected to as not proper cross-examination,"
Ellington said.

"Overruled," Judge Bagby said.

"It's further objected to in that it calls for evidence as
to the state of mind of the witness, which is something
with which we are not concerned. It calls for a conclusion, and quite obviously, the way the question is framed,
that conclusion can be based upon hearsay evidence."

"This is cross-examination, Your Honor," Mason said. "I have the right to probe the mind of the witness. He has given an opinion. I have the right to ask him what is his foundation for that opinion and whether or not he has an idea at the present time as to the exact hour the deceased met his death."

"I think that's correct," Judge Bagby said. "I think you have a right to ask that question in that way. The objection is overruled."

"Well," Dr. Cleveland said, hesitating. "I . . . I think that . . . well, probably around three o'clock in the morning."

"You found evidence indicating that the decedent could well have met his death at about that hour?"

"Yes."

"And no evidence to contradict that?"

"No."

"Thank you," Mason said. "That's all, Doctor."

"My next witness," Ellington said, "is Dorothy Selma."

The young woman who came hip-swaying to the witness stand had large, limpid eyes, curves of which she was only too conscious, and a completely innocuous countenance, as though her face were disclaiming all responsibility for the spectacle of her body.

She took the oath, seated herself on the witness stand, and regarded Ellington with wide, innocent eyes.

"Your name is Dorothy Selma," Ellington said. "What's your occupation?"

"I work in an all-night luncheon service."

"A drive-in?"

"That's right."

"You're what is known as a car hop?"

"If you wish to call it that."

"I show you a photograph which has previously been identified as a photograph of Joseph H. Manly. I ask you if you have seen that individual before."

"I have."

"Where?"

"Early in the morning of the ninth—that is, it was early on a Monday morning at a little before two o'clock —oh, say around twenty minutes before two. He drove in to the place where I work."

"And what happened then?"

"I served him."

"Did he order?"

"He did."

"What did he order, Miss Selma?"

"We have a special at that hour in the morning, a beef-steak sandwich with French fried potatoes. There's a bar-becue sauce, a heavily spiced tomato sauce which is included if the customer wants it."

"Did he order that?"

"Yes, sir."

"You served him?"

"Yes, sir."

"And then what?"

"He paid his bill, left a tip and drove away."

"Do you know what kind of car he was driving?"

"I do."

"What kind was it?"

"A jeep station wagon with a four-wheel drive."

"And you are positive that the man indicated in this photograph is the man on whom you waited?"

"Yes, sir."

"How do you know?"

"Well, I know him."

"You mean that he was a regular customer?"

"That's right."

"How many times had you seen him before, Miss Selma?"

"Heavens, I don't know. He'd drive in there—well, sometimes he'd drive in two or three nights running and then we wouldn't see him for a week or ten days, and then he'd come in again."

"Did you know him well enough to speak to?"

She laughed and said, 'Heavens, I don't have to know them well in order to speak to them. We . . . well, we sort of kid them along. It pays . . . in tips, I mean."

"Did you know his name?"

"We called him Joe. That was the only name we had. We girls have our first name on a badge on our blouse right . . . right here."

She turned to face the judge, pulled the blouse tight over her left breast and indicated with her forefinger the place where the badge went.

"I see," Judge Bagby said, with a slight smile.

Dorothy held the pose for a moment, then turned with a quick smile to Ellington. "Is that all?" she asked.

"Did you ever talk with the person shown in the photograph about what he did? About what his occupation was?"

"No, sir, I didn't. We used to kid along a little bit. He'd . . . well, you know. He'd hand me a line and I'd come right back at him, and . . . well, we always try to be cheerful."

"What are your hours?"

"I go on at twelve o'clock midnight and go off duty at eight in the morning."

"Do you ever rotate shifts?"

"Only if we want to. I like that shift. The work isn't as heavy. Of course, you don't get as many tips but every once in a while a lush comes along and if you kid him along in the right way he'll really decorate the mahogany."

"Thank you," Ellington said. "I'm working on a salary myself. I think perhaps Mr. Mason would be more interested in the mechanics of getting gratuitous remuneration from clients . . . You may inquire, Mr. Mason."

"Thank you," Mason said, smiling. "I'm quite certain the information will come in handy."

Mason turned to the witness. "Did you ever know his last name, Miss Selma?"

"Whose?"

"The man whose photograph you were shown. The man whom you called Joe."

"I never knew it."

"Did you ever notice anything peculiar about the automobile? Is there anything that would enable you to recognize it again, the—"

"Heavens, yes!" she said. "I know that the first three letters of the license were NFE. I know it was a jeep station wagon with a four-wheeled drive. It was kind of a gun-metal gray, and there was a little nick on the front left fender. I remember that."

"Do you know what model it was?"

"No, I don't," she said. "It . . . well, now wait a minute, I do, too. I think it had a six-cylinder motor and I think Joe told me that it was the first model that had come out with the six-cylinder motor."

"You remember the first three letters of the license number but none of the figures?"

"That's right," she said. "We have to write down the license number of the automobile on our orders when we take them. Then, in case anyone should drive away, we've got some kind of a hold on them—sometimes at that hour of the night people are a little bit happy and don't . . . well, they don't stay put, so on my shift at least we write down the license number.

"He saw me writing down the license number once and seemed to become terribly suspicious. He wanted to know what I was doing, so I told him that we were just keeping our records straight and keeping track of the orders, and I joked a little about the first three letters. He had said something about . . . oh, I don't know, about taking me out some night when he wasn't so busy and I wasn't working, and I kidded him about it the way we always do. You know, a girl gets lots of propositions like that and you sort of roll with the punch and keep the guy feeling good. I told him, 'Sure,' and he said, 'No fooling, eh?' Then, when he saw me writing down the numbers of the license number, I said, 'Oh, I was just making an abbreviation. Your license is NFE, and that stands for No Fooling Eh?' I got by with it for a minute but then he saw the figures and knew I'd copied his license number. Then I really had to explain.

"After that when he'd drive up he'd say, 'Well, you'd better write it down. No fooling, eh?' and we'd laugh."

"Then it was always the same car?"

"Every time I waited on him he had the same car, this jeep with the six-cylinder motor and the four-wheel drive."

"Now, are you positive about the time on this Sunday night? Let's see, it was actually Monday morning. It was past midnight."

"I'm positive. I can't tell you the exact minute, but I can tell you it was very shortly before two o'clock. He drove away just a few minutes before two, perhaps four or five minutes before."

"And how do you know?" Mason asked.

"There is an entertainer who works every night and he comes in for coffee and a sandwich when he gets off work. He gets off work at two o'clock. His place is just a couple of blocks down the street and you can count on him every night, regular as clockwork, at about five minutes past two. I remember that he drove in just after Joe had driven out."

"Thank you," Mason said, "that's all."

"If the Court please," Ellington said, "in the case of the next witness I am going to call, I would like to point out to the Court that this witness will be called for a very specific and limited purpose. I feel that counsel would like very much to go on a fishing expedition as there are other matters within the knowledge of this witness which I don't consider directly pertinent to the case, at least at this time, but counsel for the defense would doubtless like to turn her inside out.

"I am, therefore, going to be very careful to restrict my examination in chief. I am going to ask the Court to take particular note of the questions I ask and the limited field which I open up because I intend to object if there is any attempt to go on a general fishing expedition with this witness by way of cross-examination."

"Why doesn't counsel wait until I start fishing before he tries to put up the no-trespassing signs?" Mason asked, smiling.

Judge Bagby smiled. "I think that might be the better procedure, Mr. Prosecutor. However, the Court is duly placed on notice as to your intention. Call your witness."

"I am calling Mauvis Niles Meade," Ellington said.

The courtroom door opened and Mauvis Meade, accompanied by Dukes Lawton, entered the courtroom.

Lawton cupped his big hand underneath her elbow, walked up the aisle with her and opened the gate.

Ellington regarded Mauvis Meade with approval, then frowned slightly as he saw Dukes Lawton starting to follow her into the enclosure.

"Wait right there, Mr. Lawton. Take one of those seats," Ellington said. "Only witnesses and counsel are allowed behind the bar. Just sit right there."

Lawton glanced at Judge Bagby, then dropped down into a vacant seat in the front row, seating himself right on the edge of the seat, poised for swift action.

"Your name is Mauvis Niles Meade. You are a novelist and you are the authoress who wrote the current best seller *Chop the Man Down*?"

"I am," she answered in an all but inaudible voice.

"You are acquainted with the defendant?"

"Yes."

"Did she work for you?"

"Yes."

"In what capacity?"

"As secretary."

"I direct your attention specifically to Friday, the sixth of this month. Do you remember that date?"

"Yes."

"Now, I am going to ask you, Miss Meade, to limit your answers to the questions I ask. Did you have a conversation with the defendant on that day in regard to her duties over the weekend?"

"I did."

"Did you furnish her with a car?"

"I did."

"Did you give her certain specific duties, that is, a certain specific assignment?"

"Yes."

"What was it?"

"She was to go to Summit Inn and meet a writer there, a man whose name is Edgar Carlisle. I understood that—"

"Now, never mind what you understood," Ellington interrupted, "unless it was something that you told the defendant at that time."

"That's what I'm trying to tell you," she said. "I told her that he was in the publicity department of American Film Producers Studios—I thought he was."

"Now, I want to limit this part of the examination," Ellington said. "Did you have a discussion with her about when she was to come back to the apartment, and how she was to come back?"

"Yes."

"Kindly tell the Court just what you told her at that time."

"I told her to leave Summit Inn on the main highway gave her directions."

"Can you give us the directions that you gave her?"

"Yes, sir."

"What were they?"

"I told her to leave Summit Inn on the main highway and to go into the main part of town. Two blocks past the post office she was to turn right. Then after five blocks she was to turn left. This is a narrow road but it is a surfaced road that goes for about a mile on a fairly easy grade, then turns sharply and starts winding down the mountain.

"I told the defendant to set her speedometer at zero at the post office, that at nine and seven-tenths miles she would come to a fork in the road and she was to take the right-hand turn. At fifteen and three-tenths miles she would come to another fork in the road and again she was to take the right-hand turn. After that, I gave her directions about following the road to the main highway, crossing the main highway and traveling a rather narrow road through the orange groves for three miles until she came to the freeway to Los Angeles."

"The defendant made notes?"

"She did. Yes, sir."

"I am going to show you what appears to be a page from a shorthand notebook with some writing and some shorthand annotations. I will ask you if you are familiar with the handwriting of the defendant."

"I am. Yes, sir."

"Do you recognize this handwriting?"

"It is the defendant's handwriting."

"There are words here—'Received, three hundred dollars.' What does that mean?"

"I gave her three hundred dollars to apply on an expense account."

"Over the weekend?"

"Yes. Of course, she was to credit me with anything that was left over."

"Are you familiar with the defendant's shorthand?"

"I am, yes."

"Can you read these shorthand notes?"

"Not well enough to testify to each word, but well enough to testify that they are the directions I gave her for coming down the mountain and that they are in her handwriting."

"Now, do you know where this page which I hold in my hand was found?"

"Yes."

"Where?"

"In a wastebasket in the room in my penthouse which was assigned to the defendant."

"You took this out of the wastebasket?"

"Yes."

"And what did you do with it?"

"I gave it to a police officer."

"What officer?"

"Lieutenant Tragg of Homicide."

"That's all," Ellington said. "You may cross-examine."

Mason said, "What else did you talk about when you were discussing this weekend trip with the defendant, Miss Meade?"

"Just a moment," Ellington said, "if the Court please, I feel that cross-examination should be restricted to the specific ground I have covered."

Mason smiled. "It is an axiomatic rule of law that when testimony is adduced concerning a part of a conversation, the cross-examiner can call for all of the conversation if he wishes."

"Only, if the Court please, for so much of the conversation as is pertinent to the issues," Ellington said. "I am familiar with the rule and the code section, but I insist that it must have a reasonable interpretation."

"I'll lay a little more foundation," Mason said. "How long did this conversation last, Miss Meade?"

"Oh, perhaps fifteen or twenty minutes."

"And you discussed her duties with her?"

"Yes."

"And the trip she was to make?"

"Yes."

"And the trip down the mountain?"

"Yes."

"And what else?"

"I . . . I think that's all. I remember I told her that I had reason to believe this Edgar Carlisle was something of a wolf and she was to take reasonable precautions. I also told her something about the clothes she was to take and told her what car to take up there."

"And that was the entire conversation?"

"That's all I can remember at the present time."

Mason said, "You told her how to come down the mountain."

"Yes."

"Now, when you gave her those directions, did you give them from memory?"

"Yes."

"I would like to refresh your recollection a little, Miss Meade, without appearing to be unduly insistent, but isn't it a fact that you had a map which you kept in your desk and that you used this map in giving Miss Doyle the directions as to how to come down the mountain?"

"I may have."

"Where is that map now?"

"Heavens," she said, "I don't know. I . . . I just can't remember. I think perhaps I gave it to Lieutenant Tragg —No, I guess— Frankly, I think that was a duplicate map that I gave to Lieutenant Tragg. I had two maps."

"The map you used in giving Miss Doyle directions and one other?"

"Yes."

"Both covering the same thing?"

"Generally."

"You had those two maps in your possession on Friday, the sixth of this month, when you gave Gladys Doyle the directions for coming down the mountain?"

"Well, now . . . wait a minute. I'm not prepared to state that, Mr. Mason."

"Oh, Your Honor, I object to this as incompetent, irrelevant and immaterial, not proper cross-examination and already having been asked and answered," Ellington said irritably.

"Are you making any particular point about this map or these maps, Mr. Mason?" Judge Bagby asked. "Is there anything about them which you feel the Court should know about?"

"I think there is, Your Honor."

"Well, I'll overrule the objection on the strength of your assurance, Mr. Mason. I assume that it is a matter of importance, and, inasmuch as it relates to the conversation and the manner in which the directions were given to the defendant, I'm going to permit the question."

"If the Court please," Ellington said, "I'd like to be heard on that. That map is going to become a controversial point in the case, and once we open the door we're going to go far afield. Counsel will attempt to impeach the witness on a collateral matter, which, as far as we're concerned, has no great bearing on the case."

"Well, I'll permit the question, at least I'll go that far," Judge Bagby said.

Mason turned to the witness. "Did you have both maps at that time?"

"I think . . . I think I had the second map later."

"The map which you gave Lieutenant Tragg?"

"Yes."

"Does the prosecution have that map?" Mason asked, turning to Ellington.

"The prosecution has the map," Ellington said stiffly.

"May I see it, please?"

"You may not," Ellington said. "The map has no bearing whatever upon the issues involved in this case. It is purely a collateral document, it is one which the witness did not have in her possession at the time this conversation took place, it is one which came into her possession later on."

"It's in her handwriting, isn't it?" Mason asked.

"Don't examine me," Ellington said testily. "If you want to call me as a witness, wait until I've submitted my case, then you can call me as your witness and I'll answer what questions I see fit."

Judge Bagby frowned. "Counsel will please refrain from personalities," he said. "Is there some reason, Mr. Prosecutor, why this map should not be produced?"

"There is, Your Honor. Very frankly, this map is one that counsel would like to use as a springboard for a brow-beating cross-examination of this witness. He would like to try to confuse her and confuse the issues with this map. We object to it.

"The evidence will show—in fact, I am prepared to show by this witness—that this map was actually not in existence at the time that this conversation took place."

"Not even in existence?" Judge Bagby asked.

"It was not in existence," Ellington said. "The witness may have drawn this map especially for Lieutenant Tragg when she couldn't find the original map. I will state to the Court that during the absence of this witness someone had searched her penthouse apartment and had pulled out drawers, had taken clothes out of closets and left the place looking generally like a wreck.

"Lieutenant Tragg asked about this map because Perry

Mason was there and Perry Mason was anxious to see the
map. I won't say what happened, but it is quite possible
that the witness, unable to produce the map she had at
that time, drew another map which illustrated the point in
which Mr. Mason and Lieutenant Tragg were interested
and gave Tragg that map, simply stating that it was a map
showing the road in question. I certainly see nothing
wrong with that, but I realize that it is a straw at which
counsel is going to clutch with savage ferocity if he can
once get that into evidence."

Judge Bagby pursed his lips.

"May I be heard?" Mason asked.

The judge nodded.

"I am very much interested in the question of whether
the map which was in the possession of this witness
showed the cabin and the location of the cabin and the
road leading to the cabin where the murder was committed."

"It has absolutely nothing to do with the case," Ellington said. "You are simply trying to confuse the witness in
regard to that map, where it is and what happened to it
and how she happened to make another map in her
handwriting."

"And I think I'm entitled to cross-examine her on
it," Mason said.

"It has nothing to do with the case," Ellington
snapped.

"She used that map as a memo when she directed the
defendant as to the road she was to follow."

"Not that map," Ellington said. "If you want to cross-
examine her about the location of the map that she used
at that time, I have no objection. But if you want to try to
confuse this witness and impeach her and question her
veracity in regard to a conversation which took place
subsequently between her and Lieutenant Tragg, or if you
want to cross-examine her about a map which wasn't in

existence at that time, I do object. If you want to cross-examine her about any map, specify that it is the map that she used at that time, and I will have no objection."

"Thank you," Mason said. "Under those circumstances, Your Honor, I withdraw my previous question. I will ask the witness this question. You had a map at that time, Miss Meade?"

"Yes."

"Where is that map now?"

"I don't know."

"Do you remember the contents of the map?"

"Vaguely."

"What did it show?"

"It showed the road down the mountain, from Summit Inn on down."

"And where is that map now?"

"I tell you, I don't know. It disappeared."

"It was not in your apartment?"

"It was not in my apartment."

"Would you know that map if you saw it again?"

"Certainly."

"That map was in your handwriting?"

She hesitated a moment, then said, "Yes."

"And how did you happen to draw that map?"

"Someone told me about this short cut down the mountain."

"Had you ever followed this short cut?"

"I had. I'd taken it on several occasions."

"And had you ever made the turn at that fork so that you drove past the cabin—the fork which is fifteen and three-tenths miles?"

"I . . . I may have. I have been up and down that mountain a great number of times, Mr. Mason."

"And have you ever stopped in at that cabin?"

"Now there, Your Honor," Ellington said, "is an illustration of the point I was making—I was very careful to say nothing about that cabin or about that road. I limited my questions of this witness to one conversation. The question of whether she ever saw the cabin is not proper cross-examination."

"I think I'll sustain that objection," Judge Bagby said.

"But you would know that map if you saw it again?" Mason asked. "The one that you had in your hand when you gave the defendant directions how to get down the mountain."

"Yes."

Mason moved casually over toward the witness. "You had had that map in your possession for some time?"

"It was in my desk."

"Do you remember anything about that map? Was there a sketch on one side of the map?"

The witness frowned, then shook her head and said, "I can't remember."

"Perhaps I can refresh your recollection," Mason said, drawing from his inside coat pocket the map he had received in the mail and placing it on the rail in front of the witness. "I will ask you, Miss Meade, if this is your handwriting."

Mauvis Meade looked at the map Mason was holding and went white to the lips.

Ellington, seeing the expression on her face, jumped to his feet and started hurrying to the witness stand.

Mason folded the map, put it back in his pocket. "Is that your handwriting?" he asked.

"If the Court please," Ellington said, "I am entitled to see the document that counsel has produced and with which he is facing the witness. I want to know what's on it."

Judge Bagby nodded.

"I have no intention at the present time of introducing it in evidence," Mason said. "I was simply asking her to identify her handwriting."

Judge Bagby looked at the face of the witness, which despite her attempt to control her expression, showed complete consternation.

"I think counsel is entitled to see any document that you show to the witness and on which you are basing your question," he said.

"Very well," Mason said, smiling urbanely, "I withdraw the question then."

"I still want to see the document."

"But the question is withdrawn," Mason said. "I will not ask any more questions on that subject."

He moved back, away from the witness, over to the defense counsel table and sat down.

"But he has asked her a question about it and I want to see it," Ellington said.

Mason smiled at the Court. "Who's going on a fishing expedition now?" he asked.

Judge Bagby's eyes twinkled. "I think that in view of the fact the question has been withdrawn, Mr. Prosecutor, there is now no necessity for exhibiting the document to either Court or counsel."

Ellington took the ruling with poor grace.

Mason turned back to the witness. "Are you acquainted with Morrison Findlay who previously testified and who appears to be the owner of the cabin where the murder was committed, Miss Meade?"

"I don't think I have ever seen him," she said, slowly shaking her head.

"Have you ever talked with him over the telephone?"

"Now, just a moment, just a moment," Ellington said, jumping to his feet. "Here again, Your Honor, we come to a point where I must insist upon the rights of the witness and the rights of the prosecution. We did not ask her anything at all about whether she had talked with Morrison Findlay over the telephone. We asked her only about one conversation with the defendant. This is not proper

cross-examination, it assumes a fact not in evidence, it is
incompetent, irrelevant and immaterial."

Judge Bagby regarded Mason with a thoughtful frown.
"On the face of it, the objection is well taken," he said.
"But, of course, under the circumstances and in view of
the testimony which has been given, the situation might
be a little . . . well, of course, the Court can see where
this might very well go to the bias of the witness, and I
believe counsel has a right to cross-examine a witness in
regard to bias."

"He can ask her about her bias," Ellington said, "but
he can't go rambling all around the lot, dragging in all
sorts of telephone conversations the witness may have had
in order to show that bias. He's got to have some specific
objective in mind."

"I have some specific objective in mind," Mason interposed.

Ellington ignored the interruption, went on smoothly as
though it had been in his mind all of the time to finish his
statement in that manner. "And specifically what he has
in mind has to be communicated to the Court so that the
Court can then determine whether it does actually give
ground for bias within the meaning of the law. Counsel
simply can't ask this witness all kinds of questions about
her early childhood, her correspondence, the people she
talked with over the telephone, and all of the hundred
thousand other things that he might think up simply on
the chance that some answer that the witness might give
would show a possible bias or show something that counsel could use as a peg on which to hang an argument that
the witness was biased."

Judge Bagby drummed with the tips of his fingers on
the desk in front of him. "I can recognize the importance
of this point to the defense," he said, "and I also realize,
of course, that this is a preliminary hearing and that
under the law, the prosecution has the right to control the

amount of proof it puts on. It does not have to put on its entire case. It is obligated only to put on enough evidence to show that a crime has been committed and there is reasonable cause to believe the defendant is connected with that crime.

"The Court itself admits that it would like very much to know a little more about this situation. It might make quite a difference. However, in view of the fact that the prosecution has announced its desire to limit the examination of this witness, and has been very careful in so doing, the Court is going to sustain the objection to the question in this form. At least at this time, Mr. Mason."

"Thank you," Mason said. "Now, Miss Meade, I am going to ask you directly whether you are the person who rented this cabin from Morrison Findlay."

"Objected to as not proper cross-examination, incompetent, irrelevant and immaterial," Ellington said.

Judge Bagby ran his left hand over his head, then down the angle of his jaw and rubbed his cheek thoughtfully with the tips of his fingers, then said, "I'm going to permit counsel to examine the witness as to possible bias, Mr. Prosecutor."

Mauvis Meade said, "I have no bias, I have no animosity against Gladys Doyle. If I knew anything that would help her, I'd be glad to say so. I can tell you that I'm triyng to protect her in every way that I can. Now, does that answer the question about my bias?"

"The specific question," Judge Bagby said, "was about whether she rented that particular cabin shown on the maps introduced in evidence, the cabin where the murder was committed."

"But that's only for the purpose of showing bias," Ellington said desperately. "The witness has answered the question about her bias."

Mason said, "Do you understand the question, Miss Meade?"

"I'm not sure."

"The question is whether or not you were the person who leased that cabin over the telephone from Morrison Findlay."

"Now, right here, Your Honor," Ellington said, "we are going far afield. This is a fishing expedition, pure and simple. I object to having extraneous matters brought in here, and I object to having this case unduly prolonged by going into all these matters and having us wait here while counsel fishes for information."

Judge Bagby said, "The distinction is very close. It's something of a hairline distinction, but I am going to sustain the objection to that question, Mr. Mason. The general knowledge, if any, of this witness is not something the Court is prepared to let you go into on *cross*-examination, particularly when the prosecution so carefully limited the *direct* examination of this witness."

"Very well," Mason said. "That's all. I have no further questions."

Judge Bagby looked at Mason with thoughtful consideration. "Do you wish the document which you showed the witness marked for identification, Mr. Mason? If you do, it will be necessary to show it to the prosecutor. Unless it is marked for identification there is no way *at any subsequent time* that the document can be identified as being the one which was shown the witness."

"The question was withdrawn," Mason said.

"And you don't wish the document marked for identification?"

"No, Your Honor."

"Very well. Call your next witness," Judge Bagby said to Ellington.

"The prosecution will call Lieutenant Tragg," Ellington said.

Lieutenant Tragg came forward, stood shrewd-eyed and

unsmiling while the oath was administered, then took the witness stand.

"You are acquainted with the defendant, Lieutenant?"

"I am."

"Did you hear her make any statement, or were you present at a time when a statement was made, concerning the events of the night of the eighth of this month and the early morning hours of the ninth?"

"I was."

"The defendant did make such a statement?"

"She did.

"You were present?"

"I was."

"What will you state to the Court with reference to any inducements, threats or promises which were made at that time?"

"There were no threats, no promises, no inducements, no abuse," Tragg said.

"To the best of your knowledge, was the statement free and voluntary?"

"To the best of my knowledge, it was a free and voluntary statement."

"What was it?" Ellington asked.

Judge Bagby frowned. "Are you going to show the other persons present, Mr. Ellington? The general circumstances?"

Ellington shook his head. "If Mr. Mason wants to object on the ground that no proper foundation has been laid, he can go into the subject on *voir dire*."

"Is there any objection from the defense?" Judge Bagby asked.

Mason said, "No, Your Honor, not in view of the statement made by Lieutenant Tragg."

Judge Bagby frowned at Mason as though trying to see beneath the surface and put together the defense strategy. Then he gave an almost imperceptible shrug and said,

"Very well. Lieutenant, answer the question. What did she say?"

Lieutenant Tragg said, "She made a statement that she was following directions down the mountain, that she came to this fork in the road fifteen and three-tenths miles from where she had set her speedometer, that she thought she had been told to turn left at the fork and she took the left-hand turn, that it was a wild, stormy night, that she came down the mountain and found herself bogged down in a mudhole. She had to leave her car in this mudhole. She said she started walking down the road in the dark, groping her way, that she had gone only a few yards when she saw a light, that she went to the light, that it turned out to be a light in this cabin, that she found a man there whom she described as being very tall with dark, wavy hair and very penetrating steel-gray eyes but whose name she doesn't know other than he told her she could call him John, that the man was rather curt with her, that she tried to get him to help her get her car free, that he refused to do so, stating that he had had pneumonia, that he didn't intend to go out and get wet, that thereafter the defendant went to bed and slept soundly, although she thinks she heard the sound of an automobile, that when she awoke in the morning she went out into the main room, that the oil stove had been turned off, the room was cold, the house seemed deserted. She said she opened the door of the other bedroom and found a body on the floor, that she knelt down and felt for a pulse, that she then noticed a .22 rifle on the floor by the open bedroom window, that she picked up the rifle, thinking for a moment that perhaps she might need a weapon, that she decided against this and dropped the rifle, that she ran from the house in blind panic, that she ran up the road, that when she came to this mudhole she found that her car had been extricated from the mudhole, had been turned around and was pointing up the grade, that she jumped in the car and drove to the city. She stated that she went to the penthouse where she lived and found that Miss Meade, whom she wished to see, was absent, that the place had been thoroughly ransacked, that in very much of a panic and without changing her clothes, she went at once to the office of Perry Mason, that Mr. Mason arranged to have her borrow some clothes from Della Street, his secretary, and that Mr. Mason notified the police of the murder."

"Did you find her co-operative?" Ellington asked. "Was this statement made for the purpose of facilitating your investigation?"

"She was not co-operative and the statement was not made for the purpose of facilitating our investigation but for the purpose of trying to explain away certain facts after we had discovered those facts and asked her for an explanation."

"What facts?"

"Well, for one, her clothes. We discovered that the clothes she was wearing had the cleaning mark that was issued by the Excelsior Cleaning and Dyeing Company to Miss Della Street. Therefore, we surmised what had happened, got a search warrant for Miss Street's apartment, found clothes there which the defendant admitted were hers. Thereafter we asked questions and finally received this statement."

"All at one time or piecemeal?"

"We had to drag it out of her a bit at a time, then afterward she tried to put it all together for us in a consecutive narrative."

"You say you found clothes belonging to the defendant at Miss Street's apartment?"

"Yes, sir."

"Did the defendant make any statement with reference to the ownership of those clothes?"

"She admitted they were hers."

"Did you notice anything significant about those clothes?"

"They were processed in the laboratory."

"Were you present at the time?"

"I was."

"What did you yourself notice, Lieutenant, not what anyone else at the crime laboratory may have noticed?"

"There was a rather large blood spot on the hem of the skirt, there was a blood spot near the bottom of the left sleeve. There was another spot of blood on the slip."

"These bloodstains were typed by the laboratory?"

"I believe so."

"You yourself were not present when that was done?"

"No, sir."

"Did you examine the .22 rifle which was found in the cabin for fingerprints?"

"I did."

"And where was that done, if you know, Lieutenant?"

"It was processed at the police laboratory."

"Were you present?"

"I was."

"Were there any latent fingerprints on that rifle?"

"There were several. Only one, however, was sufficiently clear so that it could be identified."

"Did you work on that fingerprint yourself on the identification?"

"I worked on it myself and I worked with the fingerprint expert while he was developing, photographing and identifying the print."

"And did you check the work of this fingerprint expert?"

"I did."

"Do you know of your own knowledge whose fingerprint that was?"

"I do."

"Whose hand made that fingerprint, Lieutenant?"

"The right forefinger of the defendant, Gladys Doyle, left that fingerprint on the gun," Tragg said.

"Did you make any attempt to check her story as to another person being in the cabin?"

"I made what check I could."

"Did you find anything that would tend to disprove that story of hers?"

"That question calls for a conclusion of the witness, if the Court please," Mason said.

"I'll withdraw the question," Ellington said. "Did you find anything that would substantiate that story?"

"Nothing," Tragg said.

Ellington bowed. "I think, under the circumstances and in view of counsel's objection, I will leave it to Mr. Mason to elicit exactly what Lieutenant Tragg means by the last answer. Your witness, Mr. Mason. You may cross-examine."

Mason smiled urbanely. "No questions."

"That's all, Lieutenant Tragg," Judge Bagby said. "Call your next witness, Mr. Ellington."

"There are no more witnesses as far as the prosecution is concerned," Ellington said. "That's our case. We have made a prima facie case and we ask the Court to bind the defendant over on the ground that a murder was committed and there is reasonable cause to believe the defendant was connected with that crime."

Mason jumped to his feet. "On behalf of the defense, I ask the Court to dismiss the case against the defendant on the ground that there is no proof connecting her with any crime."

Judge Bagby shook his head.

"I would like to argue the motion," Mason said, with an eye on the courtroom clock.

"There's no need for argument," Judge Bagby said. "The prosecution has proven a murder. It has proven that the defendant was in the cabin where the murder was committed at the time it was committed, and that the defendant's fingerprints were on the murder weapon, that there was blood on her clothing, that she consulted an attorney before making any attempt to notify the authorities.

"The Court will admit that by the time the case reaches the superior court the prosecution will doubtless want to put on more evidence, indicating motivation perhaps, and perhaps more statements made by the defendant. However, for the purposes of a preliminary examination, it certainly seems that there is sufficient evidence, if that evidence is unexplained, to bind the defendant over. Now, if the defense wishes to make any showing, the defense of course has the right to put on witnesses and to make any showing that it desires."

Mason said, "It is nearly twelve, Your Honor. If we could take a recess for lunch at this time, I—"

"I think not," Judge Bagby interrupted. "There is a very great backlog of criminal cases, and I want to expedite matters as much as possible. Let me ask you frankly whether the defense intends to make any showing."

"The defense does," Mason said.

"Then go ahead and call your first witness."

"I'll call Lieutenant Tragg as my witness," Mason said.

"Very well. Come forward, Lieutenant Tragg. You're a witness called by the defense," Judge Bagby said.

Ellington showed surprise. He exchanged a swift glance with Lieutenant Tragg, then Tragg, his face a perfectly expressionless mask, came forward.

"You've already been sworn," Judge Bagby said. "You don't need to be sworn again. Proceed with your examination, Mr. Mason."

"You were up at this cabin on Monday after the rain had ceased?"

"Yes, sir."

"Did you, at that time, have the story told by the defendant?"

"Not at that time. That came later."

"But during the same day?"

"Yes."

"Did you check automobile tracks in the vicinity of the cabin?"

"I did what I could."

"I notice that you were not asked about those tracks on direct examination," Mason said. "Therefore, I am going to ask you to describe those tracks at the present time."

"If the Court please," Ellington interrupted, "this is incompetent, irrelevant and immaterial. It is quite apparent that counsel is simply fighting against the clock. He is asking Lieutenant Tragg to describe these tracks because, by so doing, he can stall his case along until the noon adjournment. If the defendant wants to make any showing, the proper procedure is to call the defendant to the stand, have her story and then, after that story is before the Court, try to establish any facts which may substantiate it."

"That may be *your* idea of the proper procedure," Judge Bagby said, "but I know of no rule of law which determines the order in which a defendant should put on his case. The defense counsel is now asking for certain automobile tracks in the vicinity of the cabin, and the Court will confess that that is a matter which occurred to the Court. The Court wondered why this witness was not asked about tracks. The Court is very interested in hearing the testimony of this witness. The objection is overruled. Answer the question, Lieutenant."

"Well," Lieutenant Tragg said, "there were just so many tracks around the place that it was impossible to keep them all segregated. Cars had been up and down that road and left tracks. Cars had turned around and there were jeep tracks and automobile tracks, and you just couldn't keep them all straight. We tried to, but it couldn't be done."

Judge Bagby leaned forward with quick interest. "All of this traffic was after the ground had been softened by the rain?"

"Yes, Your Honor."

"Could you determine how fresh those tracks were?"

"They had been made after the ground became soft."

"Were there tracks indicating a car had been stuck in that mudhole on Sunday night?" Judge Bagby asked.

"There the situation depends on what sort of evidence would be taken as indicating that," Lieutenant Tragg said. "There was a mudhole, all right, with the ground churned up to about the consistency of thick hotcake batter. There was a deep hole in the center which could have been made by the spinning wheels of an automobile, but there's no way of telling *when* it was made. There were tracks of more than one automobile, and there were tracks down the road where automobiles had been turned around. That much we could decipher. But there were other tracks interspersed all through, and it was difficult to get them straightened out."

"Did you try to check the marks made by the tire treads with known automobiles?" Judge Bagby asked. "The car driven by the defendant, for instance?"

"We did."

"Were you able to do so?"

"We were able to prove that the defendant's car, that is, the car owned by Mauvis Meade but driven by the defendant, had been through the mudhole on the downhill side.

"Whether the car had been left there, as is claimed by the defendant, for some time before the tracks below the mudhole were made, we don't know. We do know that the car driven by the defendant had unquestionably been below the mudhole. We can't tell how far.

"We also know that the car which the defendant claimed she was driving, the station wagon belonging to Mauvis Meade, had been driven both down and up the grade. Therefore, if the defendant's car was left in the mudhole while it was headed downhill; it must subsequently have been driven through this mudhole down the hill and then driven back up the hill and through the same mudhole which the defendant claimed stuck the car going *downhill*."

"Yet it went uphill through that same mudhole without getting stuck?" Judge Bagby asked.

"That's what the tracks show, Your Honor."

Judge Bagby's expression became one of cold finality.

"There were other tracks?" Mason asked hurriedly.

"Yes."

"Footprints?"

"There were many traces of footprints, but for the most part they were not clear. Where the mud was hard it was slippery, and the prints were blurred. Where the mud was soft it was too soft to yield much in the way of prints."

"Did you find any footprints of the defendant?"

"We couldn't tell they were her prints. There were many tracks made by a woman's shoes, or by the shoes of more than one woman. We couldn't get any prints that were clear enough for identification."

"Footprints of men?"

"Yes."

"How many?"

"You mean, made by how many men?"

"Yes."

"We couldn't tell. There had been people up there, both men and women—or at least one man and one woman. We couldn't tell when the tracks had been made, nor could we find footprints we could identify."

"Now how about automobile tracks?" Mason asked.

"There were quite a few tire tracks," Lieutenant Tragg said. "There's a flat about fifty yards below the cabin, and quite apparently this flat had been used as a place to park cars for some time. There was hard-packed road leading up to it and places where cars had been parked and turned around and driven out."

"And there were fresh tracks there?"

"There were."

"And could you determine any sequence or order in connection with those tracks?"

"No, sir."

"Were they jeep tracks?"

"Some of them had been made by jeeps. However, it was a little difficult to determine. The tracks indicated a certain amount of traffic."

"What do you mean by a certain amount of traffic?"

"Several cars had been in there—including the defendant's car."

"During the last storm?"

"We can't tell as to that. The ground was shaded and we don't know how long the mud had been sufficiently soft to take and retain tire tracks, but *if* the ground hadn't been soft until after the storm started, then there was quite a bit of traffic up and down the road *after* the storm started. However, rainfall figures show that there had been another very good rain about three days before this particular storm and another very intense storm about a week prior to that. We just don't know whether that ground had been soft and had remained soft."

"In other words, you couldn't tell as to the freshness of tracks?"

"Not absolutely," Tragg said. "My personal opinion was that they were fresh, and—that is, most of them—"

"Just a moment," Ellington said. "If the Court please, I move to strike out that last part of the answer as not being responsive to the question and on the ground that it is incompetent, irrelevant and immaterial, that the witness is testifying to a conclusion and assuming a fact which has heretofore not been put in evidence. This witness is a police officer, that doesn't mean he's an expert on tracks."

"I think it does, Your Honor," Perry Mason said. "However, if there's any question I'll qualify him. Lieutenant Tragg, how long have you been a police officer?"

"Just a minute, just a minute," Ellington said, jumping up. "If the Court please, I realize now I was playing right into the hands of defense counsel. He is just looking for an opportunity to prolong this examination. In order to save time, I'll withdraw the objection. I'll stipulate that Lieutenant Tragg is an expert on tracks. I'll stipulate to just about anything the defense counsel wants him to testify to—now, let's get on with this and get it over with."

"Well," Judge Bagby said, smiling, "I don't think, Mr. Prosecutor, that the situation calls for any dissertation on your part as to the tactics of the defense counsel. However, the Court will note that the hearing has been somewhat delayed because of your objections, and, in view of the fact that it now appears the defense does intend to put on some evidence so that the matter will not be disposed of during the morning session and leave the Court free for another case during the afternoon, the Court will now take its usual morning recess. Will it be convenient to reconvene at one-thirty, gentlemen?"

Mason shook his head, and said, "I have a great deal of checking to do, if the Court please. I would prefer to reconvene at two o'clock."

Judge Bagby hesitated, then said, "Well, of course, we *are* pressed for time. But if we couldn't save an entire half-day for some other case, we probably aren't going to gain anything by getting an extra half-hour this afternoon. You feel that you can conclude your case well within the afternoon session, Mr. Mason?"

"I hope so," Mason said.

"Very well, we'll take a recess then until two o'clock," Judge Bagby said.

When the judge had left the bench, Ellington grinned at Mason and said, "That's a prize piece of stalling, putting Tragg on the stand as *your* witness."

"I thought you'd subject him to grueling cross-examination when I got through with him," Mason said.

Ellington laughed. "I'll stipulate anything that you want Tragg to testify to right now. All I ask is that you tell me what you expect him to testify to, that Tragg says that's correct and we'll stipulate that's evidence in the case."

"I can't do that," Mason said. "I want the judge to see the evidence as it unfolds."

"What the hell are you stalling for?" Ellington asked.

"I'm sure I don't know," Mason said, with a disarming smile. "Come on, Della, I think we'd better get some lunch . . . Where's Paul?"

"In the telephone booth," Della Street said.

"Well, come on," Mason said, "we'll get him and go to lunch— Did you get any gas in the car this morning?"

She shook her head and said, "We have about a quarter of a tank."

Mason said, "We'll get the car filled. We may want to use it this afternoon."

"Go ahead and fill it," Ellington laughed. "But you aren't frightening me at all, Mason. You're just stalling along, hoping that something's going to turn up. It's a good even-money bet that when you walk back into court this afternoon, you'll state that Lieutenant Tragg is your only witness—I'll bet you two to one right now that you're afraid to put the defendant on the stand."

"How much do you want to bet?" Mason asked.

"Well, now, wait a minute," Ellington said. "You'd put her on the stand just in order to win the bet. I . . . I'll still make a fifty-dollar bet."

"Fifty dollars against twenty-five?" Mason asked.

Ellington hesitated, then nodded.

Mason grinned. "I wouldn't want to tip my hand over a small bet like that. Let's go, Della, find Paul and eat."

13

■

PERRY MASON, DELLA STREET AND PAUL DRAKE left their car in a parking lot, with instructions that it was to be filled up with gas and the oil, water and battery checked and be all ready to go.

Walking down the street toward the restaurant, Mason said, "Paul, what about the handwriting expert?"

"Nothing to help there," Drake said. "The typewriter used on those rental letters was a Smith-Corona."

Mason frowned. "There was a Smith-Corona in Mauvis Meade's penthouse, Paul."

Drake said, "Sure. Mauvis Meade was the one who rented that cabin all right. Ellington is trying to clam up on it right now, but you can force his hand on your case.

"Get samples from Mauvis Meade's typewriter and they'll show the rental remittance letters were typed on her machine."

Mason pursed his lips. "I wish I knew a little more about that cabin deal, Paul. I hate to go into it blind, but it's almost a safe bet Mauvis rented that cabin, and Manly spent quite a bit of time there . . . Paul, you're worried about something. What is it?"

"I hope it's nothing," Drake said, "but . . . I'm debating what to do, Perry. I don't know whether to try and head something off or what."

"Come on," Mason said, "get it off your chest, Paul."

"I hate to bother you at a time like this, and yet it's information that you should have—I am worried."

"Come on, come on, Paul, let me have the worst."

"Well, it may be that there's no necessity for it. That's what bothers me, Perry. Let me ask you something. Ellington has rested his case?"

"That's right."

"He doesn't intend to put on any more evidence?"

"Gosh, no," Mason said. "He's put on more evidence now than he wanted to. He's trying to get just enough evidence to get the defendant bound over and not enough to tip his hand. Of course, my strategy is to try and find out everything I can. There's no question about the outcome. Judge Bagby has indicated his mind's made up, but he's leaving the door open for the defendant to take the stand."

"Would it do her any good to take the stand?"

"Not a bit," Mason said. "Even if the judge believed her story, he'd still bind her over. You see, for the purpose of a preliminary hearing, a judge is inclined to take the evidence presented by the people. He isn't a jury and he isn't called on to make the decisions that a juror is called on to make. Therefore, a judge is pretty apt to reason that the prosecution has made out a good case, that the evidence presented proves the defendant guilty, that the story told by the defendant is at the very most only an explanation. If the story is true, it's consistent with her innocence. But the question is, is her story true or is it false?

"Now, there are some judges who *will* try to determine whether the explanation would satisfy a jury and give the defendant the benefit of the doubt. But, for the most part, once it appears there's a real conflict in the evidence and the district attorney wants the defendant bound over, the judges bind the defendant over and pass the buck to the jury to decide what's to be done. You see, a district attorney can always dismiss a case if he can't get more evidence, but a judge never knows when more evidence may show up."

"Well," Drake blurted, "the thing that bothers me is this fellow, Kelton."

"What about him?"

"He's fidgeting."

"In what way?"

"He was talking with one of the newspapermen this morning. He told the man that he was right at the fork of the road, that he had to make a decision that might determine his entire future in the detective business. He said that he always tried to be loyal to his clients but that a man had his career to think of and that he couldn't violate the law— In short, he seemed terribly worried."

"You think he's worrying about that stuff we found and didn't turn in?" Mason asked.

"Of course he is," Drake said. "Now then, the newspaper reporter thought it over, then rang up my office to try and find out what it was Kelton was talking about. The newspaper is on the trail of a story.

"Well, of course, I tried to get in touch with Kelton as soon as I heard about it. I had the office working on it— that's why I was on the telephone so much this morning.

"We couldn't get a line on the guy at all, and finally I had another operative ring up his wife and say that he was a detective out of Homicide and he had to get hold of Kelton right away for the district attorney. I just wanted to see what Mrs. Kelton would say.

"She fell for it hook, line and sinker and said, 'Why, Mr. Kelton is at the district attorney's office now—at least, I think he is.'"

"Oh-oh," Mason said.

Della Street glanced up at the lawyer in swift dismay.

"Well," Mason said, holding the door of the restaurant open, "here's where we turn in. Let's try Selkirk's today."

"I was planning on going down to Tony's," Paul Drake said. "They make a special today of—"

"And it's loaded with garlic," Mason interposed. "Come on, let's try Selkirk's. They have a very fine saddle of lamb here."

"What difference does it make to you?" Drake asked. "All you eat is a pineapple and cottage cheese salad."

"I don't dare to drug myself with food when I'm going into court," Mason said.

"How about Della?"

"She can eat," Mason said. "And she will."

"I want to keep on speaking terms with my stomach," Della said. "My breakfast this morning consisted entirely of two cups of black coffee."

A headwaiter came forward and bowed deferentially.

Mason said, "What about the small dining room, Pedro?"

"You mean the private dining room for twelve?"

"That's right. Anyone in it?"

"No one in there. I will look to see if there are reservations—Mr. Selkirk doesn't like to let it go for a small party . . . but for you, Mr. Mason, I'm sure it will be all right."

Mason looked over the head of the waiter, caught the eye of the manager and said, "Hi, Jim."

Selkirk came hurrying over. "They want the small private dining room," the headwaiter said.

"Well, give it to them," Selkirk said. "What are you waiting for?"

"Yes, sir, yes, sir," the headwaiter said. "Right this way, please."

"Thanks, Jim," Mason said.

Selkirk smiled and nodded.

"You have a telephone jack in there?" Mason asked the headwaiter.

"Two of them."

"Then bring in two telephones," Mason said. "We're going to be busy."

The lawyer turned to Drake and said, "All right, Paul, you get busy on one of the telephones and keep in touch with your office. I want you to find out everything you can about Kelton. This may make quite a difference."

"Will Ellington use the evidence if he gets it?"

"You're damn right he'll use it," Mason said. "He'll use it on several counts. One of them is that by putting Kelton on the stand under oath he ties him down and gets him so he can't change his story. The other one is that if Kelton should skip out before the case comes to trial, he can show that he can't find Kelton within the state and then seek to use his evidence given at the preliminary examination. The advantage of that is that if he catches me by surprise, my cross-examination may not be quite as vigorous, quite as forceful, quite as purposeful or quite as effective as the cross-examination I can think of later."

The waiter appeared with two telephones, started plugging them in.

Mason said, "Hang it! I just can't understand why we haven't heard from that man."

"What man?"

"The one who was in the cabin," Mason said. "I was betting that he'd come forward—unless, of course, he's the murderer."

Drake was skeptical. "You think there really was a man in the cabin?" he asked.

"Sure there was," Mason said. "My client says there was."

"That's all the evidence there is to indicate it," Drake said. "He didn't leave any fingerprints."

Mason said, "They only found one of the defendant's

fingerprints, and that was on the gun— If she'd been in the place turning on water faucets in the bathroom, drinking out of a cup . . . why didn't they find *her* fingerprints?"

"I never thought of that," Drake admitted. "You mean her fingerprints had been removed?"

"There's a darn good chance," Mason said, "that somebody removed a lot of fingerprints— Of course, we have to remember that there was high atmospheric humidity at the time and, as I understand it, that's not conducive to keeping fingerprints."

The headwaiter appeared in the door and said, "Pardon me, Mr. Mason, but there is a telephone call for you. I said I didn't know whether you could receive a call or not, I said that I didn't even know you were here. But the man was most insistent and said that you were here and he wanted to talk with you right away."

Mason exchanged glances with Paul Drake and Della Street. "Either of you say where we were going to eat lunch?" he asked.

Della Street shook her head.

"We didn't even know," Drake said. "You were the one who was calling the shots. Frankly, I thought we were going to eat at Tony's."

"Then who would know I'm here?" Mason asked.

He gave the problem frowning consideration for a moment.

"Shall I say you are not here?" Pedro asked.

"Hell, no," Mason said, picking up the telephone. "I'll take the call."

He said to the operator, "There's an incoming call for Perry Mason. This is Mason. I'm in the small private dining room. I'll take it here. Can you put it on?"

"Surely," the operator said. "Just a moment."

A moment later the operator said, "There's your party. Go ahead, please."

"Hello," Mason said.

A man's voice, speaking in a low monotone, said, "Perry Mason?"

"That's right. May I ask who's talking?"

"Never mind my name," the man said. "I've got a tip for you. When the police fingerprinted that cabin they found remarkably few fingerprints. Someone had apparently rubbed off a lot of fingerprints, but there was a stainless-steel teakettle in the cupboard above the stove. Now, don't make any mistake about this. There was an aluminum teakettle on the wood stove, a rather battered kettle, but there was a stainless-steel teakettle on the upper shelf, and——"

"Just a moment," Mason said. "Excuse me." And then, in a loud voice, "Please don't disturb me at the moment. I'm talking over the telephone. How's that——"

Mason clapped his palm over the telephone and motioned to Paul Drake. "Get busy and trace this call, Paul," he said. "This is pay dirt."

Drake moved so rapidly that he toppled his chair backward as he raced for the door of the private dining room.

Mason, removing his hand, engaged apparently in an altercation with someone. "I'm sorry. I tell you, I can't be disturbed now. I'm talking on the phone. Will you please leave me alone . . . ?" Mason closed his right eye in a wink at Della Street and said, "Della, can you take care of this? I want to be free to talk on the phone. This is my confidential secretary, Miss Street. She'll take care of you."

Then Mason said into the phone, "You'll pardon me. I had a most annoying interruption. Now, what was it?"

The voice at the other end of the line, speaking so hastily that the words tumbled all over each other, said, "Look, Mason, you're smart. That may have been on the square. It may have been a stall to trace this call. Don't try it. There was a stainless-steel teakettle, there were prints on that teakettle. The police couldn't identify those prints. Make Tragg produce the prints. Start from there."

The receiver banged at the other end of the line, and the telephone went dead.

Mason slowly and thoughtfully replaced the receiver on the hook.

"A tip?" Della Street asked.

"More than a tip," Mason said, his eyes narrowed in concentration. "A break. It's the break I've been looking for."

"What was it?"

"A man's voice giving a tip about something that the police have kept very well hushed up. If that information is true, it's of the utmost importance—he says the police found fingerprints on a stainless-steel teakettle that was in a cupboard above the stove. The police haven't been able to identify all of those fingerprints."

"Do you suppose there's anything to it?"

"I think there's a lot to it," Mason said. "But more than the fingerprints, Della, is the question of who this man is, how he got his information and how he happened to call me here."

The door from the main dining room opened and Paul Drake came in and said dejectedly, "He was too smart for us, Perry. He hung up before I could get to first base."

"I know," Mason said, as the tips of his fingers drummed on the table. "Hang it, Paul, that's the break I've been waiting for. Now, how did he know where to find us?"

"I'll bite," Drake said. "How did he?"

"We picked this restaurant on the spur of the moment," Mason said. "We were followed here, Paul."

"I guess so," Drake admitted.

"Then it was an expert tailing job," Mason went on.

Abruptly Mason pushed back his chair, "All right, Paul," he said, "we're taking fifteen minutes out."

Dismay showed on Drake's face.

"We leave here," Mason said, speaking rapidly. "You turn to the left, Paul. You turn to the right, Della. I'll cross the street and try working both sides as best I can. Go into each place you see, look for a phone booth, ask if a man recently used the telephone, ask if he was a man six feet tall with big shoulders, a slender waist, wavy dark hair and steel-gray eyes. The eyes will be the most important part of his face. Get busy."

"I don't get it," Drake said. "I—"

"Got it, Della?" Mason asked her.

She nodded.

"All right," Mason said, "let's go."

They pell-melled out of the restaurant. Mason said to the headwaiter, "Hold the private dining room. We'll be back."

He gave the man a ten-dollar bill.

"All right, Paul, you left. Della, right. I'm crossing the street."

Mason dashed across the street, entered a liquor store.

"Phone booth?" he asked.

The man shook his head. "We have a public phone there, but—"

"Anyone use it within the last two minutes?"

"Not within the last half-hour."

Mason hurried into a candy store, asked the same question, got the same answer, walked on down the street, covering store after store until he noticed a parking lot. He started to walk past, then saw a telephone booth back against the checking stand.

Mason walked into the parking lot.

The man came forward. "Got a ticket?" he asked.

Mason shook his head. "I'm after information. That

telephone booth. Do you remember anyone going in it in the last few minutes?"

"Could be," the attendant said, looking at him curiously. "Why?"

"A man about six feet tall," Mason said, "wavy dark hair, very light steel-gray eyes. He has a strong, rugged face and—"

"I didn't see him use the phone," the checker said, "but he sure parked a car here about five minutes ago."

"Is there any chance you'd be able to point out the car?" Mason asked.

"Look, Mister, we're busy. We have a stream of cars and . . ."

The checker started to move away as a car drove in.

"I'm sorry, ma'am we're full up," he said. "Didn't you see the sign? . . . You'll have to back out now . . . I'll watch for you. Come on back."

The woman backed the car out.

Mason said, "Look, this is important. If you're full up now, that must have been about the last car that squeezed in."

"Well?" the man asked.

Mason handed him a five-dollar bill.

"That's different," the fellow said. "That gray car over there."

"That's the one?"

He nodded.

"All right. Cover me for a minute," Mason said.

"Now, wait a minute. What is this? You can't move that car."

"I just want to look at the registration," Mason said.

The lawyer walked across to the car, jotted down the license number, opened the door, looked on the steering column and found the certificate of registration wrapped in a cellophane container.

Mason took out his notebook, copied the data from the

certificate of registration: "Richard Gilman, 2912 Moss-wood Apartments."

Mason walked over to the telephone booth.

"Find what you wanted?" the parking attendant asked.

"I think so," Mason said. "I take it you don't have a very good memory?"

"Poorest in the world."

"You've forgotten all about my being here?"

"I'd forgotten all about you by the time I got that five bucks in my pocket— I just work here, you know."

"That's fine," Mason said. He walked into the telephone booth, found the number of Selkirk's, called it and asked to speak with the headwaiter. When he had him on the line, he said, "This is Perry Mason. I'm at Crestwood 6-9666. As soon as either one of the parties who were with me come in, tell them to call me at this number. It's important."

The waiter assured him that he would, also that he was holding the private dining room.

Mason took a blank subpoena from his pocket, filled in the name of Richard Gilman as a witness for the defense in the preliminary examination in the case of the People of the State of California versus Gladys Doyle.

The lawyer opened the door of the telephone booth and waited, standing at a point where he could see the gray automobile and also where he could hear the ringing of the telephone bell.

It was ten minutes before the telephone bell jangled.

"Hello," Mason said.

Paul Drake's voice came over the wire. "Perry?"

"Yes."

"I struck a blank, Perry. I covered I guess a dozen public telephones and five booths. I asked—"

"Never mind," Mason said. "I've struck pay dirt. How quick can you get a man out here to serve a paper, Paul? A really good operative."

"Oh," Drake said, "fifteen minutes on a guess, if I'm lucky and hurry."

"Get lucky and hurry," Mason said. "I'm waiting right here. This is a telephone booth in the Twenty-Four Hour Parking Lot just across the intersection. You have the telephone number. I'm waiting here. When Della shows up, you and she go ahead and order something to eat. I'll wait until your process server shows up, then I'll come over and join you.

"You see what I mean, Paul? This man I want may be here inside of two minutes or he may not be here for hours. I'll cover the place until your man comes, then I'll join you at the restaurant.

"Get him here as fast as possible."

"Okay," Drake said. "I'll have a good man out there just as fast as the law allows."

"Make it faster, if possible," Mason said, hung up the telephone and resumed his waiting.

Mason had been waiting less than ten minutes when a man, walking vigorously down the sidewalk, swung into the parking place. He was holding out the ticket for his automobile before he was halfway to the checking station.

The attendant took the check, glanced over toward the telephone booth, nodded imperceptibly, then went over and got into the gray automobile with the license number NRG 936.

The man waited impatiently until the attendant swung the car out into the driveway.

It was just as he was opening the door to get in that Mason tapped him on the shoulder.

The man whirled.

Mason extended the paper at him. "Mr. Gilman?" he asked.

"What the devil's this?" Gilman asked.

"Subpoena to appear this afternoon as a witness for the defense in the case of the People of the State of California versus Gladys Doyle. Court convenes at two o'clock. I'd like to have you there at that time, please."

"Perry Mason!" the man exclaimed in dismay.

"That's right."

"Good Lord!" the man said. "I— Look here, Mason, I can't possibly be a witness for you."

"You can't possibly get out of it," Mason said.

The man was thoughtful. "Look, Mason, where did I make my mistake? Where did I slip up? I'm certainly not that dumb and not that amateurish. I know you didn't have any idea I was following you. I— Will you tell me where I made my mistake?"

"After you've testified, I will," Mason said.

"I can't testify."

"You've been subpoenaed. You'll be there."

"I tell you, I can't. I'll have to ignore the subpoena."

Mason grinned. "Like that, eh?"

"It's like that, Mason. Now, look, let's be reasonable about this thing."

"I've been reasonable," Mason told him. "You're subpoenaed. I've been expecting you'd come forward. I didn't think that even your professional obligations would enable you to keep in the background and still have a clear conscience."

"Now, look, Mason, we've got to straighten this up someway, somehow."

"You be in court at two o'clock this afternoon," Mason said. "If there's any reason you can't be there, I'll make a showing to the judge as to what your testimony would be and get a continuance."

"You don't know what my testimony would be," the man said.

Mason grinned. "You'll testify that you were in the cabin when Gladys Doyle arrived, that her story of what happened is substantially true, that sometime after midnight you went out and got her car out of the mudhole, then drove it down the hill past the cabin, turned it around, and then, because you're an experienced and expert dirt-road driver, managed to take a run for the mudhole and worked the car through to the upgrade side of the mudhole. You may have used your jeep to help you, I don't know. You wiped the cabin clean of fingerprints, turned out the oil stove and left the place, leaving Gladys Doyle still asleep.

"I don't know what else you can testify to, but I hope it will be something that will help my client because, if it doesn't, I'm going to make you the murderer of Joseph H. Manly. And now, if you'll pardon me, I have a luncheon engagement."

Mason walked briskly away.

Back in the restaurant, Mason joined Della Street and Paul Drake, who were already eating.

"What was it?" Della Street asked.

Mason grinned. "When your process server gets there, tell him to go back, Paul. The guy showed up and I did the job myself. Come on children, hurry through your food. We're going up to court so we can be there as much before two as possible."

"What's going to happen?" Drake asked.

"A well-dressed man carrying a briefcase is going to come and talk with me," Mason said, "and then I wouldn't be too surprised if we didn't have a conference with Harvey Ellington, and there's a possibility that Hamilton Burger, the district attorney in person, will be in attendance."

Della Street turned to the puzzled Paul Drake. "He's located the man who was in the cabin with Gladys Doyle," she said.

14

PERRY MASON entered the courtroom at ten minutes to two.

A man wearing a gray flannel suit, carrying a briefcase, tall, slimwaisted, who might have been an advertising executive, arose from one of the seats near the door.

"Mr. Mason?" he asked.

Mason, striding down the aisle, turned, gave the man a swift appraisal. "That's right."

"Permit me to introduce myself. I'm Dartley B. Irwin."

Mason shook hands, said, "What's your line, Mr. Irwin?"

The man looked swiftly around, then put his hand into his pocket, brought out a leather folder and opened it to disclose a gold badge.

Mason examined the badge which was pinned to one side of the folder, the identification card which showed through a cellophane window on the other side, then nodded gravely.

"Now, look," Irwin said, "we don't want to be disagreeable about this, but you have subpoenaed one of our men."

"I have?" Mason asked, with every semblance of surprise.

"Richard Gilman," Irwin said.

"And he's one of *your* men?"

"Yes. He can't testify."

"Why not?"

"Because we're working under cover on a very important matter, and to have Gilman get on the witness stand and disclose his identity at this time, or be examined about the matter on which we're working would be fatal."

"Fatal to whom?" Mason asked.

"Fatal to the operation."

"And if he *doesn't* get on the stand and testify," Mason said, "this case may be fatal to the defendant. Have you ever stopped to think that one out?"

"I hadn't," Irwin admitted, "up to a short time ago, but within the last hour and a half I've given the matter very careful consideration."

"And so?" Mason asked.

"This is a hearing addressed to the discretion of the magistrate. The question is whether there is sufficient evidence to connect the defendant with the crime of murder. That's all there is to it. The prosecution can't convict her in this court and you can't get her acquitted.

"Now, we're willing to make a deal, Mason."

"What sort of a deal?" Mason asked.

"This hearing is addressed to the sound discretion of the magistrate. It's only a question of whether there's sufficient evidence to bind the defendant over, or rather, to connect her with the crime of murder. Now, we're willing to have Richard Gilman appear in chambers before the magistrate. Both you and the prosecution can question him as to what happened. He'll make a statement.

"That statement won't be public, it won't be a part of the record in the case. It will be made outside the presence of the courtroom, but it will be stipulated between you and the prosecution that the magistrate may consider that statement as part of the evidence in the case."

Mason shook his head.

"Why not?"

"Because that's not the legal procedure," Mason said.

"I want an opportunity to examine this witness, I want to know what's happening, and I want the hearing to be in the presence of the defendant. The law says the defendant has those rights.

"Now then, Mr. Irwin, if I start stipulating those rights away on my own responsibility and the defendant winds up in the gas chamber, I've put myself in a very questionable and a very unenviable position."

"But I don't see what difference it makes," Irwin said. "We can, of course, go one step farther, if you want. We can have the court reporter present to take down what is said, and, as far as the presence of the defendant is concerned, there's certainly no objection to that. We just don't want Gilman appearing on the witness stand, we don't want his picture in the papers, and we don't want the newspaper notoriety that would be incident to a disclosure of how we work."

Mason frowned. "I'd feel more inclined to co-operate if we had received co-operation," he said. "Why didn't Richard Gilman come forward? Why didn't he get in touch with me?"

"Because I told him not to."

"And why did you tell him not to?"

"Because I felt that there was plenty of time before trial to decide what to do. I have taken the matter up with Washington. I haven't as yet received my instructions. Until I did receive those instructions, I wanted to keep Gilman out of it."

"Regardless of what it might mean to the defendant?"

"I'd thought about that," Irwin admitted, "and I've been thinking of it a lot since Gilman reported the subpoena had been served on him. I feel that you're an officer of the court, a responsible party and that we're entitled to your co-operation.

"Now remember this, Mason. Gilman's testimony may not do your client one bit of good."

"Why not?"

"She could have murdered Manly and she probably did."

"I don't subscribe to this quote, probably, unquote, in a murder case," Mason said. "Now then, where's Gilman?"

"We can produce him, if necessary."

"I'll go this far with you," Mason said. "We'll stipulate that the hearing may be continued in chambers, that the court reporter will be present, that the defendant will be present, that the bailiff will be present. We'll stipulate that Gilman can make a statement, provided it's a full and complete disclosure of everything he knows about the case—not only the matters that I would interrogate him about in court, but any background information which you people have that might be of value to the defendant."

Irwin shook his head. "We can't divulge information. The most we could do is to have Gilman tell about the physical facts, the things that happened there that evening at the cabin."

"He was there?" Mason asked.

"He was there."

"What was he doing?"

"Getting evidence."

"Against whom?"

"I'd rather not answer that at the moment."

"All right," Mason said, his eyes narrowing. "Have your man here at two o'clock. We'll put him on the stand."

"Now, wait a minute, Mason," Irwin said. "I've approached you nicely, as man to man. We may be able to bring a little pressure to bear if we have to."

"Try bringing pressure to bear on me when I'm representing a defendant in a case," Mason said, "and see what happens. When I'm representing a client, I'm going to do what is for the best interests of that client."

"Will you do this?" Irwin asked. "Will you attend a session in chambers with Judge Bagby? Then, if it appears that you're not getting the information you think is required, we'll discuss the courtroom procedure further."

"If it's satisfactory with the defendant, I'll go that far with you," Mason said.

Irwin looked at his watch. "We have only a few minutes."

"Does Judge Bagby know anything about this?"

"Not yet. We haven't approached him."

"The district attorney's office?"

"We have approached the district attorney's office. We have been in touch with Hamilton Burger, the district attorney. We contacted him within ten minutes of the time you served this subpoena on Gilman. Mr. Burger is very much concerned."

"I hope you didn't interfere with his lunch hour."

"You'd be surprised how many people have had no lunch on account of you," Irwin said.

"All right," Mason told him, "let's go into the judge's chambers and talk with Judge Bagby. How about Ellington? I'd want him present."

"Ellington will be there and so will Hamilton Burger, the district attorney."

"You're bringing out your big guns?" Mason asked.

"As big as we can find locally," Irwin said.

Mason walked over to where Gladys Doyle was seated, awaiting the opening of court.

He leaned forward to whisper to her. "We've found the man who was in the cabin," he said.

"You have?" she asked in surprise.

Mason nodded.

"Well, then, he can vouch for my story. He—"

"Wait a minute," Mason said, "it's not that simple. We don't know yet exactly what happened. This man is a Government investigator. We don't know just what he was investigating, and they'd like to keep us from finding out, if possible. But I've served a subpoena on this man, whose name is Richard Gilman.

"Naturally the Government doesn't want to tip its hand in public. The minute Gilman gets on the stand and word gets around of what is happening, the newspapers will have photographers here. Now, the proposition has been made that we have a hearing in chambers, with the public excluded, and that Gilman tells all he knows about the case. What do you think of that?"

"What do you think of it?"

Mason grinned. "I'm inclined to ride along. I always have the opportunity to state that I'm not satisfied with the procedure and that we're going back to court.

"If I think they are becoming unduly secretive, that gives me a weapon to hold over their heads.

"On the other hand, if I call this man as a witness in court, I've then lost all of the leverage I have, and if he is not very co-operative I can't do very much about it."

"I'm leaving the strategy entirely in your hands, Mr. Mason."

"I just wanted to be sure you understood," Mason told her.

"Will I be there?" she asked.

"In chambers?"

"Yes."

"They didn't want you there, but that was one of the conditions I insisted would have to be in the stipulation. I gather that this man, Gilman, is sympathetic and has been wanting to come forward and disclose his identity, but his superiors have told him not to until the matter can have been submitted to Washington, and apparently Washington can't make up its mind."

Mason glanced hurriedly at his watch, said, "Well, we'd better get in to see Judge Bagby before he goes on the bench."

Mason looked back to where Dartley Irwin was standing and nodded his head.

Irwin came bustling forward. Together they walked into the chambers of Judge Bagby.

Harvey Ellington and Hamilton Burger, the district attorney, were already in the judge's chambers.

Judge Bagby looked grave. "I understand the situation, gentlemen," he said, when Mason entered. "I am not certain that this is a matter which can be handled by stipulation. The law provides that hearings are to be public and witnesses are to testify in the presence of the defendant."

"That," Mason said, "was the point I had in mind."

"You're willing to proceed in chambers?" Judge Bagby asked.

"I'm willing to try it out," Mason said, "and see what happens. I want it understood that if, at any time, I am not satisfied, we can adjourn the hearing to the courtroom and I'll interrogate the witness on a basis of question and answer, and take the ruling of the Court as to whether the question calls for evidence which is competent, relevant and material."

Hamilton Burger, the district attorney, shook his head. "I don't think that stipulation is fair," he said.

"Why not?" Mason asked.

"It gives you two strings to your bow, two shots at it. You can express dissatisfaction with something and call for the hearing to be transferred back to the courtroom. Then you get a chance to go over all the same ground again. It gives you two shots at it."

"What's the matter?" Mason asked. "Don't you think this man can tell the same story twice?"

Burger flushed. "I don't see any reason why you should have two shots at it, that's all."

"Well, if that's the case," Mason said, "then we're all finished before we start. There's nothing to be gained by having a discussion in chambers. We'll just go right ahead in court."

"Now, just a moment, just a moment," Irwin interposed. "I think perhaps you're being unduly technical, Mr. Burger. That is, I think perhaps you're magnifying the possibilities of the situation."

"When you're dealing with Perry Mason," Hamilton Burger said, "you don't magnify anything. He carries his own magnifying glass."

Irwin said, "Nevertheless, we are very anxious to try it this way. That is the only condition under which Mr. Mason will proceed, and the Government is very anxious to keep Gilman out of the courtroom."

"You tip your hand to Mason like that," Hamilton Burger said angrily, "and he'll trump every ace you've got."

"Unfortunately, we don't have a chance to play our cards," Irwin said. "We're forced to put our hand on the table."

Burger yielded the point with poor grace. "All right," he said, "let's get the defendant in here and get it over with."

Judge Bagby sent for the bailiff to bring Gladys Doyle into his chambers.

While she was being brought in, Irwin stepped out into the corridor. A moment later he returned with Richard Gilman, opening the door and entering the chambers just as the bailiff was bringing Gladys Doyle through the courtroom entrance.

Gilman's grin was somewhat sheepish. "Hello, beautiful," he said.

She impulsively gave him her hand. "Hello. I knew I could count on you. I felt that sooner or later you'd come forward and clear me."

"I'm sorry, I'm afraid it's later and I'm afraid I can't clear you."

"Now, just a moment. Let's not have any further discussion until we get the record straight," Judge Bagby said. "Now, Mr. Court Reporter, I want to have the record on this. It appears that a witness who has been subpoenaed by the defense is in the employ of the United States Government. He is working undercover on a confidential matter, and the Government feels that it would be embarrassing if he should be brought into the courtroom and put on a witness stand.

"He is, however, concededly a man who knows something about the facts of the case. As I understand it, gentlemen, it is stipulated that he was at the cabin where the murder was committed on the night of the murder, and that he saw the defendant there.

"The defense wishes to examine this man as its own witness.

"The defense and the prosecution are willing to stipulate that this preliminary hearing can be had in chambers, that the court reporter will take down everything that is said, and that if counsel for both sides so stipulate, it can become a part of the record. It is further stipulated that if, at any time, counsel for the defense is dissatisfied with this procedure, he can discontinue it at any time and adjourn the hearing to the courtroom.

"Is that generally the stipulation, gentlemen?"

"I don't approve of it, but I've been pressured into it," Hamilton Burger said.

"I'm agreeable," Mason said, "but I want the defendant to pass on it."

"That's what I'm coming to," Judge Bagby said.

"Now, Miss Doyle, you're the defendant in this case. You've heard the stipulation. Is it agreeable to you? That is, is this procedure agreeable?"

"It is if it's agreeable to my attorney, Mr. Mason," she said. "I'm in his hands."

"Then let's proceed," Judge Bagby said. "Now, how do you want to handle this, gentlemen?"

Mason said, "I want Gilman to make a statement, an informal statement that will cover the whole background of this case, and—"

"All the pertinent background," Irwin said. "There are some things we will have to withhold."

"I don't want anything withheld," Mason said. "I want a statement. Then after he's made that statement, either the prosecution or the defense can question him, and it can be done informally. It won't be on the basis of a regular cross-examination. We'll just be trying to get at the evidence."

"Well," Irwin said, "we can start out on that basis."

"Now, what about swearing the witness?" Judge Bagby asked.

"He isn't a witness at this point. He's just making a statement in chambers."

"I want him sworn," Mason said.

Irwin flushed. "You're being rather difficult, Mr. Mason."

Mason surveyed him coldly. "I can," he said, "become more difficult, if necessary. This is your proposition. Do you want to go through with it or not?"

"I told you he'd start trumping your aces," Hamilton Burger said.

Irwin said, "I haven't played any aces—yet."

"No," Burger said, "Mason has played all the cards so far—and taken all the tricks."

Irwin said reluctantly, "Very well, let Gilman be sworn."

The court clerk administered the oath to Gilman.

"Go ahead," Mason said, "make your statement."

Gilman said, "We were working on some tax investigations. It was brought to our attention that Mauvis Niles Meade, who had written a best-selling book entitled

Chop the Man Down, had touched on some matters in that book which indicated she probably had firsthand information concerning certain avenues of tax dodging which are of very great interest to the department.

"It was decided to make an investigation of Miss Meade.

"It soon became apparent that Miss Meade was, from time to time, having a surreptitious rendezvous in a cabin up in the Pine Glen Canyon—the cabin, incidentally, where the murder was committed.

"I was commissioned to find out something about the cabin and what was going on there.

"I went up there on Sunday night, the eighth of this month. I started an investigation, trying to determine whether there were any papers in the cabin or any books of account which could be photostated to advantage.

"I arrived about ten o'clock in the evening. I found it rather cold and started an oil fire in the heating stove in the main cabin. I had just got to work when there was the sound of steps on the porch and someone pounding at the door.

"Quite naturally, I was annoyed and frankly somewhat apprehensive. After concealing evidences of the search I was making, however, I opened the door and found the defendant, Gladys Doyle. She told me that her car was stuck and she wanted me to get her out.

"I recognized Gladys Doyle immediately as being the secretary of Mauvis Meade, one of the persons we were investigating, and I assumed, of course, that I had walked into a trap.

"I am afraid that I was, therefore, rather unco-operative, particularly when Miss Doyle announced that she was going to take a hot shower and planned on spending the night there. So while Miss Doyle was undressing and taking the shower, I stepped outside the cabin and looked around it in order to see if there were people planted nearby. I thought perhaps I was being framed for something, either assault with intent to commit rape, or burglary. I had entered the house without a search warrant."

Mason said, "I would like to know exactly what you did after Miss Doyle arrived at the cabin."

Gilman hesitated a moment, then said, "Frankly, Mr. Mason, I wanted to be sure that I wasn't walking into a trap, so I waited until I was certain Miss Doyle was taking a shower. I felt that after she had divested herself of her wearing apparel, she wouldn't be apt to try to follow me if I went out and investigated."

"You peeked," Gladys Doyle charged.

Judge Bagby frowned. "Now, just a moment. I think that while this hearing is informal, we should keep some semblance of order. I think you should speak through your attorney, Miss Doyle, and—"

Richard Gilman hurried on. "When I was certain that she was actually taking a shower and not just stalling, I went out in the rain and went up the road to take a look and see if her car was actually there.

"Sure enough, the Mauvis Meade station wagon was bogged down in the mudhole just as she had described it. Looking the situation over, it seemed to me that it either represented a bona fide accident or that the stage had been very carefully set.

"I circled the cabin a couple of times, working my way cautiously over the ground and through the wet brush, listening and trying as best I could to make certain that there was no one staked out watching the cabin. When I had reassured myself, I returned to the cabin and then waited until I was certain Miss Doyle had gone to sleep.

"I then walked back up to the station wagon, started the motor and after some very careful driving managed to extricate it. I then drove it down past the cabin to a flat where there's room to turn, turned the car around and drove back up the grade.

"I have had a great deal of experience in dirt-road driving, and knowing exactly where this mudhole was located and the nature and extent of the hazard, I was able to get the car up through the mud and to the upper side of the mudhole.

"I left the car parked there, the keys in the ignition, all ready to go."

"Then what did you do?" Mason asked.

"I went back to the cabin, looked around and made certain everything was all right, turned off the fire in the oil stove, went back to where I had left my jeep, drove back to town and made a complete report."

"You reported about Gladys Doyle being at the cabin?"

"Certainly."

"And you were instructed to do what?" Mason asked. "To keep quiet?"

"I don't think I should betray my instructions," Gilman said.

"That would be hearsay anyway," Hamilton Burger interposed.

"What directed your attention to the cabin in the first place?" Mason asked.

Irwin said, "I think I'll answer that question, if you don't mind, Mr. Mason."

"Wait a minute," Judge Bagby said. "You're not under oath and this is all—"

"It's all informal anyway," Mason interposed. "We're simply getting a background here."

"Well, go ahead and explain it if you want," Judge Bagby said, "and then we can ask Gilman if your statement is correct, according to his best recollection."

Irwin said, "We knew that Mauvis Meade had been intimately associated with some people whom we were investigating financially. We felt that she might well be juggling funds so that it would be difficult to trace them.

"We also knew that there were other very attractive women working on some sort of a similar basis. We wanted very much to find out more about that.

"Then Miss Meade began to cultivate Manly and soon they began using this cabin as a rendezvous."

"A romantic attachment?" Judge Bagby asked.

"Frankly, I don't know," Irwin said. "That phase of it doesn't interest us as much as the purpose of the meetings and what was going on generally.

"We found that Manly was leading a double life. He'd leave home ostensibly on a business trip. Sometimes he would actually make a business trip, but quite frequently he would detour to an apartment which he maintained at the Gandarra Apartments under the name of Joe Fargo. The apartments are furnished and there is an individual garage for each apartment in the rear.

"We checked Manly's apartment and the garage and found that he was keeping a jeep station wagon stored in the garage. The registration of that jeep station wagon shows that it had been purchased in his name and registered at his home address.

"Quite naturally, we put a shadow on Manly, paying particular attention to his comings and goings from the apartment house, and so found out about this cabin up on the Pine Glen Canyon road.

"Now, I think that's all the detail we care to go into now."

"Then Mauvis Meade is the one who rented this cabin?" Hamilton Burger asked.

Irwin said, "I think you may assume that, but I won't confirm it."

Mason said to Gilman, "Now, as I understand it, when you first got to the cabin and the defendant showed up shortly after you arrived, you thought you had been trapped. Is that right?"

"I thought I'd walked right into a trap," Gilman admitted. "I recognized her as the secretary of Mauvis Meade and felt certain that I was being framed. I wanted to get out of there, but I didn't want to tip my hand."

"Subsequently, when you found out that the defendant was acting in good faith, your conscience bothered you?"

Gilman flashed Mason a look of pleading. "I don't know what you mean by saying that my conscience bothered me. I did nothing that was wrong."

He held his eyes meaningly on Mason and said, "I haven't the slightest idea how it happened that you located me."

Irwin said, "I think, Mr. Mason, that since we're co-operating with you, you owe it to us to tell us how you got a line on Dick Gilman."

Mason eyed him coldly. "You're not co-operating with me," he said. "I'm simply trying to make up my mind whether I'm willing to co-operate with you."

There was a moment of silence.

Gilman turned to Gladys Doyle and said, "You can see how I felt, Miss Doyle."

"Under the circumstances, I certainly can," she said.

Hamilton Burger said, "Your Honor, this hearing is now getting down to an informal discussion which I don't think we should permit."

"Why not?" Mason asked. "This isn't part of the courtroom proceeding. If you want to be formal, we'll go back to court."

"It suits me all right," Burger said. "Let's go back to court."

"Well, it doesn't suit me," Irwin announced. "Your Honor can see the situation in which we are placed. The minute this man goes on the stand his undercover work is ruined."

"You're doing undercover work?" Mason asked Gilman.

"Of course I am," he said. "Otherwise, I'd have—" He caught himself abruptly and stopped midsentence.

Judge Bagby looked at Gilman speculatively, then turned his attention to Gladys Doyle. "Of course, the Court hasn't had the benefit of the defendant's story," he said, "but it is beginning to look more and more as though this is a situation which is susceptible of an explanation. Mr. Gilman, do you have any idea who murdered Joseph Manly in the event we should, simply for the sake of argument, assume that this defendant did *not* do it?"

"I have only an idea," Gilman said.

Mason turned to Hamilton Burger. "Your people found some fingerprints in that cabin?" he asked.

Hamilton Burger nodded.

"Some of them were the defendant's fingerprints?"

"Yes, several," Burger said testily.

"You also found some other prints?" Mason asked.

"You'd better ask Lieutenant Tragg about that," Burger said.

"Get him in here and I'll ask him," Mason said.

"Now, Your Honor," Burger protested, "that's just the thing I was afraid of about this informal discussion. Mason is using it as grounds for a general fishing expedition. Your Honor will notice *he* hasn't committed *himself* to a thing as yet. He can stall around here, having an informal discussion, getting us to tip our hand, and then say he's decided not to play, that he's going to put Gilman on the stand anyway and walk back into court. He has everything to win and nothing to lose."

"And you don't want me to find out what evidence the prosecution has?" Mason asked.

"Naturally not," Burger said.

Mason turned to Judge Bagby and said, "And I submit, Your Honor, that's not a fair attitude for a prosecutor, in view of the fact that the case has taken the turn it has. It seems to me that we are charged with the duty of administering justice, that it's up to us to find out exactly what happened out at that cabin. If this defendant is guilty, that's one thing. If she's innocent, that's quite another."

Judge Bagby cleared his throat. "This is certainly a most peculiar situation," he said. "It would be much better, as far as the formalities are concerned, to have the hearing conducted in a regular manner in the courtroom."

"But, Your Honor," Irwin protested, "the minute that is done we have lost thousands on thousands of dollars which have been spent in preliminary work, and we subject certain people to danger. I am not in a position to state the work on which Mr. Gilman is engaged at the present time, but it is very, very highly confidential. He is placed in a strategic position as an undercover man, and to have his identity disclosed at this time would simply ruin our entire plans and play right into the hands of a gang of very shrewd criminals."

Judge Bagby turned to Hamilton Burger. "I take it that you are keeping this situation in mind, Mr. Burger."

"I don't know why I should," Burger said. "Nobody told me anything about it."

Irwin said with some heat, "Well, we certainly aren't going to go into your office and tell you every case we're working on, the investigations we're making and ask your permission to carry on our business."

"I don't like it," Burger said doggedly.

Mason smiled at Judge Bagby and said, "It seems to me, Your Honor, that we're doing all right. I think we're getting to the bottom of the case. I'd like very much to have Lieutenant Tragg brought in and ask him about those fingerprints."

"I think I'd like to hear a little more about this," Judge Bagby said, glancing at Hamilton Burger and frowning. "After all, Mr. Burger, the function of a district attorney's office is to do justice. The district attorney is not the representative of the prosecution, despite the fact that he is the prosecutor. He is, actually, the representative of the people. He's the representative of the highest ideals of justice."

Hamilton Burger, his lips clamped in a tight line of anger, jerked his head at Perry Mason and said, "Not when you're dealing with Mason—we're not even dealing. He's handing us out the cards he wants us to have, some of them from the top of the deck, some of them from the middle of the deck, some of them from the bottom of the deck and some of them he's keeping up his sleeve."

Judge Bagby smiled, turned to the bailiff and said, "Let's get Lieutenant Tragg in here."

Gilman said to Perry Mason, "I haven't the faintest idea how you got a line on me. I certainly would like to know."

"And I would," Irwin said.

"Perhaps I'll tell you some day," Mason said casually. "A great deal depends on the developments of the next few minutes."

Hamilton Burger got to his feet angrily. "Ellington," he said, "I guess you can handle this. Good day, Your Honor."

"This seems to me to be rapidly approaching a situation where it will be necessary to make a major policy decision on the part of the prosecution," Judge Bagby said coldly. "I know that you are a very busy man, Mr. Burger, but I do think that it would be advisable for you to remain, at least for a few minutes."

"Very well," Burger said. He strode off to one side, turned and motioned to Ellington.

The deputy district attorney walked over and Burger and Ellington engaged in a whispered conference.

Gilman took advantage of the opportunity to move his chair up close to that of Gladys Doyle. "I'm awfully sorry Miss Doyle," he said. "If I had had any idea of the real situation . . . well, you can see how it looked to me."

"I certainly can," she said, smiling up into his eyes. "There's no hard feelings."

"Well . . . thank you."

"There's one thing about your testimony that concerns me, however," Gladys said.

"What?"

She lowered her eyes demurely. "Your statement that you waited until you were sure I was taking a shower . . . you were watching me while I undressed."

Gilman's eyes widened. "What do you mean?"

"There was no shade on the window. You were looking in."

He shook his head. "I was waiting for the sound of water running from the hot water tank," he said. "I held my hand against the tank and felt the hot water going down and the cold water coming in. Then I knew you were in the shower, so I left."

"And you weren't looking at me through the window?"

"Certainly not."

She suddenly smiled. "Well, you missed something!"

The phone rang.

Judge Bagby answered it, then called Burger. "It's for you," he said.

Burger picked up the phone, said, "Hello," then listened for some two minutes, said, "All right, bring him up here right away."

He hung up the phone and his face was suffused with smiles. "All right," he said, to no one in particular, "let's go ahead. I find I've got a fist full of trumps, myself."

He walked over to Ellington and engaged him in a whispered conference. It was quite apparent that he was in the greatest good humor.

The door opened and Lieutenant Tragg entered the judge's chambers.

"Sit down, Lieutenant," Judge Bagby invited. "We're having something of an informal conference here. There have been some peculiar developments in this case. I understand that you found some fingerprints in the cabin, some fingerprints that were not immediately accounted for."

"We found some fingerprints," Tragg admitted.

"Were you able to account for all of them?"

Tragg shook his head. "We found some of the defendant's fingerprints, we found a few man's fingerprints . . . we weren't able to identify them. I now assume they're those of Mr. Gilman. And we found fingerprints of one other person that the expert hasn't been able to identify. He thinks they may have been left by a woman or a child."

Gilman glanced at Mason.

"Did you," Mason asked, "check those fingerprints to see if one of them had been made by Mauvis Meade?"

"Certainly," Tragg said.

"Were any of them hers?"

"No."

Gilman looked up in quick surprise.

"Do *you* know whose prints they were, Lieutenant?"

"I don't."

"Were they good prints?"

"One was a very good latent print, almost perfect."

"Where did you find it?"

"There was an aluminum teakettle on the stove," Tragg said. "It had evidently been used quite a bit. Then there was a very fine, modern, stainless-steel, copper-bottomed teakettle in the shelf, and that teakettle apparently had never been used for heating water, but it had been used apparently as some sort of receptacle. It had been handled quite a bit. There were smudges of fingerprints on it. We found several fingerprints on the cover . . . I now assume some of them were Mr. Gilman's fingerprints."

"I lifted the lid," Gilman admitted.

"And we found some prints that we couldn't identify.

As I say, we think they're the fingerprints of a child or a woman."

"They were not the defendant's?"

"Definitely not."

"And not those of Mauvis Meade?"

"No."

Judge Bagby turned to Mason and said, "I couldn't help but notice, Mr. Mason, that when you exhibited that document to Mauvis Meade when she was on the witness stand it seemed to cause her a great deal of consternation. Frankly, I expected you to follow up your advantage."

Mason merely smiled and said, "There are certain things which are matters of courtroom strategy, Your Honor, and an attorney has to play his cards as he sees them."

Judge Bagby frowned thoughtfully, said, "Well, the Court is not entirely satisfied. I'd like to have Mauvis Meade brought in here. I'm going to ask her some questions. Mr. Bailiff, will you ask Miss Meade to come in here, please?"

Ellington said, "The Court can readily see why we objected to this entire procedure. This inquiry is now getting far, far afield."

"That's all right," Judge Bagby said. "If we can't get justice on the high road, then we'll take to the fields."

Gladys Doyle looked up to find Gilman looking at her. She smiled at him. He cleared his throat, started to say something, glanced at Irwin, changed his mind and remained uncomfortably silent.

Burger leaned forward and again whispered to Ellington, then turned and said to Judge Bagby, "Very well, Your Honor, I see that my hand is being forced in this matter."

"Not at all," Judge Bagby said, "we're simply trying to get at the bottom of a rather puzzling situation."

"I know, I know," Burger said impatiently. "But nevertheless it *is* forcing my hand."

Judge Bagby flushed.

"Now, since we've got to this point, and since Mr. Mason is adopting the position of a sort of czar where things have to be done his way or he won't co-operate, I want to show that co-operation is a two-way street and that Mr. Mason is in no position to say what he'll do and what he won't do.

"I'm going to call a witness. I would like to have Your Honor hear what this witness has to say. I may say I am going to use this witness in preferring charges against Mr. Mason, not only for unprofessional conduct but for concealing evidence."

Judge Bagby said, "If you have a witness you want to call, you may go ahead and call that witness. I will permit you to reopen your case."

"Very well," Hamilton Burger said. "I'm going to call Ira Kelton. He should be in the witness room by this time. Will the bailiff bring him, please?"

Burger glanced triumphantly at Mason.

Mason's face was utterly without expression.

Judge Bagby was drumming on his desk with the tips of his fingers, a sure sign that the jurist was annoyed.

The bailiff returned with Ira Kelton.

Hamilton Burger said, "Now, Ira Kelton is an operative. He was employed by the Drake Detective Agency, which in turn was employed by Perry Mason to—"

"Hadn't you better have this man sworn if he's going to make a statement?" Judge Bagby asked.

"I'm quite willing to have him sworn, Your Honor," Burger said. "Hold up your right hand and be sworn."

Kelton held up his right hand and was sworn.

"What's your occupation?" Hamilton Burger asked.

"I'm a detective."

"Have you been employed by Paul Drake?"

"Yes, sir."

"Many times?"

"Many times."

"Were you in his employ on the ninth of this month?"

"I was, yes, sir."

"Did you go out to the cabin on the Pine Glen Canyon road, where the murder was committed?"

"Yes, sir. Several times."

"Can you tell us the circumstances under which you went out there?"

"I had been instrumental in getting a lead on the identity of the victim. I noticed that there was a pile of firewood in the backyard. I measured it. It measured almost exactly a cord, so I felt that it had been delivered recently. I made inquiries, found out who was selling the wood, found this man, a man whose name was Atkins, and learned from him that the wood had been paid for by a Joseph H. Manly. I traced down Joseph H. Manly and reported to Mr. Drake, who in turn reported to Mr. Mason."

"Then what?"

"Then I believe they called on Mrs. Manly. I'm not certain, but they got enough information to feel that they had some knowledge in advance of the police as to the identity of the murdered man."

"Then what?"

"Then they drove up to the Pine Glen picnic grounds where I was stationed. They asked if they could get in the cabin.

"I told them I thought they could get in through the bedroom window, the bedroom where the body had been found. I noticed that there was no catch on that window and that it could be raised and lowered quite easily."

"Go on. What happened?"

"Well, we three went out there to the cabin and went in and looked around."

"Now then," Hamilton Burger said triumphantly, "did you find anything?"

"Mr. Mason did."

"What?"

"Down under the cabin in a container, Mr. Mason found a scarf with a distinctive pattern and wrapped in this scarf was a box of shells, the variety known as the .22 long-rifle."

"Shells which fit the gun with which the murder was committed?" Hamilton Burger asked.

"Yes, sir."

"And what did Mr. Mason do with this very interesting bit of evidence?" Hamilton Burger asked triumphantly.

"He put it in his pocket."

"Now, you say that this scarf had a distinctive pattern. What was it?"

"It was a pattern of the classical three monkeys, one with his hands over his eyes, one with his hands over his ears, one with his hands over his mouth."

"That was a silk scarf?"

"Yes, sir."

Hamilton Burger turned triumphantly to Judge Bagby. "Now then, Your Honor," he said, "that presents a new angle. Here we have counsel deliberately tampering with evidence, concealing evidence and obstructing the administration of justice. I call Your Honor's attention to this photograph of Mauvis Meade. It is a publicity photograph taken for the purpose of being put on the dust jacket of her book.

"Your Honor will see she is wearing a scarf which is streaming out in the wind, presumably a stiff ocean breeze. Your Honor can plainly see that it is a scarf showing the traditional three monkeys. I am going to call on Mr. Perry Mason to produce that scarf and that box of shells."

Judge Bagby turned to Perry Mason, frowning

thoughtfully. "You have heard the district attorney, Mr. Mason?"

Mason gravely nodded. "I have heard the district attorney. I have also heard the witness. I believe that it is proper to permit counsel for the defense to cross-examine a witness before his testimony is taken as final."

"Certainly," Judge Bagby said, an expression of relief on his face. "If there is any misunderstanding about this situation the Court would like to have it cleared up."

"You had been out at the cabin before we made that trip?" Mason asked Kelton.

"Yes, sir."

"You were working for Paul Drake at the time?"

"I was, Mr. Mason, and don't misunderstand me. I still feel loyal to him and to you, but I cannot condone the commission of a crime. I have a license and a wife and children. I—"

"Never mind that," Mason said coldly. "Never mind volunteering information. Just answer the questions. You had been out to the cabin before?"

"Yes, sir."

"You knew the lay of the land?"

"Yes, sir."

"You had noticed that there was no catch on that window and it could be raised from the outside?"

"Yes, sir."

"That window was found open when the police first arrived at the cabin?"

"I believe it was, yes, sir."

"When we got there you opened the window and let us in?"

"Yes, sir."

"How was that window held open, incidentally? Were there window weights to balance the window?"

"No, sir. It was held open with a stick."

"In other words, you opened the window and propped it open with a stick?"

"Yes, sir."

"And where did you get that stick?"

"I found it lying on the ground outside the cabin, right near the window."

"It was a stick that was exactly the right length so that when you propped the window open with it, the window remained open?"

"Yes, sir."

"Now, we went in and looked around. The police at that time had been in and had finished with the cabin. Is that right?"

"Yes, sir."

"Then we went out and I suggested I wanted to look under the cabin. There I found a coffee can and in it was this silk scarf and a box of .22 shells?"

"Yes, sir."

"A full box?"

"No, sir, it was not. As it happened, we counted the shells and seven were missing. I believe there were six in the magazine of the automatic rifle with which the murder was committed, leaving the other shell as the one which was fired into the body of Manly."

"And was any comment made about this being evidence at the time?"

"Mr. Drake said that we would have to turn it in, and you simply put it in your pocket and said, 'I'll take charge of this and the responsibility will be mine. You folks don't need to worry about it,' or something to that effect."

"Thank you," Mason said. "That's all."

"That's all?" Judge Bagby asked incredulously.

"I want to ask Lieutenant Tragg one question in connection with this," Mason said. "You've already been sworn, Lieutenant. You can just answer this one question."

Lieutenant Tragg turned expectantly toward Mason.

"You went out to the cabin where the murder had been committed?" Mason asked.

"Yes."

"When?"

"Late in the morning of the ninth."

"You were looking for evidence?"

"Yes."

"Did you overlook any?"

"I hope not."

"Did you," Mason asked, "look in an old coffee canister underneath the house?"

"Certainly," Lieutenant Tragg said.

"And found nothing?"

"Nothing."

Hamilton Burger was unable to restrain the exclamation of dismay which marked the complete collapse of what he had intended as a devastating coup.

"Why in heaven's name didn't you tell me you had searched this old coffee canister and found it empty?" Burger asked Lieutenant Tragg.

"Why in heaven's name didn't you tell me about this new evidence?" Tragg retorted.

"Because I didn't know about it until just now," Burger said.

Tragg said with dignity, "I am glad to see Mr. Perry Mason has more confidence in my ability than you have."

Mason turned to Judge Bagby, "There you are, Your Honor. I had confidence in Lieutenant Tragg. I knew that this scarf and the box of shells must have been a plant because I knew that if it had been there when the police searched the place, Lieutenant Tragg wouldn't have overlooked it."

Hamilton Burger tried one more time.

"The fact remains, Your Honor," he said, "that it's still evidence."

"Evidence of what?" Judge Bagby asked.

"Evidence of the murder."

"Quite evidently, this material had never been placed there until after the murder had been committed," Judge Bagby said. "However, the Court is very much concerned about this. Apparently this scarf belonged to Mauvis Meade."

Hamilton Burger nodded.

"And," Mason pointed out, "the evidence that the district attorney is now presenting tends to implicate Miss Meade in the murder and therefore absolves the defendant, Gladys Doyle. I would like to ask Mr. Gilman another question."

Mason turned to Gilman and said, "You were investigating someone in connection with income tax frauds?"

"Income tax frauds and other illegal acts."

"Was that someone Gregory Alson Dunkirk?"

"Don't answer that." Dartley Irwin interposed quickly.

"Why not?" Mason asked Irwin.

"Because we can't let that information get out at the present time. We have a complete file in this case. We're almost ready to spring our trap and close the case, but any premature disclosure would, at this time, wreck our plans."

Judge Bagby said, "I think I want to ask Mauvis Meade some questions, and I definitely want to know, Mr. Mason, whether that document you showed her was a map showing the road down the mountain."

"It was, Your Honor."

"And did that map show the forks of the road at fifteen and three-tenths miles from the post office back at Summit Inn?"

"It did."

"And did the map show a left-hand turn or a right-hand turn at the forks?"

"The arrow very distinctly showed a left-hand turn."

Judge Bagby said, "Then it was your duty to have impeached her testimony with that map, Mr. Mason. You owed that to your client."

"Why did I?" Mason asked. "And how is it going to impeach her testimony? She testified that she gave Gladys Doyle directions as to a short cut down the mountain. Gladys Doyle is the one who told the officers the story about Mauvis Meade getting a map out of a pigeonhole and telling her what route to follow. But the fact that the map showed a turn to the left doesn't mean that Mauvis Meade had to follow the directions on the map. She was simply using the map to refresh her recollection as to distances. I'm satisfied that Miss Meade told Gladys Doyle to turn right at those forks."

"I think I'd like to have Mauvis Meade interrogated again," Judge Bagby said.

Dartley Irwin's reaction was close to panic. "Your Honor," he said, "if you do that, we can't possibly have Richard Gilman present. She simply mustn't see him."

"This is getting too complicated," Judge Bagby said. He turned abruptly to Hamilton Burger. "Look here, Mr. District Attorney, why don't you dismiss the case against the defendant, Gladys Doyle, then co-operate with the Government and find out what this is all about?"

Burger said, with cold dignity, "Because it is against the policy of my office to dismiss a case once I have filed it unless I am satisfied the defendant is innocent."

"You can dismiss this case," Judge Bagby said. "It's not a bar to any subsequent prosecution. If, later on, it appears that this defendant is guilty, you can have her arrested or have her indicted by the grand jury. You have the right to dismiss a case and the defendant can't claim double jeopardy."

"It has a bad effect on public relations," Hamilton Burger said.

"Well, of course," Judge Bagby told him irritably, "if

you're going to be more concerned with what the newspapers may say about your office than about the administration of justice, you—"

"You have no right to say that," Burger protested.
"That's unfair."

Judge Bagby said, "Well, *I'm* going back to court. *I'm*
going to conduct this hearing from the bench, and *I'm*
going to have proper respect from counsel on both sides.
I will excuse Mr. Gilman momentarily from attendance in
the court, despite the subpoena that has been issued. I
want your assurance, however, that you will be in attendance in an ante-room—in fact, you can wait right here in
chambers. If counsel insists on calling you as a witness in
response to his subpoena, you're going to have to take the
stand."

"But, Your Honor," Irwin protested, "we have explained the situation and—"

"I know you have," Judge Bagby said. "If it's so important to the Government, why don't you get Mr. Burger
to dismiss the case against this defendant for the moment?"

"You have seen Mr. Burger's attitude," Irwin said.

Judge Bagby got to his feet. "Very well," he said,
"we're going back into the courtroom where we'll conduct
proceedings in an orderly manner. The Court is going to
take it on itself to recall Mauvis Meade for some questions. After that, counsel for both sides will have a right
to examine her by interrogation which can be called
cross-examination or anything else you want. The Court
will remember, however, that she was called as the prosecution's witness and her attitude will be considered that of
hostility toward the defense as far as leading questions are
concerned.

"Very well, gentlemen, we're now going into court and
try to handle this thing on some sort of an orderly basis."

15

■

JUDGE BAGBY took his place on the bench, said, "I have to apologize to the parties for the delay in resuming our hearing. A matter came up which required the attention of the Court in chambers.

"Now, the Court is aware of the fact that the prosecution has rested its case and has moved for an order binding the defendant over. The Court, however, is not entirely satisfied with the evidence in its present shape, and the Court is going to recall a witness on its own motion.

"Miss Meade, will you come forward and take the stand, please? Now you've already been sworn. Just step forward and take the stand."

Judge Bagby studied Mauvis Meade thoughtfully as she walked up and took her position on the stand. He regarded Dukes, who followed her as far as the rail and then took his position once more on the edge of one of the front seats.

"Miss Meade," Judge Bagby said, "the gentleman who accompanies you and is sitting there in the front seat is in the nature of a bodyguard?"

"Yes, Your Honor."

"Why do you need him?"

"I have been disturbed a lot—that is, people annoy me. I have interruptions from people who want autographs, who want to talk with me—people whom I don't want to see."

"I understand that, but is there any other reason that you deemed it necessary to have a bodyguard—are you afraid of something?"

"No, Your Honor."

"Mr. Mason showed you a paper when he was cross-examining you?"

"Yes, Your Honor."

"Did you recognize that paper?"

She glanced helplessly about her, then said, "I thought I did."

"Was that paper a map which had been made and which had, at one time, been in your possession?"

"I . . . I didn't have it in my possession long enough to be certain just what it was. That is, Mr. Mason showed it to me and I . . . well, I just had a glimpse at it."

"But you saw it well enough so that you thought you recognized it?"

"Yes."

"Now, was that a map showing the road from Summit Inn down to this cabin where the murder was committed? In other words, on that map was there an arrow leading to the road that went by the cabin?"

"Now, just a moment, Your Honor," Hamilton Burger said, getting to his feet. "I dislike interfering with the Court's examination of a witness, but I insist that we keep the evidence within the issues and the issues within reason. The question is whether Gladys Doyle was given directions which took her past this cabin in Pine Glen Canyon, and there again the evidence can have no practical application except insofar as it tends to support the statement that she made to the arresting officers."

"You're objecting to the Court's questions?" Judge Bagby asked.

"Yes, Your Honor."

"On what grounds?"

"That it is incompetent, irrelevant and immaterial."

"The objection is overruled. Now, answer the question, Miss Meade."

"I think that was the map," she said, "and I think that map showed an arrow turning to the left. However, I am quite certain that the directions I gave the defendant were that she was to turn to the right."

"Do you know why the defendant tore those directions out of her notebook and put them in the wastebasket?"

"I don't think she did."

"You found them in the wastebasket?"

"Yes."

"Do you know who tore them out of the book?"

Mauvis Meade took a deep breath, "I did."

"*You* did?"

"Yes."

"Why?"

"Because I didn't want to have those directions left in her shorthand notebook."

"Why?"

"Because after I thought it over, I felt it would be better if no one could prove I was familiar with that cut-off road."

"You had been at that cabin before?"

"I . . . I refuse to answer that question."

"On what grounds?"

"On the grounds that the answer may tend to incriminate me."

"The Court sees no reason for you to take advantage of any constitutional rights under the circumstances," Judge Bagby said. "The Court is going to overrule your objection."

A voice from the spectators' benches in the courtroom said, "May I be heard on that, Your Honor?"

A tall, spare man with a horse face, large, expressionless blue eyes and a determined mouth, came striding forward. "Let the record show," he said, "that I am Wendell

Parnell Jarvis. I wish to represent Miss Meade. I think, if the Court please, that the Court misunderstood the scope of her objection. It was not referring to any matter in connection with the murder which was committed in the cabin but had reference to other matters which I have reason to believe are under investigation by some branch of the United States government. I am advising Miss Meade not to answer that question."

Judge Bagby sighed, said, "Very well. The Court will state, however, that it feels this situation is very confused and should be clarified before the Court is asked to make any ruling. Would the parties object to a continuance for as much as two weeks? It would, of course, have to be made on the motion of the defendant and acquiesced in by the prosecution."

"Would the defendant remain in custody?" Hamilton Burger asked.

"The defendant," Judge Bagby said, "would be released on her own recognizance."

"Then I certainly would object to it."

"May I ask a question of the witness?" Mason asked.

"Proceed," Judge Bagby said.

"Miss Meade," Mason said, "you are a badly frightened young woman, aren't you?"

There was no answer to the question.

"Aren't you?" Mason asked.

Jarvis said, "If the Court please, I think that question is completely foreign to the issues in this case."

"Your objection is overruled," Judge Bagby said. "You have no official status in this hearing. You can advise the witness as to her constitutional rights. The prosecution and the defense will take care of the record in this case. The objection is overruled because you have no right to make it. I hear no other objection. Answer the question, Miss Meade."

"But it has no bearing whatever," Jarvis said.

"It has a tendency to show her bias or mental attitude. I'm going to let her answer the question."

Mauvis Meade hesitated a moment, then slowly shook her head.

Mason said, "This bodyguard is not employed by you, is he, Miss Meade? He is employed by someone else, not so much for your protection as to see that you don't get out of line and make some statement which would incriminate others, isn't that right?"

She remained silent.

"And isn't it a fact," Mason said, "that because you knew you were in danger, you wrote a letter. That letter was to be turned over to the authorities in event of your death or disappearance. You didn't dare leave that letter where anyone who was searching your things would find it, so you put the letter in Gladys Doyle's belongings so that if anything happened to you, Gladys Doyle would read that letter.

"Isn't it a fact that someone tried to lure you out of your apartment by making a publicity date at Summit Inn in your behalf, and, having insured your absence from the apartment, carried on a search? Isn't it a fact that when you returned to your apartment and found that the place had been searched, you dashed into the room of Gladys Doyle for the purpose of finding whether that letter had been disturbed and you found it gone?"

Jarvis expostulated, "Now, if the Court please, this is entirely outside of the issue, this is an attempt on the part of counsel to crucify this witness under the guise of cross-examination. Simply because the district attorney's office is willing to sit there without making objection is no reason that this witness has to be pilloried by any such series of questions."

"She hasn't, as yet, refused to answer," Judge Bagby said.

"Well?" Mason asked.

Mauvis Meade hesitated.

Abruptly Judge Bagby leaned forward on the bench. "Look here, Miss Meade," he said, "this is a court of law. If you feel that you are in danger, if you feel that you are threatened by outside parties, will you take the advice of this Court, will you tell this Court the whole story? Will you realize that if you continue to seek refuge from the law by living without the law, you are not finding safety but only further danger and further troubles."

Abruptly Mauvis Meade said, "Yes, Your Honor, I want to tell my story. I want protection. I claim the protection of the Court."

"From whom?" Judge Bagby asked.

"From Gregory Alson Dunkirk," she said. "From this man, Dukes Lawton, who is supposed to be my bodyguard, and from this attorney, Wendell P. Jarvis, who is actually representing Gregory Dunkirk."

"Now, just a moment," Jarvis shouted. "I wish to be heard on a matter of professional privilege. I rise to that point."

"Well, sit down again," Judge Bagby said. "I'm interested in this witness. You go right ahead, Miss Meade. Tell me your story."

She said, "I became acquainted with Gregory Dunkirk. I had been acquainted with other men, but Greg was different. He was ruthless, he was powerful, and he started using me in connection with schemes that had to do with the underworld. He—"

"Miss Meade, do you know what you're saying?" Jarvis demanded.

"You sit down and stay down," Judge Bagby ordered. "You say you're representing this witness. This witness says she wants protection from you. Now, she's going to get it. One more word out of you and you're going to jail for contempt of court. Go on, Miss Meade."

She took a deep breath. "Josh Manly was mixed up in

the rackets. I don't know all of the details. Manly did. We would meet at that cabin. Sometimes we would be there together, sometimes I would come and get large sums of money which were left in that teakettle on the shelf."

"What did you do with these large sums of money?"

"I turned them over to Greg—Mr. Dunkirk."

"And then what?"

"Then," she said, "I tried to get out of it and I couldn't. I was in too deep, and . . . I became frightened. I did write the letter that Mr. Mason asked me about. I left it with Gladys Doyle. I . . . I became suspicious of that date at the Summit Inn. I rang up the American Film Producers Studios and asked them if Edgar Carlisle was in their publicity department. They said he was not, so I made arrangements to send Gladys Doyle up to keep the date in my place. I went into hiding because I felt certain —because I felt afraid."

"What were you afraid of—of Gregory Dunkirk?"

"Not exactly," she said.

"Of whom?"

"I don't want to state."

Judge Bagby frowned.

"May I ask a question, Your Honor?" Mason asked.

"Do you think you can clarify this matter?" Judge Bagby asked.

"I think I can," Mason said.

He turned to the witness. "Miss Meade, you have cultivated a manner, a seductive type of approach. Let me ask you, did you have this same approach when you were dealing with Josh Manly?"

"I tried to be myself."

"But after a while Josh Manly began making passes at you?"

"Yes."

"And do you feel it was because of those passes that he was killed?"

"I . . . I don't know."

Mason addressed Judge Bagby. "I think that the reason an attempt was made to decoy Miss Meade to the Summit Inn was so her apartment could be ransacked by someone who wanted to get that letter. I think Miss Meade had told Manly she had written such a letter. I think she did this to show him that simply removing her wouldn't bring safety to Manly and the others. Manly reported that conversation.

"If Miss Meade had gone to the Summit Inn in person, it is quite possible she would have met with a fatal accident. Her car would perhaps have been crowded over the grade.

"I think this publicity interview at Summit Inn was a trap. The minute she left the apartment, it was to be searched for the letter. The minute that letter was found, Miss Meade's life was in danger.

"The apartment was searched, the letter was found, but Miss Meade wasn't at the Summit Inn. She had become alarmed and had gone into hiding.

"But she had to go back to her apartment. She waited until she was certain Gladys Doyle would have returned, and then Miss Meade went back to her apartment.

"Not only did she find it a wreck, but as soon as certain people learned of her return, a bodyguard was brought into the picture ostensibly to protect her, but, in reality, to see that she had no opportunity to get in touch with the authorities. And I think this is the first opportunity this woman is having to tell the truth."

"Then who do you think killed Manly?" Judge Bagby asked.

"I am not making any accusations," Mason said, "but there is one fingerprint on that teakettle which has not been identified as yet by the police. Somone raided Mauvis Meade's apartment. Someone found the letter, and that letter was virtually Mauvis Meade's death warrant. It only remained to set the stage for an 'accidental' death.

"Later on, however, another person went to the apartment. That person found the door had been forced, the apartment searched.

"That person made a second search. That person found two things, a map showing the cabin, and the scarf showing the three mythical monkeys. That person took both of these things. That search was made *after* Manly had been killed but before Miss Doyle had returned to the apartment Monday morning.

"Simply because police found the lock on the apartment door had been forced and the apartment searched it was assumed *one* person had made a single search. I feel there were *two* searches made by two separate people and at two separate times.

"The scarf that was taken from the apartment must have been taken before the police knew of the murder. It was taken for one purpose—to implicate Mauvis Meade in the murder. Therefore the logical assumption is that it was taken by the person who killed Joseph Manly."

"Who?" Judge Bagby demanded.

Mason said, "I can't be certain of my deductions, but I would suggest to the Court that if Lieutenant Tragg would take the fingerprints of Mrs. Joseph Manly, he might find that the mysterious fingerprint on the teakettle had been identified."

Judge Bagby's eyes narrowed. "It is," he admitted, "a thought. Lieutenant Tragg, have you had occasion to compare that unidentified fingerprint with that of Mrs. Manly?"

Lieutenant Tragg slowly shook his head.

Mrs. Manly jumped to her feet. "You can't frame me! Suppose I *did* go to that cabin? It doesn't prove a thing!"

"It proves you were lying," Mason said.

She hesitated for a moment, then suddenly made a dash through the door of the courtroom.

Lieutenant Tragg half arose, then settled back in his chair.

"Aren't you going to follow that woman and bring her back?" Judge Bagby demanded indignantly of Lieutenant Tragg.

"Not right away," Tragg said, with a slow drawl.

"And may I ask why not?"

"Well, it's like she said," Lieutenant Tragg observed, "the fingerprint in the cabin proves she was lying but that's all. But her flight is evidence that the district attorney can use in the case against her when he's trying her for murder. So if she's foolish enough to resort to flight, I'll give her a good start before I catch her."

Slowly the look of annoyance on Judge Bagby's face was replaced by a smile. "It is always a pleasure to watch a really efficient officer at work," he said.

16

PERRY MASON, DELLA STREET AND PAUL DRAKE were gathered around the big desk in Mason's office.

Della Street plugged in the coffee percolator.

"Now," Drake said, "suppose you open up with a little information, Counselor. How did you know?"

"I didn't know," Mason said, "but I had a growing suspicion."

"How come?"

"Someone," Mason said, "was trying altogether too hard to frame Mauvis Meade. Someone wanted to drag her into it. That person was altogether too eager, altogether too persistent.

"What happens when you're shooting at big game? If you feel your bullet might miss, you shoot again, and again and again.

"I received a letter. It had been written on a typewriter. The letter enclosed a map which must have been taken from Mauvis Meade's apartment, ergo, the person who wrote the letter had taken the map.

"When we went to the Manly house, you'll remember that Mrs. Manly told us she had been cleaning the house. She was wearing rubber gloves. She took off the gloves and her fingertips were black. Now, how does one get black fingertips from house cleaning if one is wearing rubber gloves?"

"You mean the typewriter ribbon?" Della Street asked.

"Exactly," Mason said. "The smudged fingertips weren't so much of a clue as was her guilty attitude. The minute she glimpsed those smudged fingertips, she put her gloves back on.

"I noticed it at the time. The significance of it didn't occur to me until later.

"Now then, the person who typed that letter to me was trying to bring Mauvis Meade into the picture. The map which she enclosed must have been stolen from Mauvis Meade's apartment.

"The box of .22 shells wrapped in the scarf was left for the purpose of dragging Mauvis Meade into the murder. And the scarf must also have been stolen from her apartment.

"Mauvis Meade made the mistake of trying to lure everybody on. She couldn't be with a man without encouraging that man to make passes any more than she could

be thirsty without drinking. The association with Manly
was originally a business association.

"Mrs. Manly was a plain, vigorous, executive-type
woman who had probably been a highly efficient secretary
before she was married. She couldn't compete with the
seductive curves and carefully cultivated sex appeal of
Mauvis Niles Meade.

"Something happened to arouse her suspicions. She
followed her husband. She traced him to the Gandarra
Apartments where he had a jeep station wagon. Then she
traced him to the cabin. Then she saw Mauvis Meade
show up.

"Mrs. Manly went back and waited. The next time her
husband went to the cabin must have been well after
midnight on the weekend. She took a .22 rifle, waited in
the cover, perhaps twenty or thirty yards from the cabin.
Her husband went into the bedroom. The window was
open. She shot him, then wiped the gun clean of fingerprints, tossed it in through the open window and then
went back, determined to implicate Mauvis Meade in the
crime by planting evidence indicating Mauvis committed
the murder. The time element shows this took place after
Gilman had left the cabin. Gladys Doyle was sound
asleep. She may have heard Manly's car, but only vaguely. She didn't hear the shot because it was fired outside the
cabin, perhaps thirty or forty yards away. It was a single
shot from a very small caliber gun.

"Mrs. Manly, of course, had no idea Gladys was asleep
in the other bedroom. Having killed her husband, Mrs.
Manly walked up to the cabin, wiped the gun clean of
fingerprints and looked in the new stainless steel teakettle
where Joseph Manly had been leaving sums of money
for Mauvis Meade.

"Mrs. Manly took out the money and went home.
Later on, after the police had investigated the murder
without suspecting Mauvis Meade, Mrs. Manly started

planting clues to be sure Miss Meade would be convicted of the murder."

"It *always* sounds simple when he explains it," Della Street said.

"What's going to happen to Mauvis Meade and to Gladys Doyle now?" Drake asked.

Mason laughed. "You don't need to worry about Mauvis. The way Dartley Irwin and two deputy marshals came forward to escort her from the courtroom leads me to believe that Miss Meade is, at the moment, appearing before a federal grand jury, and that Gregory Alson Dunkirk is going to be plenty busy trying to save his own skin without having anything else to worry about. And you don't need to worry about Gladys Doyle. My best guess is that at the moment she's renewing her association with Richard Gilman."

"The moral of all this is," Della Street said, "that a young woman who intends to write a sex novel should be more careful in doing her field work."

"No," Mason said. "Mauvis Meade is going to come out all right. I think the fall guy is Gregory Dunkirk, and the moral probably is that when you work out a foolproof method of beating the law, you want to remember that the law isn't *always* a fool."

The Case of the
Fabulous Fake

FOREWORD

FOR many years, my Perry Mason books have been dedicated to leaders in the field of courtroom medicine For the most part, these people have been forensic (courtroom) pathologists (experts in disease and injury), whose skill in determining the *cause* of death helps convict the guilty and protect the innocent.

Cause of death is always a medical question.

Manner of death, on the other hand, is never a medical question. If, for example, the *cause* of death is a bullet through the head, the *manner* of death is whether it was self-inflicted, accidental or fired by another person in the commission of a crime.

Jack Cadman, Director of the Orange County Sheriff's Criminalistics Laboratory in Santa Ana, California, is an expert investigator in determining the manner of death.

One of his early cases dealt with a young woman who had been fatally shot in the back with a shotgun. There were two prime suspects, the husband and one of his friends. Cadman asked for the clothing that each was wearing the night of the shooting. He found microscopic droplets of flesh and blood embedded in the sweater of the boy friend, the man entered a plea of guilty, and the case was solved without even the necessity of a trial.

A short time later, a proverbial "hired" man was found

dead in a barn His crushed head looked much as if he had been kicked by a horse. Jack Cadman examined the man's hair and scalp, and discovered tiny fragments of dust and a few wood splinters. This initiated a search through a huge wood pile for a two-by-four which, Jack suggested, ". . may be three feet long." It was found, and examination under the microscope disclosed fresh depressions caused by the head hairs being pressed into the compressed wood. Hairs and micro droplets of blood from the victim's head confirmed that this was the weapon that had caused the death.

A suspect was found; robbery was the motive; and another guilty plea to murder resulted.

Jack Cadman is internationally known for developing the Cadman-Johns method for detecting alcohol in the blood stream through the use of the gas chromatograph. This method is perhaps the most accurate one developed to date. A test can be completed in fifteen minutes, whereas other methods require from one to four hours.

Cadman is in great demand as a lecturer at scientific meetings and at universities throughout the West.

He has just moved into a modern and well-equipped crime laboratory which is a real show place, illustrating what science can do in evidence that will tie a criminal to the scene of his crime.

"The solution of the crime problem has to be the field of science," Cadman said, as he surveyed his stereoscopic and ultropak microscopes, his refractometer, search and sweep tables with their vacuum attachments, and a dozen other new crime-fighting tools. "This is the space age, but crime-fighting has not kept pace with other scientific developments since World War II. Any time the American people are ready to give the problem sufficient attention and priority, we can raise the present 'solved' and 'conviction' rates from maybe 10 percent to 90 percent. When it becomes unprofitable for a criminal to commit a crime, he's going to think twice or three times about doing it.

When he knows that the odds are nine to one that he's going to get caught and going to jail, crime will lose a lot of its appeal. But until that happens, why shouldn't people continue to commit crimes? It's quite a profitable trade!"

Therefore, I dedicate this book to an outstanding leader in the field of forensic science:

JACK CADMAN
Director, Orange County Sheriff's
Criminalistics Laboratory
Santa Ana, California

ERLE STANLEY GARDNER

CAST OF CHARACTERS

The Case of the
Fabulous Fake

1

⊙

PERRY MASON looked up from his desk as Della Street, his confidential secretary, stood in the door of the office which communicated with the reception room.

"Yes, Della?"

"We have a young woman in the outer office who won't give her name."

"Then I won't see her," Mason declared.

"I understand how you feel about these things," Della replied, "but I think there's some interesting reason why this young woman won't give us the information."

"What sort of reason?" Mason asked.

Della Street smiled. "I think it might be interesting to find out."

"Blonde or brunette?"

"Blonde. She's holding on to a flat black bag in addition to a purse."

"How old?" Mason asked.

"Not over twenty-two or twenty-three."

Mason frowned. "Are you sure she's over twenty-one?"

Della shook her head. "You can't tell by looking at her teeth," she said, smiling.

"How about her hands?" Mason asked.

"And you can't tell too much by a woman's hands until after she passes thirty," Della explained.

1

"All right," Mason said, "bring her in, we'll take a look."

Della Street turned, went into the outer office and shortly returned with a young woman who was trembling with excitement as she approached the desk and said, "Mr. Mason?"

Mason smiled. "There is no need to be nervous," he said. "After all, I'm an attorney and if you are in trouble perhaps I can help you."

She seated herself across the desk from the lawyer and said, "Mr. Mason . . . I . . . I . . . I'm going to have to disappear and I don't want my parents ever to be able to find me."

Mason regarded her thoughtfully. "Why are you going to have to disappear?" he asked. "The usual reason?"

"What's the usual reason?" she asked.

Mason smiled and shook his head. "Don't cross-examine me," he said. "Let me do the questioning. Why do you want to disappear?"

"I have my reasons," she said. "I don't think I need to go into all the details at the present time, but I do want to disappear."

"And you want me to help you?"

"I want you to be in such a position that you can, if necessary, furnish the missing link which will connect me with my past life. But I don't want you to do it unless I give you permission and tell you to, or unless certain circumstances develop which will make it imperative that you do communicate with my parents."

The telephone on Della Street's secretarial desk rang and she said. "Hello . . . yes, Gertie. . . . Right away? . . . Is it that important? . . . Very well, I'll be right out."

She glanced meaningly at Perry Mason, said, "If you'll excuse me a moment," and hurried through the door to the outer office.

Mason regarded his visitor quizzically. "You're asking me to take you on trust."

"Don't you have to take all your clients on trust?"

"Not entirely. I usually know with whom I am dealing and what the score is."

"And you are usually retained to defend some person who is accused of crime?"

"Quite frequently."

"And how do you verify the fact that your client is telling you the truth?"

Mason smiled. "You have a point there," he admitted.

"You take them on trust," she said.

"Not entirely," Mason replied. "Any person accused of crime, whether guilty or innocent, is entitled to a defense. He's entitled to his day in court. I try to give him legal representation."

"But you try to make that representation effective so that you prove his innocence."

Mason thought for a moment, then, choosing his words carefully, said, "I try to make my representation effective. I'll go that far."

Della Street appeared from the outer office, motioned to Perry Mason, and walked through the door into the law library.

Mason said, "You'll have to excuse me just a moment. We seem to have some rather important matter demanding immediate consideration."

"Certainly," she said.

Mason swung around in his swivel chair, got up, walked around the desk, gave his visitor a reassuring smile, said, "I'm satisfied it will only be a moment," then opened the door to the law library.

"What's the excitement?" he asked Della Street when he had closed the door.

"Gertie, at the switchboard," Della said.

"What about her?"

"I hardly know," she said. "You know Gertie, she's an incurable romantic. Give her a button and she'll sew a

3

vest on it every time, and sometimes I think she even uses an imaginary button."

Mason nodded.

"She observed something about our visitor in there, or thinks she did, and perhaps you'd better talk with her."

"Can't you tell me what it is?"

"Of course I can," Della said, "but I can't evaluate what Gertie's saying the way you can—it makes quite a story."

"All right," Mason said, "let's go see what it is."

He took Della's arm, escorted her through the door which opened from the law library into the entrance room.

Gertie, at the switchboard, was sitting on the edge of her chair, her eyes wide with excitement, her jaws chewing gum in a frantic tempo, indicative of her inner nervousness.

Gertie had an insatiable curiosity. She always wanted to know the background of Mason's clients and, quite frequently, vested them with an imaginary environment which, at times, was surprisingly accurate.

Considerably overweight, Gertie was always going on a diet "next week" or "after the holidays" or "as soon as I return from my vacation."

Despite the fact there was no one in the office, Gertie beckoned Mr. Mason over to her desk and lowered her voice so that it was barely audible.

"That young woman who went in your office," she said.

"Yes, yes," Mason said, "what about it, Gertie? Did you notice something about her?"

"Did I notice something about her!" Gertie said, quite obviously savoring the fact that she had for the moment become the center of attention. "I'll say I did!"

"Well," Della said impatiently, "tell it to Mr. Mason, Gertie. After all, she's waiting in there."

4

Gertie said, "you noticed that black bag she's carrying with her, that she hangs on to so tightly?"

"I didn't notice her hanging on to it so tightly," Mason said, "but she has both a black bag and a hand purse with her."

"It's a kind of cosmetics and overnight bag," Della said. "In a bag of that type there's a mirror on the inside of the lid when you open it."

"And cosmetics, creams, and hairbrushes on the inside?" Mason asked.

"Not in *this* bag," Gertie asserted vehemently. "It's packed, jammed solid with hundred-dollar bills, all neatly packaged."

"What!" Mason exclaimed.

Gertie nodded solemnly, obviously enjoying Mason's surprise.

"How do you know, Gertie?" Della Street asked. "Tell him that."

"Well," Gertie said, "she wanted to get something out of the bag or put something in it. Anyway, she opened it, but it was the way she opened it that attracted my attention."

"In what way?" Mason asked.

"She turned around in her chair, her back toward me, so that I couldn't see what she was doing."

Mason smiled and said, "And the minute she did that you craned your neck, trying to see what it was she was concealing."

"Well," Gertie said, "I guess everyone has a natural curiosity, and after all, Mr. Mason, you want me to find out about the clients that come to see you."

"I was just making a comment," Mason said. "Don't let it worry you, Gertie. What did you see?"

"Well, what she didn't realize," Gertie said, "was that just as soon as she turned her back and opened the lid of the bag, the mirror at a certain angle reflected the contents of that bag so that I could look right into the mirror and see what was inside."

Mason said, "Tell me exactly what you saw."

"The whole inside of that black bag," Gertie said impressively, "was just one mass of hundred-dollar bills, all neatly stacked in piles just as they came from the bank."

"And you saw that in the mirror?"

"Yes."

"Where were you?"

"I was here at my desk by the telephone switchboard."

"And where was the young woman?"

"Sitting over there."

"All the way across the office," Mason commented.

"That's right. But I saw what I saw."

"You say she turned her back to you?"

"Yes, very ostentatiously."

"And then opened the bag?"

"Yes."

"And when the lid reached an angle of approximately forty-five degrees you could see the contents of the bag?"

"That's right."

"Now, did she very carefully hold the lid in that position so you could continue to look at the contents, or did she open it the rest of the way so the lid was straight up?"

Gertie thought for a moment and said, "When I stop to think of it, I guess she opened it the rest of the way, but I was so startled at what I saw that I didn't realize she had opened it the rest of the way until you asked me just now."

"Then she held the lid which contained the mirror for some appreciable interval at the angle of forty-five degrees so you were able to see the contents?"

"I guess she must have, Mr. Mason," Gertie conceded. "I didn't think this all out until— My heavens, you cross-examine a person so!"

"I don't want to cross-examine you," Mason said, "but I do want to find out what happened. You must admit that if she opened the lid of that bag and then held the mirror at an angle so that you could see the contents, she must have been rather anxious for you to see what was in the bag rather than trying to conceal it from you."

"I never thought of that," Gertie admitted.

"I'm thinking of it," Mason said thoughtfully.

After a second or two, he went on. "How did you know they were hundred-dollar bills, Gertie? You couldn't see the denomination at that distance."

"Well, they . . . they looked like hundred-dollar bills, all flat and—"

"But they could have been fifty-dollar bills?" Mason asked as Gertie hesitated. "Or perhaps twenty-dollar bills?"

"Well, I distinctly had the impression they were hundred-dollar bills, Mr. Mason."

"And, by the same sign," Mason said, "looking at those bills in the mirror across the length of the office, they could have been one-dollar bills?"

"Oh, I'm *certain* they weren't one-dollar bills."

"What makes you so certain?"

"Just the way they looked."

"Thanks a lot, Gertie," Mason said. "I'm glad you tipped us off on this. You did quite right."

Gertie's face lit up. "Oh, I thought I had botched it up, the way you were asking those questions."

"I'm just trying to get it straight," Mason said. "Forget all about it, Gertie."

"Forget about something like that!" Gertie exclaimed. "Mr. Mason, that woman is . . . well, she's going to lead you into *something*. She just isn't any ordinary client."

"That's quite right," Mason said. "She isn't an ordinary client, which is perhaps why the case intrigues me."

The lawyer patted Gertie on the shoulder. "You're a good girl, Gertie," he said. "You just keep an eye on these clients that come in, and if you see anything unusual always let me know."

Mason nodded to Della Street and they went through the door into the library.

"What do you think, Chief?" Della asked.

"I think Gertie saw the contents of that bag, all right, and I think it was packed full of currency. But whether it was filled with hundred-dollar bills or whether it was filled with one-dollar bills is anybody's guess. I don't think Gertie could have seen the hundred-dollar denomination at that distance while looking in the mirror."

"Gertie has a wonderful imagination," Della said.

Mason nodded thoughtfully. "But," he said, "the important thing is how long that mirror was held at a forty-five degree angle; whether our mysterious client *wanted* Gertie to see what was in the black bag and report it to us, or whether she was taking something out and Gertie's quick eye managed to get a glimpse of the contents. . . . You have to hand it to Gertie for that; she can see more in a tenth of a second than most people can see after staring for five minutes."

Della laughed. "And then her mind has a computer system all of its own by which she multiplies what she has seen by two."

"Squares it," Mason said, laughing. "Well, let's go back and see our client."

Mason and Della returned to the lawyer's private office.

"I'm sorry we kept you waiting," Mason said. "Now, let's see, where were we? You wanted to have a lawyer who would represent you in case you needed an attorney?"

"That's right."

"But you didn't want anyone to know your identity."

"I have my reasons, Mr. Mason."

"I presume you have," Mason agreed, "but that makes it rather unsatisfactory as far as I'm concerned. Suppose you want to communicate with me so I can do something for you. How am I to know that I'm talking with the same person who retained me?"

"We'll agree on a code," she said.

"All right," Mason said, "what do you suggest?"

"My measurements."

"Yes?" Mason asked.

"Thirty-six, twenty-four, thirty-six," she said.

A smile flitted across the lawyer's face, then he was serious once more. "That's not much of a code," he said.

"But if I gave you the measurements in my own voice over the telephone—you'd recognize my voice, wouldn't you?"

"I'm not certain," Mason said. "I might. Sometimes voices are rather hard to place over the telephone. What would you want me to do? That is, what do you think you'd like to have me do if I should decide to represent you and you should call me over the phone?"

"Defend me," she said.

"For what?"

"Heavens, I don't know," she said, "but the people who are trying to find me are very, very ingenious. They wouldn't go to the expense of hiring private detectives when they could accuse me of having committed some crime and put the police on my trail. *That's* what I'm afraid of.

"You see, Mr. Mason," she went on hurriedly, "I'm not at liberty to tell you all of the facts, but there are certain people—that is, a certain person who wants to find me or who might want to find me. That person is devilishly ingenious. He would stop at nothing."

"It's not easy to find a person who deliberately disappears," Mason said.

"I know," she said, "and this other party knows that, too. He isn't going to waste his time and money hiring private detectives at fifty dollars a day. He'll accuse me of some crime and get the police to find me."

9

"And then?" Mason asked.

"Then," she said, "I'd have to defend myself."

"You mean he'd actually try to press these trumped-up charges?"

"He might. He might try *anything*."

"He would be putting himself in a very vulnerable position," Mason said. "That is, unless you *have* committed some crime."

"But I haven't."

"What do you think he would accuse you of?"

"Heavens, I don't know. Murder perhaps. He's absolutely ruthless."

Mason eyed her steadily. "Or perhaps embezzlement?" he asked.

A sudden flush of color flooded her face.

"Well?" Mason asked.

"He might even do that," she said, "but I hadn't thought of that."

"That would seem to be a logical thing to do," Mason commented, making his voice elaborately casual. "If he accused you of murder he would have to have a corpse. Whereas, if he accused you of embezzlement he would only have to swear that a large sum of money was missing."

"Yes," she said, and then added slowly, "I see your point."

"And just what did you have in mind?" Mason asked.

"I wanted to give you a retainer and have it so that you'd be willing to act as my attorney, to come to my rescue in case I should telephone. . . . No matter what it was I wanted."

"How much of a retainer did you have in mind?" Mason asked.

"Would three hundred dollars do?"

"I would say that that would be a reasonable retainer," Mason said. "Of course, after you consulted me—

and in case the situation became complicated, I'd have to ask for more money."

She opened her hand purse, held it carefully so that Mason could not see the contents, and took out six fifty-dollar bills.

"Do I give them to you or give them to your book-keeper?" she asked.

"My secretary will make a receipt," Mason said. ". . . Those fifty-dollar bills look uniformly crisp."

Her laugh was nervous. "Well, I prepared myself. I don't ordinarily carry large sums of money like this. I got these for you—at my bank."

"Here in the city?" Mason asked quite casually with a quick glance at Della Street.

"No, no, not here in the city. Heavens, no."

"I see." Mason said. picking up the fifty-dollar bills and fingering them casually.

"Just what did you expect me to do for you?" he asked.

"Probably nothing. Don't misunderstand me, Mr. Mason. You are just an anchor out to windward. If all goes well you'll never hear from me again. I'll walk out of this office and out of your life."

"And if all doesn't go well?" Mason asked.

"Then you'll hear from me."

"And what will I hear?"

"I don't know. I'll be calling on you for help."

"What sort of help?"

"I don't know, perhaps advice in a tight situation."

"I can't establish a relationship with a client on that kind of a basis," Mason said.

"You mean financially?"

"In part."

"At the time I call on you for help we'll discuss additional fees. I know that you'll be fair with me and I certainly won't ask you to do anything which is unfair, inequitable or unjust."

"Or illegal?" Mason asked, with a twinkle in his eye.

11

She started to say "or illegal" but suddenly caught herself, hesitated a moment, then said, "You wouldn't do anything that was illegal, so why waste time talking about it?"

"Then you'll get in touch with me if you need me?"

"Very definitely."

Mason said, "You can reach me at this office during office hours. During the evening you can reach me through the Drake Detective Agency, which has an office on the same floor here in this building."

"I saw the sign on the door as I walked down from the elevator," she said.

"They have a twenty-four-hour switchboard," Mason said, "and in the event of any emergency—that is, if it's a *real* emergency—they can usually get in touch with me."

Della Street handed her a card. "Here are the numbers," she said, "day and night."

"Thank you, Miss Street."

Mason said to Della, "Make out a receipt, Della, for a three-hundred-dollar retainer in the form of cash. Now, do you want this made simply to the Code Number thirty-six, twenty-four, thirty-six?"

She shook her head. "I don't want any receipt." She slipped the loop of her purse over her wrist, picked up the black cosmetics bag, smiled at Della Street, said, "Thank you for seeing me, Mr. Mason," and walked out.

Mason sat watching the automatic doorstop as it closed the door.

When the latch had clicked, Mason said to Della, "You know she put on a good act."

"In what way?"

"That we'd never see her again."

"You think it was an act?"

"I'll give you ten to one," Mason said, "that within a matter of five days that girl calls us up and is in serious difficulties—difficulties which she had already anticipated."

"No takers," Della said. "It's bad luck to take the other side of a bet with you. I'll tell you one thing, however, those weren't *her* measurements. She's nearer thirty-two, twenty-four, thirty six."

Mason thought that over. "Padding?" he asked.

"Not that much," Della said, "She's using quite a bit, but not that much."

"Now that you mention it, Della," Mason said, "I see what you mean. So we have a client who is lying to us right at the start."

"Sailing under *false* colors," Della Street said, smiling.

Mason said meditatively, " 'The Case of the Falsified Tape.' "

"Let's hope it doesn't turn out to be 'The Case of the Costly Client,' " Della said. I'm suspicious of padded stories, padded expense accounts, and padded clients."

"She sneaked up on my blind side," Mason said. "I should have given her more of a third degree and broken down her story. However, it's too late now. We'll ride along with her false measurements."

2

⊙

AT TEN MINUTES after nine Mason entered his private office through the hall door, smiled a greeting at Della Street, said, "Anybody in the outer office, Della?"

She shook her head and then said, "Gertie."

"Well, Gertie is supposed to be there."

"Gertie's there, hitting on all six," Della said. "Gertie is so excited she is running around in circles."

"What's excited Gertie?"

"Your mysterious client of yesterday."

Mason's eyebrows rose in surprise. "We've heard from her again?"

"Gertie has."

"What do you mean?"

Della motioned to Mason's desk. On top of the mail was a folded newspaper, opened at the section of CLASSIFIED ADS and folded so that the so-called "Personals" were on top.

Mason walked over to the desk, seated himself in the cushioned swivel chair, picked up the paper, let his eyes glance down the section of personal columns, and noticed the ad which had been marked in the margin:

AM HERE READY TO CONCLUDE
NEGOTIATIONS ON STRAIGHT CASH BASIS.

NO CHECKS. SPOT CASH. CONTACT ME AT
WILLATSON HOTEL. 36-24-36.

"Well, I'll be darned," Mason said. "Do you suppose that's our gal?"

"Sounds like it," Della said.

"Hang it," Mason said, "that's what comes of taking a case sight-unseen. Now, that gal is mixed up in some adventure which is going to get her into trouble just as sure as shooting. And when she gets into trouble she's going to look to us to get her out."

Mason hesitated a moment, then jerked his thumb toward the telephone. "Paul Drake, Della."

Della dialed Paul Drake's unlisted number and, in a moment, said, "Just a minute, Paul, Perry wants to talk with you."

She handed the phone over to Mason.

"Hi, Paul," Mason said, "are you too busy to come down to the office for a minute?"

"Never too busy but what the scent of new business causes me to come running!"

"Come running, then," Mason said, and hung up.

Della Street said, "Is it ethical for you to tell Paul. . . ?"

"It isn't ethical for me to tell him anything," Mason said, "not at this stage of the game—at least the way I interpret ethics. But I'm going to find out something about who this gal is seeing and what it's all about."

"Any idea?" Della asked.

Mason said, "I think she came down from San Francisco."

"Why?"

"The way she's dressed for one thing," Mason said, "plus the time of day she came in. She took a plane down, checked her baggage somewhere, probably at the Willatson Hotel, took a cab, came up here. . . . And she had probably arranged to put that ad in the paper before

15

she ever came down here. As I remember it, it takes a day or two to get an ad of that sort published. . . . If that's correct, she telephoned the Willatson Hotel for a reservation."

"And so?" Della asked.

"And so," Mason said, "we're going to find out a little bit about our mysterious client, a little bit more than the three measurements."

Paul Drake's code knock sounded on the corridor door of the private office. Della opened the door. "Hi, Paul," she said. "How's the digestive system?"

"Better, thanks, Beautiful. You folks haven't had me sitting up all night on cases where I've had to eat soggy hamburgers at an office desk. I've dined out on good freshly cooked meat now for six days in succession."

"Business that bad?" Mason asked.

"Lousy," Drake said.

"Maybe we can help," Mason told him. "But this isn't a big case, it's just a routine job."

"Who's the client?" Drake asked.

"I am," Mason said.

"Oh, oh."

"He wants to find out about a client," Della said.

Drake settled himself in the overstuffed leather chair, threw his legs over the rounded arm, took out a notebook and a fountain pen, and said, "Shoot."

Mason said, "I think I let a client down, Paul."

"How come?"

Mason hesitated, spoke cautiously. "I can't tell you the details without violating the code of ethics, Paul. An attorney is supposed to protect the confidences of his client. Any statements that are made are completely confidential.

"Now then, with that in mind I want you to know that I am afraid I gave a client advice which fell short of the advice I should have given."

"Male or female?" Drake asked.

"That also is confidential," Mason said.

"Well, how did you fail this client?"

"I didn't tell the client the things the client should have known for the client's own good," Mason said. "I let the client diagnose the case and accepted that diagnosis."

"How come?"

Mason said, "Every once in a while a client wants to diagnose the case, just as a patient will come to a doctor and say, 'Doctor, I have indigestion. I want you to give me something for indigestion.'

"If the doctor simply gives the patient something for indigestion he is untrue to his profession.

"What the doctor should do is ask about symptoms connected with the indigestion. He finds out that the patient has been having pains in the chest and occasionally down the left arm, so he suspects something entirely different from indigestion. He has a cardiograph made and finds out that the patient is suffering from a high cholesterol count. He doesn't give the patient medicine for indigestion, but puts the patient on a diet consisting of no fats, no dairy foods, but high in proteins.

"The patient gets better.

"If, on the other hand, the doctor had accepted the patient's self-diagnosis, the patient would probably have been dead inside of twelve months."

"That," Drake said, "is rather elementary, isn't it, Perry?"

"I'm making it elementary," Mason explained, "because I want to show you the situation.

"This client came here and diagnosed the case and prescribed the remedy. Unfortunately, I accepted the statements at face value. I shouldn't have done that. Now then, in order to appease my own conscience, I want information."

"About the client?" Drake asked.

17

"About various and sundry things," Mason said. "They do not necessarily have any *direct* bearing on the situation. They may not even *directly* concern the client. But they are sufficiently significant so they concern me."

"All right," Drake said, "you've now reached your thumb by going all the way around your elbow. You want me to do a job. It's a job in which you are the client. You'll get the best service I can give and you'll get a discount on the bill. What do I do?"

Mason took the folded newspaper and handed it to Drake.

"That ad," he said.

Drake read the ad aloud:

"AM HERE READY TO CONCLUDE
NEGOTIATIONS ON STRAIGHT CASH BASIS.
NO CHECKS. SPOT CASH. CONTACT ME AT
WILLATSON HOTEL. 36-24-36."

Drake looked up from the newspaper. "That's the ad that interests you?"

Mason nodded.

"Your party evidently has three rooms," Drake said. . . . "No, wait a minute, thirty-six is mentioned twice. It may be two rooms, thirty-six and twenty-four, and then the person putting in the ad signs it thirty-six to show that that's the room where contact is to be made."

"Could be," Mason said.

Drake regarded him shrewdly. "And it could be some sort of a code," he said.

Mason was silent.

"Exactly what is it you want me to do?" the detective inquired.

"Find out everything you can about who put that ad in the paper and the person for whom the message was intended."

Drake said, "That may be a big job, or it may be

18

rather simple. The Willatson Hotel is a commerical-type hotel. When there are conventions in town it's probably about ninety-five percent occupied. At other times the percentage of occupancy may be sixty to seventy percent. In any event there will be too many people just to go at it blind. I can find out who's in room thirty-six and who's in room twenty-four. That may not mean anything.

"The best bet is to try to get a line on whoever put the ad in the paper by making a dummy reply in the press, saying something like:

"MESSAGE NOT CLEAR. YOU CAN REACH ME TELEPHONE NUMBER 676-2211 TO CLARIFY. AM NOT WALKING INTO ANY TRAP REGARDLESS OF TYPE OF BAIT USED."

Drake made a little gesture and said, "Of course, that's just off the top of my head, Perry. I'd have to word it a little more carefully than that. I'd have to be subtle, but even so the chances are that there'd be some false note in the reply which would alarm the quarry and let your client know that some outsider was checking."

"Well," Mason said thoughtfully, "I don't know as there's any reason why a situation of that sort should be fatal. . . . It might send the client back to me and then I could . . ." His voice trailed away into silence.

"What's the matter?" Drake asked. "Can't you phone your client at the Willatson Hotel and——"

"I didn't say I thought the person who put this ad in was my client," Mason said. "The client may well be the one to whom the ad is addressed."

"In other words, you don't know where to reach your client?"

"Come, come," Mason said, "you haven't been reading your decisions of the Supreme Court lately. Before I can be questioned I have to be advised of my constitutional rights and given an opportunity to consult a lawyer. . . . I've given you a job to do. Get busy and do it."

Drake thought for a moment and said, "This situation has overtones which intrigue the hell out of me, Perry, but, after all, you said it, you've given me a job to do. It's up to me to get busy."

Drake heaved himself up out of the chair. "When do you want reports?" he asked.

"As soon as you have something definite to report. No matter how trivial it seems to you, give me a line on it."

"Day and night?" Drake asked.

"It's not exactly *that* urgent," Mason said. "Let's say day and evening."

"Okay," Drake said, "day and evening it is. Any limit as to the number of people I can put on it?"

"Don't go over five hundred dollars until you have asked me," Mason said.

"With your discount," Drake told him, "you can get quite a bit of investigative work done for five hundred bucks. . . . I'll be in touch, Perry."

Mason and Della Street watched the detective out the door. Then Mason heaved a sigh, picked up the pile of papers on his desk and said, "Well, Della, we've done all *we* can do. I guess now we'll get to work."

"How are we going to enter this on the books?" Della asked. "You take in three hundred dollars, you pay out five hundred, and we don't even have a name for the client in the case."

"Call her Miss Deficit then," Mason said. "That will serve until we have a better name."

"Perhaps," Della mused, "it could be Miss Deceit."

"She hasn't deceived us," Mason said. "At least we don't know that she has. What we need is information. She has diagnosed her own case, prescribed her own remedy, and she may be wrong on both counts."

20

Della Street picked up her shorthand notebook and pencil. "Well," she observed, "we're only starting the day two hundred dollars worse off than when you sat down at the desk."

3

◉

THE NEXT DAY Perry Mason was in court all day defending a young Negro lad who had been accused of robbing a pawnshop.

The identification by three eyewitnesses who had seen the robber running madly down the street, jumping into a parked car, and making off at high speed was absolutely positive.

In vain Mason tried to shake the identification of the witnesses.

At three o'clock the Deputy District Attorney concluded his opening argument and Mason had an opportunity to address the jury.

"Contrary to popular belief, gentlemen, circumstantial evidence is about the strongest we have, and eyewitness evidence is about the weakest.

"Here is a tall, young Negro lad with a mustache, carrying a paper bag.

"The place in question was held up by a tall, young Negro lad, wearing a mustache, carrying a paper bag.

"It is the theory of the prosecution that the defendant made his escape, hid the money somewhere, put half a dozen packages of cigarettes in the paper bag, and then, when he was arrested, explained that he had been run-

22

ning short of cigarettes; that he went to a coin-vending machine in the neighborhood, bought the six packages of cigarettes, put them in a paper bag he had taken with him, and was returning to his modest apartment when he was apprehended by the police.

"I ask you, if he had disposed of the money so that he could conceal the evidence against him, why, in the name of reason, didn't he also dispose of the paper bag?

"A tall, young Negro with a mustache and carrying a paper bag was like a magnet to the police within a matter of minutes after the holdup when the alarm had been broadcast on an all-points bulletin.

"People get a fleeting glimpse of an individual. They remember the salient points. In this case, that he was a tall, young Negro with a paper bag and a mustache. That is all they really remember.

"Later on when they try to cudgel their recollection into producing additional facts at the insistence of the police officers, they hypnotize themselves into believing there are other things which they remember clearly. Later on they are given photographs to look at, the so-called mug shots of the police. They are asked to study these photographs carefully. They study them until they see the defendant in a line-up and promptly pick him out as the man they saw running down the street, carrying a paper bag.

"It is a case of self-hypnotism.

"It is incumbent upon the prosecution to prove its case beyond all reasonable doubt. I ask you to return a verdict of not guilty."

Mason returned to his seat.

The Deputy District Attorney in his closing argument resorted to sarcasm.

"The defendant robs the store. He puts the money in a paper bag. He is seen running down the street by three witnesses. He tried to fabricate the evidence after he has hidden the money by putting some packages of cigarettes

23

in the paper bag so that it will look like an entirely innocent transaction.

"Three reputable eyewitnesses identify this man positively. Perry Mason, who is one of the shrewdest cross-examiners in the country, has resorted to every arrow in his legal quiver to weaken the testimony of these men. They remain unshaken.

"Don't be hypnotized by eloquence. Don't by swayed by spurious reasoning. Don't be conned out of your just convictions. Go out and find this man guilty."

It was after five o'clock by the time the Judge had finished his instructions, and the jury retired immediately.

It was expected there would be a quick verdict, but the jury was taken out to dinner at six-thirty, returned at eight, and resumed deliberations. By nine o'clock the buzzer sounded and the jury announced they had agreed upon a verdict.

The courthouse grapevine promptly transmitted the news.

The jury had found the defendant guilty.

The Judge took his place on the bench, the defendant was brought into court. All was in readiness for the jury to be received when a plain-clothes officer hurriedly pushed his way through the swinging doors of the courtroom, dashed down the central aisle, approached the bench, and said something in a whisper to the Judge.

The Judge frowned, leaned forward for a whispered colloquy. Then the Court said to the bailiff, "You will keep the jury waiting for a few minutes. I will ask counsel for both sides to join me in chambers."

When the Judge had retired to chambers, he kept on his judicial robes, seated himself in the creaking swivel chair back of his desk, and said, "Gentlemen, there has been a surprising development in this case.

"The police have apprehended a man in the act of holding up a store. They found a cache of money containing one of the hundred-dollar bills taken from the

24

store in the robbery which is being presently tried before this court.

"You gentlemen will remember that the proprietor had taken the numbers of those hundred-dollar bills. The culprit has confessed to the holdup. It appears that the defendant in this case is innocent."

"What!" the Deputy District Attorney exclaimed.

The Judge nodded.

"But they've agreed on a verdict," the prosecutor blurted. "It's 'guilty.' "

"We can't let that verdict be received in court," the Judge said, "and there is a legal point. Having agreed upon the verdict, I don't know offhand exactly what the legal status of the case is. I could, of course, call the jury into court, explain the circumstances to them, and instruct them to return a verdict of 'not guilty'. But it is my present idea that the best thing to do is to tell the jury that circumstances have occurred which necessitate their discharge before any verdict is formally received in court."

"Explaining the circumstances to them, of course," Mason said.

"Certainly not!" the Deputy District Attorney objected.

"Why not?" the Judge asked.

"Because this would tend to weaken the whole fabric of identification evidence," the Deputy protested.

"Otherwise," Mason said, "the twelve people on that jury are going out and criticize the Judge and the administration of justice. It's a lot better to have the people lose a little faith in too confident, too cocksure eyewitness identification than it is to lose confidence in the administration of justice."

"I think so, too," the Judge said, pushing back his swivel chair and getting to his feet.

"Gentlemen, we will return to court. I will call the jury in, and before I ask them if they have agreed upon a verdict, I will make a brief statement to them advising them of recent developments and discharge the jury. At that time you, Mr. Deputy District Attorney, can ask for a motion dismissing the case. It will be granted."

The Deputy District Attorney accepted the Judge's decision wih poor grace. They returned to the courtroom, and the Judge made a brief statement to the jurors as to what had happened.

Mason enjoyed watching their astounded expressions as they realized the significance of what the Judge was saying.

Then the lawyer shook hands with the jurors. The jurors, after some hesitancy, shook hands with the defendant, and Mason said to his client, "Go home and shave that mustache off and never wear one again. Also never carry a paper bag."

The defendant laughed. "Tall Negro boy with a mustache. Tall Negro boy with a paper bag, yes, *sir*. I am going back home and shave off that mustache just as soon as I can get my hands on a razor, and I'm *never* going to carry anything in a paper bag again!"

Mason, tired after the long trial, nevertheless stopped in at his office on the way home.

Della Street had left a note for him:

8:45 P.M. COULDN'T WAIT ANY LONGER,
BUT WANTED YOU TO SEE THE AD IN THE
EVENING PAPER. IT'S ON YOUR DESK.

Mason picked up the folded paper, looked at the ad which had been circled.

The ad read:

36-24-36. WANT TO AVOID ANY TRAPS.
WILL BE AT HOTEL ENTRANCE IN
TAXICAB AT EXACTLY NINE O'CLOCK

TONIGHT. CONTACT ME THERE. NO
WITNESSES, PLEASE. U NO HOO.

Mason regarded the ad thoughtfully, then dialed the
number of the Drake Detective Agency.

"Perry Mason talking," he said. "Is Paul Drake in?"

"No, he isn't. Mr. Drake's out working on a case. He
said he didn't know when he'd be back."

"Anyone there know what job he's working on?"
Mason asked.

"I'm afraid not," the secretary said. "Mr. Drake said it
was extremely confidential."

"Thank you," Mason said. "I guess that's all we can do
tonight."

The lawyer hung up the phone, closed the office, went
to his apartment, and sank into deep sleep.

4

⊙

PAUL DRAKE was already at his office at nine o'clock the next morning when Perry Mason, leaving the elevator, detoured into the office of the Drake Detective Agency.

The girl at the switchboard smiled, nodded, pointed down the corridor toward Drake's private office, and returned to the telephone conversation she was holding at the switchboard.

Mason walked down a veritable rabbit warren of cubbyhole offices where Drake's operatives prepared reports on their various cases, and then entered Drake's personal office at the end of the passageway.

This also was a tiny office with a desk and a battery of telephones.

Drake looked up at Mason, grinned, yawned, said, "You and your mysterious client!"

"How come?" Mason asked.

Drake passed him over the newspaper containing the ad which Della Street had left on his desk the night before.

"Some of your work?" the lawyer asked.

"My work," Drake admitted.

"Do any good with it?"

"Yes and no."

"What happened?"

28

"Well, I had to take certain chances—that's one of the things you have to figure on in this game. I'm playing it blind. The other side has all the numbers.

"Now, either this party had already contacted the person she wanted, or she hadn't. I couldn't tell which."

"Wait a minute," Mason said. "You're using a female pronoun. Why?"

"Because she is a female."

"Go on."

"Well, as I said, either she had contacted the person or she hadn't. Then I had another horn of the dilemma. Either she knew the person by sight or she didn't. The fact that she put that ad in the paper indicated the probabilities were that she didn't know the party by sight.

"Of course, I had one other chance to take. Either the party was a man or a woman. I was in a position to hedge a little bit on that by taking one of my women operatives with me.

"I put that ad in the paper, stating that I would be parked in front of the hotel entrance in a taxicab at exactly nine o'clock."

Mason said, "I presume you had made other efforts to find her identity?"

"Of course. I went to the office of the newspaper which had run her ad. A five-dollar bill got me the information that she was a young woman, good figure, blond, blue eyes, a little bit diffident.

"I went to the Willatson Hotel and wasted five dollars. I couldn't get any lead there.

"So I decided to take a chance and put this ad in the paper. Then, with my female operative, I went to the hotel and sat in front in a taxicab."

"Why the taxicab?" Mason asked.

"So she couldn't trace the license number."

Mason nodded approvingly. "What happened?"

"Promptly at nine o'clock she walked past the car, but so did a lot of other people. However, I had it fixed so she couldn't get a real good look at either my female operative or myself. I was wearing a cap pulled down over my forehead and dark glasses. The operative was wearing a coat with a high collar and dark glasses. . . . It was all real cloak-and-dagger.

"With all those people walking past we couldn't spot her the first time, but when she turned at the end of the block and walked back we had her spotted. She did that three times, never giving us the faintest tumble; no signal, no recognition, no attempt to come up and engage us in conversation. She just walked past four times. And she was clever enough so she didn't indicate any particular curiosity. She kept her eyes straight ahead each time she passed the cab."

"And so?" Mason asked.

"So," Drake said, "we didn't press our luck. We had the cab drive away."

"You didn't try to shadow her?"

"Of course, we shadowed her. I had one operative in an automobile parked behind me, and when the girl walked past the cab the second time he spotted her the same way we did. When we moved on I gave him the signal to follow her.

"After our cab drove off she went back to the Willatson Hotel. She's registered as Miss Diana Deering of San Francisco. She's in room seven-sixty-seven."

"Good work, Paul," Mason said.

"Wait a minute," Drake told him, "I'm not finished. We put some more five-dollar bills to work with the bellboys and the phone operator. Her luggage is stamped D.D.

"Now, when a person assumes an alias they quite frequently use their own first name, and, of course, with initials on the baggage they want to get a name that tallies with the initials. So Diana Deering could well be Diana——, of San Francisco."

Mason raised his eyebrows.

"So," Drake went on, "we did a little leg work. We

30

found that our subject telephoned a San Francisco hospital from time to time to inquire about a patient, one Edgar Douglas.

"Edgar is employed by the Escobar Import and Export Company of San Francisco. He was in an automobile accident a few days ago, has a fractured skull, and is still unconscious.

"So we took the initials of Diana D. and tried Douglas as the last name. We phoned the Escobar Company and asked about Edgar Douglas, were told about the automobile accident, and asked about Diana Douglas.

"We were told she was his sister, that she was also an employee of the company, was upset about the accident, and had been given a leave of absence for a few days so she could be near him.

"We got a description. It checks. We also found out there are no other members of the family."

"Arouse any suspicion?" Mason asked.

"Not a bit. We said we were a finance company checking on Edgar's employment and credit standing, made the questions as routine as possible and asked them in a somewhat bored tone of voice."

"Then what?" Mason asked.

"So then we did leg work in San Francisco," Drake went on. "The Escobar Company doesn't seem at all alarmed, but they're having a 'routine' audit of their books. We found that out more or less incidentally."

"What's the prognosis on the brother?" Mason asked.

"Probably going to be all right, but may be unconscious for as much as two weeks," Drake said. "The guy was all set to take a business trip somewhere—that is, suitcase all packed; drove to a service station to get the car filled up; was clobbered by a car which drove through a red light and knocked him unconscious."

"Any question that it was his fault?" Mason asked.

"None whatever. Not only did the car that struck him come through a red light with several witnesses willing to testify to that effect, but the driver was pretty well potted. The police took him to jail to sober up and he's facing a citation for drunk driving."

Mason was thoughtful for several seconds. "Why should all this cause Diana to leave her brother, critically ill, come to Los Angeles, and start putting ads in the paper?"

Drake shrugged his shoulders and said, "If you want us to keep on we'll find out. Probably it's some form of blackmail which involves the family in some way."

"You say there are no other members of the family?" Mason asked.

"That's all. The parents are dead. Diana and her brother, Edgar, are the only survivors at the present time. Diana has never been married. Edgar is a bachelor, but the rumor is he's going to announce an engagement to a wealthy heiress—although that's just rumor."

"How old?" Mason asked.

"Diana?"

"No, Edgar."

"A little over twenty-one."

"Younger than Diana," Mason said thoughtfully.

"A couple of years."

"She could try to mother him a little," Mason said.

"It has been done," Drake conceded. . . . "How about you giving a helping hand?"

"To whom?"

"To me, and, incidentally, to yourself," Drake said. "If you can tell me about Diana's case and why you're interested I may be able to help both of you. At least I can save you a little money."

Mason shook his head. "I can't, Paul. I'm bound by professional ethics."

"Do you want me to keep on the job?" Drake asked.

"For a while," Mason said.

"Want me to put a tail on her?"

Mason said, "I'd like to know where she goes and who

she sees, but that's a pretty ticklish job because I don't want her to feel that she's being shadowed. If that happened it might alarm her and cause her to take steps which would be against her own best interests."

Drake said, "Then you'd better let me make a very casual shadow job of it, because on a tight shadow job the subject is quite frequently aware of the tail. It's a pretty difficult job to put on a real shadow and guarantee that the subject is completely unaware of it."

"Then make it a loose shadow job," Mason said.

"Of course," Drake went on, "where money is no object, we can use enough operatives to—"

"We haven't an unlimited expense account here, Paul, and I don't know that it's absolutely imperative that we know where this young woman goes and what she does, but I would like to keep in touch with her and I would dislike very, very much to have her become alarmed and take a powder."

"Okay," Drake said, "I'll see what can be done. We'll make a loose tail job of it. When do you want a report?"

"Whenever you have anything worthwhile," Mason said, put his hand briefly on Paul Drake's shoulder, and walked down to his own office.

5

◉

THE WILLATSON HOTEL was a commercial hotel which operated on a basis of live-and-let-live. Very little attention was paid to people who came through the doors, crossed the lobby, and walked directly to the elevator.

Perry Mason, however, felt it better to follow the procedure of being a total stranger.

He went to the desk, caught the eye of the clerk, and said, "Do you have a Miss Diana Deering registered here?"

"Just a moment."

The clerk looked through a file and said, "Seven-sixty-seven."

"Will you announce me, please?"

The clerk seemed bored. "What name?"

"She won't know the name," Mason said. "It's in connection with a social-security inquiry. Tell her it has to do with thirty-six, dash, twenty-four, dash, thirty-six."

The clerk said, "Very well," picked up the phone, rang Room 767 and said, "A gentleman is here to see you in connection with an inquiry about a number. I believe it's a social-security number. . . . What's that? . . . Very well, I'll tell him if that's your message."

He turned to Mason, said, "She is having no social-security problems. You'll have to give me a name or—"

Mason raised his voice and said, "You didn't give her the number: thirty-six, twenty-four, thirty-six."

The receiver suddenly made squawking sounds.

The clerk said, "It's quite all right. She wants to see you. She heard you give the number over the telephone. You may go on up."

The clerk hung up the telephone and returned to the task of bookkeeping with a manner of bored indifference.

Mason took the elevator to the seventh floor and knocked on the door of Room 767.

The young woman who had been in his office earlier in the week opened the door quickly, then fell back in amazement. "Good heavens!" she exclaimed. "You!"

"Why not?" Mason asked.

"How . . . how did you know where I was? . . . How did you know who I—"

Mason pushed his way into the room as she fell back, closed the door, walked over to a chair, and seated himself.

"Now, let's talk a little sense for a change," he said. "Your real name is Diana?"

"Yes."

"Diana what?"

"Diana Deering."

"Let's try doing better than that," Mason said.

"That's my name, Mr. Mason. You ask down at the desk if you don't believe it. That's—"

"That's the name you're registered under," Mason interrupted. "But that's not your name. How about Diana Douglas of San Francisco? Would that do any better?"

For a moment her eyes showed dismay, then her face flushed. "I retained you as *my* attorney," she said. "You're supposed to help me, not to go chasing around trying to uncover things about my past, trying to cooperate with . . ."

Her voice trailed into silence.

"With the police?" Mason asked.

35

"No, not with the police," she said. "Thank heavens, I haven't done anything that violates the law."

"Are you sure?"

"Of course I'm sure."

"Look here," Mason said, "I'm an attorney. People come to me when they're in trouble. I'm supposed to help them. You came to me and sneaked up on my blind side. I didn't do a very good job of helping you. I'm sorry about that. That's why I decided I'd better find you before it was too late."

"You're mistaken, Mr. Mason. I'm not in any trouble. I'm trying to—to protect a friend."

"You're in trouble," Mason said. "Does the Escobar Import and Export Company know where you are?"

"I don't know. . . . They know that I'm away on personal business."

Mason reached across her lap, picked up the black handbag.

"You leave that alone!" she screamed, grabbing his arm with both hands.

Mason kept his grip on the bag.

"Full of money?" he asked.

"That's none of your business. I want to fire you right now. I wanted an attorney to protect me. You're worse than the police. Let go of that bag. You're fired!"

"Where did you get the money that's in this bag?" Mason asked.

"That's none of your business!"

"Did you, perhaps, embezzle it from the company where you worked?" the lawyer asked.

"Good heavens, no!"

"You're sure?"

"Of course I'm sure!"

Mason shook his head. "Would it surprise you to know that the Escobar Import and Export Company called in an auditor to go over its books?"

Her face showed surprise, then consternation. Her grip

on his arm weakened. "Why, why in the world—good heavens . . . they couldn't."

"That's the information I have," Mason said. "Now, suppose you do a little talking and try telling the truth for a change. What's your capacity with the Escobar Import and Export Company? What do you do?"

"I'm a cashier and bookkeeper. I have charge of foreign exchange and foreign payments. I . . . Mr. Mason, there *must* be some mistake."

Mason said, "Let's look at basic facts. You come to my office. You have a bag that's loaded with money. You—"

"How did you know about what's in this bag?"

"My receptionist had a chance to see the inside of it," Mason said. "It was loaded with bills."

"Oh," she said, and then was silent.

Mason said, "You put an ad in the paper indicating that you were here to pay off a blackmail demand. So, let's put two and two together. You take an assumed name. You come to Los Angeles. You put an ad in the paper. You are dealing with a blackmailer. You have a large sum of money with you in the form of cash. The company where you work evidently feels some money is missing. It calls in an auditor."

Diana sat silent. From the open window came noises of traffic from the street.

"Well?" Mason asked, after a while.

"It's absolutely fantastic," she said, removing her hands from Mason's arm. "There's—there's nothing I can do."

"I'm trying to help you," Mason reminded her. "You've made it rather difficult for me so far. Perhaps if you tried telling me the truth I could put in my time helping you instead of running around in circles trying to cut your back trail. . . . Now, *did* you embezzle that money?"

"Heavens, no!"

37

"How much money do you have in this bag in the form of cash?"

"Five thousand dollars."

"Where did you get it?"

She was silent for a moment, then said, "I'm going to tell you the truth."

Mason settled back in his chair, said, "You're a little bit late with it and I don't know how much time we have, but go ahead."

She said, "The whole thing happened when my brother was injured in an automobile accident. After they took him to the hospital I went to his room to get some things for him—shaving things and things of that sort that I thought he'd need in the hospital, and I found his bags all packed and a letter addressed simply 'DEAR FUGITIVE.' The letter said that the writer was fed up with waiting around; that either he should receive five thousand dollars by Tuesday night or other action would be taken."

"How was the letter written?" Mason asked.

"In typing. It was all typed, even the signature."

"And the signature was 36-24-36?"

"That's right."

"And the postmark?"

"Los Angeles."

"So, what did you do?"

"Mr. Mason, my brother was unconscious in the hospital. I couldn't let him down. I arranged to put an ad in the paper, just as the letter said I was to do, and came down here."

"And the money?"

"My brother had the money in a briefcase in his apartment. He was all ready to go. Apparently, he was going to drive down. He had the briefcase with the money, a suitcase and an overnight bag."

"And where did he get the money?"

"Mr. Mason, I . . . I don't know."

38

"Your brother works in the same company you do?"

"Yes."

"Could he have embezzled the money from the company?"

"Mr. Mason, in the first place Edgar wouldn't ever do anything criminal. In the second place, he wouldn't have had access to the money. The cash is kept in a money safe in the vault. Only the top executives have the combination."

"But you have it?"

"Yes, it's my job to check the books on the cash—not every day, but twice a month I have to add up the withdrawal slips and see that everything balances."

"Tell me a little more about Edgar," Mason said.

"He's young. He's a year and a half younger than I am. He . . . our parents were killed five years ago. I've tried to help Edgar every way I could. He's a sensitive individual who—"

"You're both working for the Escobar Export and Import Company. Who got the job there first?"

"I did."

"What about the company?"

"It engages in exports and imports just as the name indicates."

"What kind of a company?"

"What do you mean?"

"A big company, a little company, a—"

"No, it's pretty much of a one-man concern."

"Who's the big wheel?"

"Mr. Gage—Franklin T. Gage."

"How many employees?"

"Oh, perhaps ten or fifteen altogether. There are five working full time in the office and an auditor and tax man."

"Do I understand then there are others who work outside of the office?"

"Yes, there are scouts and buyers."

"But nevertheless they are employees?"

"In a sense, yes."

"How old a man is Franklin Gage?"

"Forty-something or other. Perhaps forty-five."

"He runs the company?"

"Yes. He's the big shot."

"Who's next in command?"

"Homer."

"Homer Gage?"

"Yes."

"His son?"

"His nephew."

Mason's eyes narrowed thoughtfully. "How long after you started work there did your brother, Edgar, start work?"

"About six months."

"And what was he doing during those six months?"

"He was doing nothing. He had been let out at the place where he was working. He became involved in a lot of office intrigue and— It's too long a story to tell you."

"Who supported him?"

"I did."

"So then after six months, you got a job for him there at the company where you work. . . . Who gave him the job, Franklin Gage or Homer?"

"Franklin."

Mason regarded her shrewdly. "You didn't talk to Homer about it?"

"I talked to Mr. Gage. Mr. Franklin Gage."

"At the office?"

"No, I worked late one night and he said that I'd missed my dinner on account of working and that the company was going to buy my dinner."

"So in the intimacy of that little dinner party you took occasion to tell him about your brother and asked him if Edgar could have a job?"

40

"Yes. Only you make it sound so very . . . so very calculating."

Mason brushed her remark aside with a wave of his hand. "How did Homer react to that?"

"I didn't ask Homer."

"That wasn't my question," Mason answered. "I wanted to know how Homer reacted to it."

"Well," she said, "I think that Homer felt that we really didn't need to take on Edgar at the time."

"And what are Edgar's duties? What does he do?"

"He's a liaison man."

"Now then," Mason went on, "Edgar had been out of work for six months and you had been supporting him?"

"I'd been helping out. He had unemployment insurance and—"

"So where," Mason interrupted, "did he get five thousand dollars in cash?"

"I—I just don't know."

"Not from you?"

"No."

"Do you have five thousand dollars?"

"I . . . yes, I do."

"More than that?"

"A very little more."

"Where is it?"

"In savings banks."

Mason took mental inventory of the situation, then said abruptly, "This Homer Gage, what's his attitude toward you?"

"Friendly."

"Very friendly?" Mason asked.

"I think he'd like to be."

"Married or single?"

"Married."

"Ever met his wife?"

"Not formally. She's been at the office a couple of times to get checks cashed or something like that. She's

41

smart-looking . . . you know, very much on the ball. They say she's a bitch."

"Her husband steps out?"

"I wouldn't know. I do know his married life isn't happy."

"You see him looking at the other girls in the office. Doubtless you've discussed him with the other girls. Does he keep them after hours?"

"I don't know. I think perhaps . . . well, I just don't know."

"Does he step out?"

"I told you I wouldn't know."

"Does he step out?"

"All right, if you're going to be insistent about it, I think he does, but I wouldn't know."

"And Homer's had you stay after hours more than once?"

She hesitated, then said, in a low voice, "Yes." Then added quickly, "You see the business is very, very unconventional. It's a complicated deal of buying and selling in large lots, and quite frequently the deals are made on a spot-cash basis.

"This is particularly true in connection with Oriental goods. You see, we have to have a Certificate of Origin on goods which are taken out of Hong Kong, for instance, and . . . well, sometimes matters have to be handled with a great deal of diplomacy."

"So sometimes you work late?"

"Yes."

"And Homer has had you work late?"

"Yes."

"And taken you out to dinner?"

"Twice."

"And propositioned you?"

"What do you mean by that, Mr. Mason?"

"You know what I mean."

"If you mean has he ever come out cold turkey with a

42

proposition, the answer is 'no', but all men proposition you. They size you up. They look you over. They make a remark occasionally with a double meaning. They tell a story that's a little broad. They are quick to follow up any opening. . . . Mr. Mason, I don't need to tell you how men are. They're always on the lookout in an aggressive way, and if they get an opening they follow up and just keep pushing."

"And Homer Gage has been like that?"

"He's been like that. He isn't going to come right out in the open and make any proposition and get rebuffed and perhaps have his uncle know what is happening and—"

"The uncle likes you?" Mason said.

"Yes, he does."

"Married or single?"

"He's a widower."

"And how about him? Does he have the aggressive, masculine mannerisms?"

"No, no, Mr. Mason. Mr. Franklin Gage is very much of a gentleman. He is courteous and considerate and— well, he's an older, more mature man and his attitude is . . ."

"Fatherly?" Mason ventured, as she hesitated.

"Well, not exactly fatherly. More like an uncle or something of that sort."

"But he likes you?"

"I think so."

"Very much?"

"I think so. You see, I am pretty good at adjusting myself in a business way and I have tried to do a good job there at the export and import. And Mr. Gage, Mr. Franklin Gage, knows it.

"In a quiet way he's very nice to—to all of the girls who work in the office."

"How many other than you?"

"Three."

"Names?"

43

"Helen Albert, a stenographer; Joyce Baffin, a secretary-stenographer, but her duties are mostly of a secretarial nature—for Homer Gage; and Ellen Candler, who has charge of the mail and the files."

"Suppose a person wanted to embezzle money from the company?" Mason said. "Would it be easy?"

"Very easy—too easy for those who had the combination to the cash safe. The company keeps large sums of money on hand. Occasionally it's necessary to make deals on a completely cash basis with no voucher of any kind."

"Bribery?" Mason asked.

"I don't think so."

"Smuggling?"

"I don't think it's anything like that."

"And how do you keep your books under those circumstances?" Mason asked.

"Well, there's a certain amount of juggling with the cash so that the books are regular, but sometimes there are transactions which—well, it would be a little difficult to trace them."

"So your brother could very easily have embezzled five thousand dollars to go to Los Angeles and pay off a blackmailer?"

"Mr. Mason, I tell you Edgar wouldn't do that, and even if he had wanted to he couldn't have done it. He doesn't have the combination to the cash safe."

"Who does have the combination?"

"Franklin Gage, Homer Gage, Stewart Garland, our income-tax man, and myself."

"You found five thousand dollars in cash in Edgar's apartment?"

"Yes. I've told you that two or three times. It's the truth."

"And you knew Edgar hadn't had an opportunity to save that much out of his salary since he'd started work?"

"Well, yes."

"Where did you think he got it?"

She said, "My brother is—well, he has friends. He's very likable, very magnetic, and I think he has friends who would help him out in a situation of that sort. . . . That's what I thought."

"All right," Mason said, "let's face it. You're in a jam. You've come to Los Angeles under an assumed name. You've got five thousand dollars in cash. You're mixed up with a blackmailer. Suppose the accounts at the Escobar Import and Export Company show a five-thousand-dollar deficit?"

Her hand went to her throat.

"Now, you're getting the point," Mason told her. "There's only one thing for you to do. Get a plane back to San Francisco. Get into your office tomorrow morning.

"Now, do exactly as I say. If it turns out an auditor says there's a five-thousand-dollar shortage, just laugh and say, 'Oh, no, there isn't.' Tell the auditor that your brother was working on a company deal at the time of the accident; that you took out five thousand dollars to finance that deal; that Edgar asked you not to make an entry until he had had a chance to discuss the deal with Franklin Gage; that he thought it was going to be a good deal for the company but that you knew all about the five thousand dollars that he had and knew that it was company money.

"You go to a local bank this afternoon, deposit the five thousand, buy a cashier's check payable to you as trustee. As soon as your brother recovers consciousness, you'll see him before anyone else does. . . . Make certain of that. As a member of the family you'll have the right-of-way.

"Then you can use your own judgment."

"But, Mr. Mason, this thing is coming to a head. It isn't going to wait. This blackmailer—or whatever it is— this letter that my brother had was most urgent, imperative, demanding."

"What did you do with that letter?"

45

"I burned it."

Mason said, "There was an ad in the paper for you to make contact with a cab passenger at—"

"Heavens, how did you know about that?" she asked.

"We make it a point to read the personal ads," Mason said. "Why didn't you contact the man in the taxicab?"

"Because I didn't like the looks of the thing. There were two passengers, a man and a woman. It was night, yet they both were wearing dark glasses. I thought it was a trap of some kind. I . . . well, I decided to pass it up. When I made contact I wanted it to be where there were no witnesses."

"I see," Mason said thoughtfully, then abruptly he walked over to the telephone, asked the switchboard operator for an outside line, and got Paul Drake's office.

"Paul," he said, "I want a female operative—blonde, twenty-two, twenty-three, or twenty-four, with a good figure—to come to the Willatson Hotel and go to Room Seven-sixty-seven.

"She can't carry anything with her except a handbag. She can make purchases and have them sent in from the department stores where she buys. She'll take the name of Diana Deering, which is the name of the present occupant of the room."

"I know," Drake said.

"She'll masquerade as Diana Deering. She'll make it a point to get acquainted with the bellboys, with the clerks as they come on duty. She can ask them questions. Inquire about a monthly rate on the room. Do anything which will attract attention to herself as Diana Deering. And quit tailing the real Diana."

Drake said, "It happens that I have a girl who fits the description in the office right now, Perry. She's Stella Grimes. She's worked on one of your cases before, although I don't know if you've seen her personally. The only thing is she's a little older."

"How much older?" Mason asked.

"Tut, tut," Drake said, "you're asking questions."

"You think she can get by?"

"I think she can get by," Drake said.

"Get her up here," Mason told him.

"But what about me?" Diana asked when Mason hung up.

"You're going to get that cashier's check payable to you as trustee and then go back to San Francisco."

"And what about my baggage?"

"You'll have to wait for that."

"How will I get it out of the hotel? Don't they check people when you leave with baggage?"

"Sure they do," Mason said, "but we'll fix that."

"How?"

"I'll rent a room here at the hotel. I'll try to get one on the same floor. We'll move your baggage into that room. Then I'll check out, carrying the baggage with me, go right to the desk, and pay the bill on that room. They'll have no way of knowing that one of the suitcases I'll have with me was taken from Room Seven-sixty-seven."

"And what about this girl who is going to masquerade as me?"

"She'll deal with the blackmailer."

"And if I've turned the money in for a cashier's check, what will we pay him—or her?"

"We won't," Mason said. "It's against the policy of the office to pay blackmailers."

"But what are you going to do? How can you avoid payment?"

"I don't know," Mason told her. "We'll play it by ear. I wish to hell your brother would regain consciousness so we could find out what it's all about. . . . Get your suitcase packed."

Tears came to her eyes. "Edgar's a wonderful boy, Mr. Mason."

Mason said, "I'm going down to a baggage store and get a suitcase. I'll stuff it full of old paper, come back,

47

and check into the hotel—somewhere on the seventh floor, if possible. I want you to wait right here. Promise me you won't go out until I get back."

"I promise."

"And don't answer the phone," Mason warned.

"I . . . all right, if you say so."

"I say so," Mason told her.

The lawyer walked to the door, turned, smiled, and said, "You'll be all right, Diana."

Her eyes started to blink rapidly. "You're wonderful," she said. "I wish I'd told you all about it when I first came to your office."

"You can say that again," Mason told her. "We might have headed off that damned auditor. As it is now, you're hooked."

"What do you mean?"

"Figure it out," Mason said. "We're starting a little late. You've come to Los Angeles, registered in a hotel under an assumed name. You have a bag containing five thousand dollars in currency. And if the company where you work *should* happen to be short five thousand dollars, and if your brother *should* happen to die, and if you're arrested before you get that cashier's check—figure where you'll be."

Mason walked out as her mouth slowly opened. He closed the door gently behind him.

6

●

THE LAWYER took the elevator to the lobby, went to a baggage store two doors down the street, selected a suitcase, paid for it; then he crossed to a secondhand bookstore.

"I'm looking for some books dealing with the history of early California and, particularly, with the discovery of gold," he said.

The clerk led him to a shelf.

"Do you," Mason asked, "have paperback books?"

"Oh, yes, we have quite a selection."

"I also want to get some of those books for lighter reading," Mason said. "I'll pick out some."

Ten minutes later Mason presented himself at the checking-out desk with an armful of books.

The cashier scanned the penciled prices marked on the title pages, gave Mason the total figure, $27.85.

"All right," Mason said, "I'll . . . why not put them in this suitcase?"

The clerk, his attention drawn to the suitcase, leaned forward to pick it up and make sure it was empty, then smiled and said, "That's quite all right. Put them in there if you want."

Mason put the books in the suitcase, paid the bill, walked back to the Hotel Willatson, said, "I'm going to be here probably overnight. I'd like to have a room somewhere above the fifth floor. I don't like traffic noises."

"I can let you have eleven-eighty-four," the room clerk said, "if you're only going to be here one night, Mister . . . uh . . ."

"Mason," Perry Mason said. "I prefer to be a little lower than the eleventh floor. What have you got on the eighth?"

"We're all taken up."

"The seventh?"

"I have one room on the seventh floor—seven-eighty-nine. It's a slightly larger room than our average and a little more expensive. . . ."

"That's all right," Mason said, "I'll take it. I'm likely to be here only one night."

The lawyer registered, gave a bellboy a dollar to take his bag and escort him up to the room, waited until the bellboy had withdrawn; then put the room key in his pocket and walked down the hall to 767.

He tapped gently on the panels.

Diana Douglas opened the door.

"Mr. Mason," she said, "I've been thinking over what you said. It's—I'm afraid I'm in a terrible position."

"It'll be all right," Mason told her, "I'll take charge."

"You're going to—to need more than the money I gave you."

"Unfortunately," Mason said, "I spent a large amount of the money you gave me trying to check up on you and get back of the falsehoods you had told me. As it is now . . ."

The lawyer broke off as a knuckle tapped gently on the door.

Diana Douglas raised inquiring eyebrows.

Mason strode across the room, opened the door to confront an alert-looking young woman with blonde hair, blue eyes, and that something in her bearing which radi-

50

ated competency and ability to look after herself under any circumstances.

The woman smiled at him and said, "I recognize you, Mr. Mason, but you probably don't know me. I'm from— well, I'm Stella Grimes."

"Come in, Stella," Mason said.

The lawyer closed the door and said, "Stella, this is Diana Douglas. She's registered here as Diana Deering. You're going to take over."

"Who am I?" Stella asked. "Diana Douglas or Diana Deering? . . . And how do you do, Diana. I'm pleased to meet you."

"As far as the hotel is concerned you're Diana Deering," Mason said. "I'll let you read an ad which appeared in the paper."

Mason handed her a copy of the ad which Diana had inserted in the paper and which was signed "36-24-36."

"I see, Mr. Mason," Stella said, reading the ad carefully. Then she looked at Diana, looked at Perry Mason, and said, "Precisely what do I do?"

"You identify yourself here as Diana Deering," Mason said. "You sit tight and await developments and you report."

"Report on what?"

"On everything."

"Can you give me any line on what is supposed to happen?" she asked. "I take it that I'm supposed to be here to make a cash payment. Suppose someone turns up and wants the cash?"

"Then you stall," Mason said.

She nodded, took a card from her purse, scribbled something on it, and said, "You'll probably want one of my cards, Mr. Mason."

The lawyer took the card she had given him. On the back was scribbled, *"I've seen her before. I was the operative in the taxicab with Paul Drake last night."*

Mason slipped the card in his pocket. "Exactly," he

51

said, "I'll call you by name if I have to, but in the meantime I want you to impress upon the clerk that if someone calls and asks for you by the code numbers of thirty-six, twenty-four, thirty-six that the call is to be put through. You think you can make up a good story?"

"I can try," she said.

"What do you have in the way of baggage?" Mason asked.

"Just this purse that I brought in with me. I was instructed not to attract attention by coming in with any more than this."

"You can buy what you need at the department stores and have it sent in," Mason said.

"Any idea how long I'll be here?"

"It may be only a day. It may be three or four days. Just sit down and make yourself at home. I'll be right back."

"I'll take your suitcase down to Room Seven-eighty-nine, Diana," he said. "Later on I'll check out with it and give it to you in San Francisco. In the meantime, you take this key, go on down to seven-eighty-nine, and wait. Take that black bag and your purse with you. I'll be seeing you in seven-eighty-nine in a few minutes. You use that room until you're ready to get the cashier's check and leave for the airport. Don't come back to this room under any circumstances and don't try to leave Room Seven-eighty-nine until I give you the all-clear sign."

"Any idea when that will be?" she asked.

"When I think the coast is clear."

"Suppose the banks close before you say it's okay for me to leave?"

"Then you'll have to keep the money with you until you get to San Francisco. Get the cashier's check there, but don't enter the office tomorrow until you have that check. When the office opens tomorrow I'll be on hand to help. We'll fix up the details before we leave Room

Seven-eighty-nine. In the meantime, I want you out of here."

She nodded, said, "I want to get a couple of things from the bathroom."

Stella Grimes said to Mason, "You'd better brief *me* a little more. What happens if someone calls on me by this number, wants me to meet him with a sum of cash?"

"Stall it along and notify Paul," Mason told her.

"And if there isn't time for that?"

"Make time."

"Am I to have any idea what it's all about?" she asked.

"Nothing that I can tell you," Mason said.

"Am I the party that's being blackmailed?"

"No," Mason said, "you're a girl friend, an angel who's going to put up the money, but before you put up the money you want to be absolutely certain that you're getting what you're paying for. You're a fairly wealthy young woman, but you're rough, you're tough, you're hard-boiled. You know your way around. . . . Got a gun?"

By way of answer she reached down the V of her blouse and suddenly produced a wicked-looking, snub-nosed revolver.

"I'm wearing my working bra," she said as Diana emerged from the bathroom, her hands filled with toilet articles.

"Good enough," Mason told her. "I hope you don't have to reach for it, but I'm glad you've got it. We don't know with whom we're dealing."

"Have there been—other payments?" she asked.

"That we don't know," Mason said. "The present demand is for five grand. The probabilities are there's been one earlier payment and this is—you know, the old story, the guy hates to be a blackmailer. He wants to begin life all over again. He had intended to collect a thousand or so every few months, but he just can't live with himself

53

on that kind of a deal. If he can get five grand he's going to buy a little farm way out in the sticks and forget all about his past and turn over a new leaf.

"In that case he'll tell the sucker he'll be done with payments forevermore, and all that sort of talk. . . . You know the line."

"I know the line," she said, smiling, "I've heard it."

Mason took Diana's suitcase and said, "We're taking this down to seven-eighty-nine, Diana. You take that black bag. Be sure to follow instructions."

"And I'll see you in San Francisco?"

"That's right. I'll get in touch with you. Put your phone number and address here in my notebook. But stay in seven-eighty-nine until I give you an all-clear."

The lawyer handed her his open notebook. Diana took it and carefully made the notations Mason asked, picked up the black bag, gave Stella her hand, said, "Thanks, sister. Be careful, and keep wearing that bra."

She turned to Perry Mason and said, "You're all right. You're good. . . . Let me carry my suitcase. I'll wait. I have the key to seven-eighty-nine." Impulsively she kissed him on the cheek, picked up the suitcase, the black bag and purse, crossed swiftly to the door, opened it, and was gone.

Mason settled himself in a chair, motioned for Stella to be seated, said, "I'm playing this pretty much in the dark myself, Stella. The blackmailer will be expecting the pay-off will be made by a man. You'll have to act the part of the financial angel, probably related to the sucker. However, you're skeptical, hard-boiled, and—"

The lawyer broke off as knuckles tapped on the door.

"This may be it," he said. "Gosh, I hope Diana got down to seven-eighty-nine and out of sight."

The lawyer went to the door, opened it, and said, "Yes, what is it?"

The man who stood on the threshold was a small man in his early thirties. He had black hair which was very

54

sleek and glossy, parted in the middle and curled back from his forehead at the temples. He was wearing dark glasses and well-pressed brown slacks with a darker brown sport coat. His shirt was tan, and an expensive bolo tie furnished ornamentation.

"How do you do?" he said. "I called in response to an ad in the paper. I . . ." He broke off as he caught sight of Stella Grimes.

"That's all right," Mason said. "Come in."

The man hesitated, then extended a well-manicured hand, the nails highly polished, the skin soft and elaborately caref for.

"Cassel," he said, smiling, "C-A-S-S-E-L. I had hardly expected you would come down in person, Mr.—"

Mason held up his left hand as he shook Cassel's right hand.

"No names, please."

"All right, no names," Cassel said.

He regarded Stella Grimes appraisingly, as a cattle buyer might size up a prime heifer. There was a puzzled frown on his forehead which speedily gave way to an oily smile.

"We'll dispense with introductions," Mason said abruptly.

Cassel said, "As you wish. However, we don't put on our best performances in front of an audience, you know." He made a deprecatory gesture. "I confess *I* get stage fright," he said. "I may not be able to recall my lines at all."

Stella said, "Perhaps you two would like to have me go in the bathroom and close the door."

"No, no, no," Cassel said. "Nowhere in the room, please. I am *very* self-conscious."

Mason laughed. "Mr. Cassel and I have some very private business to discuss, Stella. I'm sorry that you and I didn't have more of an opportunity to talk, but it follows that we'll get together sometime later. I dislike

55

these interruptions as much as you do, but that's the way things go. . . . Mr. Cassel and I are going to have a business talk, and *following* that I'll be in and out for a while, but I'll give you a ring whenever I'm at liberty. However, don't wait for my call. Just *follow* your own inclinations."

Stella Grimes regarded Mason thoughtfully for a few seconds, then said, "I think I've got it," to Mason, and, turning to Cassel said, "Good-by, Mr. Cassel."

She walked casually over to Perry Mason, put her lips up to be kissed as in a pleasant but often-repeated salutation of affection, then left the room.

"Nice babe," Cassel said, eying Mason.

Mason shrugged. "I like her."

"Known her long?"

Mason smiled. "Not long enough."

"You're not handing me *that* line," Cassel said.

"I'm handing you nothing."

"You can say that again."

There was a brief period of silence.

"Okay," Cassel said, "let's quit stalling around and get down to business. You brought it with you?"

"Brought what?" Mason asked.

"Now, let's not be cagey about this," Cassel said irritably. "I don't think that you'd be guilty of a breach of faith by trying to blow the whistle but . . . to hell with this stuff, let's take a look."

Cassel strode to the bathroom, jerked the door open, looked around inside, surveyed the walls of the room, moved a couple of pictures looking for a concealed microphone.

"Don't be simple," Mason said when he had finished.

Cassel's eyes were suspicious. "I don't like the way you're going about this," he said.

"What's wrong with the way I'm going about it?"

"You want me to make statements," Cassel said. "I'm

not making statements. I'm here. You're here. It's your move."

Mason said, "I'm the one that should be suspicious. What made you so long showing up?"

"I had other matters which took me out of town for a while," Cassel said. "I called as soon as I came back and got free. . . . By the way, there was an ad in one of the evening papers. Do you know anything about that?"

Mason said, "I know enough about it to know that I wasted a lot of time giving the occupants of a taxicab an opportunity to give me the double take."

"And you received no signal?"

"No."

Cassel shook his head. "I don't like that. I don't like that at all. It means some third party is trying to chisel in on the deal."

"*You* don't like it," Mason said. "How do you suppose I feel about it? What the hell are you trying to do?"

Cassel thought for a moment, glanced at Mason, looked away, looked back at Mason again, frowned, said, "There's something familiar about your face. Have I ever met you before?"

"I don't think so."

"Well, every once in a while you— Wait a minute, wait a minute . . . I've seen your picture somewhere!"

"That's not at all impossible." Mason conceded.

"Hell's bells," Cassel said, "I've got it. Why dammit, you're a lawyer. Your name is Mason."

Mason didn't let his face change expression by so much as the flicker of an eyelash.

"That's right," he said, "Perry Mason."

"What are you trying to pull?" Cassel asked. "That wasn't part of the deal. I don't want to have any business dealings with any damn lawyer."

Mason smiled affably. "I'm not any damn lawyer," he said. "I'm a particularly special, high-priced lawyer."

"I'll say you are," Cassel said, edging toward the door.

"What the hell's the matter with you, Mason? Are you crazy? You act as though you've got the room bugged. You know as well as I do that if you're trying to blow any whistles you're cutting your client's throat. You're acting just as if this was some kind of a shakedown."

Mason said nothing.

"You know the proposition." Cassel said. "It's a business proposition. Your client doesn't have any choice in the matter but, under the circumstances, he can't have any protection. Any agreement that's made isn't worth the powder and shot to blow it up."

Mason said, "That doesn't prevent me from representing my client."

Cassel sneered. "It means that we've had our sights too low," he said. "If your client has got money enough to pay a high-priced lawyer a fat fee in a deal of this kind we've been too naïve. I don't blame you, I blame us. We aren't asking enough."

"Keep talking," Mason said. "I'm listening."

Cassel, annoyed now, said, "This isn't a payoff. This is something your client owes. . . . I'm not going to argue with you, Mason, have you got it or haven't you?"

"If you're referring to the money," Mason said, "I don't have it, and if I did have it I wouldn't pay it over on the strength of any proposition you've made so far."

"What's wrong with my proposition?" Cassel asked.

"You said it yourself. Any agreement is worthless. You could come back tomorrow and begin all over again."

"I wouldn't be foolish enough to do that," Cassel said.

"Why not?"

"Well, it wouldn't be . . . ethical."

Mason laughed.

Cassel's face darkened. "Look, Mason, you're supposed to be high-powered. You're supposed to be the last word. But all you're doing so far is making it tough for your client. He had a chance to get off the hook at a bargain price. Now, things are going up."

"Don't say that," Mason said, "or prices may go down."

"You think you can pull a rabbit out of a hat?" Cassel asked sneeringly.

Mason said, "That's what I'm noted for, pulling rabbits out of hats and coming up with another ace when it's least expected."

Cassel started angrily for the door, turned, said, "Look, Mason, let's be businesslike. Your client pays five grand and that's all there is to it."

"And what does he get in return for the five grand?"

"Immunity."

"What about the proofs?"

Cassel's face showed surprise. "What are you talking about, the proofs?"

Mason recovered easily. "The proofs of your integrity, of the fact that my client has immunity."

"Draw up an agreement," Cassel said.

"You said yourself it wouldn't be worth anything."

"Not in court," Cassel said, "and not if the right party brings the action. But it closes a lot of doors—all the doors your client needs to worry about."

"I'll think it over," Mason conceded.

"Think it over, hell! You haven't got a lot of time to think things over. This is a hot deal. If you're going to go for it, you've got to move and move fast."

"Where can I reach you?" Mason asked.

Cassel surveyed him thoughtfully. "You're asking a lot of questions."

"All right," Mason said, "where can I leave the money—if I decide to leave the money?"

Cassel said, "Look, your phone number is listed. You have an office. I don't know what you're doing here in the hotel. I'll give you a call from a pay station at your office."

"When?"

"When I get damned good and ready," Cassel said. He

59

opened the door and walked out, slamming the door behind him.

Mason went to the telephone, put a call through the switchboard to Paul Drake's office.

"Perry Mason talking, Paul. Did Stella Grimes phone in for an operative to do a tailing job?"

"Haven't heard from her," Drake said. "The last I knew she was in the Willatson Hotel. Weren't you with her?"

"I was," Mason said. "I had a man I wanted followed. I tried to give her a signal."

"If you gave her a signal, she got it all right," Drake said. "She's a bright babe. Was there any reason why she couldn't do the tailing job herself?"

"The only trouble is, the subject knows her," Mason said. "A stranger would have been better."

"Well, she probably didn't have time to phone in. What was it, a rush job?"

"It was one hell of a rush job."

"You'll be hearing from her," Drake predicted.

Mason hung up the phone, walked casually around the room, again picked up the telephone, said to the hotel operator, "Ring Room Seven-eighty-nine, please."

It was some time before Diana Douglas answered the phone.

"Yes?" she asked.

Mason said, "It took you a while to answer, Diana."

"I didn't know whether I should answer or not. How's everything down your way? I thought you were coming to—"

"We were interrupted," Mason said. "The other party to the transaction showed up."

"You mean . . . you mean the blackmailer?"

"Yes."

"What happened?"

"We stalled around for a while," Mason said, "and, unfortunately, he made me."

"What do you mean by that?"

"He knew who I was. He recognized me from the photographs he had seen in the papers from time to time."

"Is that bad?" she asked.

"It may be good," Mason said. "I think he was just a little frightened. . . . I just wanted to tell you to sit tight until you hear from me. It's *very* important that you keep under cover."

"I should be—well, shouldn't I be getting my ticket back to San Francisco? And the banks will be closed here."

"We can't hurry this now," Mason said. "There may be developments. Wait a few minutes—or up to an hour— until I have a chance to join you. Don't try to leave that room until I give you a signal that everything's in the clear."

7

MASON STRETCHED out in Room 767 at the Willatson Hotel. Despite himself he couldn't refrain from glancing at his wristwatch every few minutes. Twice he got up and paced the floor.

The phone rang.

Mason snatched up the instrument. "Yes?" he said.

Diana Douglas' voice said, "Mr. Mason, I'm frightened. Can I come down there and wait where I can be with you?"

"Definitely not," Mason said. "Sit where you are. I'll have instructions for you soon."

"What do you mean by soon?"

"I hope within a few minutes."

"I'm getting the heebie jeebies sitting here all by myself, Mr. Mason, just looking at the walls and . . . well, I feel that we aren't accomplishing anything this way."

"We're accomplishing a lot more than you realize," Mason said, "and it's imperative that you follow instructions. Just sit tight."

The lawyer hung up the telephone, walked over to the window, looked down at the street, came back to his chair, settled himself; then abruptly got up and started pacing the floor.

The doorknob suddenly turned. The door opened and Stella Grimes walked into the room.

"Any luck?" Mason asked.

"Lots of it," she said, tossing a cardboard box on the bed.

Mason raised his eyebrows.

"Clothes," she said. "I picked up a few necessities at the department store because I felt I might have to ride herd on this room. I just snatched up some things and had them wrapped up because I didn't want to keep you waiting."

"What happened?"

"Well," she said, "I got your signal all right. You wanted him followed."

"That's right."

"Well, of course, he knew me by sight. That complicated the job. I felt that the chances that he was living here in the hotel were rather slim. So I went down to the curb, hired a taxicab, and told the driver to just sit there until I told him I wanted to take off.

"Well, it was absurdly simple, so simple in fact that I feel that perhaps it may have been a frame."

"What happened?"

"Our man had his own car, a Cadillac. He had given the doorman a substantial tip to park it for a few minutes in the loading zone. It must have been a pretty good-sized tip because when he came out the doorman was all attention. He ran over and held the car door open for Cassel and bowed his thanks as Cassel drove off."

"You followed?"

"That's right."

"Get the license number?"

She took a notebook from her pocket and read off the license number, "WVM five-seven-four."

"Could you tail him?" Mason asked.

"It was easy. He went to the Tallmeyer Apartments.

Drove right into the garage in the basement of the apartment house and didn't come out."

"So what did you do?" Mason asked.

"I had my taxi driver drive three blocks to where a car was pulling out from the curb. I said, 'Follow that car but don't let him know he's being followed.' "

"Good work," Mason said.

"Well, of course, this driver got mixed up in traffic. We lost out on a traffic signal and I shrugged my shoulders and said, 'Well, that's the best we can do.' Paid off the cab and took another one and came back here to the hotel. I didn't want the cab driver giving me a double cross and tipping Cassel off, and, as it is, he thinks I'm some sort of a nut. At least, I hope he does."

Mason picked up the phone, said to the operator, "Give me an outside line," then gave the number of the Drake Detective Agency.

"Paul in?" he asked the switchboard operator.

"He just came in, Mr. Mason," she said, recognizing his voice.

"Put him on, will you please?"

Drake's voice came on the line, "Hello."

"Perry Mason, Paul."

"Where are you?"

"At the Willatson Hotel with Stella Grimes. She's back now."

"Doing any good?"

"I think we've struck pay dirt. I want to find out the owner of a Cadillac automobile, license number WVM five-seven-four, and if the owner lives at the Tallmeyer Apartments I'd like to try to find out a little bit about him without doing anything that would arouse suspicion."

Drake said, "Della was asking if it's all right to call you."

"She'd best not," Mason said. "I'll call the office from time to time and see if there's anything important. Was there something in particular on her mind?"

"I don't think so, except that you had a few appointments she had to get you out of with a story about you being called out of town on important business."

"I think that's just what's going to happen," Mason said.

"On the square?"

"On the square. . . . How long will it take you to find out about that car registration?"

"I can have that right quick."

"I'll call back," Mason said. "Get on it as fast as you can."

"How's Stella doing?" Drake asked.

"Fine," Mason said.

"Okay, if you want anything, just put in a call. It'll cost you money, but you'll get the service."

"Will do," Mason said, and hung up.

"Gosh, that guy was mad," Stella said. "You really must have pinned his ears back!"

Mason grinned. "How did you know he was mad, Stella?"

"The way he walked, the way he looked, and the way he left himself wide open."

"I guess he was disappointed," Mason said. "He was expecting a soft touch."

"I'll bet he thought he'd run full speed into a brick wall instead," she observed. "He certainly was one very mad citizen."

The lawyer looked at his wristwatch. "Hold the fort a minute, Stella," he said. "I'm going down the hall. If anything should happen that would complicate the situation hang the DO NOT DISTURB sign on the outside of the door. If Paul Drake phones while I'm down there tell him to call me in that room."

Mason walked down to Room 789 and tapped on the door.

Diana Douglas threw the door open.

"Don't do that!" Mason said.

65

"Do what?"

"Be so eager," Mason said. "Don't open that door until you find out who it is."

"I'm all on edge," she said. "I sit here and thoughts are running through my head. I just can't take this waiting game, Mr. Mason."

Mason said, "Listen very carefully, Diana. How much money do you have?"

"I told you, five thousand dollars."

"That isn't what I meant. I want to know how much you have outside of that."

"I drew out six hundred dollars from my savings account when I left. I wanted to have enough to give you a retainer and—"

"The money that you gave me didn't come out of the five thousand dollars then?"

"No."

"You don't have any idea on earth what this is all about? I want you to be frank, now."

She lowered her eyes. "Well, I suppose it's some kind of an indiscretion that Edgar—well, something he got himself mixed up with. . . . Oh, you know how those rackets go, some kind of a badger game or photographs or— Why do ask me these questions, Mr. Mason?"

"Because," Mason said, "I think we may be following a wrong trail, barking up a wrong tree. Tell me as much as you can about Edgar, only condense it."

"Well," she said, motioning for him to sit down, and seating herself on the edge of the bed, "Edgar is naïve. He's—I won't say he's weak, but he is easily influenced, and I suppose I haven't been of too much help to him trying to make things a little easier for him. I guess life wasn't meant to be that way, Mr. Mason. I guess a man has to develop himself by having things made a little difficult at times instead of having someone whom he looks up to who can smooth things out and take some of the load off his shoulders."

66

"That's what I was coming to," Mason said. "Do you think there's anything in Edgar's past that would have caused him to come to you with a sum of money and ask you to bail him out?"

"I just don't know, Mr. Mason."

"He could have been coming to you?"

"He could have been, but everything indicates he was going to come here to Los Angeles and try to deal with this thirty-six-twenty-four-thirty-six situation."

"And you have no clue as to what that situation is?"

"No."

"Your brother gambled from time to time?" Mason asked.

She chose her words carefully. "Edgar was impulsive."

"He gambled from time to time?"

"Don't all men?"

"He gambled from time to time?"

"Yes," she flared. "You don't need to cross-examine me like that. He gambled from time to time."

"Where?"

"Where do men usually gamble? Sometimes he put two dollars on a horse. Sometimes he put ten dollars on a horse."

"Las Vegas—Reno?"

"He would go to Las Vegas once in a while."

"How much did he ever win?"

"I don't know. I don't think he won much."

"What was the most he ever lost?"

"Eight hundred dollars."

"How do you know?"

"He told me."

"Why did he tell you?"

"Because I'm his sister."

"Why did he tell you?"

"I told you," she blazed back at him. I'm his sister. What are you doing, trying to break down my story?"

"Why did he tell you?" Mason asked.

"All right," she said, lowering her voice, "I had to bail him out. He only had two hundred and I had to make good to the extent of six hundred dollars. He had given a check in Las Vegas and—well, you know how they are."

"How are they?" Mason asked.

She shrugged her shoulders. "I don't know, but the story is that if you gamble on credit with professional gamblers you have to make good or else."

"And Edgar was frightened?"

"Terribly frightened."

"In other words," Mason said, "I'm trying to establish a pattern. When Edgar gets into real trouble, he comes to you. You've been something of a sister and a mother to him."

"Well," she said thoughtfully, "I guess that's right."

"So, if Edgar was in some trouble where he had to raise five thousand dollars, the assumption is he would have told you."

"Unless he—well, it might have been something that he wouldn't have wanted to talk to me about. You know, men can get into scrapes of that sort where they wouldn't want their family to know just what had happened."

"Who told you that?" Mason asked.

"Why, I . . . I've read it."

"Ever talk with Edgar about anything like that?"

"No."

"Know anything about Edgar's sex life?"

"Virtually nothing."

Mason regarded her thoughtfully. He said, "There's a United Airlines plane leaving here for San Francisco at six twenty-seven. I want you to be on that plane.

"I'm going to escort you to the elevator. When you get into the lobby, walk across the lobby casually. Don't look around as though you might be afraid someone was trying to follow you. We'll walk two blocks down the street. There's a taxi stand down there. I'll put you in a cab. Go to the Union Station. When you get to the Union Station, try to make sure that you're not being followed. Then go out, get a cab, and go to the airport. When you get to the airport, wait."

"For what?"

"I'll try to meet you just before you get on the plane. I'll have your baggage. I'll check out of the hotel within an hour or so. That'll give me time to get to my apartment and pack a bag. I'll take my bags and your suitcase and join you at the airport."

"But what about this bag that has the—you know, the money in it?"

"The banks are closed now," Mason said. "You've got to take a chance with that because I want you to be sure and have a cashier's check made to you as trustee when you walk into the office in the morning.

"The minute the banks open in San Francisco, get that cashier's check. Then go to the office just as if nothing out of the ordinary had ever happened. I'll meet you there when you come in. That should be about ten-thirty. Let's have that as the deadline. Don't arrive before ten-thirty. Don't be any later than that if you can avoid it."

The telephone rang.

Mason said, "I think that's for me."

He picked up the instrument, said a cautious, "Hello."

Drake's voice, cheerfully routine, came over the line, "Hi, Perry. Got most of the information you want. It was like rolling off a log."

"What is it?"

"The Cadillac you wanted is registered under the name of Moray Cassel, nine-o-six Tallmeyer Apartments. I've got that much. I haven't been able to find out much about Cassel's habits as yet, but he's been a resident there for something over a year."

"Well, I'll be damned," Mason said in an undertone.

"Something wrong?"

"The guy gave me his right name," Mason said. "You could certainly have fooled me. I had him sized up as a

69

blackmailing pimp, a damned good, prosperous, shrewd pimp."

"And he isn't?" Drake asked.

"That I'll have to find out," Mason said.

"You want him tailed?"

"No. The guy is either too dumb to be true or too smart to be trapped, and I want to find out which it is before I get my feet wet."

"Okay, let me know if there's anything else you want."

"Will do," Mason said, and hung up.

Diana, watching Mason with anxious eyes, said, "Is something wrong?"

Mason, frowning thoughtfully, let the question go unanswered for a few seconds, then said, "I don't know. I seem to have made a mistake in sizing up a situation."

"In what way?"

Mason said, "Thanks to good detective work on the part of the Drake Detective Agency, we have run the blackmailer to ground. His name is Moray Cassel. He drives a Cadillac automobile. He lives in the Tallmeyer Apartments, apartment nine-o-six. But when he came to call on us he gave us his real name. He had his Cadillac parked right in front of the door, having given the doorman a good tip to see that it was left where it would be readily accessible in the parking space reserved for incoming guests with baggage."

"Well, what's wrong about that?" Diana asked. "A lot of people who are on brief errands give the doorman a good tip to keep an eye on their cars. That's the way the doormen make a living. They—"

Mason shook his head. "It isn't that, Diana," he interrupted. "The man simply wasn't that kind of a citizen."

"How do you know?"

Mason said, "Well, I have to admit that this is a time when I may have led with my chin, but I sized the man up as a pimp."

"How, for heaven's sake?"

70

"His appearance. His manner. Everything about him."

"Mr. Mason, do you mean to tell me you can just take a look at a man like that, have a quick conversation with him, and know that he's . . . well, what you call a pimp?"

"No," Mason said at length, "I won't go that far, Diana. And remember when I say the guy's a pimp, I don't mean that he's actually engaged in pimping, I mean he's that type of citizen. He's one who would make his living out of representing a woman in a blackmail scheme."

"But how in the world can you possibly tell? What is there about a man of that sort, the way he dresses, that . . . I just don't get it."

"It's not any one particular thing," Mason said. "It's a combination of things. You take a man who's making his living directly or indirectly out of women, and he knows there's something wrong inside. He tried to cover it up. He tries to square himself with himself. He tries to put the best possible veneer on top of what's underneath in order to hide the rotten part.

"So he goes in for a faultless personal appearance. His shoes are always shined. His trousers are sharply creased. He wears expensive shirts and ties. His nails are always well manicured. The skin of his hands is well cared for. His hair is cut, combed, and brushed so that it makes a flattering appearance in the mirror.

"Then there's his voice. There's something about it. A voice that isn't used to carrying weight with the world in general but is sharply authoritative in dealing with a situation which he thinks he can handle. It lacks tone and timbre. You have the feeling that if he became enraged and flew off the handle his voice would rise to a sharp falsetto."

"And this man, Cassel, had those points?"

"He had those points," Mason said.

"What did he want?"

"He wanted money."

"Did he say how much?"

"He wanted the bundle, five grand."

"And what did you tell him?"

"I stalled him along."

"Did he go for it?"

"He didn't like it."

"Did he feel that you were—?"

"As I told you, he recognized me," Mason said. "I've had my picture in the newspapers too often. He knew that he was dealing with Perry Mason, an attorney, and he didn't like any part of it."

"And you never did find out what he wanted, what he had on my brother, Edgar?"

Mason shook his head. "It evidently isn't the ordinary kind of blackmail deal," he said.

"You think it was something . . . well, worse than what you call the ordinary blackmail?"

"It could have been," Mason said. "He acted as though he really had the winning hand."

"What's he going to do next?"

Mason shrugged his shoulders, said, "That's something we'll have to wait for."

"Mr. Mason, suppose it could be something—well, *real* serious?"

"You don't make a pass at a guy for five thousand bucks on squaring a ticket for parking in front of a fire hydrant," Mason said. "Whatever it is, it's something serious."

"Look, Mr. Mason, I've . . . I could raise money if . . ."

Mason said, "Forget it. It's against my policy to pay off blackmailers. To hell with them. Come on, Diana, we're going to leave here casually. We won't be carrying anything except your purse and that black bag with the money in it. I'm going to walk with you through the lobby and out the front door. As we cross the lobby, be talking and laughing. You know, the quick, nervous laugh of a woman who realizes that she's embarking on an adventure which may have romantic overtones. I don't want anyone to think that you may be surreptitiously leaving the hotel.

"Now, after we've walked across the lobby, we're going down the street a couple of blocks to a taxicab stand. You remember and follow instructions. Get in a taxicab and pull away from the curb. Go to the Union Depot. Mingle around with the crowds. Switch cabs. Go to the airport and get that plane for San Francisco. . . . Hold everything. I'll see if I can get reservations."

Mason picked up the phone and asked for an outside line. He gave the number of United Airlines, got the reservations desk, and asked for two tickets to San Francisco on the flight leaving at six twenty-seven.

The lawyer nodded his satisfaction, said, "We'll pick up the tickets at the airport. Put them both under the name of Perry Mason. . . . That's right, Perry Mason, the lawyer. I'm listed in the phone books. I have an Air Travel Card and— That's fine! I'll pick up one ticket myself. Give the other one to a Miss Diana Douglas. Hold them right up until plane time, if you will.

"Thank you very much!"

Mason hung up the telephone, said, "Everything's all set, Diana. Ask for a ticket that's held in the name of Perry Mason. I'll see you aboard the plane. I'll have your suitcase with me when I check out of the hotel here. Now, remember that if anything happens to that bag of money you're carrying, you're stuck. You're behind the eight ball. You're in trouble."

"I know," she said. "I've been carrying it with me and I . . . I can hardly sleep worrying about it. I know that if anything happens to it I'm never going to be able to work things out. But I've got by so far and, after all, Mr. Mason, who knows I'm carrying five thousand dollars?"

"Too many people by this time," Mason said grimly. "Come on, Diana, put on your best smile and we're going to go down to the lobby, out the front door, and down

73

to the taxicab stand. You're going to be laughing and talking and I'll try a wisecrack now and then. . . . Come on, let's go. I've got an idea this hotel may be a darn poor place for you from now on. . . . You'll have some time to wait at the airport, but try to be as inconspicuous as possible and get aboard the plane just as soon as the doors are open for boarding."

8

●

MASON RETURNED to Room 767 at the hotel, knocked at the door, and when Stella admitted him said, "Well, I got rid of the bait in the case. She'll join me at the airport. Let's hope nothing happens until we get off."

"You think she's in danger?"

"Not danger exactly, but this guy Cassel worries me. He may be smarter than I had him pegged. I've had an uneasy feeling about Diana ever since I arrived here at the hotel. She left too wide a back trail and—"

The lawyer paused as the sharp rap of knuckles sounded on the door. He turned back and said to Stella Grimes in a low voice, "Those are masculine knuckles and they sound imperative."

"Cassel coming back?" she asked.

Mason shook his head. "He's a soft, sneaky knocker. These are the knuckles of authority—either the house detective, or—"

He was interrupted by another knock and a voice said, "Open up, please. This is the police."

Mason said to Stella Grimes, "Let me do as much of the talking as possible."

Mason opened the door.

Two plain-clothes men, standing in the hallway, showed surprise as they recognized the lawyer.

"Perry Mason," one said, "what are *you* doing *here?*"

"The question," Mason said, "is what *you* are doing here."

"We prefer to discuss it inside rather than in the corridor," the spokesman said, and pushed his way into the room, holding in his hand a leather folder displaying a badge. "Los Angeles police," he said.

"And what brings you here?" Mason asked.

The officers ignored him temporarily, looked at Stella Grimes. One of the officers nodded at the other. "Age twenty-two, five-feet-two, a hundred and sixteen pounds, blonde, blue eyes, good figure," he said.

The other nodded.

The two officers helped themselves to chairs, and one said, "We want to ask a few questions."

"Very well," Mason said, "go ahead."

"Is your name Diana Douglas?" one of the officers asked Stella Grimes.

"Now, just a minute," Mason said. "Let's do this thing in an orderly manner. Why do you come here?"

"We don't have to tell you that."

"No, but you have to tell the young woman that. Do you suspect her of a crime?"

"We're acting on telegraphed instructions from the San Francisco police. We're trying to get some information. We want to ask some questions, that's all."

"Do you suspect this young woman of any crime?"

"We don't know. We haven't the faintest idea."

"You're acting for the San Francisco police?"

"Yes."

"Do the San Francisco police suspect her of any crime?"

"We're not mind readers. We don't know."

"Then," Mason said, "since you're acting for and on behalf of the San Francisco police, and since you don't know whether the San Francisco police suspect her of any crime, before she answers *any* questions you had better advise her as to her constitutional rights."

"As if she didn't know them," the officer said.

Mason smiled. "Tell that to the Supreme Court."

"All right, all right," the officer said. "We want you to answer a few questions, Miss. We're not making any specific charges. We're not here to take you into custody, but we do want to ask you some questions.

"You are entitled to remain silent if you wish. You don't have to make any statement. You are entitled to have an attorney represent you at all times. If you don't have money enough to secure an attorney, we will secure one to act on your behalf. However, we want it understood that anything you do say may be used against you. Now then, do you wish an attorney?"

Stella started to say something when Mason motioned her to silence. "She's got one," he said.

"You're representing her?"

"Yes."

"What are you doing here—Miss Douglas, is it?"

"She's here on business," Mason said.

"What sort of business?"

"Personal business."

"Miss Douglas, were you aware that a relatively large sum of cash was being kept in the vault at the Escobar Import and Export Company where you work in San Francisco?"

"No comment," Mason said.

"Now, wait a minute," the officer said. "You're injecting yourself into this thing and you're just making it worse for this young lady. All we're trying to do is to elicit information."

"Why?"

"Because San Francisco wants that information."

"I take it there's a crime involved?"

"We're not sure. San Francisco isn't sure."

"I think, under the circumstances, my client doesn't

77

care to answer any questions until the situation is clarified," Mason said.

"You're forcing us to report to San Francisco that there's every likelihood that your client is guilty of a substantial embezzlement."

"Indeed!" Mason said. "How much of an embezzlement?"

"The audit hasn't been completed," the officer said, "but it's a substantial amount—over twenty thousand dollars."

"How much?" Mason exclaimed, surprise showing in his voice.

"You heard me, over twenty grand."

"That's a lot of money to embezzle from one company," Mason said.

"There *have* been embezzlements involving larger sums," the officer said.

"Then there has been a crime committed in San Francisco?"

"If you're referring to the embezzlement, it looks that way."

"And San Francisco suspects my client of embezzling the money?"

"I haven't said that—yet."

"But you want to ask questions about it?"

"Listen, Mason, you're making things rather difficult and you're getting mighty hard to get along with. All we want to do is to ask your client some questions about how the cash is kept in that company, about who has the authority to draw out cash, and, generally, things about the bookkeeping end of it. For your information, that company seems to keep perfectly huge sums of liquid cash available, and we'd like to know why.

"We'd also like to know how many people have the combination to the vault and how it is possible for a company to run up a shortage of that sort without somebody checking it earlier."

"It's been going on for a long time?" Mason asked.

"We don't know," the officer said. "That's what we're trying to find out. We're simply trying to get information."

"But you think my client *may* have embezzled that money?" Mason asked.

"Not exactly," the officer said. "I'll put it this way. We won't say that we've uncovered any evidence which makes it appear that it's a physical impossibility for her to have been guilty of embezzlement, but, on the other hand, we haven't uncovered any evidence which points to her—as yet."

"Except in a circumstantial way," the other officer said.

"Well, yes," the spokesman conceded.

Mason smiled and said, "That makes it very plain, gentlemen. My client is entitled to the advice of counsel."

"That's right. We told her that. There's no question about that."

"And, as her counsel," Mason said, "I advise her to say absolutely nothing."

"You won't even let her talk about the methods of bookkeeping, about the business background of the company?"

"Not a word," Mason said. "Not even to admit her identity."

The two officers looked at each other in frustration and disgust.

"That may not be a very smart thing to do," the spokesman said to Mason.

"Perhaps so," Mason conceded. "I'm not infallible. I make mistakes every so often. . . . How did San Francisco know enough about the situation to send you two hot-footing to the hotel here?"

The officer grinned. "On the advice of counsel, I decline to answer, Mr. Mason."

The lawyer was grave. "You're absolutely entitled to

adopt that position. It's a constitutional privilege. You don't need to say a word."

The officers got up, looked belligerently at Stella Grimes.

The spokesman said, "Okay, sister, it's up to you, but let me tell you, you're not being very smart. When we walked in we just wanted information."

"What do you want now?" Mason asked.

"At least twenty grand," the officer said, and then made a parting shot at the lawyer. "Remember it won't do *you* any good to collect a fee out of embezzled money. It can be traced and impounded. . . . I guess that's all."

"See you later," Mason said.

"In court," the officer promised, and walked out.

Mason motioned for silence, said to Stella Grimes in a low voice, "Be careful what you say. They sometimes wait just outside the door."

They were silent for more than a minute; then Mason tiptoed to the door, abruptly jerked it open, and looked up and down the hall.

When he saw there was no one there, the lawyer closed the door and said, "Well, that's a kettle of fish."

"Twenty thousand dollars," Stella Grimes said.

Mason shook his head. "I don't get it," he said, "but I'm on my way to the airport. I'll take the baggage out of my room which has Diana's stuff in it and be on my way. I'm catching that six-twenty-seven flight to San Francisco."

"You're going to see Diana at the airport?"

Mason nodded, said, "She'll join me there. Hold the fort, Stella, and play it by ear. Keep in touch with Paul Drake. . . . Better have your meals sent up to the room for at least twenty-four hours. If you leave the room they may bug it."

She said, "I can get by all right now. What about the switchboard?"

"You'll have to take a chance on that," Mason said.

"But don't scatter information around like birdseed. Be cryptic when you call your office, but be sure you get the idea across."

She nodded.

The lawyer left Room 767, walked down to 789, picked up his suitcase and that of Diana Douglas, and called the desk for a boy to assist him.

"Please ask the cashier to have my bill ready," Mason told the desk clerk. "I've received an unexpected long-distance call and I've got to leave at once."

Mason waited until the boy arrived, gave him the bags and a tip, hurried down to the cashier's desk, and explained the situation. "I'm Mr. Mason in Room Seven-eighty-nine. I wanted to stay for a day or two, but I've received a call which makes it imperative that I leave at once. Now, what can we do about the room? I've only been in it a short time. I've used a couple of towels, but the bed hasn't been occupied."

The cashier shook her head. "I'm sorry, Mr. Mason, but we're going to have to charge you for one full day."

Mason made a point of protesting the charge. "But you can put in two new towels and rent the room again."

"I'm sorry, but maid service is cut down at this time of the afternoon and—well, we have a rule, Mr. Mason. I'm sorry."

"All right," the lawyer yielded. "Give me the bill."

He paid in cash, nodded to a bellboy, said, "I want a taxi."

"There's one right outside," the boy said.

Mason gave the boy a good tip, settled himself in the cushions of the taxicab, said in a loud voice, "Take me to the Union Station. Take it easy because I've got a couple of telegrams to read and I want to catch the train to Tucson."

Suddenly Mason, folding the papers which he had taken from his pocket, said, "Hold everything, driver. That telegram really does it."

81

"You don't want the station?" the driver asked.

"Hell, no," Mason said, "I've simply got to get the plane that leaves for Phoenix and Tucson, so get me to the airport just as fast as you can."

"It's a bad time of day to hit the airport."

"I can't help it, we'll do the best we can."

"When's your plane due out?"

"Five forty-eight," Mason said.

The cab driver threaded his way through traffic, found a through boulevard, and started making time.

Mason sat forward on the edge of the seat, looking at his watch from time to time, occasionally complimenting the cab driver on the time he was making.

The lawyer got to the airport. The cabby honked the horn for a porter.

Mason whipped the door open, said to the porter, "Get those two suitcases on the plane for Tucson."

The lawyer handed the cab driver a ten-dollar bill. "Get going, buddy, before some cop catches up with you. That was a swell ride."

The driver grinned. "This is all for me?"

"Pay the meter and the rest is yours," Mason said.

The driver threw the car into gear.

When he was out of earshot, Mason hurried after the porter.

"I made a mistake," he said, "I was thinking about Tucson. Darn it, I want to get in one of those suitcases. Let me have them." Mason handed the porter a couple of dollars.

"You've got your plane ticket?" the porter asked.

"I've got it," Mason said.

The lawyer went into the waiting room and made a quick survey; then went to the airline counter, picked up one of his tickets, paid for both, checked in Diana's baggage, then walked down to survey the waiting room again. Following this, he strolled casually around, then settled himself comfortably after checking the dummy suitcase in a storage receptacle, and bought a drink.

Five minutes before departure time the lawyer walked in a leisurely manner to the gate and presented his ticket.

"You'll have to hurry," the attendant told him. "The last of the passengers is getting aboard now."

"I'll walk right along," Mason promised.

Mason walked through the door, signaled to the guard, and got aboard the plane just before the portable passageway was pulled back into place.

The hostess at the door looked at him chidingly. "You almost didn't make it," she said.

Mason smiled. "I almost didn't, but it's too hot to hurry."

"There's a seat toward the rear."

"Thank you."

Mason walked the length of the plane, glancing at the faces of the passengers.

After ten or fifteen minutes he walked forward to the lavatory and again took an opportunity to study the faces of the passengers on the plane.

Diana Douglas was not on board.

Mason rode to San Francisco on the plane, took a taxi to a hotel, registered, had dinner, then called the Willatson Hotel, asked for Room 767, and when he heard Stella Grimes' cautious voice on the telephone said, "Recognize the voice, Stella?"

"Yes. Where are you?"

"San Francisco. Did you hear anything from your double?"

"Not a word."

"She was to have taken the same plane I did, but she didn't show up. She didn't leave any message with you?"

"Not a word. I haven't heard a thing."

"Anything from anybody else?"

"Nothing."

Mason said, "I think we've been given a complete

runaround on this case, Stella. I'll keep my appointment at ten-thirty tomorrow morning and if nothing happens then we'll wash our hands of the whole business."

"Okay by me. Do I report to you if anything happens?"

"Keep in touch with your employer and I'll contact him. Do you still have your working bra?"

"I have it."

"Keep it," Mason said, "and sleep tight."

9

⊙

THE ESCOBAR IMPORT and Export Company had its offices in the United Financial Building.

Mason found from the registry list that the firm had offices on the sixth floor, then retreated to a point near the door where he could watch the people coming in.

The time was 10:20.

At 10:25 Diana Douglas walked through the door.

Mason stepped forward. "Where were you last night?"

She raised tear-swollen eyes; then clutched at his arm as though she needed his physical as well as his mental help.

"Oh, Mr. Mason," she said, "Edgar passed away at three twenty-five this morning."

"I'm so sorry," Mason said, putting his arm around her shoulders. "He meant a lot to you, didn't he?"

"A lot. I was very, very fond of him."

She suddenly buried her head against Mason's shoulder and started to cry.

Mason patted her back. "Now, don't let yourself go, Diana. Remember we have a job to do. You'll have to get your chin up and face the facts."

"I know," she sobbed, "but I . . . I just don't feel that I

can take it. . . . If it hadn't been that I'd promised you I'd meet you here I . . . I wanted to telephone Homer Gage and tell him not to expect me. I . . ."

"There, there," Mason said, "we're attracting a lot of attention, Diana. Move over here to the corner and try to get control of yourself. You've got a job to do. You're going to have to go up and face the music."

"How much music?"

"Lots of music."

"What do you mean?"

Mason said, "I'm afraid you're being sucked into a game which is as old as the hills. Someone embezzles a thousand dollars from a company and skips out. Somebody else, who knows what has been going on, calmly reaches in and takes another four thousand out of the till. The man who has absconded with the one thousand dollars gets credit for having embezzled five thousand."

Her eyes, red with crying, widened as she looked at him. "You mean that. . . ?"

"I mean," Mason said, "that the Escobar Import and Export Company is now claiming there's a shortage of twenty thousand dollars."

"*Twenty* thousand dollars!" she repeated, aghast.

"Exactly," Mason said. And then after a moment went on, "How do you come to work? Do you drive or. . . ?"

"No, I take a bus."

"What about arrangements for your brother? Were there any other relatives?"

"No, I got up early this morning and made arrangements."

"Why didn't you take that plane last night as you were instructed?"

"Because I thought someone was following me. Mr. Mason, I felt certain that a man in an automobile followed my taxicab all the way to the Union Depot and then tried to follow me. I tried to lose myself in the crowd, but I don't think I was very successful. I kept having that horrible feeling that this man was spying on me and was where he could see me all the time, so I went into the women's restroom, stayed for a long time, then came out and took a lot of what I suppose you would call evasive tactics. I started through the gate for a train, then doubled back and then, by the time I got to the airport, it was ten minutes too late. The plane had taken off. So then I decided to have dinner and come in on a later plane."

"Why didn't you telephone Paul Drake's office or somebody?"

"I—I never thought of it. I knew you were coming up on that plane and I knew I'd meet you here this morning and—well, I never thought of anything else.

"Then when I got in I telephoned the hospital and found out that my brother was worse and I went up there and—I was with him—when—"

"There, there," Mason said. "You've had a pretty hard row to hoe. Now, what I want you to do is to catch the next bus, go back to your apartment, and try to get some sleep. Do you have any sleeping medicine?"

"Yes, I have some sleeping pills."

"Take them," Mason said. "Go to sleep and forget about everything. . . . Do you have that cashier's check?"

"Yes."

"Give it to me," Mason said. "I probably won't use it, but I'd like to have it. And here's your suitcase."

"What are you going to do?" she asked, giving him the cashier's check.

"I'm going up to the Escobar Import and Export Company and throw a little weight around. At least, I'm going to try to."

"Mr. Mason—twenty thousand dollars. Good Lord!"

"I know," Mason said. "It's a shock."

"But what can we do?"

"That," Mason said, "remains to be seen. The game is old but it's almost infallible. Some poor guy gets to betting on the horses, gets in over his head, takes two or three thousand dollars and skips town, and the smart guy who remains behind cleans out all the cash available and the embezzler is stuck with the whole thing. If they never catch up with him, he's supposed to have taken it all, and if they do catch up with him and he denies that he took anything above two or three thousand, no one believes him. He goes to prison for the whole thing."

Mason put the check in his wallet, then guided her gently toward the street door. "Get on your bus," he said. "Go back to your apartment and go to sleep. Leave the Escobar Import and Export Company to me. . . . Do you have a private phone or does it go through the apartment switchboard?"

"It goes through the apartment switchboard."

"Leave word that you're not to be disturbed," Mason said. "Get some sleep. I have your phone number. Tell the operator that only calls from me are to be put through. This is Friday. I'll go back to my office this afternoon. You can reach me through the Drake Detective Agency if you need me. . . . I'm sorry about your brother's death. You poor kid, you've had a lot to put up with during the last few days. Take it easy and call on me if you need me. . . . Where does your bus stop?"

"Right here," she said, "at this bus stop. And I owe you for my plane ticket, Mr. Mason. I remembered you had ordered two tickets to be charged to you. When I got to the airport I made a rush for that plane, thinking it might have been a few minutes late taking off. I was going to pay for the ticket with my credit card, but I couldn't find it. I must have lost it, and the girl at the ticket counter said that the ticket was all paid for, and—"

"That's all right," Mason said. "Forget it."

He guided her to a wooden bench at the curb. "Take

88

the first bus home. I'm going up to the office and see what can be done."

She flung her arms around the lawyer and kissed him impulsively.

"Mr. Mason, you're *so* wonderful!" she said.

10

◉

MASON STOOD in the hallway on the sixth floor surveying the offices of the Escobar Import and Export Company.

There was a display showing Oriental art goods, carved ivories, and cloisonné.

On the other side of the entrance door the display showed figurines which had a Toltec or Aztec look about them.

Double plate-glass doors opened into a rather shallow showroom in which there were glass shelves containing further specimens of art. The entrance doors had the legend ESCOBAR IMPORT AND EXPORT COMPANY, *Wholesale Only*.

Mason pushed the doors open and entered the display room. A girl seated at a switchboard smiled mechanically. "May I help you?" she asked.

Mason said, "I'd like to see Mr. Gage, please."

"Which one? Mr. Franklin Gage or Mr. Homer Gage?"

"Franklin Gage."

"He isn't in. He's out on a business trip."

"Then I'll see Homer Gage."

"What's the name, please?"

"Perry Mason."

"Did you wish to see him about a purchase, Mr. Mason, about some art goods, or . . . ?"

"It's a more personal matter than that," Mason said.

"May I ask what firm you represent?"

"I don't represent any firm," Mason said. "My name is Perry Mason. I'm an attorney from Los Angeles. I happen to be here at the moment to discuss an employee by the name of Diana Douglas."

"Oh, oh!" she said. "Oh, yes . . . yes, indeed. Just a moment!"

She plugged in a line and Mason saw her lips moving rapidly, but the connection of the telephone was so arranged that he couldn't hear her words.

A moment later a door in the back part of the room opened and a heavy-set, chunky individual came striding out, a man in his late thirties, with dark hair which had receded well back from his temples, bushy black eyebrows, keen gray eyes, and tortoise-shell glasses. His mouth was a straight line of thin determination.

"Mr. Mason?" he said.

"Right."

"I'm Homer Gage. What did you wish to see me about?"

"Diana Douglas."

"What about her?"

"She's an employee of yours?"

"Yes. She is, but she's not here at the moment. Her brother was seriously injured in an automobile accident and I am afraid she is rather upset. If it's a matter of credit rating or integrity, I can assure you that she has a fine reputation."

"It's neither," Mason said. "I wanted to talk to you about her."

"Well, I'm here."

"All right," Mason said, "if you want to talk here, we'll talk here. I'm representing Miss Douglas. What was the idea of telling the Los Angeles police that she had embezzled twenty thousand dollars from this . . ."

Gage interrupted, throwing up his hands, palms outward. "Stop right there, Mr. Mason. We never said any such thing."

"Then you intimated it."

"Mr. Mason, this is hardly the time or the place to discuss a matter of this sort."

"What's wrong with the time?" Mason asked.

"Why . . . I hadn't anticipated . . . you didn't telephone . . . I had no warning."

"Did you need warning?"

"Not necessarily."

"Then what's wrong with the place?"

"It's public."

"You picked it," Mason reminded him.

Gage opened a gate in the counter. "Won't you please step into my private office, Mr. Mason?"

Mason followed him down a thick carpet where there were further showcases on the sides, past two young women, who very frankly stopped the work they were doing to gawk at the lawyer as he walked past.

Gage held the door of his private office open, then, when Mason had entered, said, "Please be seated, Mr. Mason. I'm sorry you brought this up where the girls in the outer office could hear it."

"You left me no choice," Mason said.

"Well, perhaps I didn't . . . I'm sorry. I didn't appreciate the importance of your visit."

"I hope you appreciate it now."

"Well, Mr. Mason, the fact remains that an audit of the books shows that there is a very substantial shortage in our cash, and, of course, under the circumstances, we wanted to check on any of our employees who are absent."

"Diana Douglas was one?"

"Yes."

92

"Your uncle, Franklin Gage, is another?"

"Well, he's hardly an employee. He virtually owns the business."

"And Edgar Douglas is another?"

"Yes. He's in the hospital with a fractured skull. He has never regained consciousness since the accident. I'm afraid the prognosis is not good."

"Did you check on him, too?" Mason asked.

"We were hardly in a position to check on him. You can't question a man who is unconscious."

"So Diana Douglas was the only one you asked the police to check on?"

"Now, Mr. Mason, you're getting the cart before the horse. With a shortage of that sort showing up we quite naturally wanted to talk with Miss Douglas. That was our right. She's an employee of this company. We had assumed that she was absent from work because of the condition of her brother and was spending all of her time in the hospital with him, but inquiry disclosed that she had left rather suddenly for Los Angeles."

"And you asked the Los Angeles police to check on her?"

"The Los Angeles police were asked to try to get some information from her."

"You intimated that she might be an embezzler?"

"Certainly not, Mr. Mason. Don't try to put words in my mouth. We simply asked for a check-up."

"And how did you find out where she was staying in Los Angeles?"

"I'm afraid that's a confidential matter that I don't care to go into at the present time, Mr. Mason."

"All right," Mason said, "I just wanted you to know that I'm representing Miss Douglas; that we feel that her reputation has been damaged because she was accused of embezzlement, at least by inference, and because you asked the Los Angeles police to look her up. . . . Here is my card, Mr. Gage, and if you have any further matters

93

to take up with Miss Douglas you can take them up with me."

"You mean she is finished working here?" Gage asked.

"That is something I'm not prepared to discuss," Mason said. "I am referring only to the case she has against you for defamation of character. I would suggest you get in touch with me if you have any further activities in mind."

"Come, come, Mr. Mason. There's no need to be belligerent. You don't need to come up here with a chip on your shoulder. Did you come up all the way from Los Angeles to tell us this?"

"Why not?" Mason asked.

"It seems so futile, so— Good heavens, we don't know where the money is. All we know is that there's a shortage."

"You're sure of that?"

"Apparently so. An amount of something over twenty thousand dollars seems to be missing from the cash."

"You keep an amount of that sort on hand in the form of ready cash?"

"Yes, indeed. We have a lot more than that."

"May I ask why?" Mason asked.

"I don't know why not," Gage said. "A lot of our deals are for cash, and a great many of them are made on weekends when the banks are closed."

"And on some of them you don't want any question of having left a backtrack?"

"No, no, no, it isn't that. It's simply that we've followed a policy of buying many times for cash and then, when the deal is completed, getting . . . well . . . establishing—"

"I'm afraid I don't understand," Mason interposed.

"It's rather difficult to understand, Mr. Mason, but there are various embargoes in various countries which must be—well, taken into account. For instance, in Mexico it is illegal to export ancient artifacts, yet there is a very brisk demand for such artifacts in this country."

"And these Mexican figurines have been smuggled out of Mexico?"

"I didn't say that, Mr. Mason. I was very careful *not* to say that. I was telling you something about the reasons that we have to have large supplies of cash in our business. There are certain questions we do not ask. And when you do not ask questions, cash does the talking."

"I'm afraid I don't understand," Mason said.

"Is it necessary that you should?"

"I think it is."

Gage flushed. "After all, Mr. Mason, I have explained to you as much of our business activities as I think is required under the circumstances."

"When you talk about using cash," Mason said, "in order to get figurines across the border, I take it that you are referring to bribery."

"Not at all," Gage said. "You're a lawyer. You should be able to put two and two together."

"Perhaps I have," Mason told him.

"Perhaps you put two and two together and came up with an entirely wrong answer," Gage warned.

"In that event," Mason told him, smiling affably, "you'll have a chance to explain in greater detail in court."

"Now, wait a minute, Mason, there's nothing to go to court about, and there's no reason for you and me to get at loggerheads."

Mason said nothing.

Gage took a deep breath. "Let me explain it this way, Mr. Mason. Mexico has an embargo on shipping ancient artifacts out of the country. On the other hand, there is no embargo in the United States on importing ancient artifacts. Therefore, if someone shows up with a station wagon full of figurines from Mexico, we don't have to determine at the time we complete the transaction whether the figurines are genuine or whether they are copies.

"You must realize that there's quite an industry in

95

Mexico in copying ancient figurines and selling some of the copies to tourists, who quite frequently think they're getting a genuine prehistoric artifact."

"That still doesn't explain the cash," Mason said.

"Well," Gage went on, "put yourself in the position of the man who is driving the station wagon. He wants to sell the artifacts. He wants to get what he considers a good price for them. He knows how much he had to pay for them. He wants to make a profit. But when a man has a station wagon filled with figurines of this sort, it's only reasonable to suppose that he's in business. It isn't merely an isolated transaction.

"Under those circumstances he prefers to have no official record of the transaction. He prefers to deal on a cash-and-carry basis.

"Then there's the other end of things, the export of goods from Hong Kong where it is necessary to have a Certificate of Origin. Here again there are situations which require cold, hard cash, which is transferred by wire.

"Now, it's not necessary to make any more detailed explanation than that. We . . ."

Gage broke off as one of the secretaries entered the door.

"I beg your pardon," she said, "but Mr. Franklin Gage has just returned."

"Ask him to come in, please," Homer Gage said. "Tell him that Mr. Perry Mason, an attorney of Los Angeles, is here and that it may be we will have to consult our own legal department."

"Why don't you do that?" Perry Mason said. "I'd much prefer talking with an attorney."

"No, no, no, not yet. I simply wanted Mr. Franklin Gage to understand the situation. He . . . here he is now."

Mason turned. The tall, distinguished-looking gentleman who stood in the doorway wore an affable smile on the lower part of his face, but his eyes were appraising and unsmiling. They were eyes which were wide and round and somehow seemed to dominate the face.

He was in his late forties, wore rimless spectacles which seemed somehow to emphasize the rather wide eyes. The mouth was large, the lips rather thick, and the smile was that of a man who is accustomed to using suave tactics in getting what he wants out of life.

"Mr. Mason, Mr. Franklin Gage," Homer Gage said.

Mason stood up.

Franklin Gage gave him a hand which seemed cushioned with flesh, as though the man's body had built up a layer of insulation in the right hand.

"Ah, yes, Mr. Mason," Gage said, "I've heard a great deal about you. Your reputation is not confined to Los Angeles by any means. It's a pleasure to meet you. What can we do for you, Mr. Mason?"

Homer Gage was quick to answer that question. "Mr. Mason is calling about Diana Douglas," he said. "You'll remember she's been absent for the last three or four days.

"We weren't particularly busy at the time and I gave her some time off. Her brother was seriously injured in an automobile accident and has been unconscious."

"I understand he passed away early this morning," Mason said.

The two Gages exchanged glances.

"Good heavens!" Homer said.

"The poor kid," Franklin muttered sympathetically.

"I'm glad you told us," Homer Gage said.

Franklin Gage turned to his nephew. "The firm must send flowers, Homer."

"Certainly. I'll attend to that."

"And contact Diana and see if there's anything we can do. We must express our sympathies."

"I'm afraid Mr. Mason doesn't want us to have any direct contact with Diana," Homer Gage explained. "And

97

even if he had no objections, I don't think it would be wise—not until we consult our lawyers."

"Nonsense!" Franklin Gage snapped. "We can certainly be guided by the humanities and plain decency."

"I think you'd better listen to Mr. Mason," Homer said.

"And why should that make any difference?" Franklin inquired, his voice now losing its tone of cordiality.

Homer rushed in with a hurried explanation. "Well, it seems that Diana Douglas made a quick trip to Los Angeles for some reason and somehow word got out that she had traveled under an assumed name.

"Then Stewart Garland, in checking the cash, said that there seemed to be quite a discrepancy—a rough estimate fixed this discrepancy at some twenty thousand dollars. Quite naturally, I wanted to find out about it and I wanted to interrogate Diana Douglas."

"You mean you interrogated her about the cash shortage?" Franklin Gage asked.

"Well, not directly," Homer said. "I may have acted rather hastily, but when I found she was registered at a hotel under an assumed name, I asked a very close friend of mine on the police force what to do about it and he said he'd arrange to have her interrogated by some friends of his in the Los Angeles Police Department.

"Mr. Mason seems to feel that what we did amounted to an accusation of embezzlement against her and constituted a defamation of character."

"Tut, tut," Franklin Gage said to Homer, "you shouldn't have jumped at conclusions. A lot of people have access to that cash drawer—the way we do business, you know. I, myself, had ten thousand dollars which I took from the cash drawer in order to complete a deal I was working on. Unfortunately, the deal fell through. I returned the cash a few minutes ago."

"That would seem to leave us with a shortage of only

ten thousand dollars then," Homer Gage said, his manner greatly deflated.

"You can't tell if there's been any shortage until you check everything," the older man replied. "You know how that cash vault is. We keep large sums there and whenever any of the executives need money they simply take out what they need and then leave a note stating what they have taken out. And sometimes those notes aren't up-to-date. That is, if a man's in a hurry he won't bother to leave a note.

"In my case I was negotiating for a deal which, unfortunately, fell through. I took out ten thousand dollars and didn't leave any note stating I had done so. I had no idea that there was going to be all this talk of embezzlement. . . . The way we're organized, Homer, you should have waited until you got all of us together before you even had any idea of embezzlement or let any talk of that sort get started."

"I'm sorry, but Diana Douglas used an assumed name, went to Los Angeles, and registered in a hotel as Diana Deering. Under those circumstances I felt that we——"

"How did you find out about all this?" Franklin Gage asked.

"Well, frankly, I didn't find out about it," Homer Gage said, now quite apparently on the defensive and somewhat flustered. "I wanted to ask Diana about the cash and whether she had any slips that had been taken from the cash safe which she intended to post. . . . Well, I found she wasn't in her apartment. She wasn't at the hospital with her brother, although she had been there faithfully for some two or three hours right after the accident. Then she seemed to have disappeared.

"Well, I had this friend on the police force and I asked him how a man would go about locating a young woman under those circumstances and he said he'd run down a couple of leads.

"Well, of course, he used common sense, something

99

which I could have done if I'd only thought of it. He knew that Diana was concerned about her brother, so he went to the hospital, interrogated the telephone operator, and found that calls had been coming in regularly from Los Angeles to find out about Edgar Douglas' condition. A number had been left to be notified if there was any change. The officer found that number was the number of the Willatson Hotel in Los Angeles and that a Diana Deering had put in the calls. By checking her description he soon had it pretty well established that Diana Deering was Diana Douglas, so then he suggested that it would be a good plan to question her because—well, you can see the position I was in."

"I'm not going to make any comment at this time," Franklin Gage said, "but Diana Douglas has been a very loyal employee and I have the utmost confidence in her integrity. I'm sorry that Mr. Mason has adopted the attitude there has been any defamation of character. I also feel that we had better check up rather carefully on that cash situation before we talk about *any* shortage. . . . You will understand, Mr. Mason, that at times there is as much as a hundred thousand dollars in our cash safe."

Mason raised his eyebrows.

"I know that seems large to you," Franklin Gage went on, "but it seems small to us because this is a very unusual type of business.

"This isn't like dealing in automobiles where there is a registration number and a pink slip. In this business the person who has possession of the articles is to all intents and purposes the owner—unless, of course, he has stolen the articles—and that is a chance we have to take.

"However, we have a regular clientele with whom we do business, and we have been very fortunate in dealing in property which was not stolen."

"But smuggled?" Mason asked.

"I wouldn't know," Franklin Gage said, shaking his

head. "I wouldn't want to know. And, of course, smuggling is only a minor crime. There are embargoes against exportation. If a shrewd operator ships a dozen figurines out of Mexico without alarming the Mexican authorities, and then presents them at the United States border as copies which he has picked up for a nominal consideration in a Tijuana curio store, nobody is going to bother about it because there *are* curio stores selling copies of ancient figurines.

"Then when they get to this country, if it should turn out that the figurines are actually genuine, ancient figurines, we certainly aren't going to ask how it happened that they were released from the embargo in Mexico. We simply say, 'How much?' And if the price is right and if we are satisfied as to the quality of the merchandise, we close the transaction."

"Then these ancient figurines in your display windows are copies?" Mason asked.

Franklin Gage shook his head. "We don't deal in copies, Mr. Mason. We deal in genuine, authentic articles."

"But they come across the border as copies?" Mason asked.

"We have no idea how they come across the border, Mr. Mason. . . .

"Now, may I say that we are genuinely concerned about Diana's misfortune, the loss of her brother. I know that they were very close. I take it that this is a poor time to communicate with her, but, after the funeral, Mr. Mason . . . I think you will agree with us that this whole discussion should be postponed until after the funeral?

"Personally, I don't see how any good can come of trying to intensify the feeling of grief, on the one hand, or of injured feelings on the other. Mr. Mason, I ask you please, as a favor to the company, as a personal favor, to hold this matter in abeyance for a few days. This is the

101

end of the week and, as you say, Diana's brother has passed away. That will mean funeral arrangements, and the poor girl has— Homer, see if you can get her on the phone and ask her if she wants any money. Ask her if she needs an advance."

"Don't try it today," Mason said. "I have advised her to take sedation and shut off the telephone."

"Yes, yes, yes, I see." Franklin Gage said, "and, of course, tomorrow is Saturday but— I think it might be a little better, Homer, if you had one of the other girls in the office—surely someone must know her intimately and have a friendship with her, someone who could ring up in a few hours and express our sympathy in a perfectly natural way."

Homer Gage shook his head. "Not Diana. She's something of a loner as far as the others are concerned, but I'll see what I can do."

Franklin Gage arose and again held out his flesh-cushioned hand to the lawyer. "So nice to have met you, Mr. Mason, and thank you so much for dropping in to tell us what you had in mind. I am quite certain that it won't be necessary for us to adopt any adversary position —not that I agree with you in any way, but—well, we'll work out something somewhere along the line.

"And please don't get the idea that we are engaged in an unusual type of business. I can assure you that every importing and exporting business these days has problems, Mr. Mason, and I think everyone has contacts."

"What do you mean, contacts?" Mason asked.

"Well, brokers," Franklin Gage said with a wave of his hand. "You know, Mr. Mason, we don't give money to every Tom, Dick, and Harry who shows up with a load of curios. But we have certain people with whom we deal, and those people, in turn, deal with other people and . . . well, it's not at all unusual for me to walk out of here, picking up five, ten, or perhaps fifteen thousand dollars in cash and contacting one of our brokers who will have a shipment of curios that we feel we can dispose of at a profit—Mexican figurines, carved ivories, or good jade.

"We know that the broker is only a middleman, and, of course, he is making a profit on the deal. We try to see that his profit is not exorbitant, but, on the other hand, we want him to make a fair profit because in this business everyone has to make a fair profit. . . . Well, you can understand how it is."

"I see," Mason said.

Homer Gage did not offer to shake hands. He stood somewhat aloof and dignified.

Franklin Gage held the door open for Mason. "Thank you again for coming in, Mr. Mason. It's nice that you felt free to come and explain the situation to us. I feel that it can be worked out. Good day, Mr. Mason."

"Good day," Mason said.

The lawyer walked across the office and, on his way out, paused momentarily at the counter to look at a piece of the carved ivory which claimed his attention. A small slip of folded paper had been placed by the carved ivory figure. The slip of paper had Mason's name typed on it.

Mason leaned forward to study the figure more closely. As he did so his right hand unostentatiously closed over the paper. When he straightened he placed the folded paper in the right-hand side pocket of his coat.

Mason went through the gate to the outer display room and paused again to look at some of the figurines in the outer cases.

"They're really very beautiful," the girl at the switchboard said, smiling at him.

"Indeed they are," Mason said. "They grow on you."

The lawyer left the office, walked out to the corridor, and halfway to the elevator removed the small piece of paper from his pocket. A typewritten message was in his hand when he unfolded the paper.

The message read:

Don't let them pull the wool over your eyes. Diana is on the level and tops. There are things going on here that they don't want you to know about. Be sure to protect Diana.

The message was unsigned.

Mason folded the typewritten slip of paper, put it back into his pocket, went to his hotel, and checked out.

11

⊙

ON MONDAY morning Mason fitted a key in the lock of
his private office and swung back the door.

"Well, hello, stranger!" Della Street said.

Mason smiled. "It isn't *that* bad!"

"Pretty close to it, what with running up and down to
San Francisco and working with detectives. What do you
know?"

"Not a darn thing," Mason said, "except that this
Diana Douglas is a problem. I feel like throwing her
out."

"Why don't you?"

"Well," Mason said, "I have a professional obligation."

"She's lied to you all the way along the line," Della
Street said. "And when she hasn't been lying, she's tried
to conceal things."

"I know," Mason said, "but the poor kid certainly was
all wrapped up in her brother."

"The one that had the automobile accident?"

"He died early Friday morning," Mason said. "I guess
the funeral is this morning. I told Diana to take some
sleeping pills Friday; to go to sleep and forget the whole
mess."

"And you went to see the Escobar Import and Export Company?"

"I met a couple of very interesting men," Mason said. "I'd like to know something about the inside operation of that company. I met Homer Gage and Franklin Gage and there you have a couple of real characters."

"Smooth?"

"Puzzling. . . . Homer Gage has to control himself with an effort every once in a while. Franklin Gage is synthetically suave. He gives you the impression of having tried all of his life to keep from showing his real feelings. When he shakes hands with you you feel there's a cushion of flesh on his hand, a sort of sponge-rubber insulation that he uses to keep any magnetic current from penetrating."

"From him to you?" Della asked.

Mason thought for a moment, then smiled and said, "Both ways. . . . We're getting into a deep subject, Della, but somehow when you shake hands with a man you can tell a lot about him from his grip. There's a certain magnetic something you can feel."

"I know," she said. "Some hands are firm and sincere and others are—well, sort of evasive; it's hard to describe."

Mason was thoughtful. "Shaking hands is a peculiar custom. It consists in clasping a part of two bodies together so that a vibration or magnetism or whatever you want to call it is exchanged from one to the other. . . . Well, we'd better go to work."

Della Street shook her head. "You had two appointments for this morning, and when I didn't hear from you Friday afternoon I canceled them."

"I should have let you know," Mason said, "but I got up there and had this session with the Escobar Import and Export Company and I had a peculiar experience."

"What?"

"One of the stenographers left this note with my name

on it beside a piece of carved ivory I had been looking at."

"Oh, oh," Della Street said. "So that's why you stayed over in San Francisco Friday night!"

Mason grinned. "It wasn't that kind of a note. Take a look."

The lawyer took the note from his notebook. Della Street looked at it, said, "I think it was done on an electric typewriter. Did you notice which of the secretaries had electric typewriters?"

"I didn't," Mason said. "I was noticing the decorations in the office—figurines, carved ivories, jade. They must have had half a million dollars' worth of stuff on display."

"Did they offer you anything at a discount?"

"Wholesale only," Mason said thoughtfully. "I'd like to know something about who their customers are and I'd like to know a lot more about where they get their stuff. . . . You say you canceled all my appointments for this morning?"

"That's right. They weren't important, and I rang up Friday afternoon and canceled."

Mason said, "After I got out of the Import and Export Company I went out to Fisherman's Wharf and had a good crab lunch—or I guess you'd call it dinner—and then went down to the airport. . . . Friday afternoon at a San Francisco airport. I was lucky to get home at all. I didn't get in until five-fifteen and then I didn't want to bother you. . . . I'm going down to Paul Drake's office and see if our stakeout has heard anything."

"Our stakeout?"

"Stella Grimes," Mason said, "the operative who's registered under the name of Diana Deering at the Willatson Hotel. Somehow I have an idea we may be a bit behind on developments.

"For your information Franklin Gage seemed to adopt a rather casual attitude toward a shortage of twenty thousand dollars. Actually it was only ten thousand, because Franklin had taken out ten thousand to use in a business deal that he hadn't consummated, and he had put the money back when he came in the office Friday morning."

"But he reported what he had done?"

"Yes, as soon as his nephew told him there was a shortage."

"Well, that was opportune," Della Street said.

Mason nodded. "The way they keep their cash is certainly cool and casual. I have an idea that Franklin Gage would a lot rather absorb a reasonable loss than have the matter come into court where he would be cross-examined about the reason they keep such a large amount of cash on hand and what they do with it. . . . There could be an income-tax angle there, too . . . and I'm willing to bet there's a lot of customs regulations that are being by-passed."

"You think they're smuggling?"

"I think people with whom they deal are smuggling, and there's an atmosphere of complete irregularity about the whole thing. . . . Some of those art objects they have on display are *really* beautiful. . . . I'm going down and have a chat with Paul Drake for a minute, Della. I think he's in this morning. Then I'll come back and get my nose ready for the grindstone."

"You have three rather important appointments this afternoon," she reminded him.

"Okay," Mason said, "I'll take a quick look; then back to the salt mines. . . . I guess Edgar Douglas' funeral is this morning. After that we may hear from Diana. And then again we may never hear from her again. I have an idea our Franklin Gage will be at the funeral, and he may tell Diana the whole embezzlement idea was a false alarm.

"Diana certainly looked a wreck. She had taken a plane up from Los Angeles, gone to the hospital, was with her brother when he died about three o'clock in the morning; then had to make funeral arrangements and meet me at the Escobar Import and Export Company at ten-thirty and—say, wait a minute, I told her to get a cashier's check. She had it for me."

Mason took the leather wallet from his inside coat pocket, pulled out several papers, and said, "Well, here it is. A cashier's check made by the Farmers' Financial Bank of San Francisco to Diana Douglas as trustee in an amount of five thousand dollars. She may have cut corners with us, Della, but she followed instructions on that check at a time when her heart must have been torn to ribbons. She was really fond of that brother of hers. I guess she's sort of been a mother to him as well as a sister. . . . If anything turns up in the next ten minutes, I'll be down at Paul Drake's office."

"No hurry," Della Street said. "I'll call if there's anything important."

Mason walked down the corridor to the offices of the Drake Detective Agency, said hello to the girl at the switchboard, and jerked his thumb in the direction of Paul Drake's office.

She smiled in recognition, nodded, and said, "He's in. He's on the phone at the moment. Go on down."

Mason opened the spring-locked gate in the partition which divided the waiting room from the offices and walked down the long corridor, flagged by little offices in which Drake's operatives made out their reports, until he came to Drake's office.

Paul Drake was sitting in his little cubbyhole behind a desk on which were several telephones. He was just completing a telephone conversation when Mason opened the door.

The detective indicated a chair and said, "Hi, Perry. This is intended as a place of command from which to direct multitudinous activities, not as a place of consultation."

Mason settled himself in the chair. "What have you got on those phones—a hot line to police headquarters?"

"Darned near," Drake said. "We handle a lot of the stuff at the switchboard, but on delicate assignments when we have cars cruising with telephones in them, there are lots of times when there just isn't time to go through a switchboard. I give the operatives an unlisted number. They can call me direct and be absolutely certain that they're going to get me here."

"But suppose you're not here?" Mason asked.

"Then there's a signal on the switchboard and the switchboard can pick it up, but I'm usually here. When you run a job like this you have to sit on top of it, and that's particularly true with men who are cruising with cars that have telephones. . . . What's on your mind, Perry?"

"This thirty-six-twenty-four-thirty-six case," Mason said. "Diana Douglas is the sort of girl who will go to a doctor to get medicine for the flu; then go home, take the advice of the janitor, take two aspirins with a hot lemonade, and throw out the doctor's medicine. Then a friend will drop in who'll tell her that what she needs is a lot of vitamin C and whiskey; so she'll take five hundred units of vitamin C and a hot toddy. Then somebody will tell her she needs hot tea and quinine and she'll take that. Then when the doctor comes to see how she's getting along she'll push the whiskey bottle and the teapot under the bed so he won't know she's taken anything on her own and say, 'Doctor, I feel terrible!' "

Drake grinned. "You're just describing human nature, Perry. What's she done now?"

"Nothing," Mason said. "She was very, very much attached to her brother who was in that automobile accident. He passed away early Friday morning. But up to that point our little Miss Douglas did all kinds of things, or rather didn't do all kinds of things. She was supposed to go up to San Francisco with me on the plane, but she

110

didn't make it. She said she had a feeling that someone was following her.

"Ordinarily I'd have accepted that as the gospel truth, but in view of her record I'm inclined to doubt it. Anyway, Paul, we'd better get our double out of the Willatson Hotel, and then we'll sit tight on the case for a while."

"Can you tell me any more about it without violating ethics?" Drake asked.

Mason shook his head. "Remember, Paul, I was your client in this case and all that you found out about Diana Douglas came from the detective work you did.

"Let's give Stella Grimes a jingle. Tell her to pack up and come on home."

Drake picked up the telephone, said, "Call the Willatson Hotel and get Room Seven-sixty-seven for me."

A moment later he said, "Hello, Stella. I guess the job's over. You'd better pack up and— What's that? . . . Are you sure. . . ?

"Hold on a minute, Stella."

Drake looked up at Mason and said, "Stella thinks there's something funny going on. She went out to get breakfast and a man followed her. She's pretty certain there's a man on duty at the end of the seventh-floor corridor keeping an eye on the elevator."

Mason looked at his watch. "Tell her we're on our way down there, Paul."

"Gosh, Perry, I can't get away. I can send an operative if—"

"I can handle it," Mason said. "I just thought you might like to go along. I'm free this morning, and if our friend Moray Cassel has got one of his little pimp friends waiting to throw a scare into the occupant of Room Seven-sixty-seven, it'll be my great pleasure to tell the guy where he gets off."

"Take it easy, Perry," Drake warned. "Some of these guys are vicious."

111

"I'm vicious myself," Mason said, "when some pimp starts shoving a woman around."

Mason left Drake's office, said to the girl at Drake's switchboard, "Ring my office, will you please, and tell Della Street that I'm out on an errand for an hour, that I'll be back then."

"An errand?" the girl at the switchboard asked. "Just that?"

"Well," Mason said, grinning, "you can tell her it's an errand of mercy. Also, if she gets inquisitive, tell her that I've had to sit in a position of command and let the troops do the fighting for so long that I'm getting rusty. I think I need to get out on the firing line myself."

"You want me to tell her that?"

"On second thought." Mason said, "you'd better not. Tell her that I'll be back in an hour."

The lawyer took the elevator to the ground floor, picked up a taxicab, gave the address of the Willatson Hotel, went up to the seventh floor, and noticed a man with a hammer and chisel doing some work at the end of the hall. Otherwise he saw no one.

The lawyer walked down to Room 767, tapped gently on the door, and said, "Oh, Diana."

Stella Grimes opened the door. "Come in, Mr. Mason. And don't ever give me any more assignments like this one."

Mason said, "You mean you're alarmed because somebody is following you?"

"Heavens, no," she said, "I'm bored stiff. Did you ever sit in a hotel room hour after hour waiting for something to happen and nothing happens? You turn on the radio and have a choice of two stations. You listen to a lot of inane jabbering until you get tired. You move from one chair to another. You have meals served in your room, and don't leave the phone because you're afraid that someone may want you on something important. You don't dare to call up anyone because you don't want to

112

tie the telephone line up in case the boss wants you. I'll bet I've slept enough in the last two or three days to last me for a month. I went out this morning for the first time in days. The chambermaid was getting suspicious, so I phoned the office switchboard that I'd be out for forty-five minutes and went out for some air.

"Next time I hope you can give me a job that's got some action to it."

"Where you'll have a chance to use your official bra?" Mason asked.

She smiled and said, "I never have had to actually *use* it. I've pulled it a couple of times when the going got tough. I . . ." She broke off as knuckles sounded on the door.

"Don't tell me nothing ever happens," Mason said. "We're calling things off too soon. Even money that's our friend Moray Cassel."

"And if he finds me here again?"

"Look guilty," Mason said. "Be the party of the second part in a surreptitious assignation. . . . And then be very careful. The guy will want to sign you up as a part of his stable of call girls."

Knuckles sounded heavily on the door again. Mason nodded to Stella Grimes. "It's your room," he said.

She crossed over and opened the door.

Two men who were standing on the threshold pushed their way into the room. They were not the same officers who had called previously.

"Is this your credit card?" one of the men said. "Did you lose it?"

He handed Stella Grimes a BankAmericard credit card, then saw Mason and said, "Who's your friend?"

"Better ask your questions one at a time," Stella Grimes said. "Which comes first?"

One of the men turned belligerently to Perry Mason, said, "Who are you?"

The other man kept pushing the credit card at Stella

Grimes. "All right," he said, "*is* it your credit card or *isn't* it?"

Stella Grimes glanced at Mason, said, "This seems to be a BankAmerica credit card issued to Diana Douglas."

"Is it yours or isn't it?"

"I..."

"Don't answer that," Mason said, his voice sharp as the crack of a whip.

"Now, just a minute, Mac," the man said. "you're sticking your nose into a ..."

"Wait a minute, wait a minute, Bill," the second man warned, "this is a lawyer. I recognize him now. This is Perry Mason."

"What the hell are you doing here?" the man asked.

"What are *you* doing here?" Mason countered.

"We're trying to find out whether this credit card is the property of this young woman."

"A credit card made out to Diana Douglas?" Mason asked.

"That's right. Diana Douglas."

Mason, suddenly thoughtful, said, "If you are investigating any crime it is incumbent that you warn the suspect and tell her of her constitutional rights."

"All right," the man said, "we're plain-clothes police. Homicide squad. Here are our credentials."

He took a leather folder from his pocket, opened it, and displayed a badge and an I.D. card. "Now then, young lady, you're entitled to remain silent if you want to. If you answer questions anything you say may be used against you. You're entitled to have an attorney at all stages of the proceedings."

"She has an attorney," Mason said. "I'm her lawyer. Now, tell her the specific crime of which she is accused."

"She isn't accused of anything yet," the man said, "but we're following a hot lead. For your information we want to question her about the murder of Moray Cassel, who lived in the Tallmeyer Apartments in Apartment Nine-o-six. Now then, you want to talk or don't you?"

"Just a minute," Mason said, "let me think."

"You'd better think fast," the man said. "We're not out to frame anything on anybody, but unless this young lady can explain what her credit card was doing in the apartment with the murdered man she's in trouble. If she can explain it, we're perfectly willing to listen and to check on any leads she gives us."

Mason said, "When was this man, Cassel, murdered?"

"Now, *you're* asking questions," the man said. "We're the ones who are asking questions and we want some answers fast."

Mason said, "If you want some answers fast, you'd better grab that man at the end of the hall who's working down there with a hammer and chisel and find out where *he* fits into the picture."

The man grinned and said, "Don't worry, buddy, he's one of our men. We've had this room under surveillance since early this morning, hoping that somebody would come in. We were sort of looking for a male accomplice. You triggered our visit."

Mason said to Stella Grimes, "Show him your credentials, Stella."

Stella Grimes reached for her purse.

"Now, take it easy, you two," one of the officers said, "nothing fast or there's going to be a *lot* of trouble. Just hand *me* your purse, sister, and I'll look in it first."

She handed him the purse. He looked through it, then handed it back to her and said, "Okay, pull out your credentials."

Stella Grimes pulled out her license as a private detective.

Mason said, "For your information, I'm baiting a trap myself. Stella Grimes is a private detective, an employee of the Drake Detective Agency, and she's been here masquerading as Diana Deering from San Francisco."

115

The officer regarded the credentials thoughtfully. Then said, "And Diana Deering is an alias for Diana Douglas?"

"I didn't say that," Mason said.

"You didn't have to."

There was a moment of silence. Mason said, "I believe I have a professional obligation as an attorney and as a citizen to cooperate with the police in investigating serious charges.

"Since you apparently thought this was Diana Douglas I advised you as to her true identity and occupation. That's as far as we're going."

"Why did you want a double?" the officer asked.

"No comment."

"Anything to do with Moray Cassel?"

"No comment."

"Now, look," the officer said, "if this Diana Douglas happens to be your client—oh, oh, that's the angle, Bill. . . . Or is it?"

The officer addressed as Bill disgustedly pushed the credit card back in his pocket. "Well." he said, "we've tipped our hand now."

The other officer said to Mason, "Any attempt on your part to communicate with Diana Douglas will be considered as a hostile act by law-enforcement officers and may make you an accessory."

Mason said to Stella Grimes, "Take the phone, Stella, put through a call for Diana Douglas."

The officer called Bill threw a shoulder block and pushed her out of the way of the telephone. He picked up the phone, said to the operator, "This is a police emergency call. Get me police headquarters in San Francisco immediately."

The second officer stood guard, protecting the telephone.

A moment later the officer at the telephone said, "This is the Los Angeles police, Bill Ardley talking. We want you to pick up a Diana Douglas for questioning. She works for the Escobar Import and Export Company. She has a BankAmerica credit card issued in her name. . . . You folks gave us a tip that she was in Los Angeles at the Willatson Hotel, registered as Diana Deering. That's a bum steer. She's probably in San Francisco at the present time. Pick her up for questioning, and then notify us in Room Seven-sixty-seven at the Willatson Hotel. . . . You got my name okay? This is Bill Ardley of— Oh, you know me, eh? . . . That's right, I worked with you a year ago on that Smith case. . . . Well, that's fine. I'll appreciate anything you can do. Get on this immediately, will you? And when you pick her up ask her first rattle out of the box where her BankAmerica credit card is. If she says she lost it, find out when she lost it. . . . Okay. G'by."

The officer depressed the connecting lever with his finger rapidly several times until he got the hotel operator. Then he said, "This is the Los Angeles police, operator. Put this phone out of service until we stop by the switchboard and give you instructions to the contrary. We'll take all incoming calls. No outgoing calls, no matter who makes the call, unless it's identified as being police business. You got that? Okay."

The officer hung up the telephone, settled himself spraddle-legged across one of the straight-back chairs. "Okay, my lawyer friend," he said, "now suppose *you* start doing a little talking."

"On the other hand, suppose I don't," Mason said.

"We wouldn't like that," the officer said.

"Start not liking it, then," Mason said. "I'm leaving."

"Oh, no, you aren't! Not for a while."

"Do I take it," Mason asked, "that you're intending to hold us here?"

The officer smiled affably, nodded. "I'm going to do the best I can."

"Now, that might not be very smart," Mason said. "If

117

you put me under arrest you're laying yourself open for suit for unlawful arrest, and this young woman is—"

"Take it easy," the officer interrupted. "I'm making this play for your own good. You may thank me for it later—both of you."

"That credit card," Mason said, "is that a clue in the murder?"

The officer said, "What do you think of the Dodgers' chances this year?"

"Pretty good," Mason said.

"Now then," the officer went on, "we'd like to know when was the last time you saw Diana Douglas, what you talked about at that time, and what you told her."

"You know I can't betray the confidence of a client," Mason said. "What do *you* think of the Dodgers' chances?"

"Pretty good," the officer said. He turned to Stella Grimes. "You don't have any professional immunity," he said. "You're a private detective, you have a license. You have to cooperate with the police. What brought you here?"

Stella Grimes looked helplessly at Mason.

"He's right," Mason said, "tell him."

She said, "Mr. Mason telephoned the Drake Detective Agency where I work and asked for me to come over here and go under the name of Diana Deering, and if anyone asked for me at the desk using the code figures thirty-six twenty-four thirty-six I was to answer."

"Anybody come?" the officer asked.

Again she looked at Mason.

"Tell him," Mason said. "You're a witness. He's investigating a homicide."

She said, "A man came here and acted rather peculiarly."

"In what way?"

"He acted as if he might be trying to put across some sort of a blackmail scheme."

118

"And what did you tell him?"

She said, "I didn't tell him anything. I let Mr. Mason do the talking."

"And what did Mr. Mason tell him?"

"I wouldn't know. I left the room. I got a signal to act as Mr. Mason's girl friend who had been enjoying a rendezvous in the hotel and I went over to him, kissed him, and walked out."

"Leaving Mason and this man alone?"

"Yes."

"What did the man look like?"

"He was about—well, in his middle thirties. He had slick, black hair and was—well groomed. His trousers were creased. His shoes were shined, his nails manicured."

The officer frowned. "Did that man give you any name?" he asked.

Again she looked at Mason.

Mason nodded.

"He said his name was Cassel."

"I'll be damned," the officer muttered.

There was silence for several seconds. Then the officer said, "So, you left the room and left Mason and this man alone here?"

"That's right."

"Where did you go?"

"Tell him," Mason said.

She said, "Mr. Mason gave me a coded signal to follow the man who left here. I found it was absurdly easy. He had parked his Cadillac automobile right in front of the entrance and had tipped the doorman to take care of it for him. I got the license number of the automobile. It was WVM five-seven-four. I hopped in a taxicab, and when this man came out and got in his Cadillac automobile I told the cab driver to follow."

"And you followed him?"

"Yes."

"To where?"

"To the Tallmeyer Apartments."

"Then what?"

"Then I used a few evasive tactics so I didn't lay myself wide open to the taxi driver so he could pick up a good fee by tipping off the driver of the Cadillac that he had been followed."

"Then what?"

"Then I came back and reported."

The officer looked at Mason. "Take it from there, Mason," he said.

Mason said, "I'm an attorney, acting in a professsssional capacity, representing a client. I have no information in which you would be interested except that I have no comment on what this young woman has said."

"But," the officer said, "you immediately traced the license number of that automobile, did you not?"

"No comment."

"And found out it was registered to Moray Cassel in Apartment Nine-o-six at the Tallmeyer Apartments?"

"No comment."

"And," the officer went on, "if it appears that you passed that information on to Diana Douglas we've got just about the most perfect, airtight murder case you ever encountered. Even the great Mason isn't going to beat this one."

"Still no comment," Mason said.

The officer took out a pack of cigarettes, selected one, offered a smoke to Stella Grimes, then to Mason, and last to his brother officer.

"Well," he said, "we seem to have uncovered a live lead."

They smoked in silence, the officer quite evidently thinking over the information Stella Grimes had given him.

There was more desultory conversation for some twen-

120

ty minutes. Then the phone rang. The officer answered the phone. A slow smile spread over his face.

"Okay," he said.

He turned to Mason and waved toward the door. "You and this young woman are as free as the air," he said. "Go any place you want."

Mason held the door open for Stella Grimes. "Bring your things," he said. "We've finished. That means they've picked her up in San Francisco."

12

⊙

PERRY MASON sat on the edge of the seat of the taxicab
counting the minutes until the driver reached his office
building. Then he tossed the driver a five-dollar bill, said,
"Keep the change, cabbie. Thanks for speeding it up as
much as possible."

The lawyer sprinted across the foyer of the building
into the elevator, then hurried down the hallway to his
office.

"Well, hello!" Della Street said as he made an ex-
plosive entrance into his private office. "What's the
rush?"

"Heard anything from Diana Douglas?" Mason asked.

She shook her head.

"Any collect call from San Francisco?"

Again she shook her head.

Mason sighed his relief, picked up the telephone, said
to Gertie, "If any call comes in from San Francisco
reversing the charges, I'll take it. Put the call right
through to me."

The lawyer settled back in the swivel chair at his desk,
took a deep breath, and said, "If we don't hear within the
next fifteen minutes, we'll call the San Francisco police
and make a demand on them, and if that doesn't do the

trick we'll start a writ of *habeas corpus* in San Francisco."

"What's happened?"

"They've arrested Diana Douglas."

"On the embezzlement?"

Mason shook his head. "The embezzlement is a minor matter," he said, "although they *may* try to arrest her on the embezzlement so they can hold her up there in the hope that she'll talk. If they do that I'm going to have to get right back to San Francisco in a hurry. . . . The charge they are putting against her is the murder of Moray Cassel."

"What!" Della exclaimed.

Mason nodded. "Somebody got into Moray Cassel's apartment, killed him, and made an exit."

"And the police think it was Diana Douglas?"

Mason nodded.

"When was this done?" she asked.

"There's something of a problem. The police will probably try to show it was done Thursday afternoon. The body probably wasn't discovered until today. That's going to make a ticklish problem with experts giving various opinions, contradicting each other, and all of the stuff that goes with it."

Della Street was thoughtful for a moment, "And our client was to have met you on the plane Thursday night at six twenty-seven and didn't show up?"

Mason nodded.

"Do you suppose there's any chance she could have been— But no, she isn't that kind of a girl."

"How do you know she isn't?" Mason asked.

"You have ideas?" Della Street asked.

Mason said thoughtfully, "When I saw her in San Francisco she told me that when she got to the airport she didn't have her credit card which she intended to use to pay for her ticket. Then she remembered that I had ordered two tickets charged to my account, so she picked up one of those tickets and said she'd adjust with me."

"And?" Della Street asked, as Mason hesitated.

"And," Mason said, "two officers from homicide showed up at the Willatson Hotel, barged in on Stella Grimes, shoved a BankAmerica credit card made out to Diana Douglas at her, and asked her to please identify the card."

"Did she?"

Mason said, "I stepped into the picture, told her to keep quiet, and then it suddenly developed we were playing for much bigger stakes than the embezzlement. This was a murder investigation and I didn't dare to carry on the deception any longer. So I had Stella Grimes identify herself to the officers, and then they rushed through a call to San Francisco as soon as they got the sketch and left orders to pick up Diana Douglas immediately on a charge of homicide."

"And you're expecting she'll telephone you?"

Mason nodded. "If she'll just follow instructions for once, keep her head, and keep her mouth shut—but they're going to bring her down here and really try to work her over."

"And so we enter into the picture?" Della Street asked.

"We enter into the picture," Mason said. "We—"

He broke off as his phone rang, and, motioning to Della to monitor the conversation in shorthand, Mason picked up the receiver and said, "Perry Mason talking."

A harsh voice said, "You're attorney for Diana Douglas, an employee of Escobar Import and Export Company?"

"Right."

"She's under arrest and is asking for an opportunity to communicate with you. We've given her that opportunity."

"Put her on," Mason said.

"It's a collect call," the official voice reminded.

"Quite right," Mason said.

A moment later Diana's frightened voice said, "Mr. Mason, I don't understand. They're charging me, they claim that—"

"Shut up," Mason said. "Don't talk. Listen!"

"Yes, Mr. Mason."

Mason said, "They're going to charge you with the murder of Moray Cassel. They will offer to take you before a magistrate in San Francisco before taking you to Los Angeles. I want you brought down here. Keep your mouth shut. Don't say anything to anyone about anything. Just use two words, 'No comment', and then add, 'I answer no questions. I make no statements except in the presence of my attorney, Perry Mason.' Can you remember that?"

"Yes."

"Can you do it?"

"I think so."

"Let me talk to the officer in charge," Mason said.

A moment later the official voice came on the line once more.

Mason said, "I'm attorney for Diana Douglas. I have instructed her to make no statement except in my presence. We waive any hearing in San Francisco in favor of a hearing before a magistrate in Los Angeles County. We make no objection to being transported from San Francisco to Los Angeles. Aside from that we make no stipulations, no admissions, no concessions, and as attorney for Miss Douglas I insist that I be present at all interviews and at all questioning. I wish to be notified the moment she arrives in Los Angeles."

"If you'd let us talk things over with her, we might be able to straighten this out," the officer said. "We don't want to bring her down to Los Angeles unless there's some real reason for it. If she can explain some of the circumstantial evidence in the case, and I certainly hope she can because she's a very nice young woman who seems to have had a lot of trouble lately, we'll turn her loose."

"That's certainly nice of you," Mason said. "It's a wonderful line. It's caused a lot of people to talk themselves into prison. For your information, I have instructed Diana Douglas not to talk unless I am present, and I am instructing you not to interrogate her except in my presence. I don't want her interrogated by anybody unless I am there. I am making a record of this conversation so that any further attempts to get information from Miss Douglas will be a violation of her constitutional rights. I think you understand the situation."

"Well, as her attorney, will you explain certain things that we'd like to clear up?" the officer asked.

"I explain nothing," Mason said.

"Do you know when your client first noticed that her BankAmerica credit card was missing?"

Mason laughed into the telephone.

"What's so funny?" the officer at the other end of the line asked.

"You are," Mason said, and hung up.

13

◉

In the consultation room at the County Jail, Diana regarded Mason with tear-swollen eyes.

"Have you had any trouble with the police?" Mason asked.

"They've been wonderful to me," she said, "just so kind and considerate and— Mr. Mason, it wouldn't hurt to tell them certain things, would it?"

"What things?"

"Well, about finding the money and about Edgar and about why I put the ad in the paper and—"

"And where would you stop?" Mason asked.

"Well, I suppose I'd have to stop somewhere. I suppose you'd want me to."

"Of course," Mason said, "you wouldn't want to talk yourself right into the gas chamber. You'd want to stop sometime before you got there, but the trouble is you wouldn't know where to stop."

"Yes," she said, "I suppose I'd have to, but they've been so nice and considerate and—"

"Sure," Mason said, "that's part of the technique. With some people they're nice and considerate. With some women they're perfectly gentlemanly and fatherly. Then, if that doesn't work, they try the other tactic. They become hard-boiled and try all sorts of things.

"In recent years the courts have frowned on some of these police tactics, and the result is that they try to work up a case by getting the evidence rather than forcing the defendant to incriminate himself. But if anyone is willing to talk they're always willing to listen and many a person has talked himself right into the penitentiary, and I mean many an innocent person. He's made statements without knowing all of the facts."

"But I know all the facts," she said.

"Do you?"

"Yes."

"Who killed Moray Cassel?"

She winced at the question.

"Did you?" Mason asked.

"No."

Mason said, "Look here, Diana, you can be frank with me. I'm the only one you can be frank with. It's my duty to see that you have a defense whether you're innocent or guilty.

"Now then, you were to meet me on that six twenty-seven plane Thursday night. You didn't do it. I saw you the next morning and you had quite a story about having been followed by someone whom you couldn't shake off, someone who frightened you so you resorted to all sorts of evasive tactics and got there too late to catch the plane.

"Actually, you didn't even try to catch that plane. That story that you made up about someone following you was a lie to account for what you had done with your time.

"I gave you the information that the blackmailer was Moray Cassel. I gave you his address. You decided that I was never going to pay off a blackmailer and that might not be the thing that your brother wanted. So, you took it on yourself to second-guess my play. You took a taxicab to the Tallmeyer Apartments. You went up to see Moray Cassel. While you were up there something happened. You opened your purse, perhaps to take out a gun. When

128

you opened your purse, your BankAmerica credit card fell out and you didn't miss it at the time.

"Later on you went to the airport. You wanted to buy your ticket to San Francisco and pay for it yourself, and that was when you missed your BankAmerica credit card for the first time.

"Now then, the police either know this much or surmise this much or can get evidence which will come pretty close to proving this much."

She shook her head.

"Yes, they can," Mason said. "The police are unbelievably clever. You have no idea what dogged footwork will accomplish in an investigation. They'll find the cab driver who took you to the Tallmeyer Apartments."

She gave a sudden, quick intake of her breath.

"Oh, oh," Mason said, "that hurt. . . . You little fool, do you mean that you took a cab directly to the Tallmeyer Apartments and didn't try to cover your tracks?"

"I was in a terrible hurry," she said. "I wanted to see him and then catch that plane with you. I thought I had time enough to pay him a quick visit and if . . . well, if . . . I was going to use my own judgment."

"In other words," Mason said, "if you felt that you could clean up the whole business with a five-thousand-dollar pay-off instead of putting that five-thousand dollars into the bank and getting a check to yourself as trustee, you were going to pay him the five thousand dollars and try to make a deal with him by which your brother would be out of trouble."

"Well, yes . . ."

"Why didn't you do it?" Mason said.

"Because he was dead."

"Go on," Mason told her.

She said, "I got into the apartment house. It was one of these hotel-type apartment houses where they have a doorman on duty at the elevator, but he was busy parking a car for somebody and I slipped right on by him into

129

the elevator. I went up to the ninth floor. I found apartment nine-o-six. I tapped on the door.

"Nothing happened, so I tapped again and when nothing happened I tried the knob. I don't know what in the world possessed me to do that but I did and the door opened and . . ."

"Just a minute," Mason said, "were you wearing gloves?"

"I . . . no."

Mason sighed and shook his head. "Go on," he said.

"I got in there and at first I didn't see him. I didn't see anybody, but I said, 'Who-whoo, is anybody home?' and walked in. And then I saw him lying there on his back on the bed. Oh, Mr. Mason, it was terrible, terrible. Everything was soaked in blood and . . ."

"Was he dead?" Mason asked.

She nodded.

"How do you know?"

"I picked up his hand and it was cold."

"Then what did you do?"

"I ran out."

"No, you didn't," Mason said. "You opened your purse. Why did you open your purse?"

"Heavens, I don't know, Mr. Mason. I . . . it's just . . . I suppose I was crying or something and wanted a handkerchief. . . . I can't begin to tell you how I felt. It was . . . I was almost nauseated."

Mason said, "You damn little liar. I have a notion to grab you by the shoulders and shake the truth out of you. Why did you open your purse?"

"I've told you, Mr. Mason. I've told you the truth."

Mason said, "You either opened your purse to take out a gun or to put a gun into it. Which was it?"

She looked at him with sullen resentment. "You always try to cross-examine me!"

"Because you always try to lie to me," Mason said. "Which was it?"

"I picked up the gun," she said.

"That's better," Mason told her. "Now, why did you
ick up the gun?"

"Because it was Edgar's gun."

"How do you know it was?"

"I know it. He had a twenty-two revolver that he used
) carry with him when he'd go out on his fishing trips on
ccount of rattlesnakes and things of that sort. It had a
olished wooden handle or grip, or whatever you call it,
nd a little piece was chipped out and . . .

"Mr. Mason, it was Edgar's gun. I know it when I see
. Edgar always wanted to teach me to shoot, and I've
ot that gun hundreds of times."

"So you picked up the gun and put it in your purse?"
Mason said.

She nodded.

"And then what?"

"Then I tiptoed out of the room."

"And what did you do with the gun?"

"I'm all right on that, Mr. Mason. Nobody's ever going
find that gun. You can rest assured of that."

"They may not need to find it," Mason said.

"What do you mean?"

Mason said, "Every bullet which is fired through the
arrel of a gun has certain distinctive striations or
ratches that are made by peculiarities in the surface of
e barrel. If the bullet that killed Moray Cassel was not
eformed by striking bone and if the police can find
here your brother had been target practicing, they can
nd some of the bullets which are embedded in a tree or
bank or whatever you used as a target. Then they can
ut those bullets in a comparison microscope and they
ay—mind you, I'm telling you they just *may*—be able
prove that the fatal bullet was fired from Edgar's gun
ithout ever having the gun."

Her face showed dismay.

"However," Mason said, "with a small-caliber bullet

131

there's not so much chance of that. Only you say yo|
fired hundreds of shots. What did you use as a target?"

"Edgar had a target. He used to put it in the car. We'|
put it up against a bank."

"What kind of a target?"

"He used a dart target," she said. "He had an ol|
target that was made of some kind of a heavy cork, o|
something of that sort, and used it when he was shootin|
darts. Then after he quit shooting darts for pleasure, h|
put a backing of some kind of plywood on this target an|
then made some paper facings with a compass."

"He was a good shot?"

"A wonderful shot, and he trained me so I became |
pretty good shot."

"Always with his gun?"

"Always with his gun. He was sort of a nut on wantin|
his women to be able to protect themselves. He wante|
me to be an expert shot."

"You don't own a gun of your own?"

"No."

"You've never had a gun of your own?"

"No."

"Now, let's be sure about that," Mason said. "You'v|
never made an application to purchase a revolver of an|
sort. Never had anyone give you a revolver?"

She shook her head in the negative.

Mason was silent for a while.

She said, "I don't think you need to worry too muc|
about that revolver, Mr. Mason. They're never going t|
find it. Do you want me to tell you what I did with it s|
you can rest easy and—"

Mason held up his hand "Keep quiet," he said. "Don|
tell me. Don't tell anyone."

"But if I tell you, it's in confidence, isn't it?"

"Some things you can tell me are in confidence,|
Mason said. "But some things you can tell me woul|
make me an accessory after the fact. I don't want t|

now where that gun is. I don't want anyone to know
where that gun is. I don't want you to ever tell anyone
nything about a gun or about being in that apartment.
ust keep completely quiet. Say that your attorney
oesn't want you to make any statement at this time, that
complete statement will be made sometime later.

"Then if they ask you how much later or anything of
hat sort you can tell them that it will be up to your
ttorney to fix the date.

"Where did Edgar keep this target that you mention?"

"I don't know. Somewhere in his garage."

"He had an individual garage?"

"Yes. The apartment house where he had his apart-
nent was one of those where they had individual garages
ather than a central basement garage."

"And his car?" Mason asked.

"That was all smashed up in the automobile accident
nd was towed away by the police, I believe."

"Did you see the car after the accident?"

"No."

"Did you look in the trunk?"

"No."

"You don't know whether this target might have been
n the trunk?"

"No."

"It could have been?"

"Yes."

Again Mason was thoughtfully silent. Then abruptly he
ot to his feet. "All right, Diana," he said, "your future
epends in large part upon keeping quiet and on an
lement of luck.

"You have taken it on yourself to disregard just about
very bit of advice I've given you so far, and to try to
ubstitute your own judgment in place of mine. Now
ou're in a jam."

"But I *had* to see Cassel," she said. "Don't you under-
tand, Mr. Mason? You can't afford to take chances with

133

a blackmailer. You say that you don't pay them and all that, but you know as well as I do that that's a high-risk game.

"I didn't want you to fight with this man and take a chance on doing something that would wreck Edgar's life. . . . And, of course, at that time I thought Edgar would recover."

"The way you planned it," Mason said, "would have been the high-risk game. You don't get rid of a blackmailer by paying him off. That simply makes him more eager. It postpones the time of the next bite for a few weeks or perhaps a few months, but eventually the blackmailer is always back. He regards his hold on his victim as a certain capital asset, just like owning a government bond or having money in the bank."

She shook her head. "I know that's what lawyers always say but you can't be sure. You don't know what he wanted. You don't know what his hold on Edgar was. It may have been something that . . . well, something that I could have protected him on."

"In what way?"

"By paying off, I could have had negatives and prints of pictures and all that."

"Negatives," Mason said, "can be duplicated. Pictures can be copied. When you take the word of a blackmailer that you're getting evidence, you're trusting the integrity of the blackmailer and, for the most part, that's a mighty poor risk."

The lawyer pressed a bell button, signaling that the interview was over.

"What's going to happen to me?" she asked.

"That," Mason said, "depends upon many things. But I can tell you one thing, if you start talking, if you try to explain your actions, if you start confiding in the police, you're either going to walk into the gas chamber or spend the better part of your life in the confines of a prison."

134

"Can't I be released on bail or something?"

Mason shook his head.

A deputy slid open the door. "All finished?" he asked.

"All finished," Mason said. He turned and waved a reassuring hand to Diana Douglas.

14

⊙

On his return to his office, Mason sent for Paul Drake.

"How does it look?" Della Street asked.

Mason shook his head. "The little fool!"

"What's she done now?"

"Lied to me. Used her judgment in place of mine. Probably left a back trail that the police can follow, but still thinks she's the smart little mastermind that can get away with it."

Drake's knock sounded on the door and Mason nodded to Della.

She opened the door.

"What is it this time?" Drake asked.

"I'm afraid," Mason said, "this is an end to your well-cooked restaurant meals, Paul. I'm afraid you're going back to sitting at the desk during long hours and eating soggy hamburgers which have been sent in from the drive-in on the next corner."

"What now?" Drake asked.

Mason said, "Diana Douglas."

"What's she done now?"

"I don't know," Mason said.

"Well, if you don't, I don't know who would."

Mason said, "I can tell you what the police think she did. The police think she went to the Tallmeyer Apartments on Thursday afternoon, that she went up to the ninth floor, had a conference with Moray Cassel, that Moray Cassel was trying to blackmail her, or perhaps her brother."

"But she paid off?" Drake asked.

"She paid off with a twenty-two-caliber revolver, shooting a particularly powerful brand of twenty-two cartridge."

"And they recovered the bullet?" Drake asked.

"Probably."

"Striations?"

Mason shrugged his shoulders.

"How many times? I mean, how many shots?"

"One, as I understand the facts," Mason said. "The man lived perhaps for some time, but he was unconscious and was unable to move. There was considerable hemorrhage."

"How do they know it's a twenty-two caliber?"

"Well," Mason said, "I'll amend that. They say it's a small caliber. I think probably they mean by that it's a twenty-two caliber. And the police claim that when little Miss Mastermind opened her purse and pulled out the gun she inadvertently jerked her BankAmerica credit card out."

"Which the police have?"

"Which the police have."

"And she claims the shooting was in self defense, or what?"

"She doesn't claim. She's silent."

"Anybody see her go into the apartment?" Drake asked.

"I don't know. She may have left a back trail that can be followed and proven. I'm only telling you what the police claim at the moment. The police claim that her BankAmerica credit card fell out of her purse on the floor without being noticed."

"Fingerprints?" Drake asked.

137

"I wouldn't know," Mason said.

Drake regarded him shrewdly. "A good possibility they do have fingerprints?"

"Could be."

"And you want me to find out?"

Mason said, "I want you to find out everything you can about the case, Paul. And particularly I want to find out about the victim, Moray Cassel."

"Personal habits, friends, contacts?" Drake asked.

"Everything," Mason said. "Paul, I sized that man up as some sort of a pimp. He's the sort who is making a living out of women or off of women some way and he's trying to disguise the rotten part underneath by a well-groomed exterior.

"Now, I'm particularly anxious to find out about his woman."

"Woman, singular?" Drake asked.

"Well, let's say women, plural," Mason said, "because the guy may have more than one of them. . . . And, of course, anything you can find out about the police case is something I want to know."

"How soon do you want to know?"

"At once. Relay information just as soon as you can get it."

"Costs?" Drake asked.

Mason said, "I *think* I can get costs out of my client, Paul, but I'm going to share the expense on this one, and if necessary I'll carry the whole load."

Drake raised an inquiring eyebrow.

Mason said, by way of explanation, "This case slipped up on my blind side, Paul. I gave a client the wrong advice right at the start."

"Forget it!" Drake said. "You never made a legal mistake in your life."

"I didn't make a mistake in advising her in regard to the law," Mason said, "but I made a mistake in letting her stick her neck way, way out; and then, notwithstand-

138

ing the fact that I had been warned about her tendency to disregard a lawyer's advice and do things on her own, I let her out of my sight during the most critical period of all."

"When was that?" Drake asked.

"Confidentially," Mason said, "it was probably the time Moray Cassel was being murdered."

"Okay," Drake said, heaving himself to his feet, "we'll give you the usual trade discount and go to work, Perry."

15

◉

JUDGE CHARLES JEROME ELLIOTT looked down from the bench and said, "This is the time fixed for the preliminary hearing in the case of People versus Diana Douglas, charged with the murder of one Moray Cassel. The defendant is in court and is represented by counsel?"

Mason arose. "I am representing the defendant, if the Court please."

Judge Elliott nodded. "And the prosecution?" he asked.

Ralph Gurlock Floyd arose. "I am the trial deputy who will handle the prosecution, Your Honor."

"Very well," Judge Elliott said. "Now, I want to make a statement to both counsel. I am well aware of the fact that in the past counsel for the defense has made spectacular courtroom scenes in connection with preliminary hearings. I don't approve of trying a case at a preliminary hearing.

"The object of a preliminary hearing is to try to find whether there is a crime which has been committed and if there is reasonable ground to connect the defendant with that crime. In that event the defendant is bound over to the Superior Court for trial before a jury.

"Now then, gentlemen, I am *not* going to test the credibility of witnesses in this Court. I am going to take the evidence at its face value. Once it has been established that a crime has been committed and once evidence has been introduced tending to show the defendant is connected with that crime, this Court is going to make an order binding the defendant over regardless of how much evidence there may be in favor of the defendant.

"In other words, I am not going to try to decide the weight of the evidence or the preponderance of the evidence. Of course, it is understood that in the event the defendant can introduce evidence completely destroying the prosecution's case the situation will be different. But you gentlemen will understand that the chances of that are quite remote.

"Now that we understand the situation, you may go ahead, Mr. Prosecutor; put on your case."

Ralph Gurlock Floyd, a dedicated prosecutor, who had been responsible for more death-penalty verdicts than any prosecutor in the state, and was proud of it, apparently felt that this prosecution of a preliminary hearing was somewhat beneath his dignity. But, having been assigned by Hamilton Burger, the District Attorney, to prosecute the case, he went about it with the savage, vindictiveness which was so characteristic of his courtroom manner.

His first witness was a chambermaid at the Tallmeyer Apartments.

"Did you," he asked, "know Moray Cassel in his lifetime?"

"I did."

"When did you last see him alive?"

"On Tuesday, the tenth of this month."

"At what time?"

"At about four o'clock in the afternoon."

"When did you next see him?"

"On the evening of Sunday, the fifteenth."

"Was he alive?"

"He was dead."

141

"What did you do?"

"I notified the manager of the apartment house, who notified the police."

"Cross-examine," Floyd snapped.

"No questions," Mason said.

A police officer was called as a witness, then a deputy coroner. A diagram was introduced showing the position of the body on the bed as of 9 P.M. on Sunday, the fifteenth, when the body was discovered and the position of the various articles of furniture in the apartment.

Floyd next called William Ardley, the police officer who testified to searching the apartment for significant clues.

"What did you find?"

"I found a BankAmerica credit card issued to one Diana Douglas of San Francisco."

"What did you do with that card?"

"I marked it for identification by punching two small holes in it in certain places which I selected."

"I show you what purports to be a credit card from the Bank of America and ask you if you have seen that before."

"That is the identical credit card."

"You're positive?"

"The card is the same and the pin holes are in the exact location that I placed them."

"Cross-examine," Floyd said.

"No questions," Mason announced cheerfully.

Floyd regarded him thoughtfully, then put a fingerprint technician on the stand who testified to finding quite a few latent fingerprints in the apartment. Some of them were the fingerprints of the decedent. Some of them were the fingerprints of the maid who cleaned the apartment twice a week.

"Any other fingerprints?" Floyd asked.

"There were some we couldn't identify."

"Any others that you could?"

"Yes, sir. Two of them."

"Where were they?"

"One of them was in the bathroom on the mirror of the medicine chest. The other one was on a nightstand table by the side of the bed where the body was lying."

"Did you determine the identity of these fingerprints?"

"We did, yes, sir. One of them is the middle finger of the defendant's right hand. The other is the thumb of the defendant's right hand."

"You're positive?"

"We have more than enough points of similarity and several unusual characteristics."

"Anything else in the bathroom?"

"There was a towel with blood stains on it, a moist towel where someone had evidently washed—"

"Objected to as conclusion of the witness," Mason said.

"Sustained," Judge Elliott snapped.

"A bloody towel," the witness said.

"You have that here?"

"Yes, sir."

"Produce it, please."

The witness produced a sealed paper bag, opened it, and took out a hand towel with the words TALLMEYER APARTMENTS embroidered in the corner. The towel was stained a faint rusty color.

"We offer to introduce it in evidence as People's Exhibit B," Floyd said.

"No objection," Mason observed casually.

"You photographed the latent fingerprints?" Floyd asked.

"I did."

"Will you produce those photographs, please?"

The photographs of the latent prints were produced and introduced in evidence. The prosecutor then introduced a whole series of photographs, showing the decedent on the bed with blood which had saturated the pillow, dripped down to the floor, and spread over the carpet.

An autopsy surgeon was called as a witness. He testified that he had recovered the fatal bullet from the back of the skull; that the bullet was of a type known as a .22-caliber, long rifle bullet; that it had penetrated the forehead on the median line about two inches above the eyes; that there had been a very considerable hemorrhage.

"When did death occur?" the prosecutor asked.

"In my opinion, making all of the tests we could, death occurred sometime between two o'clock on the afternoon of Thursday, the twelfth and five o'clock in the morning on Saturday, the fourteenth."

"Was death instantaneous?"

"No, I don't think so. Unconsciousness immediately followed the shot, and there was probably no movement of the body. But, despite the fact the victim was unconscious, the heart continued to pump blood into the brain which accounted for the very extensive hemorrhage. Death may have resulted in a period of ten or fifteen minutes after the fatal shot, or it may have been an hour. I can't tell."

"You say you recovered the fatal bullet?"

"Yes, sir."

"What did you do with it?"

"I delivered it to the ballistics expert in the presence of two witnesses."

"Could you determine the weapon from which that bullet had been fired?"

"Not definitely at the moment. We knew that it must have been fired from one of several makes of guns and we rather suspected that it had been fired from a gun with a long barrel because of—"

"Move to strike out what the witness rather suspected," Mason said.

"It will go out," Judge Elliott ruled. "Stick to facts, Mr. Witness."

"Very well," Floyd said with a triumphant smile. "We'll withdraw this witness for the moment and put on other witnesses, then recall him. I will call Miss Smith, please."

Miss Smith turned out to be a neatly dressed young woman in her early thirties.

"What is your occupation?"

"I am employed at the ticket counter of United Airlines at the Los Angeles Terminal."

"Were you so employed on Thursday, the twelfth of this month?"

"I was."

"I will ask you to look at the defendant and tell us if you have ever seen her before."

"Yes, sir, I have."

"Where?"

"At the ticket counter on the evening of Thursday, the twelfth."

"At about what time?"

"It was exactly six-forty P.M."

"Did you have a conversation with her?"

"Yes."

"And what was that conversation?"

"She was very anxious to know if the plane which was due to leave at six twenty-seven had left on time or whether it would be possible for her to get aboard. I told her that the plane had left only about five minutes late, that she would have to wait approximately an hour and twenty minutes and take a flight leaving at eight o'clock."

"What did she do?"

"She asked for a ticket to San Francisco."

"And then?" Floyd asked, his manner triumphant.

"Then she produced her purse and said, 'I'll pay for it with a BankAmerica credit card.' Then she raised her purse so I could briefly see it and suddenly dropped it down out of sight."

"You say, suddenly?"

"Suddenly and self-consciously."

"Was there any reason for such action?"

"She had a gun in her purse."

"What sort of a gun?"

"A long-barreled gun with a wooden handle."

"When you say a gun, you mean a revolver?"

"Yes, sir."

"Then what happened?"

"Then she fumbled around in her purse, keeping it below the counter so I couldn't see inside of it, and said, 'Oh, I seem to have misplaced my BankAmericard.' Then she thought for a moment and said, 'Did Mr. Perry Mason, the lawyer, leave a ticket here for me?'

"I told her that Mr. Mason had left two tickets which had been charged to his air-travel card. One ticket he had picked up, and the other one he had left to be picked up by Diana Douglas.

"Her face showed relief and she said, 'I am Diana Douglas. I'll take the ticket, please.' "

"So you gave her the ticket?"

"Yes."

"And then what?"

"Then she left and I made it a point to look at the purse she was carrying. The gun in it distorted the purse's shape and—"

"Move to strike out that it was the gun that had distorted the purse's shape," Mason said.

Judge Elliott hesitated, then said, "That may go out. The witness can state whether the purse was distorted."

"The purse was distorted by some object which had been thrust into the purse, an object so long that the purse was out of shape."

"Cross-examine," Floyd said.

"Did you," Mason asked, "ever pick the defendant out of a line-up?"

"No, I didn't."

"You didn't see her from the time you talked with her at the ticket counter until you went into the courtroom today?"

"I identified her picture."

"But you didn't pick her out of a line-up?"

"I did not. That wasn't at all necessary, Mr. Mason. After the manner in which my attention had been attracted to the defendant, I would have picked her out anywhere."

"That's all," Mason said.

Floyd put on his next witness with an air of triumph. He was a middle-aged individual who gave his occupation as part of a crew who cleaned up airplanes for the United Airlines.

"Are you familiar with the plane which left the Los Angeles Airport Terminal at eight o'clock on the evening of Thursday, the twelfth of this month, and arrived in San Francisco approximately an hour later?"

"Yes, sir."

"Did you clean that plane?"

"Yes, sir."

"Did you find anything unusual?"

"I did."

"What was it?"

"It was a gun."

"Where was that gun found?"

"The gun had been concealed in an opening underneath a pile of towels in one of the lavatories. I may state that these towels are placed in piles in the containers and are replenished from time to time. On this particular occasion I wanted to get at one of the connections for the plumbing, and in order to do that I had to remove the towels and insert my hand in the opening in the back of

147

the towels. When I did that I felt some foreign object in there and drew it out, and it was this gun."

"Did you take any steps to identify the gun?"

"I took it to my supervisor."

"And what did the supervisor do?"

"He notified the police and, at the request of the police, we took down the statistics on the weapon."

"What were the statistics?"

"This was a twenty-two caliber single-action revolver, having a nine-and-three-eighth-inch barrel and a wooden handle. On the gun was stamped Ruger twenty-two, with the words single six, the number, one-three-nine-five-seven-three and the name of the manufacturer, Sturm— S-T-U-R-M—Ruger—R-U-G-E-R—and Company, Southport, Connecticut. The initials E.D. had been carved in the handle."

"I'll show you a gun and ask you if that is the gun that you found."

Floyd came forward and handed the witness the gun.

Diana Douglas' hand clutched Mason's leg, the fingers digging in so hard that the lawyer surreptitiously lowered his own hand to loosen her grip.

Diana's face was tense, tight-lipped and chalky.

The witness turned the gun over in his fingers, nodded and said, "This is the gun."

"What was the condition of the gun when you found it?"

"It was fully loaded except for one shell which had been discharged."

"This is a single-action gun, and, in other words, it has to be cocked and then the trigger pulled. It isn't the so-called self-cocking gun?"

"No, sir, it is what is known as a single-action gun."

"Cross-examine," Floyd said.

"You have no idea how long the gun had been in that receptacle?" Mason asked.

"No, sir. I know when I found it, that's all."

"Thank you," Mason said, "no further questions."

Floyd introduced in evidence the sales register of the Sacramento Sporting Dealers, Inc., showing that the Ruger gun in question had been sold five years earlier to Edgar Douglas.

His next witness was a young woman who identified herself as a hostess on the eight o'clock plane to San Francisco on the night of Thursday, the twelfth. She had noticed Diana, observed that she was a passenger, had observed the peculiar shape of the cloth purse she was carrying when she boarded the plane. She stated that Diana was carrying a sort of overnight bag as well as the cloth purse, and when Diana went to the lavatory she noticed that she carried both the overnight bag and the purse with her, which the stewardess thought was rather peculiar. Aside from that, however, she could contribute no evidence. She hadn't paid any particular attention to the purse after Diana had been in the lavatory.

Then Floyd pulled his trump witness, the ballistics expert who stated that the fatal bullet which had killed Moray Cassel had come from the gun which had been registered in the name of Edgar Douglas.

This expert was followed by the manager of the San Francisco apartment house, who stated that after the automobile accident which had rendered Edgar Douglas unconscious and had resulted in his going to the hospital, his sister, the defendant, had been given a key to her brother's apartment and had been in and out, straightening things up.

Next Floyd introduced the doorman at the Tallmeyer Apartments. He had, he admitted, not seen the defendant when she entered the apartments, but he had seen her when she left; he noticed she had been carrying a black type of overnight bag and a black cloth purse. The purse was stretched to the limit by some rigid object which was within it. He had noticed the purse particularly.

Floyd introduced a purse which was identified as the

property of the defendant and asked the doorman if he recognized the purse. The doorman answered in the affirmative. It was either that purse or one that was an exact duplicate of it.

Judge Elliott glanced at the clock and cleared his throat. "Gentlemen, it is nearing the hour of adjournment and it would certainly seem there is no use in prolonging this inquiry further. There is undoubtedly evidence that a crime has been committed and an abundance of evidence connecting the defendant with the crime. In fact, the Court has been rather surprised at the amount of detailed evidence put on by the prosecution."

Floyd said, "The prosecution is all too well aware of the reputation of defense counsel and wishes to leave no possible loophole."

"Well, it would seem that you have left no loophole," Judge Elliott said, smiling. "I think, gentlemen, we can adjourn the hearing and bind the defendant over."

Mason arose. "If the Court please," he said with respect but very firmly, "the defense may wish to put on some testimony."

"Why?" Judge Elliott asked.

"Because I believe it is our right."

"You have a right to subpoena witnesses, that is true. But this Court is not called upon to judge the credibility of witnesses. This Court is not called upon to weigh questions of reasonable doubt. You certainly can't claim that a *prima facie* case has not been established."

"The question of whether a *prima facie* case has been established," Mason said, "depends upon the evidence at the conclusion of the case and any attempt to decide a case without giving the defendant a day in court would be—"

"Oh, all right, all right," Judge Elliott said impatiently. "We'll continue the case until ten o'clock tomorrow morning. I want to warn counsel, however, that we have a busy calendar and the Court does not take kindly to fishing expeditions or attempts to try a case on the merits at a preliminary hearing. The Court warns counsel that this Court will not weigh the credibility of witnesses and that any question of conflicting facts will be determined in favor of the prosecution as far as this hearing is concerned. However, the Court will try to do nothing which will preclude the defendant from having a fair hearing on the merits before a jury in the Superior Court, at which time the credibility of witnesses can be raised and the doctrine of reasonable doubt will apply.

"It is simply a case of differing procedures in different courts. Do you understand that, Mr. Mason?"

"I understand it," Mason said.

"Very well. The case is adjourned until ten o'clock tomorrow morning."

Mason placed a reassuring hand on Diana's shoulder. "Keep a stiff upper lip, Diana," he said.

"They're going to bind me over to the Superior Court?"

"Probably," Mason said, "but I want to find out as much about the case as I can before the Court makes its order."

"And what happens when I get to the Superior Court?"

"You are tried by a jury. You have the benefit of any reasonable doubt."

Mason bent forward to say in a low voice, "Where did you get that gun?"

"Just as I told you, Mr. Mason. It was on the floor with blood on it. I took it in the bathroom and washed the blood off and then put the gun in my purse. I had a hard time getting it in, and I guess that's when I lost the credit card."

"And you hid it in the airplane?"

"Yes, I took out the towels and felt all around in the back of the towel compartment and found this little open-

151

ing way in back. I thought they'd never find the gun in there."

Mason said, "Tell me—about the girls in the San Francisco office. Do you know who could have written that message to me?"

"It might have been any one of them."

"It was written on an electric typewriter."

"All the typewriters are electric," she said.

"All right," Mason told her, "keep a stiff upper lip. I'll see you in the morning."

The lawyer picked up his briefcase and left the courtroom.

16

○

PERRY MASON, Della Street, and Paul Drake were hud-
dled around a table in an Italian restaurant which was
near the courthouse and where the proprietor was accustomed to devoting a small private dining room to the
exclusive use of the trio.

"Well," Drake said, "it looks as if the judge has his
mind made up, from all I could hear."

Mason nodded. "What have you found out, Paul?"

"Not a whole lot," Drake admitted, "a lot of detached
bits of information. I don't know whether they'll do you
any good. . . . As you, yourself, have remarked, your
client is an awful liar."

"She is and she isn't," Mason said. "She lied to me
because she wanted to save her brother's reputation. She
thought there was something that was hanging over his
head, something that he'd pay five thousand dollars to
eliminate. She wanted to carry out his wishes.

"Therefore, she acted independently of my advice and
she tried to deceive me, but when it came to a showdown
I don't think she did try to deceive me. At least, I think
there's a possibility she's telling the truth.

"That's a duty that a lawyer owes to his client. Regardless of how many times he has been lied to in the
past, he always has to keep the faith. He always has to

believe that in the final showdown, the client is telling the truth and putting the cards face up on the table."

Drake said, "She can't be telling the truth on this one, Perry. She went down there and tried to buy him off. She couldn't do it and she killed him."

"What have you found out?" Mason asked, detouring the subject.

"Well," Drake said, "you probably had Moray Cassel pretty well pegged. The guy lived a mysterious life, and no one knows his real source of income or how much his income was.

"This much I did find out. The man was always armed. He carried a thirty-eight-caliber, snub-nosed revolver in a shoulder holster under his left armpit. His clothes were tailor-made, and for years the same tailor had been making his clothes and making them so that there was an extra bit of room under the left armpit so the bulge made by the gun wouldn't be conspicuous."

"The deuce!" Mason said.

Drake nodded.

"And that gun was on him at the time his body was found?"

"It must have been," Drake said.

Mason's eyes narrowed. "Now, isn't it interesting that the police described everything in the room, showed photographs of the body lying fully clothed on the bed with a bullet hole in the forehead, the blood all over the pillow and down on the floor, and no one said anything about the gun?"

"Did you ask them?" Drake inquired.

Mason grinned. "I didn't ask them. I wouldn't have thought to have asked them about a gun, but I certainly should have thought to have asked them what was found in his pockets and whether anything significant was found in the room. . . . What about the source of income, Paul?"

Drake shook his head. "The guy did everything with

cash. He wore a money belt. There were four one-thousand-dollar bills in the money belt. He had a leather wallet that was pretty well crammed with hundred-dollar bills. As nearly as can be found out he had no bank account. He bought that Cadillac automobile and paid for it with cold, hard cash."

"Women?" Mason asked.

"Women came to see him from time to time."

"The same woman or different women?"

"Different."

"What did you find out about the note that was placed on the display case in San Francisco where I'd pick it up?"

"The note was written on an electric typewriter," Drake said. "They're all electric typewriters, but this particular note, as nearly as I can determine, was written on the typewriter of Joyce Baffin.

"For your information, Perry, if it's worth anything, Joyce Baffin left the import-export office at noon, Thursday, pleading a terrific headache. She was, however, back on the job Friday morning, and Joyce was and is very popular with the officials and employees of the company and was at one time very friendly with Edgar Douglas. In fact, he had quite a crush on her. But so did lots of other people. Perhaps Franklin Gage, who is a widower, and Homer Gage, who has a predatory eye, would have liked to enjoy a closer relationship with Joyce Baffin."

Mason, sipping a cocktail, digested that information.

Drake went on. "I have some more odds and ends of various bits of information. I spent quite a bit of time and a fair amount of money with the telephone operator at Tallmeyer Apartments. I found out that Moray Cassel put through a lot of telephone calls to a local number. I found that number was the apartment of one Irene Blodgett, twenty-seven, blond, Millsep Apartments, divorced, employed steadily during the daytime at the Underwood Importing Company. At night she's something of a gadabout but never anything spectacular. Quiet, refined, good-looking, popular—I've got operatives working quietly on her, but if there's anything phony she's pretty well covered.

"The only thing is that this Underwood Importing Company does have some dealing or has had dealings with the Escobar Import and Export Company."

Della Street, watching Mason's face, said, "You have an idea, Chief?"

"Just this," Mason said. "At the time of his death, Moray Cassel was either standing by the bed or sitting on the edge of the bed. He was shot in the forehead by one shot from a high-powered, single-action, twenty-two-caliber revolver with a nine-and-three-eighth-inch barrel. The murderer must have been facing him."

"Well?" Drake asked. "What's so peculiar about that? Diana Douglas went to call on the guy. She rang the bell. Cassel let her in. She tried to bargain with him, then he got tough with her. She knew at that time that blackmailers never quit. Once they get a hold on a victim they bleed him white. Diana was obsessed with the idea she had to protect her brother."

Mason held the stem of his cocktail glass, watching the liquid on the inside as he twisted the glass between his thumb and forefinger.

"You got into Cassel's apartment?" he asked the detective.

"Sure, after the police were through with it. That seemed to take an awful long while. They went over the whole place dusting for fingerprints, testing for blood stains, and all that."

"What about the fellow's wardrobe?" Mason asked. "Was he meticulous with his clothes as I thought?"

"Boy, you've said it," Drake replied. "It was a fairly large-sized apartment with lots of drawer space. The drawers were filled with monogrammed shirts. He even

156

had monograms on his underwear, and the closet was pretty well filled with tailor-made clothes."

"You checked with his tailor?"

"Sure. The tailor told me that Cassel always paid him in cash, seldom wore a suit over six months, and was very fastidious. And, of course, there was that bit about tailoring the suits so the bulge didn't show where the revolver was carried under the left armpit.

"The tailor got quite friendly with me, said that he always had an idea Cassel was a gangster of some sort, and was very certain that Cassel was cheating on the income tax. But, of course, it was none of the tailor's business, and, believe me, the tailor loved to get that money in the form of cash. . . . I wouldn't be too surprised, Perry, if perhaps the tailor didn't do a little cheating on the income tax himself."

"What about overcoats?" Mason asked. "Were those tailor-made, too?"

"Everything," Drake said. "Now, wait a minute, Perry, there's one exception. There was one overcoat in there that Cassel had evidently used for rough-and-tumble stuff when he was loading or unloading things in an automobile."

"What makes you say that?"

"Well, it was an overcoat that wasn't tailor-made and the labels had been cut out from both the neck and the breast pocket."

"The deuce you say," Mason said. And then, after a while, "How did it fit, Paul?"

"How should I know?" Drake asked. "The corpse was being dissected in the medical examiner's office at the coroner's by an autopsy surgeon. I couldn't very well go in there and try on an overcoat. . . . He couldn't have had it on since late spring. It had been hot for the whole week of the murder. . . . What difference does the one coat make?"

Mason sat for a long moment in contemplative silence,

then abruptly changed the subject. "You have the various telephone numbers of the personnel at the Escobar Import and Export Company?"

Drake nodded.

Mason said to Della Street, "See if you can get us a telephone, Della."

When a telephone had been brought into the room and connected, Mason used his credit card, saying, "This is a credit-card call. I want to talk with Franklin Gage at this number in San Francisco."

Mason took Drake's notebook and read the number of Franklin Gage's residence.

"It's a person-to-person call. No one else if he's out."

The lawyer drummed with the fingers of his right hand while he held the telephone to his ear. "Let's hope we're in luck," he said.

A moment later he heard the suave voice of Franklin Gage on the telephone.

"This is Perry Mason, the lawyer," Mason said. "I take it that you are somewhat interested in this case against Diana Douglas, who is working for you . . . for your company, that is."

"Well, in a way," Gage said cautiously. "It depends upon what you want."

"Has an audit been completed of the cash shortage of your import company?"

"Yes, it has."

"Would you mind telling me what it shows?"

"In round figures," Gage said, "it shows a shortage of ten thousand dollars."

Mason said, "Would you be willing to do something which might prevent a miscarriage of justice, Mr. Gage?"

"What?"

"I would like to see that Joyce Baffin is present in court tomorrow morning when the case against Diana Douglas is called up."

"Well, of course, if you want to pay her expenses down

nd back," Gage said, "I would give her a leave of ↵bsence."

"It's not that," Mason said. "She might not want to ↵:ome."

"Well, I certainly can't force her to come."

Mason said, "She has been in your employ for some ↵ime?"

"Yes, all of the secretaries have been with us for quite ↵:ome time. We don't have a turnover with help, Mr. ↵Mason. Our business is highly specialized, and after we ↵⁀ave trained a young woman to perform competent secre- ↵arial duties we try to keep her."

Mason said, "The reason I am calling you personally, ↵Mr. Gage, is that it is tremendously important that Joyce ↵Baffin be here. I can't begin to tell you how vital it may ↵⁀e. I am going to ask that you and your nephew, Homer ↵Gage, come down to Los Angeles to the trial, that you ↵⁀ersonally get in touch with Joyce Baffin tonight and tell ↵⁀er that it is highly important that the three of you come ↵⁀own."

"The *three* of us!" Gage echoed.

"Exactly," Mason said. "I have reason to believe that ↵⁀ you ask her to come down by herself she might not ↵:ome. She might even skip out. And, if only one of you is ↵⁀oming with her, she might again become suspicious. But ↵⁀ both you and your nephew are coming down ostensibly ↵⁀o see what you can do to help Diana Douglas—"

"If she's guilty, she's not entitled to any help," Gage ↵⁀nterrupted sternly.

"But suppose she isn't guilty? You've had a chance to ↵⁀tudy the young woman. You've had a chance to know ↵⁀omething of her loyalty. Do you think that she's the type ↵⁀f a woman who would commit a murder?"

"Well, of course," Gage said cautiously, "you never ↵⁀now what a person will do when they're hard pressed, ↵⁀nd she always tried to protect her brother, but— Do you ↵⁀eel this is really important, Mr. Mason?"

"I feel that it is highly important. I feel that it is vital," Mason said.

There was silence at the other end of the line.

"If you can do exactly as I suggested," Mason said, "I feel that it will be possible to eliminate certain questions which might otherwise come up in court."

"What sort of questions?"

"Oh, about the Escobar Import and Export Company, the nature of its business, the large amount of cash that it keeps on hand, and all of those things that are business details which you *might* not care to have your competitors know about."

"Very well," Gage said quickly, "if I can have your assurance that you feel this will keep the business affairs of our company out of evidence, Mr. Mason, and if you assure me that it is vital to the case of your client, Homer and I will do our best to induce Joyce to come with us and I feel that we can be successful. . . . Where and when do we meet you?"

"You take a plane tonight," Mason said, "so you will be sure to get in. You go to a hotel. All you have to do is to ring up the Drake Detective Agency and Paul Drake will send a car to escort you to the courtroom tomorrow morning, see that you are given admission, and properly seated."

"The Drake Detective Agency," Gage said.

"That's right," Mason said, and gave him Paul Drake's number.

"Very well. We'll do it."

"I can depend on you?" Mason asked.

"You have my word," Franklin Gage said with dignity.

"That's good enough for me," Mason told him, and hung up the telephone.

"Now, what the hell?" Drake asked.

Mason picked up the cocktail glass, drained it, and smiled. "I think," he said, "I'm beginning to see daylight . . . A shortage of *ten* thousand dollars."

160

"The original figure was twenty thousand," Drake said.

Mason nodded. "Remember, however, that when Franklin Gage entered the office he said that he had been working on a business deal and had taken ten thousand dollars out, that the deal had fallen through and he was in the process of replacing the ten thousand dollars in the cash drawer."

"I don't get it," Drake said.

"If we can get those people in court tomorrow morning perhaps we'll get lucky," Mason said.

"But you assured them that those business matters wouldn't come out."

"I think they won't," Mason told him. "Now then, I'm going to have another cocktail and then we're going to order one of these fabulous Italian dinners and relax while we eat it."

17

◉

RALPH GURLOCK FLOYD arose with something of a flourish when the case of the People vs. Diana Douglas was called.

"I think, if the Court please, we can rest the prosecution's case."

"I certainly would think so," Judge Elliott said. "In fact, I think this whole matter could have been disposed of yesterday afternoon. I take it there is no defense."

"Indeed there is a defense," Mason said.

"I want to repeat that this court is not interested in fishing expeditions, Mr. Mason. I am not going to preclude the defendant from putting on any legitimate defense, but it would seem virtually mathematical that there is no defense and can be no defense to the array of facts which have been marshaled this far by witnesses."

"If the Court please," Mason said, "I would like to recall one of the officers for just one or two questions on further cross-examination."

"That's irregular," Floyd protested. "That motion should have been made earlier."

"Oh, come, come," Judge Elliott said, "one thing is certain. I'm not going to preclude this defendant from an opportunity to cross-examine any witness of the prosecution. I take it, Mr. Mason, there's some particular significance in connection with this?"

"There is, Your Honor."

"Recall the witness," Judge Elliott said.

Mason motioned to the officer. "Take the stand," he said. "Remember you've already been sworn. Now, you have the bag which has been identified as the cloth purse which the defendant had in her possession when the ticket seller at the airlines saw the gun in the purse, the same purse which the stewardess noticed on the airplane?"

"That's right."

"You have both the gun and the purse," Mason said. "Now, have you tried putting the gun in the purse?"

The officer smiled patronizingly. "Of course we have. It fits so snugly that the cloth is stretched tight and the purse is bulged out of shape. That's why it was so noticeable."

"Please put the gun in the purse," Mason said.

The clerk handed the two exhibits to the officer. He took the purse, opened it, inserted the muzzle of the gun, then gradually worked the gun into the purse, explaining as he did so, "You can see what a snug fit it is and how it is necessary to twist the cloth of the purse so it fits over the grip of the gun, which, of course," he added with a quick look of triumph at the Deputy District Attorney, "explains why the defendant lost the credit card out of the purse when she was taking the gun out."

"All right," Mason said, "you have the gun in the purse now."

"That's right."

"And you can close the purse?"

"Yes, you can barely close the purse, and," the witness went on, "when you open the purse anyone who looks in it can see a part of the gun . . . the wooden butt of the weapon."

163

"Exactly," Mason said. "Now, a gun has two outlines, the convex outline and a concave outline, does it not?"

"I don't understand what you mean," the officer said.

"Well," Mason said, "a gun is made generally on a curve so that when you hold the butt of the gun in your hand in a shooting position the barrel of the gun is elevated so that you can aim down it."

"Oh, certainly, that's right."

"And, by the same sign, when you turn the gun over, the position is reversed. That is what I would call the concave position."

"All right," the officer said.

"Now then," Mason said, "you have put the gun in the purse in a concave position. Could you reverse that position and put it in a convex position?"

"Not and close the purse," the officer said. "The fit is too snug. In fact, I don't know if you could even get the gun in the purse in what you refer to as the convex position."

"All right," Mason said, "now, it's taken you a little time to get the gun in the purse."

"It's a snug fit," the officer admitted.

"Now, take it out," Mason said. "Let's see how fast you can take it out."

"What do you mean, how fast I can take it out?"

Mason turned up his wrist and consulted the second hand of his wristwatch. "Let's see exactly how long it takes you to take the gun out."

"Oh, I see," the officer said, "one of those tests, uh?"

He started pulling frantically at the gun in the purse, managed only to jam it tighter against the cloth. To get the gun out, it was necessary for him to take the top of the purse and start pulling the cloth back a fold at a time.

"Five seconds," Mason said.

The officer fumbled frantically.

"Ten seconds," Mason said. "Twelve seconds. Now

you have the gun out. Now, it is in an upside-down position. If you wanted to shoot it you'd have to turn it around in your hand. Please do so."

The officer shifted the gun rapidly in his hand.

"Now, that is a single-action gun," Mason went on. "It can't be cocked and discharged by simply pulling the trigger. You have to pull back the hammer. Do that."

The officer did so.

Mason smiled. "Do you think you could beat that time?"

"Oh, sure, I could," the officer said, "now that I know what you're getting at I could beat it all to pieces."

"All right," Mason said, "put the gun back in the purse, close the purse; then get ready, pull the gun out of the purse, turn it to a firing position, cock the hammer of the gun, and pull the trigger. Start when I say 'ready', and we'll time it until the trigger clicks."

"I'm afraid I don't see the object of this test, interesting as it may be," Judge Elliott said.

"It is simply this, Your Honor," Mason said. "Moray Cassel, the victim, was shot in the forehead by one bullet. Moray Cassel was wearing a revolver in a shoulder holster at the time of his death. I understand that he habitually carried this weapon with him.

"Is it reasonable to suppose that he stood there inactive while the defendant fumbled with her purse and—"

"I see, I see," Judge Elliott said. "Go ahead with the test."

Ralph Gurlock Floyd was on his feet. "We object, Your Honor. It's not a fair test. It is not conducted in accordance with conditions as they existed at the time of the crime. How do we know that the defendant had the gun in what Mr. Mason calls a concave position in her purse when she entered Cassel's apartment. She might have stood outside of the door and done all of the fumbling before Cassel oppened the door.

165

"In that event she would have had the gun in her hand, ready to fire."

"Nevertheless," Judge Elliott said, frowning thoughtfully, "it's an interesting hypothesis and the Court is not going to preclude the defendant the opportunity to advance it. Go ahead, let's make the test and take the time."

This time the officer, knowing what was required and working frantically, was able to cut the time down to approximately seven seconds.

Judge Elliott, who had been watching the performance, said, "The Court gets it at about six seconds."

"Between six and seven seconds," Mason said, "to the time of the click. However, that's good enough."

"Your Honor," Floyd protested, "this is absolutely meaningless. The defendant could have had the gun out of the purse, cocked and ready to shoot before pressing the buzzer so that Moray Cassel would have opened the door to find himself helpless."

"And what happened then?" Mason asked Floyd.

"Don't try to cross-examine me," Floyd snapped.

Mason said with a smile, "I will address my remarks to the Court. The idea of having the defendant ring the buzzer with a gun, loaded and cocked and ready to shoot, would necessitate that the decedent be shot while he was at the door. In place of that the decedent was shot at the far end of the apartment, either while he was standing by the bed or sitting on the bed, and he was shot from some distance since there is no powder tattoo around the edges of the wound."

"We'll argue the case at the proper time," Judge Elliott said. "You have made your point, Mr. Mason."

Floyd said. "The defendant could have had the drop on him and forced him back a step at a time."

"For what purpose?" Mason asked.

"In order to intimidate him," Floyd said. "Who else

would have had her brother's gun and— Oh, this is absurd, too absurd to even waste time on."

"Then why are you wasting it?" Mason asked.

"Don't try to question me," Floyd shouted irritably.

"I beg the Court's pardon," Mason said. "I was merely retorting to a retort."

Judge Elliott smiled. "Proceed with your case, Mr. Mason. Do you have any questions of this witness on further cross-examination?"

"I have one or two more questions of this witness, if the Court please," Mason said.

He turned to the officer. "You made a careful examination of the apartment?"

"I did. Several of us did."

"And you noticed the wardrobe of the decedent?"

The officer smiled. "I certainly did."

"It was rather elaborate?"

"That's an understatement. It was *very* elaborate."

"And did you notice that the clothes were tailor-made?"

"The outer garments, yes sir. The under garments were also, I think, custom-made, at least they were initialed."

"And in that collection of outer garments would you say that *all* of them were tailor-made?"

"Yes, sir, all of them."

"*All* of them?"

"All— Now, wait a minute. There was one overcoat in here that didn't have a tailor's label."

"And did you notice that overcoat, try it for size to see whether or not it would have fit the decedent?"

"Well," the officer said, "we didn't try it on the decedent, if that's what you mean."

"How long," Mason asked, "would it take to have this coat brought into court?"

"Oh, Your Honor," Ralph Floyd said in the tone of voice of one whose patience has been taxed to the limit, 'this is absurd, this approaches the ridiculous. *I* don't know where this coat is. I suppose it's somewhere in the coroner's office. . . . The Court has said that it wouldn't encourage fishing expeditions and if this isn't a fishing expedition I don't know one when I see it."

Judge Elliott started to nod his head, then frowned thoughtfully and glanced at Mason. "Do you care to make a statement, Mr. Mason?"

"I care to make a statement," Mason said. "I would like to have that coat brought into court. I think it is a vital clue in this case. I have one more question to ask of this witness and then I am finished with my cross-examination. I will start to put on the defendant's case. The first witness will be Stella Grimes, a private detective. Before her testimony is finished, I think that coat should be in court. I also have subpoenaed the tailor who made all of Moray Cassel's clothes, who will testify that this overcoat was not made by him and would not have fit Moray Cassel."

"Go ahead, finish your cross-examination of this witness," Judge Elliott said, "and the Court will direct the prosecution to take steps to have the coat in question brought into court. . . . If this is a fishing expedition it is certainly using most unusual bait.

"Go ahead, Mr. Mason."

Mason said, "You were present in the laboratory when the gun which was recovered from the airplane was tested and examined?"

"Yes."

"For fingerprints?"

"Yes."

"Were there any fingerprints you could find?"

"Nothing that was identifiable. You must understand, Mr. Mason, that regardless of popular fiction stories, the finding of a fingerprint upon a gun—that is, an identifiable latent fingerprint—is not only the exception but it only happens once in a very great number of cases."

"I understand," Mason said. "Now, there are other tests to which the gun was subjected."

"You mean the ballistic tests?"

"No, I meant tests for blood."

The witness hesitated, then said, "Yes, there were tests for blood. There are very sensitive tests which show up blood even when the blood can't be classified."

"The benzidine test?" Mason asked.

"That is one."

"Was a benzidine test performed upon this gun?"

"It was."

"With what result?"

The witness hesitated, then chose his words carefully. "There were widespread reactions. Evidently the gun had been exposed to blood over almost its entire surface. More probably it had been exposed to a concentration of blood and then someone had attempted to wash that blood off very hastily with water or with a damp rag."

"That concludes my cross-examination," Mason said.

"Any redirect?" Judge Elliott asked Ralph Floyd.

"Certainly not," Ralph Floyd said. "We consider these so-called points completely extraneous."

"Now, you have a case to put on for the defense, Mr. Mason?"

"Yes, I will call my first witness, Miss Stella Grimes."

Stella Grimes came forward, gave her name, age, occupation, and residence.

"When did you first see the defendant in this case?" Mason asked.

"It was at night. Mr. Drake and I were in a taxicab. We both wore dark glasses. Mr. Drake had put an ad in the paper suggesting that the person who had money to pay could make the payment to a person in a taxicab at a certain place."

"Did you talk to the defendant at that time?"

"No, she walked past two or three times, but gave no

169

sign of recognition, no indication that she wished to convey any message."

"When did you next see her?"

"The following day."

"Where?"

"At the Willatson Hotel."

"What room?"

"Room Seven-sixty-seven."

"And what happened while you were there?"

"I was instructed to take over as the occupant of that room."

"And the real occupant of that room was the defendant?"

"That's right."

"And what was done with her?"

"You had rented another room down the hall. You took the defendant down to that room."

"Then what happened?"

"Then there was a knock at the door and the decedent paid us a visit."

"By the decedent, you mean Moray Cassel?"

"Yes, sir."

"And what was the conversation?"

"It was very apparent that he was expecting a payment of money, that he expected this from a man, that when he saw that two people were in the room he became suspicious and thought perhaps a trap was being laid for him."

"So, what did you do?"

"I followed a code signal from you, Mr. Mason. I pretended that I was simply a girl friend who was paying you a visit for purposes of affection. I gave you a casual kiss, departed, but, in accordance with your code signal, I rented a taxicab, watched the exit of the hotel so that I could follow Mr. Cassel when he left, and did so follow him to the Tallmeyer Apartments.

"I then reported to you, giving you the license number

of the Cadillac owned by the decedent and the address to which he had driven."

"And then?" Mason asked.

"Then I returned, and continued to occupy the room, waiting for someone to get in touch with me seeking a blackmail payment."

"When the defendant was in the room did you see her purse?"

"I did."

"The purse which has been introduced in evidence and which I now hand you?"

"It was either this purse or a similar one."

Mason said, "I now put the gun which is supposed to have fired the fatal bullet into this purse and ask you if, in your opinion, that gun could have been in that purse at the time that the defendant left the room."

"It definitely could not have been in the purse, not that gun. I would have noticed the manner in which the purse was bulged out of shape."

"Cross-examine," Mason said to Ralph Floyd.

Floyd said, "The defendant could have had the gun someplace else, in her suitcase or concealed somewhere on her person and put it in her purse at a later date."

"Mr. Mason took her suitcase," Stella Grimes said, "to smuggle it out of the hotel. She was to take with her nothing but her purse and a black sort of overnight bag."

"And that gun could have been in the overnight bag?"

"It could not."

"Why not?"

"Because that bag was full of money with which to pay a blackmailer."

"How much money?"

"I didn't count it," she said, "but it was full of money. I saw that much."

Floyd hesitated a moment, then said, "I guess that's all."

"If the Court please," Mason said, "I notice that an

officer has handed the bailiff an overcoat. I believe this is the overcoat that was taken from Mr. Cassel's closet, the one which didn't fit him?"

"*I* don't know that it didn't fit him," Floyd snapped.

"We'll very soon find that out," Mason said. "Mr. Ballard, will you come forward and be sworn, please."

Ballard, a very short, thick-set individual in his early forties, came to the witness stand, moving with surprising swiftness and agility for one of his build.

He gave his name, address, occupation, age, and then turned to face Mr. Mason.

"You knew Moray Cassel in his lifetime?"

"Yes, sir."

"How long had you known him?"

"About seven years."

"What is your occupation?"

"I am a custom tailor."

"Did you make clothes for Mr. Cassel?"

"I did."

"How many clothes did you make?"

"Heavens, I don't know. He seldom kept a suit over six months, and I know that he had a very extensive wardrobe. I made literally dozens of suits for him."

"And you kept his measurements on file?"

"Certainly. I didn't want to have to measure him every time he came in. He would pick out the material, tell me what he wanted, and I would have the clothes ready for the first fitting within a few days."

"I show you an overcoat which I will mark for purposes of identification as Defendant's Exhibit Number One and ask you if you made that overcoat."

The witness fingered the overcoat. "I certainly did not."

"I ask you if that overcoat could have been worn by Moray Cassel."

The witness pulled a tape measure from his pocket, made a few swift measurements, then shook his head.

172

"Moray Cassel would have been lost in that overcoat," he said.

"Cross-examine," Mason said.

"I certainly have no questions about this overcoat of this witness," Floyd said.

Mason said, "In view of the fact that this overcoat which has been marked for identification as Defendant's Exhibit Number One is one that was produced by the prosecution as having been found in the closet in Moray Cassel's apartment, I now ask that this be introduced in evidence as Defendant's Exhibit Number One."

"Objected to as wholly incompetent, irrelevant, and immaterial," Floyd said.

"I would be inclined to think so," Judge Elliott said, "unless counsel believes it can be connected up. The Court would be glad to hear your theory of the case, Mr. Mason."

Mason said, "Before I give my theory of the case, I would like to have this overcoat tried on by someone who will fill it out. I have two witnesses here in court whom I expect to use. I think they will be willing to volunteer. Mr. Franklin Gage, will you step forward, please, and try on this overcoat?"

Franklin Gage hesitated, then got to his feet, came forward, took the overcoat, looked at it, and put it on. It instantly became apparent that the sleeves were too short and the overcoat too full.

"That won't do," Mason said. "Mr. Homer Gage, will you step forward please and put on the coat?"

"I see no reason to do so," Homer Gage said.

Mason looked at him in some surprise. "Is there any reason why you *don't* want to?"

Homer Gage hesitated for a moment, then said, "All right. It looks like it's about my size, but I've never seen it before."

He stepped forward and put on the overcoat. It instantly became apparent that the coat was a perfect fit.

173

"Now, then, Your Honor," Mason said, "I will give the Court my theory about the overcoat. . . . Thank you very much, Mr. Gage. You may take the coat off."

Homer Gage squirmed out of the overcoat as though he had been scalded.

Mason folded the overcoat and put it over his right arm.

"Now then, Your Honor," he said, "if a person approaches a man who is armed and dangerous and wants to be absolutely certain that he gets the drop on him, he must necessarily have a gun in his hand, cocked and ready to fire.

"The best way to do this without being detected is to have a folded overcoat over the right hand, which can hold the gun under the folds of the overcoat. . . . If you'll hand me the gun which is the exhibit in the case, Mr. Bailiff . . . thank you. I will illustrate to the Court how it can be done."

Mason folded the coat, placed it over his right arm, and held his hand with the gun in it just under the folded overcoat.

"Now then, if the Court please, I will make my opening statement. It is my belief that a young woman who was a friend of a girl who worked with Moray Cassel got into that condition which is generally known as being 'in trouble.' I believe that an executive for the Excobar Import and Export Company was responsible for that condition. I will refer to this man as Mr. X.

"Moray Cassel was a very shrewd, adroit blackmailer. He found out about what was happening and what company the man worked in. He wasn't too certain of some of the facts, but he saw an opportunity to make a few easy dollars. I believe the young woman had no part in the blackmail scheme.

"She had gone to some other state to have her baby. But one of Cassel's scouts learned of the facts in the case and probably knew that the young woman used a code in communicating with her lover. Mail was probably addressed simply to thirty-six-twenty-four-thirty-six, Escobar Import and Export Company, and signed the same way—and these may well have been the measurements of the young woman in the case.

"So Moray Cassel took a chance on making some quick and easy money. He wrote a letter to the Escobar Import and Export Company and probably said something to the effect that if thirty-six-twenty-four-thirty-six wanted to escape a paternity suit it was incumbent to have five thousand dollars in spot cash. He probably said he was related to the young woman.

"Mr. X was married. He couldn't afford to have the true situation come out. His marriage was not a happy one and he knew that his wife would sue for divorce and for large alimony if she could find some good legitimate reason to prove infidelity.

"So Mr. X went to Edgar Douglas and persuaded him for a financial consideration to pretend to be the man responsible for the woman's condition, to go to Los Angeles and make the payment to Moray Cassel. He furnished Edgar Douglas with five thousand dollars in cash with which to make that payment.

"It happened, however, that when Edgar Douglas was getting his car filled with gas, preparatory to his trip to Los Angeles, he became involved in an automobile accident which rendered him unconscious and he remained unconscious until the time of his death.

"Mr. X, knowing that Moray Cassel was getting impatient, didn't dare to try to find another stooge. He took five thousand dollars in cash, but he also took a gun, which as it happened, although he probably didn't know it at the time, was a gun belonging to Edgar Douglas. He went to Los Angeles feeling that he would make a payoff if he could be absolutely certain that there would only

175

be one pay-off. If he couldn't be certain there would only
be one pay-off, he intended to kill the blackmailer.

"He went to Moray Cassel's apartment. They had a
conversation. Mr. X was a man of the world. He knew a
blackmailer when he saw him, and Moray Cassel was a
shrewd blackmailer who knew a victim who would be
good for any number of payments when he encountered
him.

"Very calmly, very deliberately, Mr. X killed Moray
Cassel, left the gun on the floor in a pool of blood, and
returned to San Francisco.

"The defendant entered the apartment some time
later, found a gun which she recognized as her brother's
gun on the floor in a pool of blood. She hastily washed
off the blood, wiped the gun with a damp rag, put it in
her purse, and returned to San Francisco."

Judge Elliott leaned forward. "How did this Mr. X get
hold of the gun that belonged to Edgar Douglas?" he
asked.

Mason looked at Joyce Baffin and said rather kindly,
"Edgar Douglas was a nut on guns and on the protection
of his women. He wanted any woman in whom he was
interested to know how to shoot and loaned one young
woman his gun for target practice. I think that Mr. X
probably had some influence over the woman to whom
Edgar Douglas had last loaned his gun. He may have
seen it in her apartment. . . . Do you care to make any
statement, Miss Baffin?"

Homer Gage got up and said, "I guess everybody's
done with me," and started hurrying out of the courtroom.

Judge Elliott took one look at the white-faced Joyce
Baffin, at Homer Gage, and said to the bailiff, "Stop that
man! Don't let him out of the door. This Court is going to
take a half-hour recess and the Court suggests that the
Deputy District Attorney in charge of this case use that
half hour to advantage—bearing in mind, of course, that

176

the parties are to be advised of their constitutional rights in accordance with the recent decisions of the United States Supreme Court.

"Court will recess for thirty minutes."

18

◉

MASON, Della Street, Paul Drake, Franklin Gage, and a starry-eyed Diana Douglas were gathered in the private dining room at Giovani's.

"How in the world did you ever get all that figured out?" Diana asked.

Mason said, "I had to put two and two together and then find another two that seemed to fit into the picture. A net shortage of ten thousand dollars in the revolving cash fund indicated that there could well have been *two* withdrawals of five thousand dollars each. With Edgar dead there was no need to explain the first five-thousand-dollar shortage. The explanation would be that Edgar was an embezzler and he might as well have been pegged for a ten-grand theft as for five thousand. . . . Actually, I don't think your nephew would ever have given himself away, Mr. Gage, if it hadn't been for your presence."

"It is a tremendous shock to me," Franklin Gage said. "I had no idea . . . no idea at all of what was going on."

"Of course," Mason said, "handling it as we did, Ralph Gurlock Floyd wanted to button the whole thing up quick. He didn't want to be characterized in the press as one who had prosecuted an innocent person. Therefore, he was willing to make a deal with your nephew for a

178

plea of guilty to second-degree murder and call every-thing square."

Diana said, "I know that my brother wouldn't have had anything to do with getting this young women— I mean, because of . . . well, the way you said."

Mason said, "But I couldn't count on that. I was working fast and I didn't dare to share your faith without the evidence of that overcoat.

"Apparently, Homer Gage was in a situation which could have cost him his position, his social prestige, and a lot of alimony. Moray Cassel found out about it and put the bite on him, but Moray Cassel wasn't entirely certain of his man. He knew that he was an executive in the Escobar Import and Export Company, that the woman in the case prided herself on her perfect measurements and that the man used to address her as 'Dear Thirty-six-twenty-four-thirty-six.' So Cassel used those code words in putting the bite on his victim.

"And," Mason went on with a smile, "Diana tried to live up to the description."

Diana blushed. "I did the best I could without seeming to overdo it."

"So," Mason went on, "Homer Gage made a deal with Edgar by which Edgar was to take the rap, so to speak. He was to go down and identify himself as the culprit, state that he had no funds anywhere near the amount in question but that he had embezzled some funds from the company and was going to try to make restitution before the shortage was noticed.

"In that way, Moray Cassel would have very probably been content with the one payment. . . . Of course, if Cassel suspected that his real target was a prosperous executive of the company, he would have kept on making demands. And that is why Moray Cassel is dead.

"When Edgar had his accident and nothing was said about the five thousand dollars Homer Gage had given him, there was nothing for Homer Gage to do except take another five thousand out of the rotating cash fund and make a trip to Los Angeles to size up the man with whom he was dealing. He very definitely intended to make a payment if he felt he could make one payment and get out. And he very definitely intended to commit murder if he couldn't make a deal.

"He had that overcoat with him and he became afraid he'd be noticed if he wore or carried an overcoat on a very warm, sunny day so he cut the labels out of the overcoat, and when he had finished with the killing, he simply hung the overcoat in with Moray Cassel's clothes and tossed Edgar's gun down on the floor."

"But what," Franklin Gage asked, "became of the five thousand dollars which was given to Edgar by my nephew?"

Mason said, "Diana recovered that, thought that the blackmail involved her brother's reputation, came to Los Angeles to pay off, and then, following my advice, deposited the money in cash in San Francisco, getting a cashier's check payable to Diana Douglas as trustee."

Franklin Gage thought for a minute, then said, "I think, under the circumstances, the best thing you can do with that check, Diana, is to endorse it over to Mr. Mason for his fees in the case."

There was a moment's silence, then Paul Drake pressed the button. "Hold still, everybody, we're going to have a drink to that," he said.

Diana Douglas smiled at Perry Mason. "You have the check," she said.

And Franklin Gage, producing a fountain pen from his pocket, said, "And I have the pen."